Through FIRE

FREYA BARKER

Cover Design:
RE&D - Margreet Asselbergs

Editing:
Karen Hrdlicka

DEDICATION

To all women struggling and scrapping to build a better life for themselves.
Whether battling emotional, economical, or health-related issues, women have an endless reserve of strength to draw from when overcoming negatives in their lives.
Just because we sometimes get stuck in a place we didn't choose for ourselves, doesn't mean we don't have the ability to change it. Because we do.
We have the power to change our paths—We have the strength to create a meaningful future.

6

TABLE OF CONTENTS

CHAPTER ONE

Ruby

Madre de Dios!

The place looks like a box of crayons exploded. My eyes scan the colorful space as I follow Viv through the sparsely furnished apartment.

When she first suggested I could rent her apartment, I didn't take her seriously. Why would I? I've never rented an apartment in my life. I've never had a space to call my own. Not in all my forty-four years. I certainly have never had someone offer me anything, without there being an ulterior motive. Something in return. So I was suspicious. But after Pam—my counselor at Florence House, which has been my home now for close to six months—explained that Viv was simply paying it forward, I started thinking. Maybe I could let my guard down a little. Maybe it was safe. So far I haven't seen any sign of *them* and I've been very careful. I never catch the bus to work at the same stop twice in a row, which means I sometimes have to walk a bit, but I don't mind, even though it's getting pretty cold out. Initially, I'd been nervous about working in a bar, but it's not the type of establishment I would ever expect to see anyone I know. Still, so far I've been careful to keep my head down most of the time. I'm slowly starting to relax a bit, thinking maybe they've forgotten about me.

I don't trust easily. Hell, it took me an entire month of daily sessions before I gave my story to Pam. The story I decided going with, that is. A hint of truth. Just enough to explain why I came there in the first place.

Six months ago I knocked on her door, while keeping an eye on the street behind me. I'd heard about Florence House from one of the girls who used to work with me. "A safe place for women," she told me. A safe place is what I needed and Pam seemed to recognize that the moment she opened the door, pulling me in as she herself scanned the street behind me. She didn't ask anything at first, just asked if I had something to sleep in, and if I needed a toothbrush, before showing me to a tiny bedroom with only a single bed and a little table as nightstand. She apologized for needing to look through my tote bag but assured me it was standard procedure to ensure the safety of all the residents. Finding only the few clothes I'd managed to grab, and my single picture frame, she handed me back my bag and showed me the bathroom. When she went to grab a few towels for me, I couldn't help flipping back the covers on the bed to find to my surprise: the sheets were clean and smelled fresh. I think that may have been the first time since I was a little girl back home that I slept soundly.

Pam is also the one who set me up with the job at The Skipper, a local pub out on Holyoke Wharf. Viv is the manager there. She had some personal stuff going on when I started working, so it was a few weeks before I even met Viv. She's nice, just like most everyone else there. But I've seen *nice* before; it often masks something darker. I don't really trust *nice*.

Tending bar and waiting tables is not new to me and it was pretty easy to slip into the routine. My first payday felt good. I never held a fistful of bills I could keep. I've saved most of it in the toe of my winter boots. Every now and then, I take it out and count it, not quite able to believe it belongs to me. What little I brought with me, when I landed on the doorstep of Florence

House, fit into a large tote bag. The additions to my limited wardrobe were courtesy of the local Goodwill store and Pam. She's not a small woman either, although much taller than I am. Luckily over the years, I've become handy with needle and thread and was able to hem the hand-me-downs to fit me better. Having my own money is a different experience. Gunnar, my boss, said he didn't have a problem paying me cash, as long as I understood that at some point, when I have my shit together, I'd have to go on the books. When that time comes, I know I'll have to move on.

"So what do you think?" Viv prompts, propping her hands on her hips and smiling. She stands in front of the big window, with view of the water, in the living room and looks at me expectantly.

"Beautiful," I agree with her honestly, making her smile even bigger.

"Perfect." She claps her hands before continuing, "I'm sure you'll love it. If only for being close enough to work you can walk it."

"Thank you," I quietly say, watching her face turn serious when she spots me pulling out the stack of bills I've saved up. "But I checked some of the other apartment listings, and I think you made a mistake. The rent you mentioned is much too low." I slowly count out the bills on the kitchen counter, to make up first and last months' rent, for an amount I found to be more accurate than the $500 Viv quoted me. When I look up, she is glaring at me. By reflex, I lower my eyes immediately.

"Ruby." Her smoky voice is soft yet threatening. "Ruby, look at me." Slowly I raise my eyes to find hers softer but slightly irritated. "We agreed on $500, no last month needed. What you counted out is enough for four months." She walks over and places her hands on my shoulders, bending down to look me in the eyes. "Trust me. I'm not ready to sell this place, and if not for you, it would just sit empty. We're both benefitting here."

Trust me.

"Okay," I concede on a whisper.

-

It's late by the time I let myself into Florence House with the key Pam provided to me a couple of months ago, when we negotiated new terms for my stay here. She'd offered to let me stay here indefinitely, until I had a chance to find my feet, and I would clean the house and help take care of the new girls that came in from time to time. That was something I was good at, looking after the girls. I have a lot of experience dealing with the inevitable range of emotions that comes from finding yourself somewhere you'd never expected to be. Not to mention the physical and emotional scarring, which inescapably was part of why they showed up in the first place.

I'd also tried my hand at cooking, but was soon dismissed of that task after only a handful of disasters in the kitchen. The same kitchen I could now see light coming from. It softly illuminates the hallway. I head that way after hanging my coat in the wardrobe closet. Pam is bent over her book, a hand loosely draped around a mug. The lone light over the stove is barely enough to read by, but Pam seems to dislike bright lights. Hence bending over her book to be able to discern the words.

"You're gonna spoil your eyes," I warn the older woman. She lifts up her head, apparently not having heard me come in, which is odd. She slaps the book closed, but not before I spot the torn envelope I see tucked between the pages. "Everything okay?" I ask her, a little worried at the suspicious shine in her eyes.

"Late shift?" She turns the tables on me, obviously trying to avoid my question, and I let her. It's not my place. I've felt a deep sadness from her since I met her, but this is the first time I see the evidence.

I dump my tote bag on the table and pull out a chair. "Yes. I stayed late because I went with Viv to look at her place this afternoon."

Immediately a bright smile lightens up her face. "You did? I'm so glad. Cute place, right? What did you think?"

"I like it," I tell her. "But she's insisting on the rent price." I lean with my elbows on the table. "I know she can get at least double that."

"So? Not like she needs it and besides, like I told you, she doesn't want to let go of the place completely. I'm sure she's thrilled to have someone she knows live there."

Her tone is firm, but I have trouble fully believing it. Good fortune is not something I'm accustomed to, and I'm pretty sure Viv wouldn't be so thrilled if she really knew me. I don't say any of that. I know better than to try and argue with Pam.

"I told her I'd take it. It even has some furniture, so I only have to bring over my bag. She said I could sleep there tonight, but I want to wait until the weekend." I look down at my clasped hands, not wanting to give away that I'm really nervous. Terrified, really. I don't think I've ever been truly alone. Oh, I've been lonely, but never without someone to share a house or apartment with. In fact, most of the places I'd lived had been so crowded, I would often dream what it would be like not to have to answer to anyone, to truly be alone.

Pam's dark hand lands on my lighter ones with a light squeeze. "Girl, you're free to take as much time as you need," she says, understanding in her dark eyes. She sees more than I'm comfortable with. "Although, I will say, I'm gonna miss having you around. Especially with the new girls; you have a real connection with them."

"I will miss you too. Everything…I mean…without you…"

"Hush," Pam cuts me off. "Not like you're moving across the country, for Christ's sake. You're a few measly blocks away, and I'm hoping you'll pop in to continue our sessions for a bit longer. As for the girls…perhaps if you have time in your schedule, you can help out from time to time. Get them settled in when they get here."

"I would like that." I give her a little smile before pushing back from the table. "I hope you don't mind, I'm tired, I think I'll head upstairs."

"Night, Ruby."

"Good night," I wish Pam over my shoulder as I walk into the hall.

It isn't until I reach the bathroom, up on the third floor, that it occurs to me I'll soon have a bathroom to myself for the first time in my life. If I want, I can take a bubble bath this weekend. Something I've always dreamt of.

-

"Yo, Ruby! Two drafts, please?"

I turn around from the sink where I was rinsing glasses to find a familiar face. Ike is Viv's husband and always sits at the far end of the bar when he comes in. But the order came from the man sitting beside him. Tim. I don't think I ever caught his last name, not that it matters, since other than putting in his drink order occasionally on the Wednesdays he comes in, he doesn't pay me much attention. That's fine with me. It's Ike that smiles and thanks me when I drop the drafts on the coasters in front of them, taking away their empties. I give him a little smile back but ignore the large man beside him.

Every Wednesday he's here, shooting the shit with Viv's man. They've been friends for years, from what I picked up. When I first started here, he would come in with a whole group of men. I later learned they all play baseball together. Gunnar and Ike, too. Apparently the season is over because the last few times I've only seen this guy. Did I mention he's huge? Big, meaty, and blond. Not fat, mind you, just…big all over. Big chest, big hands, and big voice.

It carries, his voice does. It does now too, which is why I can clearly hear him behind me. "I don't think Betty Boop likes me much."

Betty Boop. That's what I've heard him call me before. I know what he means, I'm not skinny. I'm not even slim. I have curves that have curves of their own and I know it. I put them there on purpose, and I don't give a damn if he makes fun of me.

"Asshole." I hear Ike respond as I dunk their empties in the sink for a wash. "She's got a name. Try not to be such a dick, and maybe she'll give you one of those sweet smiles one of these days."

I dip my head down so my hair covers my smiling face. Ike is nice. Not creepy nice, but nice in a kind way. Almost brotherly, although I really have nothing to compare it to, since I never had a brother but if I did; I would want him to be like Ike, or maybe Gunnar or Dino. Dino scares me a little, though. He's angry a lot. He also sometimes says things that make me wonder if he knows me from before. That would be really bad.

"Ruby. Kitchen." Dino's head pokes around the doorway before disappearing.

I manage to get Matt's attention, yapping on the other side of the bar with one of the regulars. I point to the doorway, which he seems to understand, judging by the chin lift. Viv is clearing the tables, now that the dinner crowd has thinned out, which means Dino is in the kitchen alone. Quickly wiping my hands on a towel, I walk down the hallway leading to the kitchen: Dino's kingdom. Well, unless either Viv or Syd, Gunnar's wife, are cooking, which they regularly do to give him a break. When I walk in, I find him sitting at the large kitchen table, a pile of notes in front of him.

"Sit," he says curtly. I don't hesitate pulling out a chair and sitting down, my hands folded in my lap. If there is one thing I know, it's how to follow orders.

"Ruby…" His voice is much gentler now, and I lift my eyes to find his curious gaze on my neatly folded hands. "I've been a bear. Sorry. Shit's going on at home…I'm just…" He closes his eyes and shakes his head as if to clear it. His eyes back on me, he takes in a deep breath before he goes on. "You know Syd had her baby and had some complications, which is why Gunnar hasn't been around much either. He's looking after them at home. Viv's been busy taking up Gunnar's slack, and with Ike not around to maybe lend a hand, she doesn't have time for the kitchen. So I'm turning to you."

A sick feeling sprouts in the pit of my stomach. Kitchen? Me?

"I need a couple of days this weekend to sort out some personal stuff. I need you to run the kitchen. I have every recipe written out. Viv will be around if you have questions, and I'll leave you my number. I've precooked some of the stews and soups, but other stuff needs to be made the day of. It's really not hard." He says the last staring into my panicked face.

"I…I don't know," I manage to stutter. "I don't do too well in the kitchen. Maybe Matt?"

"Please, Ruby. Matt is a disaster in here, but he can hustle the work of two out there. I wouldn't ask if I wasn't desperate."

The pleading look on the big man's face goes a long way to soothing his last words. Desperation made him turn to me. I should be used to that, and yet it stings. But only a little. "Of course," I reply quickly, watching the instant relief wash over his expression. I'll manage. *Madre de dios!*

CHAPTER TWO

Tim

"This is where you're taking me?"

Brenda's nasal whine is already getting on my nerves as I push open the door to The Skipper. She'd been fishing for a date for weeks. Ever since we met at a project meeting for a few new proposed hotels going up in the Old Port area. Granted, I hadn't missed the tall, stacked blonde, who'd given an expert presentation for one of the hotels, but had dismissed her as too young. Didn't seem to bother her much, though, she was persistent.

Oh all right, I didn't really work all that hard at avoiding her. She caught me in the parking lot on Wednesday. I'd just gotten in my car, ready to head out for my weekly beer with Ike, when she cornered me, leaning into the car with her tits just about rolling out of her low cut top. What can I say? I'm a guy with a serious dry spell going. A good half year, if not more. "Dinner Friday?" had come tumbling out of my mouth before I could check it.

Brenda took about two seconds to pull out a business card, her address and cell number already scribbled on the back. She came prepared. "I can be ready at six," she hummed in a come-hither way that instantly had me doubting my sanity.

When I told Ike about my dilemma that night, he suggested I bring her here, to The Skipper. He said that if she didn't fit in, it would likely show within the first five minutes. I think she broke the record, complaining before we even stepped inside.

But here we are. I ignore her comment and with a hand on her elbow, lead her to my regular spot. The far side of the bar where Viv is holding court. The place is filling up.

"Sorry," Viv smiles apologetically, trying hard not to make a face when she spots my date. "Dino is off and we're struggling to keep up," she adds.

"No worries," I assure her. "We'll wait." I stay standing, minding my manners while I wait for Brenda to take a seat, but she has other plans. With a flair of drama, she starts digging through her purse until she comes up with a packet of wet wipes. I look on in stunned amazement as she starts wiping down the seat of her barstool, before she takes a fresh wipe and tackles the bar in front of us. I catch Viv's eye and her eyebrows shoot straight up to her hairline. I'm a big fucking idiot. I can read it all over Viv's face. With a roll of her eyes, she turns her attention to Arnie, a regular sitting at the other end of the bar.

Apparently deeming the place sanitary enough to finally plant her ass on the stool, Brenda starts snapping her fingers at Viv. I quickly grab her wrist and lower her hand as I take the seat beside her. "What's with the service here?" she says out loud instead.

"Chill," I say, shocking her as her eyes go large as saucers and her mouth falls open in disbelief. "Now, what can I get you?"

"Chardonnay," she finally manages.

I get Viv's attention easily—the minx, I'm sure she was purposely ignoring Brenda—and place our drink order. "What's the special?" I ask her when she hands over some menus.

"That would be a good choice. Dino is off for the weekend, but he made a hearty stew before he left." She leans over the bar and says a bit quieter, "He asked Ruby to take kitchen duty, and from what I can tell, it's not her forté. She's determined, I'll say that for her."

"Special it is," I confirm, handing back the menu without opening it.

Viv turns to Brenda. "And what can I get you? Would you like the special as well?"

The woman visibly shivers at the suggestion. "I'll have a Caesar salad. Dressing on the side." She barely looks at Viv as she hands back the menu. No thanks, no nothing. This'll be the fastest date ever, because the moment she's had her meal, I'm driving the chick home. Don't have time for that kind of high maintenance.

Viv is obviously suppressing a smile as she turns to give the kitchen our order, but almost bumps into Ruby, who is just coming through the door with a tray and two plates. I can't quite make out what Viv tells her as she takes the tray from her hands, but I do notice the stress on the smaller woman's face as she shakes her head vehemently. Viv turns around and without another word, goes to deliver the order.

"Seriously," the nose-talker beside me stage whispers. "Where do they find help like that?"

I slowly turn my attention to her. "Vivian is the manager and Gunnar is the owner. Both are very close friends of mine," I bite off, no longer bothering to check my irritation.

Brenda wisely snaps her mouth shut and doesn't say a thing when Viv sets a draft in front of me. Not even when Viv places an empty wine glass in front of her, unscrews the top from the bottle, and sloshes a good serving of wine, before walking toward Arnie at the other side of the bar again. I'm fighting to keep a straight face and lift my glass to take a swig. This girl is going home. Alone.

My eyes are drawn to the doorway, where Ruby stands, holding another tray and looking furtively in my direction. I'm guessing that's our food. I'm sure she'd prefer Viv to serve our order, but she is serving customers at the other side. Her shoulders pulled up, almost touching her ears, the woman tentatively approaches. She balances the tray on the edge of the bar and slides a plate in front of Brenda and a bowl of fragrant stew in front of me. A small plate with a hunk of fresh bread appears beside it. Her eyes never come up as she turns and heads for the doorway.

"What the hell is this?"

I turn to my regrettable date, who is staring in abject horror at her plate. "What?"

"There is onion in my Caesar salad. Who puts onion in a Caesar salad? I can't eat this," she whines and suddenly I'm fed up.

"Then don't," I snap at her, taking a healthy bite of my excellent stew. Damn lettuce munchers. I feel her eyes burning a hole in me. With a sigh I put my spoon down and turn to face her. "Look, this was obviously not one of my best ideas. Give me a minute and I'll drive you home."

"Home?" she asks incredulously, already sliding off her stool.

"Home," I confirm. "Just let me take care of the bill." I look up to find Viv's amused eyes on me. Fucking Viv. I gesture for the bill and she waves it off, her hands full with drink orders.

Brenda is already halfway to the door when I hear a crash followed by a muffled cry coming from the kitchen. Having had some unwanted excitement here before, I motion to Viv to stay put, just in case. With one last look at my date, I make my way to the back.

Ruby is on the far side of the kitchen, on the floor by the stove on all fours, trying to scoop the contents back into the large pot she obviously dropped. I stop in my tracks at the sight of her round, ample ass sticking up, the air in my lungs suddenly expelling in a *whoosh*. Soft muttering reaches my ears and gets me moving.

"Here, let me," I offer, when she tries to scramble up but slips in the slick mess on the floor. I grab her arm and haul her off the floor, ignoring her protests. Some of her hair has come loose from the elastic band holding it back and curtains her downturned face. "Are you okay?"

"I'm sorry," she whispers, not elaborating and appearing to turn in on herself. She's holding her right arm tight to her body.

"Did you hurt yourself?"

"I'm okay," she mumbles, but I'm not buying it. Reaching out I gently pull her arm toward me. A large red mark is swelling up from her skin.

"You burned yourself. Let's get some cold water on you." Holding her arm out, I turn her in front of me and shuffle her to the sink, trying hard to ignore the ripe ass mesmerizing me just moments earlier, rubbing against my crotch. I just have her forearm under the cold water when Matt comes flying in.

"Ruby, I need…" He comes to a stop in the middle of the kitchen, taking in the mess. "What the hell happened?"

"Sorry," she mumbles again, without turning around.

"No worries," he says easily, looking from Ruby, who is mostly hidden by my body, to me. "I just need the order for table three when you have a minute. I'll leave you guys to it." With a smirk on his face he walks out.

Ruby

I can't believe I did that. Burn myself and drop the pan. Just my luck to have Tim come storming in. The one man who has made ignoring me an art. *Pinche estúpida!*

"Are you calling me names?" I can feel the rumble of his voice against my hair as he bends his big body over me, forcing my arm under the cold water. I said that out loud?

"No, no—Me. I'm the idiot," I hurry to explain, as I feel the heat of embarrassment crawling up my neck. I pull my arm from his hold and twist around, forcing him to take a step back. "I have to get the order for table three." I take one step toward the stove when he holds me back by the shoulders.

"You sit down for a minute. I'll get it."

"But…" My protest is futile as he forces me down onto the nearest kitchen chair.

"Sit. Now, what did they order?" He looms over me, and for the first time, I look up to his face. Expecting anger, I'm surprised to see only mild irritation. I ramble off the order from memory and he sets about getting it together following the detailed instructions Dino taped up on the wall. But not before he gets a large bag of frozen peas from the freezer, wraps it in a towel and presses it on the inside of my arm.

I don't cry. Not anymore. But I get close, feeling the burning in my eyes as I watch the big man pull together the order with apparent ease. In no time, he has a tray together and is walking out the door. "Stay right there," he says over his shoulder before he disappears. I defy his order and shoot up, dropping the frozen peas on the table, to get the mess on the floor cleaned. I feel guilty enough as it is, I'm not about to have someone else clean up after me. I *know* I can clean. I've done enough of that.

Tim stays away longer than I thought, and by the time he walks into the kitchen with a tray of dirty dishes, I have the pan in the sink and the mess cleared from the floor.

"Didn't I tell you to sit?" he challenges, as he walks up and takes the rag from my hand.

And that's what he has me do. For the next hour, I watch him get order after order together, better and faster than I could have. I don't speak, unless spoken to, and am trying hard not to think about what happened to the woman with him. Not my business. Occasionally, Matt or Viv would stick their head around the door with a new order but those are slowing down.

By the time the last dinner order is served, it's closing in on nine o'clock. I've been sitting in this chair for near two-and-a-half hours. My ass is getting numb and I need to use the facilities. Before I can get up, Tim plops down in the seat across from me.

"Tell me," he starts, making me uncomfortable under his penetrating blue eyes. "How is it that you were left in charge of the kitchen?"

I try to shrug off the question, but he just stares me down. "Gunnar is looking after Syd and the baby. Ike had to go out of town for work, and Viv already does the lunch crowd…" I let my words trail off before deciding to cut to the chase. "He was desperate to have a few days off. I thought I could help. These people have been good to me." My voice is starting to feel rough as I feel the need to justify myself. "I thought I could help…" I repeat, sounding pathetic even to my own ears. I look up to find him looking at me quizzically. I'm not quite sure what to do with that, so I glance back down at my hands, clenched in front of me on the table.

"What time do you start tomorrow?"

My eyes snap up. The question surprises me. "I start at noon. Viv comes in early to do lunch prep. I told her I'd help with serving. I'm supposed to do dinner."

Tim nods his head. "I'm gonna be here at three. We'll make sure we're well prepared for the dinner rush," he announces.

"You're coming back?"

His low chuckle is unexpected and I snap my mouth closed. "Don't sound so surprised. I used to help out here quite a bit, and I'm not half-bad in the kitchen."

That's true. I've watched him in action all night. He may have to study the notes Dino left up, but his shovel-sized hands are sure and confident. Unlike mine, they were shaking so hard, I almost cut my fingers off a few times.

"I can't cook," I blurt out stupidly.

"You don't say?" I look up to find his blue eyes dancing with amusement.

"I never learned. I always wanted to." To stop myself from saying anything more, I push up off the table and turn toward the sink. Grabbing the spray bottle of bleach solution and the roll of industrial strength paper towels from the cupboard below, I get ready to clean the stove when he speaks up behind me.

"Why didn't you?"

I turn, a little taken aback by the straightforward question. There is no judgement in his expression, just curiosity. "I never had the chance," I confide to him softly but honestly, before turning back to my task. I wait for a more probing question, but it doesn't come. I spray down the stove and wad up some of the paper towel when I feel a slight squeeze on my shoulder.

"Tomorrow, Ruby," he says, walking out the door.

"See you," I manage to get out, but I doubt he hears me; he's already gone.

Tim

"I'll be here at three," I notify Viv, when I walk into the bar. "What?"

"Got nothing on this weekend, and it looks like your kitchen could use the help again."

"I was gonna take dinner shift as well tomorrow. Get Ruby up here and maybe call in Frankie to give us a hand." Viv stands with her feet spread, her hands on her hips almost in a challenge.

"Don't." I'm not sure what makes me say that. I walked out of that kitchen with a sense of sadness I'm not sure the origin of. Maybe it was the feeling of urgency behind Ruby's words when she tried to convey her need to help out. Maybe it was the regret I could hear in her voice when she told me she never had a chance to learn to cook. Something about the woman makes me feel sad.

Viv's raised eyebrow and keen eyes make me slightly uncomfortable. "Give her a chance," I add.

"Sure," she finally concedes after a very pregnant silence.

With a lift of my chin, I head out to my car, shaking off the strange vibe this whole night gives me.

By the time I get home, I think I've sorted through the date that spelled disaster from the start. A disgruntled Brenda, who was trying hard to salvage the night, even as I was guiding her out to the taxi I'd called. She'd still been waiting by the door when I brought around that order for table three, expecting me to follow her outside. Call me an ass, but the woman had been on the wrong side of unpleasant, bordering dangerously close to abrasively rude. I'd lost any obligation I might have felt to bring her back home when she started in again on The Skipper and all her perceived downfalls of the place.

I'd even sorted and tidily filed away the events in the pub's kitchen. The woman I'd barely spared a glance prior, who suddenly was able to invoke such strong feelings of protection in me. Safely tucked under the label, *helping a friend,* something I've been known to do with regularity.

My mind was settled when I took a quick shower, brushed my teeth, and hit the sack. When I turn off the light, folding an arm behind my head and tucking the other hand to cup my dick, I see chocolate brown eyes staring back at me. Where before Ruby was simply a shadow in the background, somehow tonight she's become a person. An intriguing one at that. Some of the things she said weigh on me. The sight of those lush globes of her ass seem engraved on my retinas. The hair…her mouth. Heck, even the little pointy chin I'd never noticed before is now forefront in my mind. *Fuck.*

I often go to sleep with lingering fantasies of Viv floating through my head but tonight, instead of her long athletic lines, it's the small, luxuriously rounded body of Ruby that heats me. I'll be damned if the memory of the scent of spicy coconut, coming from her dark brown curls, doesn't make my dick go hard.

CHAPTER THREE

Ruby

"How's the arm?"

My hands still as Tim's voice rolls through the kitchen, where Viv's showing me how to slice and dice the vegetables for tonight's special. She'd noticed my hesitation when she'd come into the bar, where the lunch crowd had dwindled to a only a few tables. With a firm hand on my wrist, she'd pulled me away from the bar, telling Matt he was on his own for a few. After last night's fiasco, I wasn't eager to get back into the kitchen. Somehow Viv had picked up on that. To be honest, I can't figure out why she'd want me in there again to begin with, but she seemed determined. Not one to question, I quietly followed her patient instructions on how to prepare the large pot of Chicken Cacciatore.

The moment our companionable silence is broken by Tim's appearance, Viv puts down her knife and grabs a towel to wipe her hands.

"Good. You can take over." She turns around to him. "Recipe is here. Veggies are about done, as soon as Ruby finishes with the carrots, and she knows what to do with them. Right, Ruby?" She turns to me, an eyebrow raised.

"Right," I respond, with much more confidence than I feel. Despite the fact the instructions are simple, I'm terrified I'll do something to mess things up.

My hands resume their task of cleaning the carrots. I focus on the long strips, curling on the cutting board, as I peel the outer skin. I haven't turned to look at him yet. He confuses me. Until last night, I'd been invisible to him, which suited me just fine since he scares me a little. With his attention suddenly focused on me, I was uneasy. Unsettled. His indifference was something I could easily deal with. His consideration, not so much.

"Can I see?" His voice is right behind me now, and I can almost feel the heat coming off his body.

Still without turning, I drop the peeler and hold my arm out to the side, slowly pulling up the sleeve of my sweater. He steps into my field of vision and wraps one of his large hands around my wrist, pulling my arm out further so he can see. It's nothing. At least nothing compared to some marks I've carried. Still, the hiss of his breath over the raised blister on my forearm seems to burn itself into my skin, and I lightly tug at my arm. He releases it instantly.

"Did you put something on it?"

He settles his back against the counter, his arms crossed over his chest. It would be rude not to look at him. Although his voice sounds gruff, almost curt, his blue eyes only convey concern.

"I did," I confirm. "It doesn't hurt. Much," I add, not quite sure why I felt the need to.

"Have you taken anything for the pain?"

I shake my head forcefully. "No." No way in hell will I take any drugs. Not even if my arm was on fire.

I can feel him examine me closely, and I keep my eyes focused on what my hands are doing. "Make sure to keep it clean. When those blisters open, it can easily get infected," he finally says.

This time I simply nod. He seems satisfied with that, and takes a look at the recipe, while I pick up the peeler again.

For the next half-hour we work in relative silence as we finish cutting the ingredients and toss them in the large pan, which is now ready to go in the oven. Tim's easily taken charge. It's obvious he is no slouch in the kitchen. I have to admit I feel more relaxed today than I did yesterday. Or even this morning, when I should've been excited about meeting Viv at her apartment—my apartment now—but was worrying about the day ahead instead.

"I can teach you." Tim's statement, out of the blue, startles me. "Cooking, I mean. I'm no chef, but I can handle the basics."

I'm not able to mask the flash of excitement at the prospect. Pam had tried, but with the constant interruptions at the shelter, I'd had a hard time staying on task. I quickly straightened my face, though, the moment I started thinking about the logistics. It would mean being alone with this large man for stretches of time. And where? At the apartment? Here at The Skipper? No. I can't. I'm smart enough to know that if a man offers you favors, it's for good reason. Usually favors in return. Otherwise what would he get out of it?

"Why?"

He seems a little taken aback by my question. "Because you want to learn. You said so. Never too late to start. If I've learned anything in my years, it's that regret is the one true failure. Besides," he says with a shrug of his massive shoulders. "I like cooking. I don't do it often enough."

"Okay." I slap my hand over my mouth, but it's too late to hold back the inadvertent response.

His eyes twinkle with amusement. "Good." He nods with a smile, before turning back to the stove.

What have I gotten myself into? *Idiota.*

Tim

Fuck me sideways.

Don't know what the hell I'm thinking. But those soft-spoken words, in that slight Latin-American accent of hers, "*I never had the chance…*" have been playing through my head all morning. Most of last night, too. Something about the way she said that stuck. A resignation that just doesn't sit well with me. I mean the woman is a grown-up. She's got to be at least forty, if not more. Her skin seems soft enough, but life has left its mark in the fine lines around her eyes and mouth; in the creases between her eyebrows. By the looks of it, it hasn't been an easy one. Not that I expected anything else; she does live in a shelter from what I heard. She's one of Pam's charges. Which should be another reason for me to get my head examined for throwing that offer down. Trouble, with capital letters, is what that spells.

Now that the offer is on the table, I'm not about to go back on my word. I noticed the light go on in her dark eyes before I saw it dull. Little Ruby was excited with the prospect before she curbed it.

"About the cooking," I begin, as I watch her walk into the kitchen, a tub of dirty plates in her hands. We'd managed the dinner demand pretty well together, although Ruby had focused more on plating and serving than cooking. She'd left that up to me. "I was thinking maybe on your day off? It's Mondays, right?" She nods her head in confirmation. "I work until five, but could pick you up. I've got a decent kitchen at my house. We could get groceries on the way." This time there is no nod or answer, just a long, scrutinizing look that makes me feel two feet tall instead of my six foot three.

She lowers her eyes, but not before I see a flash of disappointment, or maybe anger, in them. Only then does she give me words and they sound flat. Resigned. "That would be fine."

I said something wrong, but I'll be damned if I know what it is. I watch her rinse and load the dirty dishes into the industrial dishwasher, without sparing me another glance. Yup. I fucked up somewhere along the line. Preoccupied, I turn back to the grill, flipping the late order of hamburgers over one last time before I slide them on the ready buns.

Without a word, Ruby finishes adding sides and relishes, picks up the tray and moves toward the door.

"Ruby…"

She stops in her tracks but she doesn't look.

"Look. I'm sorry if I said something wrong. You seem…I don't know. Upset?"

I watch her shoulders straighten and then she turns her head, a big, very fake smile plastered on her face. "Not at all. I'm fine," she assures me, in an artificially perky tone, before walking right out the door.

Oh yeah. I pissed her off. I must be coming down with something, because I'll be dipped in shit if that hint of temper doesn't turn me on. I'm liking it a lot better than the guarded, almost demure, front she puts on most of the time.

By the time she gets back with another load of dishes, I have the grill and stove cleaned off. There are no more orders outstanding and it's just after ten. The kitchen closes at ten on weekends. I take off the apron I had wrapped around to catch the bulk of the splatter from the grill and look at Ruby. I'm hit with the sight of that memorable ass on full display again as she bends over to load another tray in the dishwasher. So fucking tempting, but as much as I'd like to discover the wonders of curves like hers, I'm not sure she'd be receptive. So instead of asking her what she'd like to cook on Monday, as I had intended, I keep it short. "Heading out. I've got stuff to do. Five o'clock on Monday?"

"Of course. Thank you so much." This time the words as well as the smile are genuine; the difference is night and day.

"Don't worry about it. So Florence House, right?"

"Oh. No, actually, I have a place now," she says, a hint of pride in her voice.

"Good for you. So where should I pick up?"

"I'm just on the other side of the alley. Viv's old place, I just brought my stuff there this morning."

The happy smile on her face is not quite enough to stop the stabbing sensation in my gut at the mention of that apartment. One I am more familiar with than I care to remember.

"See you at five," I confirm with her, as I grab my jacket and exit out the back way. I don't feel much like socializing tonight.

-

A cold wind hits my face, the moment I step outside. Winter is not far off. Tucking up my collar against the chill, I set off down the alley to the parking lot beyond. I find my eyes wandering to the sparse lighting along the way. Ruby has to walk home in this. The realization makes me think maybe I should've waited for her. Make sure she gets across to her new place okay.

By the time I get to my car, I've stopped to turn around and changed my mind again several times. Ridiculous. For months I haven't once thought about whether she'd be able to get home safely. Let alone thought much of her at all. With a final shake to clear my head, I click the locks on my car and slide behind the wheel. Just as I'm about to peel out of the parking lot, Ike's Expedition pulls in, stopping alongside my brand new Audi S5. I hit the button for the window, just as he does his.

"Thought you were out of town?"

"I was," he says with a shit-eating grin. "But since my wife is here, I cut that shit short. Surprising her."

I'm glad to note our friendship is back to the same level of comfort we've always had. It was rough going for a while there, when Ike settled into town permanently and swooped Viv off her feet. You snooze—you lose, and I'd been snoozing for too long. Truth is, Viv and I probably always were better friends than anything more. Doesn't mean I was happy to have Ike snatch her up. Whatever. It's all water under the bridge now.

"What about you? What are you doing here on a Saturday night?" he continues.

"Giving them a hand in the kitchen, with Dino gone."

"I thought Ruby was doing that," he says, eyebrows raised.

"I think she was in over her head. Bit of a disaster last night, actually. Just thought I'd relieve the pressure. Not like I haven't jumped in before." I realize I'm sounding a tad defensive when I see a smirk tugging at his mouth. "Shut up," I add unnecessarily, which only makes him laugh out loud.

"Was wondering when you'd finally take a good look," he teases.

"Not looking. She's not my type, you should know that."

"Correction: she's not the type you can safely bang and bail on. The type you've been going for to avoid any annoying entanglements. No…Ruby is the kind of woman you wouldn't want to walk out on, once you got in there. She may well be your kind of woman," he points out.

"Bullshit." That's what comes out of my mouth, but his words have a ring of truth. Other than perhaps Viv, I've always kept to very superficial engagements. No promises, no commitments, and no entanglements. Something that just doesn't fit with Ruby, and that brings me back to this rare need to protect. "Talking of Ruby, keep an eye on her when she leaves? Apparently she moved into Viv's old place, as of this morning, and there isn't a hell of a lot of lighting out here."

"Why don't you just wait for her? You can see to it she gets home yourself, and in the meantime have a drink with me."

"Nah. Gotta get home," I say, coward that I am, as I watch Ike shake his head slowly with a big smile on his face at my expense. The sharp horn of a car pulling up behind me gives me a welcome excuse. "Best get going. See ya later." With a flick of my fingers I slide up the window and pull into the street.

Ruby

"Go home. Go enjoy your new place."

Viv had been on my case since finding me alone, killing time in the kitchen. She seemed surprised Tim had left without saying goodbye.

I've been delaying, because even though part of me is excited to have an actual home to go to, another, larger, part is afraid. So far fear is winning, keeping me at The Skipper, puttering around.

"It's clean, Ruby." Viv grabs the rag from my hands when I move to wipe down the bar one more time.

It's pretty quiet for a Saturday night. No doubt the sudden cold weather is to blame for that. During the warmer months, this place is busy until the wee hours of the morning. Other than Ike, who is deep in conversation with Arnie and a few other regulars, the bar is empty and it' s only eleven.

Viv tosses the rag in the sink and puts her hands on my shoulders, bending down to look me in the eye. "You're stalling," she points out. "Are you having second thoughts? About the apartment?" she gently probes, obviously picking up on my reluctance to leave.

"No. No second thoughts. It's just…strange. Going to a new place with just myself as company."

Sliding her arm around my shoulders, Viv gives me a brief hug. "I remember the first time I was alone in the apartment. I'd felt safe staying with Pam at Florence House, and then here upstairs, in the rooms above the bar. When I got the place across the street, I thought I was ready to stand on my own two feet, but it scared me shitless. The closest I'd come to being on my own had been in college, in my own room in a dorm. But I muscled through my first night, and when I woke up in the morning, and was able to drink my own coffee, from my own mug, watching the sun come up over the water from my own apartment, I felt on top of the world." She smiles as she's remembering. Viv has told me a little about some of the things that happened to her, but I've been too scared to share.

"I've never been on my own," I confess, surprising myself. "Not ever." With that, I snap my mouth shut before I part with too much information.

Viv smiles in understanding. "Don't worry. One of these days, you'll be ready. It doesn't have to be today. Today you take your first step, and you'll find once you've managed that, the others will soon follow."

I take a deep breath. She's right. Up to the moment I ran, my life had been decided on by others; when to eat, when to sleep, what to wear, how to behave. Time I learn to think and do for myself.

"Thank you," I respond to Viv, giving her a little smile. "I think I'll go home now."

"Good." Viv squeezes my shoulder again before she turns to grab a pen and piece of paper, scribbling furiously. "Here." She pushes the paper in my hand. "The phone in the apartment is still hooked up. I'd left if like that for when my brothers would come to visit. This is my number. You need me, you call. And for the record, you seriously need to get a cellphone."

I roll my eyes. The cellphone issue is one that has come up before. Just about everyone I've met, since arriving in Portland, has reacted in shock when they discovered I don't have one. Never had one. I confessed to Pam that I didn't want any accounts. That I was afraid it would make it too easy for me to be found. I still am scared of that.

With a little wave to the guys at the end of the bar and a "see you later" for Viv, I head out the back door.

-

The alley is quiet. And dark.

I look up ahead and see one of the lights halfway down is not working. It was working last night when I walked to the bus stop.

I pull my jacket closer around me against the cold. My breath mists when it hits the much cooler air. Definitely time to look for a proper winter coat. A sound behind me has me stop and swing around, but I don't see anything except the end of the wharf. The only sounds now are the faint clanging of a chain against a dock pile and an occasional gull's cry. Not unusual for rats to scour the wharf and alley for scraps of food, in the shelter of night.

I shiver against the chill as I step out of the passage and start crossing the parking lot. My feet are moving faster now, eager as I am to get out of the cold and into the warm apartment. I promised myself a bubble bath tonight. With the place partially furnished, and Viv kind enough to let me use the bedding she had kept there for the large bed, there hadn't been much to do this morning to get myself set up. The bed is made, and my sparse toiletries are set up in the bathroom, along with the bottle of bath soap I'd picked up along with a handful of groceries. There's nothing left to do but to fill the tub and sink down in the bubbles.

I reach for the door to the apartment building as I turn around to have one last look behind me. Force of habit. It all seems quiet. Almost too quiet for a Saturday night, but a freezing gust of wind quickly reminds me summer is over. Something I'm sure is keeping others warmly indoors tonight. Inside, I ignore the elevator and opt for the stairs instead. Once the door closes on an elevator there is no escape. I don't like them.

The heat inside the apartment is welcoming as I walk in, locking the door behind me immediately. I just stand there for a moment, taking in the couch and coffee table, and beyond that, the breakfast bar and stools in the kitchen. I'd left a few lights on earlier. I'm grateful for that now. It feels friendly. It also feels odd not to hear evidence of other people. I'm so used to the sounds of footsteps, doors, and voices, sometimes quiet and sometimes loud. Screaming, even.

I finally drop my bag on the couch and shrug out of my coat. My first stop is the bathroom, where I put the stop in the tub and run the hot water, before heading into the kitchen. There I heat some water in the electric kettle Viv left behind. From the cupboard, I pull one of the two mugs and a package of hot chocolate, an indulgence I allowed myself in the grocery store this morning. It's the perfect night for a little indulgence.

By the time I slowly lower myself into the fragrant bubbles, lie back, and sip my chocolate, I can feel the blessings of a new life settle around me.

CHAPTER FOUR

Tim

"You're moody," my brother, Mark, observes from behind his bottle of beer. His words draw the attention of my mother, sitting in her lazy chair opposite the couch.

This morning I woke up late, feeling hung over. Probably because I downed half a bottle of scotch when I got home last night. My solution to the uncomfortable, unfamiliar, yet persistent thoughts of Ruby running through my mind. Not that it worked. With each sip of the warming alcohol, my resistance relaxed even further; until I found myself in bed, my hand fisting an almost painful erection my preoccupied mind had caused. *Fucking hell.* My fast and intense release had sapped me, and after a quick clean up, it plummeted me into a deep sleep the moment my head hit the pillow.

So yeah, I am out of sorts.

Dragging my ass over to my parents' place, for our perfunctory weekly lunch and ballgame, was something I could've easily done without today. To top that, Brady was fucking disastrous today: he's already been sacked three times and we've just hit half time. The Giants are wiping the field with them. All is definitely not good in my world.

"Is it work?" Mom voices her concern, as I knew she would when Mark piped up. Mom's goal in life is to see my brother and me happy.

When we're not, she feels it as a personal affront, throwing herself with gusto into fixing whatever ails us. Nothing to fix.

Just a quiet, short, olive-skinned and dark-haired woman, who suddenly decided to burrow under my skin like a fucking tick.

"No, Mom. Work is fine. I'm just a bit tired." At her dubious eyebrow lift, I decide to give her enough of the truth to tide her over. "Had a bit of a late night helping out at The Skipper." Not entirely the truth, but not a lie either, since it had been late when I went to bed, and I had been helping at the pub. "As you know, Gunnar's spending some time looking after Syd and the new baby, and Dino had some stuff to take care of this weekend."

"How are Syd and little Caden doing?" My mom jumps on the red herring I threw her way when I mentioned the baby, just like I knew she would.

"They're fine. Baby is healthy and mom is getting there. She just had a bit of a rough go of it after Caden was born."

Syd dodged a bullet when they weren't able to stop the bleeding after she had the baby. They had to rush her into surgery, only hours after the birth. Not that they would've necessarily had more kids—Gunnar had been a wreck those last few months, trying to keep Syd off her feet and swore there'd be no more—but to have that choice taken from a woman has to be tough to deal with. Not to mention the fact she was now not only recovering from childbirth, but from major surgery as well.

"Good. That's good," Mom mutters. "Emily's probably been worried sick."

I roll my eyes at Mark, who is softly chuckling beside me on the couch. Both of us know where this is leading. Emily is Gunnar's mother and an old friend of my mom's. Mom never passes up on an opportunity to let my brother and I know how much she envies the woman for having grandchildren. Obviously, neither Mark nor I have produced any offspring, and as Mom points out as regularly as she can get away with, she wants grandbabies of her own.

Mark had come close once, having done the whole marriage thing. However, he lost interest when his wife, at the time, decided she could do better than the moderate salary a police officer brought in and left for greener pastures. Those came in the form of a hospital administrator with a six-figure income.

Of course, I hadn't even been in the ballpark yet, avoiding the whole committed relationship like the plague. To Mom's great disappointment.

"You know…" Mom starts, and this time I can't hold back the chuckle either. She knows we're onto her when she shoots us both irritated looks. "Well, it would be nice to be able to bounce a grandchild on my knee before all the bounce is gone. At this rate, I'll be dead and buried before either of you bless me with babies." She huffs out her displeasure and part of me feels bad for her.

Dad however, who's been sitting beside me in his recliner, watching half-time commercials with great interest as he sucks back his own brew, has heard enough. "Leave the boys alone, Jane. I told you to look into that volunteer job at the hospital. Lots of babies there need cuddlin'. You can get your fill there."

This, of course, deteriorates into another common Sunday theme, the bickering parents.

I shoot a glance at Mark, who is rubbing his palm over his forehead. "Come on." I nudge him. "Let's grab another beer." With a little lift of his mouth, he follows me into the kitchen. He knows what's coming. After pulling two more bottles from the fridge, he follows me through the laundry room off the kitchen into the garage.

"You know I'm an officer of the law, right?" he jokes when I pull a small plastic tub from its hiding place under the workbench. Dad hasn't been in this garage in probably twenty years, and it's probably that long we've been sneaking in here for a Sunday afternoon toke.

"You know as well as I do, before the end of this year, pot will be legal in Maine. Lighten up," I mumble as I'm lighting up the joint.

"I know," he says, accepting the offered blunt and taking a hit. "It'll be different not having to waste valuable manpower when there's much more serious stuff out there we should spend our time on." I'm surprised at the bitter tone in his voice as he hands me the smoke.

"Something going on?"

He shakes his head. "Nothing out of the ordinary. Just a case that's messing with my head."

"Want to talk about it?" I take another hit and offer it back, but he waves it off.

"Nah. Wouldn't do any good. Humanity sucks, that's all. Gang shootings. People preying on innocents, making a living off their suffering. It just all makes me sick." He puts his bottle to his mouth and gulps down his beer.

"Whoa, buddy," I ease him, when he slams the empty bottle down on the workbench. "What brought this on? I thought you enjoyed being a cop?"

"I do," he sighs, as he runs a hand over his short-cropped head of hair. "It just gets to me sometimes. Just the other day, I picked up this girl in Harbor View Park. A witness had spotted her being sexually assaulted. We were around the corner, so we took the call, a second unit coming in behind us. They took up chase when two guys came running from the brush." Mark rubs both hands firmly over his face. "She was just a kid, man. No older than maybe sixteen, if she was a day. Swear to God. Her face covered in blood, tears, snot, fucking jiz."

"Christ," I hiss at the image.

"Yeah. But get this, the chick swears up and down the guy was her boyfriend. Even with the witness reporting he saw one guy forcefully holding her head as he was fucking her face. The other threatened him with a knife when he tried to interfere, and told him to get lost. Still the girl won't press charges. She seems more scared of us than the two thugs we ran off. Next thing I know, an FBI contingent waltzes into the precinct and takes over." I stay quiet as he reaches over and picks the roach from my fingers, taking the last hit. "Took all of five minutes for them to whisk the kid off to places unknown. But I'm telling you, I can't get the haunted fear marring her face, as they marched her past me, out of my fucking head. The girl was petrified." He stubs out the smoke and tosses the butt in the container, hiding it back under the bench.

"Jesus, man, that's tough." I clap his shoulder sympathetically, knowing full well it'll do dick to ease his mind.

"Yeah," he says, as he opens the door to the laundry room. "Pretty fucked up when dead bodies barely touch you anymore, but the sight of a waif of a girl with dirt and some sick fuck's cum on her face messes you up."

The last is mumbled as he walks ahead of me back into the house, but I hear every word. From the slump in his shoulders, it's obvious the job is getting to him.

From the look Dad shoots in our direction when we sit back down to watch the third quarter, he's well aware of what we were up to in the garage. Nothing has changed since we were younger; not the parental shake of his head, nor Mom's soft snoring, having dozed off in her chair.

I sit back, put my feet back on the table and slowly get sucked back into the game. As per usual, with some brilliant passing in the last five minutes, Brady and the Pats pull another squeaker out of their ass.

Ruby

If I had his phone number, I'd cancel tonight.

I hadn't had much time to think about Tim yesterday. With unusually warm and sunny weather for the time of year, people had taken advantage and flocked to the waterside. A lot of them ended up at The Skipper for a drink or a quick bite. It was busy, even with Dino back in the kitchen for the dinner rush. I felt a huge rush of relief when I saw him sauntering in at three, even though it was clear his mood was dark. For someone so in tune with everyone around him, he's pretty closed off himself. My friendly, "Is everything alright?" was met with a curt, "Fine." Obviously not prepared to elaborate, he'd thrown himself into his normal routine, and I tried to avoid the kitchen as much as possible the rest of my shift. None of my business.

Normally I have Sunday nights off, but because of the unexpected crowds, I stayed until after the dinner rush. At a little after nine, Viv finally sent me home. Again.

I didn't sleep much on Saturday night, despite my leisurely bath, it being a new place with new sounds to get used to and all. But I did enjoy my Sunday morning coffee overlooking the wharf. Enough so, I was looking forward to doing it all again the next morning. Except this time after a good night's sleep. I was dead on my feet, walking home with my mind zoned out, I hadn't noticed the guy in the dark SUV when I crossed the parking lot. Not until I heard a car door open and a deep voice say, "Excuse me, miss?" That's when I started running, ignoring the calls to *stop* behind me. I didn't stop until I locked the apartment door after me. Panting and panicked, I stayed with my back pressed against the door until I was sure there was no movement outside in the hallway. Then I snuck up to the window, overlooking the wharf. From there I can see most of the parking lot, but there was no sign of the SUV.

A slew of different scenarios went through my mind, none of which were very reassuring. The longer I thought about it, the less likely it seemed I'd been found. Surely he would've followed me into the building. Perhaps I was just being paranoid, and the man had simply wanted to ask for directions, or the time, or something. By the time midnight came around, I'd come to the conclusion that I was overreacting and finally crawled into bed, exhausted.

When I woke up this morning, I was surprised I'd slept at all, but I did. All night long.

Then tonight's plans with Tim popped in my head. It followed me into the shower and now, sitting on a stool at the breakfast bar looking out the window, it's plaguing me still. In my experience, men don't offer anything unless they want something out of it. Who am I kidding? Men don't offer help—not to me. Period. So it confuses me that a handsome guy like Tim would suddenly reach out.

There's so much about it that concerns me. Not just the idea of being alone with a man—especially *that* man—but the worry he might discover who I am. What I am. I know I worry too much. When I was little, Mamá used to tell me all the time, "*te preocupas demasiado!*" Even as a young girl, I'd always seen the danger in everything. Until as a teenager, the dazzle of a handsome man had blinded me. I shake my head to clear those memories before they have a chance to take root. Too many years gone by and too much time wasted on *what ifs* already. Even though I'd been paying my dues for my mistakes for thirty years, it would never be enough to bring my parents back.

No. Getting too friendly with anyone is too dangerous. The people I work with have stopped trying to get me to join them for social events, knowing I will pass every time. The only time I've spent time with anyone from work, outside of the pub, was when Viv showed me the apartment. Other than that, Pam and her girls at the shelter are the only ones I spend any time with. It's better this way. Better for them, but also better for me.

That's why this was a bad idea from the beginning.

I reach for the house phone again, thinking I might call Viv to ask for Tim's number, but at the last minute pull my hand back. I tell myself, calling Viv would likely result in questions, but part of me *wants* to learn to cook. Learn to be independent. At least that's what I tell myself.

-

I'm just pulling on my coat, to go wait outside, when a knock at the door freezes me. I was under the assumption Tim would pick me up outside.

The first thing I think is that the guy from the parking lot is back. When the knock comes again, this time followed by Tim's voice calling my name, I finally move toward the door, taking a quick peek through the peephole in the door. Seeing it's really him, I slide back both locks that haven't been opened since I slammed them shut last night.

"Hi." My voice sounds breathy as I tilt my head back to look up at the towering man.

"Ready?" he says casually, looking very handsome in a charcoal grey overcoat, a hint of a dark suit and grey tie underneath. Thirty years ago, I would've swooned at the sight. Nowadays, I seem to prefer a more casual look, especially on him.

He catches me looking him over. "Sorry about the monkey suit." He shrugs. "I came straight here. Was in meetings all day." With one hand, he keeps the door open and with the other, he grabs the keys from my hand. Guiding me into the hallway, I'm surprised to find him closing and carefully locking my door before handing me back my keys. "Just making sure your place is safe," he explains, when he notices my confusion. I've never had someone do that before. Not ever.

"Thank you."

With his hand on my elbow, he walks me to the elevator, where I stop dead in my tracks. He turns to me, a confused look on his face.

"I don't like elevators," I admit to him in a small voice. I feel a rush of embarrassment stain my cheeks.

He squints his eyes and looks at me oddly for a moment, before taking my hand and walking to the stairwell at the end of the hall. "Stairs it is," he says easily.

A little uneasy, with his big hand holding on to my sweaty one, I toddle along behind him down the stairs and out to the car. I'd nervously cleaned the already spotless apartment, top to bottom, to kill time today. Knowing the possibility of what might be expected of me, I'd freshened up with a shower and shaved meticulously.

Nothing comes without a price, that's something else Mamá would say. And boy, how right she had been on that one.

"Have you thought about what you want to cook?" Tim breaks the silence, as he opens the passenger door of a shiny black, expensive looking car.

"No. Not really. Sorry," I confess.

"No worries." He smiles as he closes the door and rounds the car to get in the driver's side. "We'll figure it out when we get to the store."

"What about Chiles Renellos?" I suggest, as we drive onto the grocery store parking lot. "Mamá used to make those. They remind me of home." I snap my mouth shut the moment the words leave my mouth. I'm already breaking my own rules of divulging too much.

"Mexican. I was wondering about your heritage. I thought it might have been, but I couldn't be sure. I barely hear any accent."

He gets out of the car, and before I have a chance to open my door, he is right there opening it for me. Not having much experience with being treated respectfully, I have to say it feels nice.

"Chiles Renellos is maybe something we can try next week? They'll take a little time, and I'll be able to take off a little early next Monday," Tim continues, as he casually grabs my elbow again, not seeming to notice how the mention of another *cooking lesson* has me stumble a bit.

We end up getting ingredients for simple and fast fajitas. At least that's what Tim says, because I really wouldn't know if they are simple to make or not. There is a moment at the cash register when I pull some bills from my wallet to pay. Tim's big hand comes down over mine, and he bends down so his mouth is close to my ear. "You don't pay when I'm with you."

I open my mouth to protest, but an intense glare from his blue eyes has me snap it shut immediately.

I stay quiet the rest of the way to his place; a nice brick, two-story house, surprisingly only blocks from the shelter. When we pull into the driveway, I start getting nervous. What does he expect?

Once inside, I take a moment to take in the space: a large L-shaped room, the short side an open kitchen at the back of the house. Very masculine, with dark brown, worn leather on the couch and love seat, and a beautifully crafted harvest dining table, with the same dark brown leather seats on the rustic wooden chairs. Dark browns and several shades of grey make up the entire color palette. Although it is beautiful, it's drab compared to the cacophony of color in my sparse apartment.

In the kitchen, Tim wastes no time pulling the produce out of the bag and hands me a colander to rinse the peppers and zucchini.

"Are you okay cutting these in strips?" He wants to know, placing a cutting board and large knife next to me on the counter. "I'm just going to quickly change out of this suit," he says, one hand already tugging at the tie around his neck, while he gives me a squeeze on my shoulder with the other.

I'm rattled. I don't know whether he wants me to do what he says, or what his actions tell me. "I…uhh…I'm not sure what you want." I turn my back to the sink and suddenly find myself facing the broad expanse of his chest. He's managed to tug his tie loose and is already halfway done unbuttoning his shirt. Dark reddish blond chest hair shows between the spread sides of his shirt. I'm tongue-tied.

"I'm not sure either," he says quietly. When I lift my head back and look up, I find him scanning my face intently.

Lust is something I recognize, so when the full heat in his eyes hits me, I think I have my answer.

With my body wedged between the counter and his big frame, I lower my eyes to a familiar sight. The hard bulge of his cock is something I know what to do with. I slowly let myself sink to my knees, my hands already reaching for his belt. He doesn't move when I pull the belt from the buckle, or when I open the top button on his fly. But the moment my hands smooth over the large bulge underneath, he hisses and steps back.

"What the fuck, Ruby?"

My eyes fly up to find a look of disbelief on his face. For countless seconds, time seems to be suspended as I get back to my feet, while watching his expression go through a host of emotions. It finally settles in a tight pinch of his lips and a clenched jaw.

That's when mortification hits me. I rush past him, grabbing my coat on my way out the door.

"Ruby!" is the last thing I hear as my feet start pounding the pavement.

CHAPTER FIVE

Tim

What the fuck just happened?

One minute we're unpacking groceries, and the next, I have Ruby starting to unwrap the persistent erection that had surged to life in the store. A loose curl of her luscious hair had stroked my cheek when I bent close to stop her from pulling out her damn money. That's all it took for me to lose the tight reign on my body. I'd been affected all the way home in the car, and was about to withdraw for a moment to give myself a stern talking to, when she went down on her knees. She floored me. For a woman so skittish, she sure had some direct moves. I'll admit, the sight of her big, liquid brown eyes, looking up at me from her position in front of me, was a huge turn on. Not that I needed an extra dose, just smelling her coconut scent and her mere presence seemed enough. When it hit me that her face was a mask of resignation and her actions seemed by rote, heat was quickly replaced with shock.

I don't really know much about her. Hell, she only just confirmed she was of Mexican descent. Though I know she must've had a rough life for her to end up in the shelter, I have no idea what her history is. It hadn't been difficult to figure out she didn't have a good experience with some guy, but the look on her face just now, hinted at something deeper.

Standing frozen in the kitchen, it takes the front door slamming shut for me to start moving. I run to the door in my socks and yank it open. Stepping out on the porch, I can just see her running toward the corner of the street. She doesn't even slow down when I yell her name. *Christ*, what a clusterfuck. Rushing back in, I snag my car keys, throw off my tie, jam my feet into a pair of old work boots, and snag my leather jacket off the coat rack. It takes only seconds, but when I get back outside, Ruby's gone.

I'm in my car, driving in the direction I last saw her, when it occurs to me where she may have headed, likely on her way to Florence House. The shelter is only a five-minute walk from my place, and I wonder if I shouldn't just let her go and turn my car around. Something about that just doesn't sit right with me. I don't know what that little scene in the kitchen was all about, but I want to find out.

I spot her turning onto Preble Street, no longer running but walking fast.

"Ruby," I call out when I roll down my window and pull up beside her. "Get in the car."

She doesn't slow her stride, but throws a glance in my direction. I suspected her to be upset, or angry, but the look of blatant fear on her face is a complete surprise. Without thinking, I pull up to the curb and turn the engine off. Getting out of the car, I see she's already at the gate to the shelter, and I just catch up as she steps up to the big, ornate, wooden door.

"Talk to me." I step up right behind her, noticing how she pulls her head down between her shoulders defensively. *Jesus*. "Ruby, please," I try. Her only response is that the fist, which was poised to knock on the door, is now suspended mid-air. I talk fast. "I'm not sure what happened. I'm sorry if I upset you, but you caught me by surprise. I didn't expect you to…I mean…*Fuck*. I suck at this." Frustrated, I run both hands through my hair. I'm not sure what the hell I'm trying to say, I just know I have to fix this. "I like you," I blurt out. "I just…Ruby?" Looking at her rigid back, I can't see her face and don't know what she's thinking. So I put my hands on her shoulders and turn her around just as the door opens.

"You might want to take those shovels you call hands off my girl, or I'll help you."

I look over the top of Ruby's bent head, straight into the unmistakable barrel of a gun. "Jesus, Pam. Put that damn thing down. You've known me long enough to know I'd never harm her."

The statuesque woman only shrugs her shoulders before dropping her eyes down to where Ruby, at maybe five foot one or two, is wedged between us. We dwarf her.

"Ruby?" Pam gentles her voice as she tries to get her attention. "Are you okay?"

Ruby's head comes up slowly and she turns at Pam's probing. The sharp intake of breath is evidence the sight of the weapon Pam is still aiming in the vicinity of my head startles her. In a surprising move, she steps into me and raises her arms as if to shield me. "It's my fault," she blurts out. "I made a mistake. Don't hurt him." Panic is clear in her voice, and I put my hands on her hips in an attempt to reassure her.

"She's not going to shoot me, woman," I mutter into her hair. Her body stills when she suddenly comes aware of my proximity. She immediately moves away. Pam seems to observe the interaction with a keen eye and finally lowers the damn weapon.

Truth be told, I don't think she'd shoot, but looking down the barrel of a gun is fucking unnerving.

"I need to talk to Ruby," she says, looking directly at me. "Alone," she adds pointedly.

When Ruby takes another step toward Pam, it's clear she's made up her mind. "Okay," I direct at Ruby, whose back is turned to me. "I'll leave you alone. For now. But you're a friend, Ruby. We're gonna have to talk at some point. Soon." With that,

I give Pam a nod and turn to head back to my car, hearing the door close somewhere behind me.

Ruby

"You like him."

It's not so much a question as it is a statement of fact, so despite the fact Pam's words startle me, I don't bother denying them.

I do. Like him, that is. I also know it counts for nothing. Not when the careful balance of my reality could be jeopardized with one wrong word. Not to mention the possible danger I'd put him in if I spent too much time with him. This whole thing was a big mistake right from the beginning.

Pam places a steaming mug on the kitchen table in front of me and takes the seat across. "Have you eaten?" she asks, casually sipping her tea and looking at me from under her eyebrows. The question draws a snicker from me.

"I'm not hungry," I claim and when one of her eyebrows raises in question, I explain.

I tell her about the fiasco in the pub's kitchen, Tim's unexpected help, and finally his offer to teach me to cook.

"I'm sorry," Pam says to my surprise.

"I don't understand?"

"I could see how eager you were to try your hand at it, and when you were struggling in the kitchen, I just took over instead of offering to teach you. I should've made the time…"

"Don't," I caution her, reaching to touch my hand to hers. "I didn't even realize at the time how much it was something I wanted to learn. Besides, you have more important things to keep you busy than to worry about teaching me."

"Fair enough," is her simple response. "So are you ready to tell me what happened?" she asks after a pregnant pause.

I don't bother hiding my big sigh. I knew she'd probe. It's what she does. "I'm not good at reading men. Well." I shrug, correcting myself. "I thought I was, but maybe I was wrong."

Sipping hot tea and sitting at the table in the warm, comfortable kitchen, I tell Pam everything from the start. The disaster at The Skipper, letting it slip to Tim that I never had the chance to learn cooking, and the sequence of events after. I even tell her about wanting to cancel, but not having his number, and being too chicken to ask Viv. When I finish with the embarrassing moment on my knees in front of him, my hands still cupping his big erection, Pam leans forward with her elbows on the table and her chin resting on her folded hands.

"You know he's not a John."

Her observation doesn't surprise me. Over the past months, she's pried loose enough information to know the world I've been running from. The violence I'd witnessed that put me in danger. She's even aware of the life I've lived. At least in large part. In all these months, Pam never pushed me to go to the police, and for reasons I'm keeping to myself, I never did. She is the only person I know who doesn't seem to judge me by what she knows, but life has taught me not to expect that kind of acceptance from anyone else. It's rare.

"I know," I admit. And I do, but it's hard not to taint every man by what you've known most of your life.

"He's a good man, Ruby. A decent man." Pam's voice has gone soft as she smiles gently at me.

"I know," I say again.

"A man like that doesn't expect you to go down on your knees. A man like that has no interest in forcing himself on you. Trust me when I say that Tim is quite able to find willing volunteers, if all he wanted was to get off. He certainly wouldn't have to go out of his way to teach them to cook first. Yeah?"

"Yeah," I whisper, seeing her point. "But it's difficult, believing that not everyone sees you as only good for one thing. That in the end, they don't all want what for years you've freely given."

The sharp knock on the table has me snap my eyes up to look into Pam's angry ones. "Not freely. We've talked about this, Ruby. You weren't exactly given a choice, even though you didn't always have a gun to your head. You used what you had to in order to survive, but you never chose to be there."

Pam knows I was forced into prostitution at a very young age, and despite the fact I never elaborated on the circumstances, she's aware I was only fourteen when I was seduced with promises of a beautiful life. Instead found myself in a living nightmare. One that I'd become accustomed to over the years and that ended six months ago with a single gunshot. But it was only replaced with the prospect of a different kind of hell. So I ran.

"I don't know what to do," I mumble, dropping my head on my folded arms. "I don't know where to go from here."

"You're already doing it," Pam says, switching chairs so she's sitting beside me. She puts a hand on my back. "You're slowly reclaiming your own life. You've got your own place now. You've got a job. There's nowhere to go but up, honey."

"I'll lose it all, if they find out," I whisper, voicing my biggest fear; that the life I'm building will be gone in a heartbeat, once anyone finds out where I've been. What I've done.

Pam makes a hissing sound, admonishing me, "You underestimate them. I can't blame you, but you're wrong. There are many people in this world, the bulk of people, who are kind, who don't judge, and who are ready to embrace anyone without judgement. It's a tragedy that you've never had a chance to experience that. But in the life you have now? You just need to open up to let it in. Have a little faith." Her voice becomes more impassioned and I raise my head. "Start small," she encourages. "Viv often comes here to help with the group sessions, you know that. She's heard every story there is to hear. That woman doesn't have a judgmental bone in her body. Start with her."

-

The alarm shows two in the morning.

I've been rolling around in bed ever since Pam dropped me off at home. She'd offered for me to stay the night at the shelter, but I wanted to go home. The concept of *home* still feels unfamiliar, but I want to embrace it. It symbolizes independence. Something I've not had before.

The thoughts running through my mind have kept me up. Everything is so complicated. If I tell people where I come from, if I let them in, I may put them at risk. I feel stuck in place. Every time I think of taking a step forward, there are consequences, and not just for me, for those around me too. People I've come to care about, even if they don't know who I am.

I know Pam is right. The only way forward is to take a step, otherwise I'll stay caught in this vacuum. I know the first step I should be taking is going to the police and telling them what I know. That would be the right thing to do. It would also bring my entire past to light, for everyone to see, and will eliminate any chance I have to build a life for myself.

That jump-starts my mind on thoughts of Tim and his demand for a *talk*. The scene outside Pam's door had been intense. I believed him when he said he was sorry he upset me, and I'd surprised, even myself, when I tried to shield him from Pam. It doesn't matter that I am attracted to him, that I like him, because he made clear he sees me as a friend. I can do that. I think. I've never really had friends before, certainly not male friends, but I could try. I want to try.

With the memory of Tim's big hands spanning my hips and his heat behind me, I finally fall asleep.

CHAPTER SIX

Ruby

"Are you going to the shelter tonight?"

It's Wednesday afternoon, and I've finally worked myself up to approaching Viv, as Pam suggested.

She turns to me with a smile. "Planning to. Are you ready to join the group? Want a ride?"

I shake my head. "Someone has to stay here."

"Right," she says, smacking herself in the forehead before turning curious eyes back on me. "So why were you asking?"

I look behind me to make sure we're alone in the kitchen. Matt is out front and Dino won't show for another hour. I have time. "Pam suggested I maybe talk to you."

"Okay," she says easily and waves at a kitchen chair. "Sit. Want some coffee? I just made a new pot. Decaf, though," she says with a grimace, her hand instinctively covering her lower abdomen.

Oh.

"I had no idea," I blurt out, staring at her hand. Viv looks down at herself, and then furtively at the door, before her eyes come to rest on me. She lifts her index finger to her lips.

"It's new and we're keeping it to ourselves for now." She winks with a very happy smile on her face.

I pretend to turn a lock against my lips, as I fight off the twinge of jealousy. "I won't say a word," I promise. "And I'd love to have a decaf."

When Viv sits down across from me, I suddenly get cold feet. I keep my head down but can feel her eyes on me.

"You know," she starts. "If you're not ready to talk about whatever is on your mind, we can always do it another time."

I look up and see only friendly concern on her face. "No," I declare firmly. "I have to start somewhere…"

Viv's quiet laugh startles me. "I'm guessing that's me? Bring it on, honey." Her face turns serious as she leans forward. "I swear I can take it."

I taken a moment to fortify with a sip of coffee before speaking. "My life…before I came to Portland… It was not a good life."

That's it. That's all I manage to say before the words get stuck, but then Viv grabs my hand across the table.

"Figured as much, honey. But I also figure that you're good people. Pam doesn't vouch for anyone she doesn't believe in one-hundred-percent. So I know. I *know*." She enforces the last word with a squeeze of my hand.

"I'm a prostitute. A *puta*. A whore." The distasteful words fly out of my mouth with force.

"Were…" Viv says softly, not letting go of my hand.

"Sorry?"

"You *were* a prostitute," she points out. "I'm guessing the reason you ended up at Florence House is that you no longer wish to be."

"I never did," I jump in. "I made a really bad decision when I was young and got caught up in something I never thought I'd be able to escape." I can hear how flat and emotionless my voice sounds.

"How young?" Viv's voice sounds strangled. I'm surprised to see tears in her eyes. Tears that have long ago dried up in mine.

"Fourteen."

A gasp from the doorway has me up and on my feet instantly. When I whirl around, I'm mortified to find Syd with little baby,

Caden, in her arms, and Gunnar behind her in the doorway, his hand on her shoulder. Syd is looking at me with shock, but Gunnar's face looks angry. Before they have a chance to react, I do. And I do it running, slipping through the door and out the back, where I run into the solid mass that is Dino, just coming in.

"Whoa," he rumbles, grabbing onto my upper arms. "Where's the fire?"

"Let me go!" I struggle against his hold when Gunnar's voice sounds behind me.

"Ruby." His tone is stern and invites no argument. When I turn to face him, Dino's hands still on my shoulders, giving me unexpected support, his face is not angry but seems almost sad. Still, I flinch when his hand comes up, making him hesitate before he gently cups the side of my face. "Your age was a shock, but the rest of it? It wasn't exactly a huge revelation. In fact, it explains a lot." His hand slides to the back of my neck where he takes a firm grip and pulls me toward him. "There are two women in that kitchen, who know a little bit about needing to drag yourself through fire to find your peace. Talk to them." With that he wraps his arm around me, and I let him guide me back through the door, down the hall, and into the kitchen. I stop just inside the door and blink against the burning behind my eyelids. Gunnar walks past me into the kitchen and reaches for his son before turning to Dino. "Office. You, Caden, and I have a menu to discuss." He walks out with Dino closely on his heels, leaving me to look after them open-mouthed.

"Never mind those caveman antics," Syd says, as she slides her arm around me and moves me toward the table, where Viv is still sitting in the same spot, her eyes red-rimmed. "But I heard what he said, and he's right. You can talk to us."

I'm stunned silent by their reaction, so instead of pushing me to talk or asking me questions, Syd and Viv do most of the talking. Their stories are so heartbreaking, I have to swallow a few times before I manage to start talking. In large lines, I tell them how I was kept in a *training* house, with other young women, for two years. I tell them about being moved around from city to city, and hotel to hotel, for years until I was of more value working behind the bar of a gang-run club, and looking after the new girls that occasionally would be brought in, than I was on my back. I even tell them that when I was a witness to a violent incident, I grabbed a single moment of opportunity and ran.

What I don't tell them is that because of me, my parents were murdered. I also don't tell them any specific locations or names, hoping that way I wouldn't put them at risk. By the time I've shared all I feel I'm able to, there's a half-empty box of tissues in the middle of the kitchen table. But a tiny seed of hope for redemption has been planted.

Dino walks in, with Gunnar right behind him holding Caden, effectively shutting down any lingering conversation.

"Sorry," Dino rumbles. "If I don't get prepping now, I won't be able to keep up with the dinner crowd." Without looking at any of us, he walks into the cold storage.

Gunnar walks up behind me and puts a hand on my shoulder. "You good to work?" he asks when I twist around to look at him.

"I think so. Do you mind if I give Dino a hand first?" The request surprises me as much as it does Gunnar, but I feel empowered. No time like the present to learn the workings of a kitchen. I messed up my last opportunity.

"Fine by me. Viv?"

"No problem," she agrees with Gunnar before turning to me. "I'll holler when we need you up front?"

"Thank you," I say to her, for more than just that.

"We'd better be off. This little one will be wanting to nurse soon." Gunnar looks adoringly at the little sleeping face in the crook of his arm. "And the other two are likely raiding the fridge, as we speak. I just popped in to pick up some paperwork to do at home."

Syd gets up, rounds the table, and surprises me by opening her arms and wrapping them around me. I feel awkward in her embrace and clumsily pat her on the back a few times, telling her *thanks*. "Anytime, Ruby," she offers, before following Gunnar out the door.

Next is Viv, who just grabs my hand and gives it a squeeze. "That took guts," she mumbles under her voice, making sure only I can hear. "We can talk more anytime you like." With a wink, she's gone too.

"You gonna stand there, or give me a hand?" Dino's gruff voice spurs me into action and until the first orders start coming in, I learn how to slice and dice like a chef. When I finally show my face in the pub, I do it smiling.

That little seed of hope is sprouting.

Tim

"What are you up to?"

My brother's standard question has me roll my eyes. "I'm pulling on my boots to go out. At least I was until you called. What are you up to?"

"I need a drink," he says, sounding beat.

"You're in luck, I'm heading out to The Skipper just for that reason. Meet me there?"

I'm not kidding. I need a drink myself after the fabulous start to the week I've had. Brenda was obviously still pissed I ditched her last week. She's been busy these past few days, making my life difficult. My own damn fault. I knew it was a bad idea to begin with and took her out anyway. This morning one of our engineers, Brad, nudged me when we were leaving the boardroom after a project meeting. One in which Brenda had made it blatantly clear to everyone present, with batting eyelashes and overly familiar gestures, that we have a relationship that goes beyond professional. I tried to ignore her, but it had obviously not been missed by Brad.

"You tap that?" was what he said to me. Son of a bitch. I told him, "Absolutely not," but I could tell from the smirk on his face he wasn't buying. To add insult to injury, my boss was standing six feet away and had obviously heard the exchange, raising his eyebrow at me. *Great.*

I'd holed up in my office the rest of the day, trying to keep my head down, wondering if I should confront her or whether that would just fuel the fire.

"I can be there in an hour," Mark says. "I've got some paperwork to finish up and need to stuff something in my mouth. Haven't eaten since fucking breakfast."

"Grab something at the pub," I suggest.

"I can do that. See you in a bit." He hangs up before I have a chance to answer.

Maybe I should get his opinion. Mark's got a good head on his shoulders, he may have some thoughts on how I should handle this.

-

I spot Ruby behind the bar the moment I walk in. There's a decent crowd for this time of year, and it looks like Matt and Ruby are busy. No sign of Viv though, but Ike is sitting at the end of the bar in his usual spot.

"Where's Viv?" I ask, and sit my ass down on the stool beside him.

"Group therapy. She was gonna come back here after."

I grunt in response, but my eyes have been on Ruby from the moment I walked in. Watching her in action is something else. Smiling and chatting up the customers is a far cry from the almost shy and reserved Ruby I usually get. Except the scene the other night. That one was so far out on left field, I still don't know what to make of it. The woman is a walking contradiction. Even now, I know she saw me come in, but she still avoids looking at me.

"Ruby? Can I get a draft?" Her eyes flick to me at the sound of her name, but she only nods in response.

"What'd you do?" Ike asks, looking between Ruby and me. "Did you piss her off?"

I groan as I drop my head in my hands. "Seems to be a going trend," I mumble, but Ike hears and the moment Ruby places my beer in front of me he pounces.

"Talk."

I glance to see if we're out of earshot before I start talking. I tell him how I made the mistake of asking Brenda out, ended up bringing her here, and the fiasco that followed Friday night. I also describe what my week at the office has been like so far.

"Sounds like your Brenda doesn't like rejection much," Ike says in a dry tone.

"She's not *my* fucking Brenda," I bite off, just as Ruby walks by, a slight hitch in her step when she obviously hears me. Just fucking wonderful.

"Easy, my friend." Ike's soothing tone does little to settle my aggravation. But Ruby's warm brown eyes, now turned to me with obvious concern, do. This time she doesn't look away and I'm caught in her gaze, feeling my heart rate slow down. "Really?" I hear Ike mumble beside me. When I reluctantly drag my eyes away, I find the question plastered on his face. "You went there? Christ you've been busy."

A quick look reveals Ruby now has her back turned, giving me the opportunity to lean into Ike. "Pushing all the wrong buttons tonight, *friend,*" I spit out under my voice. "I'm having a hard time keeping my seat, so better fucking check what you say about her."

With a firm hand in my chest, Ike pushes me out of his space. "Calm your tits. All I'm saying is she is not one to mess around with. There's a reason she ended up with Pam. Whatever brought her there is not out of her system yet."

"Funny," I point out with a smirk. "Would seem that not that long ago I was telling you something similar about Viv." That got a smile out of Ike.

"Yeah. And she's wearing my wedding ring now." His smug look is soon replaced with a more serious face. "Seriously, man. No offense, but this one is not even your type."

I regard him for a minute before letting my eyes drift to Ruby again. Short, round, dark little Ruby, so different from my usual fare of tall, slim, and blonde, and who confuses the hell out of me. "I know," I mutter.

"Talking about offense, did you catch the game on Sunday? Fuck, that Brady has some serious butter fingers. Last three games, I thought I was gonna have a coronary before he finally managed to turn things around. Viv had the phone ready with her finger poised to dial 911."

"Almost did too. Several times." Viv's smoky voice sounds behind us, and Ike turns around to catch his wife in his arms. "Hey, honey," she says, when Ike finally lets her come up for air. "You boys playing nice?"

"Always," Ike lies with a sideward glance at me.

"Yup," I confirm, when Viv's eyes turn to me squinting.

"I'll take your word for it," she says, making it clear she's not convinced. Her attention zooms in on the line forming at the other end of the bar, where Ruby is trying to keep up. "Better give these guys a hand."

With a last kiss for Ike, one I could've gladly done without, she's gone, and we continue our commiserating on the Patriots QB's lackluster performance thus far this season.

Three beers later, a heavy hand falls on my shoulder.

"Mark, how've you been?" Ike directs over my shoulder. I'd totally forgotten he was supposed to meet me here.

About two hours ago.

I turn around on my stool and take in my brother's bedraggled appearance. "Took you long enough," I poke at him a little. A tired grin tells me he takes it as the friendly ribbing I intended.

"Work is just…" He shakes his head as he lets his words drift off.

"Day got even tougher?"

"Yeah. Sorry," he says, pulling up a stool on my other side. "Remember that girl I told you about on Sunday?"

I nod with a wince. I remember it all too well.

"Call came in, just as I was about to leave. She'd been tucked away in a safe house, and they found her dead this afternoon. Sixteen fucking years old. She'd pocketed a paring knife from the kitchen, locked herself in the bathroom, filled the tub, and sat there slicing her forearms from wrist to elbow. By the time the agents broke down the door, it was already too late." His head slumps down on his arms. "I lost it when I heard. May have done some damage to the captain's office." He lifts up and looks at me with turmoil in his eyes. "I was suspended, pending psychiatric assessment."

"Jesus, Mark. For getting upset?"

"Not the first time," he softly admits, dropping his head down. "Job's been getting to me. Today was just the last straw." He chuckles, "Guess tossing his computer through the window was the last straw for the captain."

Nothing I can say, so I reach out and give his neck a squeeze. I don't think I've ever appreciated the pressures and the frustration of being in law enforcement. Having to look at the underbelly of humanity every day, dealing with victims of violent crimes, with the animals committing them, that's got to do something to you.

I spot Ruby and wave her over. She walks up, a look of concern on her face as she eyes the back of my brother's head once again on the bar. I'm struck by the compassionate warmth in her brown eyes. "Think we need something stronger than beer here. Scotch? Bring the bottle, honey. And three glasses."

As Ruby turns away, Mark lifts up his head and vigorously rubs his hands over his face.

"Sounds tough," Ike directs at him.

"I've had better days," he responds with a wry smile. "Hers must've been much worse, though." With affirming grunts from Ike and myself, Mark gets up and pushes away from the bar. "Right back. Gotta hit the can."

I watch my brother walk through the door to the restrooms, the weight of the world a bit heavier today, judging by the more pronounced slump in his shoulders.

"He doesn't look good," Ike points out.

"I know," I agree. "I've always worried the job might eventually get to him, but it was his dream to be a cop since he was five-years-old." I chuckle at the memory. "I'd wanted to be a lumberjack for Halloween, my dream at the time, but Mark was adamant; he wanted to have a police uniform, complete with badge and billy club. Whined for days when Mom couldn't find one in Portland, until she finally drove into Boston to a specialty store to get him what he wanted."

"Lumberjack? You?" Ike chuckles.

"You know, I liked building things with my hands," I admit. "My father had that wood shop in the garage and used to build birdhouses and bookcases. Remember, he'd let us help cut the wood with a handsaw sometimes? When I got older, we started building side tables, spice racks, all kinds of smaller wood furniture. I got pretty good at it."

"I knew that, but never realized how much you love it." Ike looks at me surprised.

"Yeah, well, Mark dreamed of catching bad guys ,and I dreamed of building furniture for the children I was going to have. Then I grew up and got a real job." I shrug, ignoring the long forgotten pang of regret.

I'm glad to see Ruby approach with three glasses and a bottle. A welcome distraction in more ways than one. "This okay?" she asks, holding up a full bottle of Gunnar's *prime* collection. Both Ike and I chuckle, knowing he'd flip his lid if he knew.

"Perfect," Ike answers for me. "Tim here will replace it before Gunnar even knows it's gone. Ouch!" He flinches when I elbow him in the ribs. Hard. "That hurt," he adds unnecessarily.

"Just leave it here, Ruby, and is it too late to get something from the kitchen for my brother? He hasn't eaten yet."

Her eyes light up with interest when I mention my brother and with a quickly mumbled, "Of course," and a hesitant smile, she disappears down the hallway.

I'm still focused on the spot I saw her disappear, when Mark's large frame blocks my view. "What were you staring at?" He wants to know when he takes his seat beside me. I dismiss his question with a shrug of my shoulders, as I crack the bottle and pour us all two fingers, but Ike is more than happy to oblige.

"Your brother has developed an interesting fascination with Ruby," he volunteers with a smile, eliciting a groan from me.

"Who's Ruby?" Mark turns to me with one eyebrow raised.

Again Ike feels the need to answer. "The luscious brunette, about five foot nothing, who started a few months ago. Took a while, but I think he's finally recognizing a rare treasure when he sees it."

"I have to see this woman," my brother says, twisting around on his stool. I drop my chin down on my chest, exasperated, yet knowing when I'm outnumbered.

"Here she is. Bringing you a plate," Ike helpfully points out.

"You?" Mark's voice sounds surprised.

A sharp intake of breath and the sound of something breaking has me sharply snap up my head. Mark is half out of his seat, and Ruby has her hands clasped to her mouth, her face a sickly white. The plate with Mark's dinner in pieces around her feet.

"What the…" Before I have a chance to finish, Ruby whips around and tears out of the bar.

CHAPTER SEVEN

Ruby

"Whoa. Where you running to twice in one day?"

The voice belongs to Dino, against whose chest I bumped for the second time. This time, I can't afford to let him hold me back. Struggling in his grip, I don't register the footsteps behind me until two strong arms band around my waist and a voice sounds in my ear, "I've got you."

"You sure, man?" Dino asks, not sounding too sure himself, as I let myself go limp in the firm hold around my body.

"Positive," he answers, taking all of my weight when Dino slowly lets go of my arms.

With my eyes closed and my head down, I let him shuffle me down the hall. I don't open them until I hear a door click shut behind me and his voice whisper my name. "Ruby?"

I'm in Gunnar's office, and Tim is walking me over to the love seat where he pushes me down. Sliding down on his knees in front of me, he places his big hands firmly on my legs, keeping me tethered in place.

"How do you know my brother?"

I flinch at his question, but there is nothing but concern in his voice. No threat, no accusation, just concern and probably confusion. I'm confused too. "I don't," I whisper the truth.

"But you recognized him. Hell, he recognized you."

"I know. I've seen him before. Just this weekend. He talked to me in the parking lot, when I was walking home. I thought…" I stop myself from telling Tim I ran from him, thinking perhaps they found me. "I was afraid," I say instead.

"Of Mark?" His disbelief cuts me and instead of answering, I just shrug.

"But he's a cop. He works for the Portland PD."

"He does?"

I realize Tim probably expects that to alleviate my fear, but it does the opposite. My experience with the police has not been good, so that bit of news doesn't instill a feeling of safety.

Before either of us have a chance to say anything, the door opens and the topic of conversation walks in, closing the door behind him.

"I thought you looked familiar," he says, with his arms crossed in front of him and his back against the door, looking relaxed for all intents and purposes. But the intense scrutiny in his eyes contradicts that.

"Mark…Give us a minute?" Tim's hands haven't left my legs. In fact, he's only tightened his grip to the point of pain.

"No," I interrupt, not wanting to cause trouble between Tim and the brother he so obviously loves. "It's okay," I assure Tim, the feeling of empty resignation hollow in my chest. Then I turn to the man by the door. "I saw you outside my apartment building."

"You did. I'd just responded to a domestic disturbance call and was on my way back to the precinct when I spotted you. Thought I recognized you from your picture, but wasn't sure until your reaction just now."

I try to stay calm, but panic starts closing off my airway. "Picture?" I manage, my voice sounding as ragged as my thoughts.

"Single potential witness to a gang-related execution, close to seven months ago, in Boston. Closed video surveillance shows what looks to be a woman hiding behind a stack of crates in a warehouse on Shipyard Point. On the footage, you can count the number of shots fired out of range of the camera, based on the woman's response to each one. All eight of them. One for each arm and leg, one to his jewels, one in the gut, another one in the chest and the final one, the one that finally killed him, right between the eyes. Then the woman runs, and when she turns around for one last look, her face is in perfect view. Snap!"

With every word from his mouth, I'm transported back to the warehouse. I am hearing each one of the shots he describes and the screams that resulted. Except the last one. That one was followed by an eerie silence, in which I held my breath, trying desperately not to make a sound. When I'd heard footsteps going in the opposite direction, I left my shoes and ran.

When Mark barks out the last word, my body jerks as if someone punched me. I hear a rushing in my ears that all but drowns out Tim's loud protests. "What the fuck, man! What the hell is wrong with you?" he yells at his brother, while at the same time sitting down beside me and wrapping his arms around me.

My body shakes uncontrollably and I'm gasping for air. I can't breathe.

Tim

I'm still glaring at Mark when I feel her body go limp. I can barely grab her as she slides off the edge of the couch, managing

to pull her up and swing her legs on the seat. Then Dino bursts into the office, with Ike and Viv right behind him.

"Outta my fucking way!" Dino bellows, as he shoves me hard on the shoulder, dropping on his knees beside Ruby.

I feel angry and useless and force my attention on Mark. "That's how you guys treat potential witnesses? No fucking wonder she was terrified, you asshole. No wonder she's on the run, if this is the kind of treatment waiting for her. Fuck you, man! Fuck you!" I realize I'm out of control, and about to lay my brother out, when Ike grabs me from behind and Viv gets in my face.

"Honey. Calm yourself. You're not helping the situation."

Normally it would've been Viv's smoky voice that would've settled me, but not this time. This time it's Dino's low, deep, threatening rumble. "You lot, get the fuck out of here. Take them to the kitchen, Ike. Fucking knock some sense into either or both." When I turn around, I see the big man sitting on the couch with Ruby's body curled up in his lap, her hands clutched in his shirt. The sight hits me in the gut.

"Let's go," Ike says, keeping his arm around my shoulder as he guides me out of the room.

-

"Tim."

I ignore my brother's voice, focusing instead on my clenched fists on the kitchen table. Anger still courses freshly through my blood, a million questions through my mind. And to top it all, sitting heavy in my chest, is jealousy: irrational, unexpected jealousy.

I take a few deep breaths to calm down when Viv slides a coffee on the table in front of me, after checking on the pub. Matt's closing shop, brushing off the last remaining patrons.

"Thanks," I automatically reply, and her hand gives my shoulder a quick squeeze.

"Was that necessary?" I ask a guilty-looking Mark, when I finally trust myself to speak. His eyes meet mine over the table and I can see regret in his eyes.

"No," he admits quietly. "It wasn't."

"Look," Ike pipes up. "Why don't you tell us what that was all about?"

"It's this damn case," Mark says, his hands running restlessly through his hair. "This young girl, a witness. She was found dead this afternoon. She was sexually assaulted just days before. She wouldn't talk, wouldn't testify, and within hours, the FBI walked in and took custody of her."

"You told me that," I remind him. "It doesn't explain why you went off on Ruby."

"Seven months ago, Carlos Delgado was shot execution style in a warehouse, just outside Boston. Delgado was a big man in the Boston sex trade. Owner of three clubs, and by all accounts, controlled most of the street action in Boston. A witness to his murder was captured on video and later picked up. She was questioned by local police and released after seventy-two hours, when they had nothing to hold her on. She disappeared from sight and her picture has been circulating police departments up and down the coast for months. It's a picture of Ruby"

A sharp intake of breath from Viv draws my attention. Her face is ashen and her hands are covering her mouth.

"What?" Ike wants to know, tilting his wife's face with his hands.

"She told us," she mumbles behind her hands. "She said she'd witnessed a violent incident and ran."

"What else did she say?" Mark jumps on it, but Viv shakes her head.

"Try asking her," she bites off, challenging him.

Mark is the first one to break their stare down and looks up at me with a mix of regret and frustration on his face.

"What does Ruby have to do with that sexual assault victim?" I ask him, my eyes never leaving his.

"Nothing. Everything. I don't know, but I know the FBI had the girl listed as a potential informant in the Delgado case."

"And she's dead," I point out unnecessarily, reeling with the information and trying to sort out what it all means.

"Dead?" Ruby's soft voice sounds from the doorway, where she stands with Dino's large frame behind her. His hands resting on her shoulders.

Mark pushes up from his chair, just as I get up from mine. But by the time I move around the table, Mark has beaten me to her. With eyes as big as saucers, she looks from one to the other. Ignoring my brother, I step around him, grab Ruby's hand and gently pull her away from Dino. I don't miss the way the corner of his mouth twitches. Asshole. I also don't miss the way she takes a wide berth around Mark, her body instinctively pressing against mine. Not going to complain about that.

"Come sit," I coax her to the chair next to the one I was sitting in and leave my arm to rest on the back of it.

Mark sits down again across from us. "I'm sorry I went off on you earlier."

"Who's dead?" Ruby's voice is soft, but filled with determination, as she chooses to ignore Mark's apology.

"A young girl. Victim of sexual assault." This time he is much more careful with his words, and his tone, as he briefly explains. Still Ruby winces at the words, but before she can react, Mark continues. "Why did you run?"

Her derisive snort sounds harsh in the kitchen as everyone quietly listens. "No offense, but the ones I've come in contact with over the years have hardly been upstanding citizens. There was no help to be found there," she states matter-of-factly, before shrugging her shoulders. "Doesn't matter now."

"Why do you say that?" Mark wants to know.

"Because you'll take me in. Hand me over to the Boston PD, and that'll be the end of that," she says with unexpected heat, as she leans forward on the table.

"Hold on," I direct her. "No one is taking you anywhere." The last I accompany with an unmistakable glare at my brother.

"He's right," he directs at Ruby, rubbing the back of his neck. "I'm hardly on good terms myself. I'd still like to know what happened."

After a heavy silence, and a long look around the kitchen at every person present, Ruby seems to come to a decision when her eyes land and stay on Mark. "Tell me something?" she asks. "In those reports you've seen, was there any mention of arrests being made? Any mention of the men I identified and named? I did, you know?" she states, as disbelief is evident on Mark's face. "I knew three of them. I named them. Several times. When the detective who was interviewing me shrugged it off, not once, but a number of times, I realized I was on my own." She looks down at the hands clasped in her lap. "When they let me go after three days in their holding cell, one of those three men was waiting across the street from the police station. And then I knew—I couldn't trust anyone. Especially not the police."

In the silence that follows, the list of questions in my head grows. What was she doing there with Delgado? Why? Those seem to be the ones that dominate the many others. I'm surprised by the lack of tears. The woman sits there dry-eyed, her face almost devoid of color, her back ramrod straight; the only outward sign of distress, the shaking of the hands in her lap. But I can see the hopelessness underneath the unemotional exterior; smell the fear thick in the air.

"Someone tipped them off," Mark bites off.

"It would seem so," Ruby answers with deceptive calm.

Ruby

Last time I checked my alarm, it was three in the morning. This time it shows only half an hour has passed since.

I rolled into bed a few hours ago, exhausted, but the moment my head hit the pillow my brain went into overdrive.

I'd opened up all right. All over the table, in a kitchen full to capacity. If ever I could trust anyone, it would be the people gathered at that time. With the exception of Tim's brother—for obvious reasons.

Tim's arm had stayed around my back the entire time. At some point, he even covered my hands with one of his own. Discussions were flying around, everyone weighing in with their ideas, their opinions. I just shut down. Resigned to have my future, or lack thereof, in the hands of these people. In the hands of one cop.

It surprised me when Mark was the one who suggested someone take me home. I faintly registered the ensuing tug of war over whether I should go with Viv and Ike, have Dino drop me off at the shelter, or even go with Tim to his place. Finally I announced I'd be going home—to *my* place. I didn't have the energy to fight Tim when he announced he'd stay with me. I have to hand it to him though, he never asked a single question. Despite the fact I could see each and every one of them playing out on his face.

Not a single one. All he said was, "Get some rest," before grabbing the throw from the back of the couch and stretching out, a small red pillow tucked behind his head. That was hours ago. A soft snore from the direction of the living room was proof at least one of us was getting some shuteye.

Grudgingly I get out of bed, the urge to pee becoming impossible to ignore. After taking care of business, I dry my hands on the towel and walk into the bedroom where the sight of Tim sitting on the edge of my bed stops me in my tracks. My first reaction is to look down at my state of dress, which is minimal at best. Nothing but a large men's t-shirt, bought for three dollars at a thrift store and serving as nightshirt, and a pair of white cotton undies. At least my torso and ass are covered, but the dimples covering my substantial thighs are not. *Wonderful.*

"Can't sleep?" Tim's voice, raspy with sleep, drags me from the intense study of my cellulite.

"No," I respond, tugging uselessly at the hem of my shirt. "What are you doing here?" They say the best defense is offense, and I'm putting it to the test. Unfortunately, Tim doesn't seem impressed.

"You've got to get some sleep, Ruby," he says, completely ignoring my question as he gets up and takes a few steps toward me. I try hard to ignore the way his undershirt stretches across the expanse of his chest. He must've taken off his sweater last night. Socks and boots too, from the look of the nice-looking bare feet, sticking out of the legs of his jeans. *Gracias a Dios,* he's still wearing jeans.

Putting his arm around my shoulder, he guides me to the bed and urges me to lie down. He pulls the covers over me, and to my surprise, lies down next to me on top of the bedding. I'm not sure what to make of it. Under any other circumstances, having a man crawl in bed with me would have crystal clear implications. But this is Tim, and I've already made the mistake once of trying to anticipate his expectations. I won't be doing that again.

"Would it help to talk about it?" he asks tentatively.

"About what exactly?" The sarcastic tone I can't hold back doesn't escape Tim's notice. From his position, with his arms folded behind his head, he turns only his eyes to me.

"How about we start with what is keeping you up?"

"Nothing. Everything." I roll on my side so I face him. "I keep waiting for a knock on the door, announcing the police are here to take me away."

"You don't have to worry about that," he says, settling on his side, facing me with one hand tucked under his pillow.

"But your brother…" I start before he cuts me off.

"Was suspended from active duty today," he fills me in.

"Oh."

We lie there, quietly looking at each other. It feels weirdly intimate, despite the fact our bodies aren't touching anywhere. His eyes are slightly red-rimmed from sleep, making the blue stand out even brighter. Lines fan out from the corners, witness to years of laughter. In contrast, the furrow between his heavy eyebrows shows those years were not all worry-free. Deep crescent-shaped grooves curve around his strong mouth, and his square chin sports a greying, dark russet scruff.

"Sleep," he mutters, his voice almost willing my eyelids to close.

CHAPTER EIGHT

Tim

The silent vibration of my cell, in the pocket of my jeans, wakes me up.

I'm still in the same position I was in when I finally fell asleep, which was well after Ruby's eyes closed and her breathing slowed down.

I can't remember ever experiencing anything like those minutes we spent studying each other's face. There'd been nothing furtive about it. It felt like we were trying to *learn* each other. Touching without hands or mouths, and yet feeling oddly connected.

Ruby did move in her sleep, having kicked off the blankets that are now twisted around her legs. Her hands are tucked under her cheek, and one leg is stretched, while the other is pulled up to the side. Both modest and wanton at the same time, much like the contradiction that she is.

My eyes follow the lines of her legs, from her small feet and narrow ankles, to the muscular calves and soft, thick thighs. I don't allow myself to linger on the dark hint of pubic hair behind the white cotton of her panties. The sight of a mark on the tender inside of her leg has me lean in a little. A tattoo is my first thought, but as I get closer, I can see the skin is raised. A circle with on the inside two elegant letters: C and D. *Jesus.*

I must've said that out loud, because the next thing I know Ruby is scrambling for the covers.

"He branded you?" I grind out between clenched teeth, as I jump out of bed and glare down at her. It's no surprise to see fear on her face. "Like cattle? He marked you as his?"

Recognizing my anger is not directed at her, she pulls herself into a sitting position, carefully keeping her bottom half covered. She looks me straight in the eyes as she nods. "At first, every year to keep it from healing," she says in a soft but steady voice. "For protection, he said. All the girls in his stable have this."

I sag down on the edge of the bed, my head in my hands. Every year? All the girls in his *stable*? Holy fucking hell.

"All his whores," she states bluntly. When I look at her, there's a challenge in her eyes. Daring me to react. I can't help it, I can feel the twitch of my face before I can stop it, but it's too late.

Her eyes turn down as she flips back the blankets, gets up from the bed, and walks into the bathroom, closing and locking the door behind her.

Somehow I feel like I've been tested. I failed miserably.

-

"Veldman! My office in five."

The last few days of this week haven't gotten any better, and my boss calling me into his office at the end of the afternoon on a Friday, does not bode well for my weekend. Call it the cherry on top.

Yesterday morning, I'd sat stupidly on the side of Ruby's bed, waiting fruitlessly for her to emerge from the bathroom where she'd holed up. When after ten minutes of silence I'd heard the shower start running, the message was clear. Already cutting it close for the site inspection scheduled for that morning, I got dressed and beelined it home for a shower and change. By the time I parked my car across from the lot, I could see the team already assembled on the other side of the street. A car door slamming shut behind me drew my attention. I almost groaned out loud when I saw Brenda walk toward me, a takeout coffee in each hand, and a predatory little smile on her carefully made-up face.

"Well, hello, handsome," she virtually cooed, sending an involuntary shiver down my back.

"Morning." I tried to convey a business-only attitude, but I don't think she got the message. She pressed the coffee into my hand, making sure to drag her fingers along the backs of mine.

"Just the way you like it." If I had any doubts about her intentions, her suggestive voice and words would've taken care of those. The lady was determined, I had to give her that.

Shaking my head, I'd followed her exaggerated sway of hips across the street where Steve Cletor, my boss, was closely observing our approach.

"Glad you could join us," he said, not bothering to hide the sarcasm from his voice, as he looked pointedly at the twin Starbucks cups we were holding.

Things had gone downhill from there.

After inspecting the site and discussing a proposed construction schedule, we walked back to the parking lot. I'd been distracted by the memory of the sad resignation on Ruby's face, as she disappeared into the bathroom this morning, and the sharp pang of regret in the pit of my stomach that resulted.

"No thanks, I'll just get a ride with Tim."

Brenda's annoying voice pulls me out of my head, and I'm surprised to see her turn away from Steve and march my way.

"My car won't start," she explains.

It was a load of crock. I knew it, she knew I knew it, but with my boss watching our interaction closely, I waved to the passenger side. "Get in."

By the time I dropped her off at her hotel, I'd told her in no uncertain terms that whatever she was hoping to accomplish—I was not interested. It was obvious she wasn't happy in the way she slammed my door. Back at the office, Steve had cornered me, coming out of the elevator.

"Anything I should know?" He didn't need to explain what he was talking about.

"Other than that I'm not looking forward to spending the next year working with that woman? No. There is absolutely nothing for you to know." I could tell he was taken aback. I've always presented an even keeled, almost laid back attitude, but this time my temper got the better of me.

The entire rest of my Thursday was spent buried under a pile of work, with clear instructions not to disturb me for anything. It wasn't hard to put the scene with Brenda out of my head but much harder to forget about certain chocolate brown eyes, openly reading my face in the dim light of dawn. Not to mention the recollection of that ugly mark on those soft, creamy thighs. And all that implied.

I stayed in the office late, but I spent most of my time thinking.

By this morning, after a rather restless night's sleep, I'd come to the conclusion that taking some distance from Ruby and The Skipper might not be a bad idea. I needed my life to be predictable, organized, and safe. That's how I designed it. Growing up with parents, who were just two aging hippies, still living the seventies free love movement, even within their marriage, had made for almost constant emotional chaos. That's why instead of pursuing dreams, which is what my folks existed on, I opted for a dependable existence. Regardless of any emotional involvement I might feel, any physical attraction I might have, Ruby's life and history screams chaos. No, I was going to have to keep her firmly in the friend zone.

Of course the rest of my day was spent reconsidering.

-

"Steve," I announce myself, as I walk into my boss's office. "You wanted to see me?"

The older man lifts his head and indicates the chair on the other side of his desk. "Sit," he says, folding his hands in front of him on the desk.

Twenty minutes later, I am escorted to my car by a security guard, with a box of my belongings in my hands. Numb, I drive my brand new Audi off the lot, after handing in my badge and parking pass at the gate. I hesitate only for a second, before turning in the direction of the water.

I'm not quite sure how I got here, but one thing stands out in the blurred haze of my mind as I push open the door to The Skipper.

"Do you want to see the menu?" A tight, tremulous smile greets me when I sit down at the bar.

Ruby.

Ruby

I should be hurt. Disappointed at the very least, but the moment Tim walks in with confusion in his eyes, and the weight of the world resting on his shoulders, all that disappears.

Hurt had been my first reaction Thursday morning. But then Viv had shown up, checking in on me. I'd hurried to the door, thinking perhaps Tim had come back. Hoping maybe the connection I'd felt to him in the early hours of the morning, had not just been one-sided. I had to fight to keep the disappointment from my face when I found Viv on the doorstep, coffee and a bag of pastries in her hands.

She asked how my night had been, to which I simply answered it had been fine. With a pronounced lift of her eyebrows, she asked about Tim. Without going into detail, I told her he'd slept on the couch and left first thing this morning. She almost seemed disappointed, but quickly covered it by offering me the day off.

I took it and ended up spending some time at Florence House that afternoon, filling Pam in on all that had happened. I didn't hold anything back from her. Talking it through helped put some things in perspective. Pam pointed out it was hardly fair to Tim to expect him to embrace my background without thought. That it was completely normal for him to react with shock.

Today I'd come into work at my regular time. Did my regular things. Part of me felt that everything should've changed somehow, that with all the revelations of Wednesday night, people would certainly look at me differently. I was surprised, no one did.

Matt's, "Hey, Ruby," was the same as every other day, as was Viv's, "Morning!" Only when Dino walked into the kitchen, took off his coat, and walked over to pull me in a tight hug, did I feel a shift.

"You good, girl?" he rumbled, with his chin on my head.

"I'm good." I smiled into his chest, surprised to find his embrace comfortable. Brotherly.

"Are you gonna help out here again?" he asked as he released me.

"Let me check with Viv."

She had no problem with me working dinner prep in the kitchen, which is what I'd been doing all afternoon, listening to Dino's deep voice explain cooking techniques and recipes.

When the door opens, and I see the familiar blond head walk through, all emotions come rushing back. My first instinct is to hide out in the kitchen, but I remember Viv's off to the store to pick up some limes we've run out of. I can't leave the bar.

I'm shocked when Tim lifts his face. I see deep lines and grooves carve his face into a mask of hurt. What the hell happened to him?

His eyes flit around the pub until they find me and settle there.

"Do you want to see the menu?" I stupidly ask. He doesn't say anything, just shakes his head no. Without thinking, I grab the half-full bottle of scotch from Wednesday night, and pour him a drink. He barely registers the glass when I set it down in front of him.

"What happened?"

His mouth opens and closes a few times, but nothing comes out. Instead, he grabs the tumbler of scotch and tosses the contents back, slamming the glass back down on the bar—empty. "More," he instructs me, his voice raw. I do as he says and pour another, but when I try to put the bottle back, he grabs my wrist. "Leave it."

Oh boy. I know what that means. With a quick glance at Matt, who is observing Tim's odd behavior from the other end of the bar, I leave the bottle and slip down to the kitchen. If the man is going to tie one on, he won't be doing it on an empty stomach.

"Do you have anything ready?" I ask Dino as I walk in.

"Like what?"

"Food. Anything that would give a good base to a bender," I suggest to him, pulling open the fridge to see what I can put together.

"Who's going on a bender?" Dino asks, his hands on his hips.

"Tim. Something's wrong with him. Something's happened, he's acting strange. Aiming to finish up that bottle of scotch, by the looks of it."

"You get back out there," he waves me to the door. "I'll get a plate together. I'll be right out."

I don't waste time and head back to see if there's any way I can stop what seems to be a runaway train.

One look at the bottle, Tim is keeping uncapped in his hand, tells me he's had at least one or two more in the short time I was gone. Determined, I step up to the bar, grab the discarded cap, and screw it back on the bottle.

"Don't bother," he says, his eyes on me dark with emotion. "It won't stay on long."

I hold his eyes, searching for something, anything, I don't know what. Answers? An explanation to why he blows in on a Friday afternoon at three o'clock, when he would normally still be at the office, intent on getting plastered? Just before he lowers them, I see his clear blue eyes start blurring.

"Do me a favor?" Dino's voice sounds behind me, as he reaches around me and puts a wooden board with slices of cold cuts, cheeses, and a little bowl of olives in front of Tim. "I'm trying out some things to go on the after-hours bar menu Gunnar wants me to prepare. Antipasto. Give it a whirl." Without waiting for an answer, he returns to the kitchen.

"I know what you're doing," Tim says, his eyes now back on me. I opt not to answer and leave him, his bottle of scotch, and his platter of protein to tend to customers on the other end.

Clever Dino. Even though Tim shoved the board aside initially, I notice he'll occasionally snatch a piece of cheese or some meat, until the food is almost gone, save for the dish of olives. I keep my eye on him, while holding court with Arnie, and more often than not, find him looking at me. When I see him pop the last of the cheese, I casually walk over.

"Don't like olives?" I say, as I pinch one and pop it in my mouth. His eyes follow the olive as it disappears between my lips before looking at me.

"Not particularly, although I have newfound appreciation for them," he admits, as he leans forward and with his thumb, brushes a drop of oil from my bottom lip. My tongue unconsciously slips out to follow the tingle left behind. Slowly Tim drags his gaze up from where it's been fixed on my mouth. The darkness in his eyes is replaced with unexpected heat. *That*, I recognize, having seen it all too often in the eyes of nameless faces hovering over me. I just didn't expect it to find it in Tim's.

It's like the air is sucked out around us, as the sounds of the bar seem to disappear, and I'm left in a vacuum, getting lost in the deep blue pools of his eyes.

"I'm back. I can't believe I had to stop into three different places to find limes. Crazy. Those things practically roll down the streets in the summer time, but disappear like the sun in the winter." Viv's ramble, as she gently nudges me aside to put away her purchases, is enough to snap me back to reality. I slowly blink and watch Tim do the same.

"Back again?" Viv teases Tim, who tries to smile back, but is not too convincing. "You okay?" I hear her ask, as I start washing and slicing a couple of the limes, putting the wedges in the fridge for later use. His response is no more than a monosyllabic mumble.

With patrons needing refills on the other side of the bar, and Matt waving for a hand, I lose track of what's being said and instead focus on serving food and drinks. After all, that's what I'm here for. I'm not his lover, counselor, or even his friend, and if he chooses to talk to Viv instead of me, it should be no skin off my nose. Except it is. It stings—especially after sharing yet another of those intimate moments.

Aside from a few cursory glances at his broad back, bent over the beer I'm glad he changed to, I try not to pay him much mind. It isn't until I'm wiping down tables after much of the dinner crowd has left, that I notice Ike sitting next to him, one of his hands in the middle of Tim's back.

With a tub full of the dirty dishes I've collected, I head to the kitchen, where Dino is putting on his coat. The large clock on the wall says it's ten o'clock already.

"How's he doing?"

I lift my head from the dishwasher. "Not sure. He never said anything." I shrug, going back to my task of stacking dirty plates in the trays.

"How are *you* doing?" Is his next question. I glance at him; leaning against the counter, holding on to the ends of his scarf, appearing very relaxed. But I can see a darkness in his eyes too. Seems like everyone is hurting these days.

"Does anyone ever ask you?" I counter, answering his question with one of my own. He looks surprised. "Don't think I don't notice how you seem to have a sixth sense about everyone else, not to mention the ability to get anyone talking, but you don't seem to share much of yourself." I tilt my head slightly when I see my words must've held some truth, because Dino immediately lowers his eyes and finishes tying the scarf around his neck. "I guess that's a no. I can tell how uncomfortable it makes you to be the focus of attention."

In two steps, he's in front of me and leans down to touch his forehead against mine. "You see too much," he mutters with a little smile.

"Pot meet kettle."

He lifts his head a little and smirks. "Smartass." Placing his hands on either side of my neck he presses an unexpected kiss to my forehead. "Look after him," he mumbles against my skin. "You're good for each other."

With that he lets me go, leaving me lost for words. My eyes snap to the door when I hear a muted exchange and am surprised to find Tim leaning against the doorway.

"I got fired today."

CHAPTER NINE

Tim

*"Look. I don't know what exactly happened between you, and
I don't for a minute believe the accusations, but the reality is, this
multimillion dollar project is very important for the city. One we
can't afford to lose. After consulting with the legal department,
the only acceptable option is to terminate you, effective
immediately. Security will escort you out."*

His words are on perpetual replay in my head.

Terminate you, effective immediately.

The logical side of my brain tells me it was the city's only
possible option, but the rest of me revolts against the injustice of
it all. A complaint of sexual harassment was filed against me, and
unless I was *dealt* with internally right away, legal charges would
be filed against me and the city. The large international hotel
conglomerate Portland had just signed a contract with, would be
no match for the municipality.

What had seemed like a minor glitch in judgement had turned
into a fuck up of epic proportions.

Sexual harassment.

The bitter taste of bile fills my mouth. How ironic, seeing as
the only person in this equation guilty of any type of harassment
would be the one crying foul. A rush of anger at the hungry bitch,
unwilling to accept rejection, burns my stomach.

Twenty years…twenty fucking years of hard work and
loyalty, of coloring inside the lines—reduced to this?

I'm not sure why I sought Ruby out. In that first wave of
shock, all I knew was I needed to ground myself in her warm

dark eyes. I'm a fucking selfish bastard, to look for some kind of comfort from her after the way I treated her.

Yet here I am, halfway drunk, with hours of Ike's brand of comfort under my belt, watching Dino kiss her and hating that even more. I glare at Dino when he passes me on his way out the door, but he stops and puts his hand on my shoulder.

"Not what you think, brother," he cautions under his breath before heading out the door.

"I got fired today," I blurt out when Ruby turns around and spots me.

Her mouth falls open and she immediately takes a few steps toward me. "I'm so sorry," she whispers, stepping a little closer. "What happened?"

She asked that question earlier, but I couldn't get the words to form then. Now they're wanting out. "It's a mess," I start, closing the gap between us. As if it is the most natural thing in the world, she slips her arms around my waist, puts her cheek against my chest and hugs me tight.

Her body pressed against me is soft all over. Cushiony and inviting. Without thinking, my arms slip around her and I bend my head down to rest against her hair. My eyes close as I let the comfort of holding her wash over me. Too soon, she releases her hold and I have to let her go.

"Sit," she says, indicating a chair as she turns to grab two coffee mugs off the shelf. "Tell me."

And I do. I tell her everything, from the first moment I realized Brenda had set her sights on me, the lapse of judgment when I finally asked her for dinner, to the utterly demoralizing walk to my car, accompanied by security and toting the sparse accumulation of twenty years on the job in a single box. I don't even stop to drink the coffee she slides toward me as she sits down. I wince at the now lukewarm temperature when I finally take a sip.

She quietly listens until I'm done. "I can't believe it. That is so unfair," she says then, shaking her head in disbelief.

I feel about two feet tall. This woman, who just days before opened herself to my judgement, didn't hesitate to step up to my defense. And what had I done? I'd walked out of her apartment, avoided her for days, and left her to believe she wasn't worthy.

"I'm so fucking sorry," I apologize, leaning over the table to grab her small hand. "I've been a fucking dick to you and here you are, being nothing but supportive."

The tight smile and shoulder shrug show me it still stings, and makes me feel even more of an ass.

"What are you going to do?" she asks me, clearly eager to steer the conversation in a different direction. I let her hand go as she sits back in her chair.

"Not much I can do. I have a week to go over the written dismissal with a lawyer. From what I remember him telling me, I get twelve months severance and will keep what I've paid into my pension, if I sign an agreement of non-disclosure. They don't want me fighting it or talking with anyone." I rub my hands over my face. I'm so goddamn tired all of a sudden. "Guess I have to figure out if fighting them for wrongful dismissal is worth it."

"The best way to eat an elephant is one bite at a time," she says, and I have no idea what the fuck she's talking about. It must've been clear on my face because she smiles and clarifies, "Pam tells me that whenever things seem too big or too overwhelming for me to overcome. A reminder to break problems into manageable pieces and tackle them, instead of trying to solve them all at once."

Good point. One I understand on a rational level but am not so sure is easy to implement.

I can't contain a yawn and immediately Ruby jumps up. "You should get home. Get some sleep." I push my chair back as well.

"What time are you done?"

She takes a quick glance at the clock before turning back to me, a faint blush staining her cheeks. "Now," she admits, quickly followed by, "but you should go ahead."

"Ike took my keys. Says he'll drive me home when I'm ready to go." I curb my smile when I see her fidgeting. "And I won't be ready until I see you home safe. It's across the road, Ruby," I enforce, when she opens her mouth to object. "I'm walking you to your door."

Grumbling, she follows me to the bar where I grab my coat and tell Ike my plans, while Ruby gets her things and says her goodbyes.

Once outside, I drape my arm over her shoulder and tuck her into my side. I tell myself it's to protect her from the sting of the wind, but the truth is, I like the feel of her body against mine.

When we get to her building, she slips from under my arm and sticks her key in the door. "Thank you for seeing me home," she says over her shoulder, in an attempt to dismiss me. I choose to ignore her and push the door open for her, following her inside the lobby. Her response is an eye-roll that draws a chuckle from me. I like her even better with her claws out.

"Home is to your front door, Betty Boop." Her eyes grow big at my use of the name, and I smile in response. "I see you've heard it before. You remind me of her. Dark curls, full lips, big eyes and curves that go on forever. It suits you," I inform her, watching her face soften as I lean in. "I may have had a little crush on her when I was younger." I put my hand in the small of her back and lead her to the far side of the lobby.

"You remembered," she says quietly, as we pass the elevator and move into the stairwell.

"Nothing about you is easy to forget."

Walking down the corridor on her floor, I slip my hand under the mass of hair to cup her neck and when we reach her door, I use it to turn her to face me. She glances up at me through the thick lashes that shield her eyes, but they can't hide the look of uncertainty. Her hand comes up to rest on my chest, almost without thought, and equally mindless, my head dips down and my lips brush hers. Full, soft, and sweet, and I go in for another taste. This time I stroke the tip of my tongue along the swell of her bottom lip. When I pull back, her mouth is slightly open and her eyes shine with curiosity. Leaning in for the third time, I slant my head a little when my mouth covers hers, slipping my tongue inside. Sweet spicy heat. That's what she tastes like; the rich flavor of a dark *mole poblano*.

Her hands clutch my shirt, but other than that her response is surprisingly timid. Still, the tentative touches of her tongue against mine are fuel to my fire. If I don't put a stop to this now, I may not be able to rein it in. She deserves more than a quick groping against her door, and I need some time to sort my head. She may have had a hard life, but that doesn't mean she can't be hurt. Last thing I want to do is hurt her, so I have to figure out where my mind is at.

"I'd better go," I whisper against her lips, feeling her stiffen up immediately and dropping her hand from my chest. "Don't," I caution her, taking both of her hands in mine and lifting them against my chest. "You are hard to resist, Betty Boop, and it kills me to walk away, but if I don't, I'm no better than any other man you've ever encountered." She pulls at her hands, but I'm not letting her go. "I want to have a clear head when we go there. I need you to *believe* it's you I want to be with. I need you to *feel*

it. With all that's happened this past week, I think we both need
to clear our heads."

Ruby's eyes are down, but she nods her head in
understanding. I let go of her hands and place mine on either side
of her neck, lifting her chin with my thumbs before pressing a
last, soft kiss on her lips.

Ruby

"He hasn't been around at all?"

We just finished cleaning up after last night's Christmas
dinner. Something Pam apparently does every year for the
women and children, who happened to be at the shelter at that
time. I hadn't celebrated Christmas, in any form, since I was a
young teenager and had it not been for Pam's insistence I join her
this year, I probably would've just stayed in, doing my best to
ignore the overt family festivities everywhere. I'd already turned
down both Syd and Viv's offers to join them. If I had to admit,
part of me was waiting to see whether Tim might have plans that
included me. When Pam asked what he had been up to yesterday,
I told her I didn't know. Pam's expression was incredulous at the
news I hadn't seen Tim in two weeks.

The first few days after the episode outside my door, I'd been
grateful for the respite, still reeling from the unfamiliar and
somewhat disturbing feelings his touch had invoked in me. In all
the years I was forced to allow men inside my body, I was able to
avoid kissing. I know it seems ridiculous, when I'd had other

parts of their anatomy in my mouth, but the intimacy of stroking someone's tongue with my own had been my way to keep a small part of me pure. Futile, I know, when the rest of me was so liberally used and abused. It felt important. Maybe it had something to do with the fact the last person who kissed me had been the one to force me into that life. A promise to myself I'd never allow myself to be seduced against my will again. I don't know. It's one of many trains of thought my mind has been occupied with, since Tim broke that seal and caused long forgotten sensations to course through my body.

Pam has helped me talk through some of it after I sat down with her and rehashed everything that happened. She pointed out that perhaps it wasn't disgust and rejection I saw in his initial reaction to my past, but shock or even anger at what happened to me. But when after a couple of days of silence, Tim didn't show up for his regular Wednesday night, I started to doubt again. His parting words had planted a seed of hope. They'd seemed genuine. The more time passed, though, the more I wondered if it was just too much for him to overcome my history. God knows, I wouldn't blame him if it was.

Yesterday had been the second Wednesday Tim had not been in, and I came to Pam looking for some wisdom.

"Not in almost two weeks," I confirm.

Pam is quiet for a bit. Thoughtful. "What does Ike say? Have you talked to him about it? Has he seen him?"

"No," I admit. I wanted to, but every time I tried to approach him, or even Viv, I'd stop myself from asking about Tim. Part of me is afraid to find out that they do know—that they've seen or spoken to him. That it's me specifically he's staying away from. Maybe he regretted walking me home that night—regrets the kissing—and is now just avoiding me. I shake my head, driving myself nuts with all these confusing thoughts and feelings.

"Hmmm," Pam hums, her long index finger tapping her chin and her dark eyes seeing right through me. "Knowing you, I'm guessing you worry this has to do with you—him disappearing like that—but have you considered that maybe the fact the man has just seen his twenty-year career go down the drain and he needs to regroup? Maybe he's gone off somewhere on his own, to work out how he can recover from this. What he wants to do with the rest of his life. For a man his age, losing a job can mean losing his identity and can be a pretty big blow to the system. Men have a tendency to have singular focus. They prioritize issues and tackle them one by one. As women, we can't seem to avoid looking at everything as being connected. Always with the big picture in mind." Pam pushes back from the table and grabs the coffee pot from the counter, holding it up for me to see.

"Yes, please," I answer her unvoiced question of more coffee, while thinking to myself how ironic it is for someone who's spent most of her life in the company of men, I have so little understanding.

"Tim has had two major changes in his life, in a matter of days: losing his job and discovering all that is you," Pam says with a soft look in her eyes when she sees me flinch. "He likely wants to figure out one before he feels he can pursue the other."

Huh. I hadn't really thought of it that way. "I guess it's possible," I admit, watching a smile stretch over Pam's face. I feel a little lighter myself.

"How about his brother? Mark, right? "

An involuntary shiver runs down my spine. I'm actually surprised he hasn't shown up since that night. Him being a cop, even one who's technically not active, I fully expected he would've come knocking by now. It's unnerving to have that hanging over my head. More than once, I've been tempted to pack up and run, but for the first time in my life, I'm starting to feel a sense of belonging. The thought of leaving these people, who've shown nothing but kindness and unexpected acceptance, makes me sick to my stomach.

"Not a sign," I sadly tell Pam.

"Have you ever thought about approaching him?" My eyes shoot up to find Pam calmly meeting my glare.

"No! Of course not." To which she simply shrugs her shoulders.

"Oh, I don't know. If he intended to drag you in by the hair, I figure he would've done it by now. Might not be a bad idea."

I shake my head forcefully. "I can't take that chance."

"What then, Ruby? Live in the shadows the rest of your life? Wondering when the sky is going to fall on you? That's no way to live."

I take in her serious face and consider her words, but the risk I'd be taking is so much bigger than she even knows. "It'd be no different from the past thirty years of my life," I finally say. "It's all I know."

-

The rest of the day, after leaving Florence House, and all during my shift at The Skipper, which is surprisingly busy the day after Christmas, her words loop around in my head.

"Hang on, Ruby," Matt says, when I get ready to go home. The guys haven't let me walk home alone once. Even Gunnar, since coming back to work this past weekend, has taken a few turns. I think one of the others filled him in on what went on during his absence, because he'd called me into his office the day after he came back. I was prepared to be shown the door, but to my surprise he said he just wanted to assure me that nothing had changed. But everything had. Where before I simply went about my work and managed to keep myself mostly unnoticed, now I seem to be the focus of everyone's attention. Making sure I'm okay, asking if I need anything, walking me home in the dark. Caring about me. The weight of guilt is building on my shoulders, because I don't deserve any of it.

That's why I turn to Matt and easily wave him off. "I'm good, Matt. Thanks for the offer." Without waiting for a response, I step out the backdoor into the alley.

The wind is frigid, blowing in from the water and roaring in my ears. My breath forms clouds in the cold air, as I duck my head and pull my coat tightly around me. I try to keep my focus on the light in the parking lot ahead, refusing to think about the shadows I'm passing. Still, a sense of relief hits when I step from the cobblestones onto the asphalt, where the streetlamp brightly lights my path.

My keys ready in my hand, I close the last few steps to the door, when a sudden shift in the air raises the hair on my neck.

"Ruby?"

The keys clatter to the ground and my knees buckle at the sound of that familiar voice.

CHAPTER TEN

Tim

"Jesus, you look like shit," Ike points out when I walk into the diner. "Sit your ass down. Have you even slept this past week? Oh, and Merry Christmas by the way."

God it had sucked. Lying in bed, wide-eyed, and then when sleep finally would come; I managed only a few hours at a time. The days were fucking long, longer than I knew what to do with. Especially now that my lawyer had confirmed what I already suspected, any kind of recourse against the city for wrongful dismissal would at best net me fifty cents to the dollar. At best. Worst case scenario was that that bitch Brenda would press charges anyway. That'd look good on my resume: sexual harassment.

I've run the gamut of emotions. Been angry enough to punch holes in my walls, and break a few things, but most of the time I've just been staring into space. Then I somehow always end up with Ruby on my mind. I can't stop thinking about her taste or the innocent way she responded to my kiss. How a former hooker can be innocent, I don't know, but she is. I've avoided her and The Skipper since that night. I don't think I have the stomach for sympathetic questions or even glances. Yesterday I even lied to my parents, telling them I wasn't feeling well and was sorry I'd miss Christmas but would try and stop in soon. Of course, Mom had ended up on my doorstep with food and presents, making me feel like the lying fraud I am. Especially when I saw the disappointment on her face, as I basically took the stuff from her at the door, without letting her come in. I've been living like a pig for over a week. No need for her to see that, it would only worry her more. The sad look on her face, as she turned away from the door, reminded me of Ruby, and I grabbed another bottle of beer from the fridge. Not particularly caring that it was only ten o'clock in the morning.

I've got so damn much on my mind, I don't want to risk saying something inconsiderate or judgmental to Ruby. Like: *How does a sweet woman like you end up fucking men for money?* Easiest thing would be to walk away and ignore whatever feelings she's eliciting from me. But after testing that option this past little while, I'm pretty sure walking away is not an option. That's part of why I finally answered one of Ike's calls and decided to meet him this morning. I want to see how Ruby is doing, but I also want to talk to him about something my lawyer asked me in our meeting yesterday afternoon. I want to pick his brain.

"Not much," I finally respond, after the waitress hands me a menu and pours me a coffee. "Had a lot to think about."

"I'll bet," Ike says. "I've gotta say, that lumberjack thing you've got going on looks impressive. Pretty badass for an upstanding citizen like yourself." He points to my growing beard and casual attire of a flannel shirt and the ratty old jeans, which I've been wearing for a week. The chuckle that escapes me sounds rusty, but the smile lingers.

"I'll try to remember to put on my Sunday best, next time."

"Nah. This fits you better than the monkey suits." He shoots me a meaningful look.

We're interrupted by the waitress, who is back to take our orders before I've even looked at the menu. "I'll just have the special," I tell her and wait for Ike to put his order in. When she's gone again, I lean forward on the table. "That's one of the reasons

I wanted to see you. On Monday, I signed the release in my lawyer's office." Ike's eyes shoot up at this.

"You're not fighting it?"

I shake my head. "I've been assured it's futile. That I'd end up with less money and still won't have a job after. And that's the best possible outcome. He did say something that got me thinking," I explain. "He pointed out that the severance pay, on top of what I've got squirreled away, is a significant amount of money. I've never had a family to care for, just myself, and other than a new car every few years, I've really never indulged in luxuries. What I put aside was well invested, and the net sum is enough to tide me over for a long time. He asked if there was something I've always wanted to do. Something I can feel passionate about. He suggested now might be the perfect time to explore that."

I watch Ike's eyes go big as comprehension hits him. "Your furniture?" A smile cracks his face. "Fuck yes, man! Damn I'm so gonna be your first customer. Viv's been nagging for a dining table like yours. That's gonna earn me some decent brownie points."

I laugh at his outburst. "Like you need anymore brownie points when it comes to Viv, you lucky bastard."

He shrugs his shoulders and winks. "Wouldn't hurt just in case."

"So, I'm guessing you think it's a good idea?" I just want to make sure.

"You kidding me? I know your heart was never in your job. Don't get me wrong." He lifts his hand in defense when I try to object. "I realize your position with the city provided you with the security and dependability you craved, but fuck, Tim…doing something you can be passionate about is so much better."

"Are you passionate about your job?" I'm curious to know.

"I love my job. But I'm passionate about my life. About Viv. About our future." He smiles at me. "I have no regrets and wouldn't change a thing."

"Good. That's good. That reminds me," I segue into the other thing on my mind. "How's Ruby doing?"

The significance of my question is not lost on Ike, as his eyes light up. "Rattled. I'm thinking now that perhaps the reason she's had her eye on the door this entire past week is becoming clearer. I thought she was nervous about the cops showing up, although I'm sure that was part of it, I bet it was mostly to see if you'd walk through. Am I right?" he asks, and I flinch a little. "Did you start something and then walk away?" His expression has turned serious and tone is almost accusatory.

"I like her," I admit. "I didn't want to. It kind of surprised me at first, but I really like her. It's just···" I scratch at my beard, considering how to voice this, without sounding like an ass. "I'd no sooner admitted it to myself, and all hell breaks loose. For both of us. I wasn't sure…Hell. I'm still not sure how to work through all of this."

"You're talking about her being on the run, or the fact she worked as a prostitute?"

Of course the waitress chooses that exact moment to stop at our table with our breakfast. With a curious glance from Ike to me, she quickly slides our plates on the table and scurries off.

"Both," I admit to him honestly.

He looks at me for the longest time before bending down to his breakfast. I follow suit and dig into mine, but a few bites in, I shove my plate away.

"I'm not judging you," Ike mumbles, around a mouthful of hash browns. "I'm looking for a way to say this without pissing you off." He takes a gulp of his coffee before taking a deep breath. "You're a fucking moron," he says without blinking, shocking the snot out of me. "Think about it. Did you ever question if Syd was good enough for Gunnar, given her history?" He raises one eyebrow in question.

"Fuck no. You know that," I spit out, pissed he would even suggest such a thing.

"Right," he says calmly, chomping on a piece of bacon. "And what about Viv? Ever look at her and see anything more than what she is today? I mean, talk about having a history, right?"

"You got a point?" I bite off through clenched teeth, to which Ike leans over the table, shoving his own plate out of the way.

"Yes, I've got a point, asshole. It being that you're coming *this* close to painting Ruby with her history, things she had no control over, when you don't judge anyone else by where they come from. Are you sure that's your problem when it comes to Ruby? Think maybe it's not the fucked up life she was forced to live, but your own hang ups?" He's angry. I can see what he's saying, but my mind gets stuck on one thing.

"Forced to live? Things she had no control over? What are you saying?" I don't notice my hand gripping his wrist until he twists it free.

"I see you only got part of the story," he says, his voice distinctly gentler. "My guess is you didn't ask her? How she happened to end up in that life?"

I shake my head, stunned, Ike seems to know more than I do. I hadn't asked. Hadn't wanted to appear too judgmental and realize that in doing so, I'd been just that. I should've asked for an explanation.

"Normally, I'd suggest you get your answers directly from her, but seeing as your head is seriously fucked up right now, it might be better you know before you think of approaching her again." Ike sighs deeply. "She talked to Viv, and she shared with me after that scene with your brother. I don't have details on what exactly happened, you'll have to get those directly from Ruby, but the gist of it is that some guy took advantage of her innocence when she was just a kid. Fourteen fucking years old." The few bites I'd had of my breakfast work their way back up at his words. I have to fight to keep them down. Ike's expression is solemn as he tells me what he knows in a soft voice. It's gut-wrenching, even without all the details. I have a clear enough understanding of the evil, alive and well in this world, to be able to fill those in myself. An innocent child when her life was ruined. The mark on her thigh, the brand, even more poignant now with that knowledge. Branded, like fresh cattle. *Jesus.*

I pull my wallet out and toss some bills on the table when Ike stops me. "Where are you going?"

"I've gotta talk to her," I snap, pushing away from the table when Ike's hand shoots out and fists in my shirt, pulling me back down.

"Sit your ass down. Don't know what's in your head and I doubt you do. Not a good time to seek her out, buddy. Get your head on straight before you do." He easily holds my angry glare, just waiting me out, and not letting go of my damn shirt. Finally I give in, albeit grudgingly. He's right, I'm not thinking straight. I wouldn't even fucking know what to say to her, or even whether I should.

"Have you heard from your brother?" Ike asks, as he holds his cup up to the waitress for a refill.

"He's been calling. So has Mom, since I've bailed on two of the obligatory Sunday afternoons, as well as Christmas dinner at Casa di Veldman. I've avoided them both," I admit, knowing if I don't get in touch with them soon, they'll be knocking down my door. I realize I've been pretty self-absorbed, not giving much thought to my brother, who had his own rug pulled from beneath his feet. I should call him. Find out where his head it at and maybe get a bit more background on the douche Ruby was working for. The kind of trouble she might be in.

Yeah, I should probably start there.

-

Not ten minutes after sending him a text, Mark is standing on my front step.

After breakfast, I'd come back here and did some research online to see what I could find out about Carlos Delgado. It wasn't much, other than what I'd already been told. I'd wanted to go talk to Ruby, see how she was doing, since I left her standing outside her apartment, and basically disappeared. That part was normal standard behavior for me, the walking away when things looked to get complicated, but I can't say I've ever felt such a strong sense of loss after. Or this kind of need to know everything there is to know about a woman. Not even with Viv. So I sent a message to my brother, in hopes he could enlighten me some.

"You look like you crawled out of your hole," he says, looking pretty damn ratty himself.

"Yeah? Well, at least I'm in good company: you look like you just came off a three-week bender," I retort.

"Pretty much." He drops down on the couch and props his feet up on the table. "So what's new in your life?" he mocks. "Thanks for bailing on Christmas, leaving me to deal with Mom and Dad alone."

With a deep breath, I catch him up on my fucked up situation, to which he reacts with predictable anger. That means, the next ten minutes I have to talk him down from wanting to *rip that bitch a new one*. He admits my comment about the bender had not been too far off the mark, but only by a week. He apparently discovered that at our age; it's a lot harder to keep up, and a shitload more painful when you finally smarten up.

By the time Mark leaves, it's dark out, my house is littered with empty pizza boxes, beer bottles, and the dining table is covered with notes and sketches. Also, I know more about the gang controlled sex trade than I ever wanted to.

It's already past nine, and if I want to catch Ruby, I'm going to have to get moving.

Ruby

"Didn't mean to scare you."

I hold myself up against the doorpost as Tim bends down to pick up my keys.

"It's okay," I say, but I'm lying. My knees still wobble like jelly and my heart is firmly wedged in my throat, trying to beat its way out. His responding grumble tells me he's not buying it. With a steadying hand on my arm, he uses my keys to open the door, and once again marches me past the elevator and up the stairs. "Wait," I insist, with a restraining hand on his chest as he prepares to unlock my apartment. "What is going on?" With the initial scare gone, a surge of anger flares up. "Are you gonna drop me at my door and disappear for weeks again? Because if you are, spare me, okay? It wasn't worth the heart attack." I snatch the keys from his hand and swiftly unlock and push open the door, fully intending to slam it behind me. Tim is faster, though, forcing himself inside, behind me, before closing the door firmly.

"We need to talk," he says, shrugging out of his coat, and for the first time I have a good look at him. I'm initially distracted by the pretty substantial beard he's grown, the unkempt hair, and his unusually casual attire, before my eyes zoom in on the lines in his face and the dark circles under his eyes. I instantly feel my anger fade. It's pretty obvious the man's not having an easy time. So instead of arguing, I take off my coat, kick off my shoes, and sit down in a corner of the couch, not saying a word.

Finally, after observing me from his vantage point by the door, he heels off his boots and follows me inside. Instead of the couch, he chooses to sit down on the coffee table facing me, running a hand through his messy hair. Slowly his eyes come up to meet mine and he clears his throat.

"I don't know what I'm doing," he starts, surprising me. "I don't," he repeats. "My life was pretty set. I thought I knew what I did and didn't want out of it, but now I'm not so sure."

"Because you lost your job," I clarify.

"Not just because of that, although I will admit; it's a fucking sobering experience to think you're sitting safe with twenty solid years under your belt, only to have it disappear like *that*." He snaps his fingers for emphasis. "These past few weeks have felt like my world's been tilted on its axis, changing my entire perspective. It's unsettling. I couldn't even handle Christmas. It didn't start with getting fired, though," he says leaning forward with his elbows on his knees. "It started when I first saw you."

I can't stop the snort escaping, despite the hand I slap in front of my face. "Please. I find that hard to believe," I scoff. "We never even spoke more than a few words since I started working at the pub. Not until a few weeks ago anyway."

"True," he admits. "Doesn't mean I didn't see you." I wave my hand in the air dismissively, not ready to buy into that.

"Will you tell me about it?" he asks, switching direction completely and throwing me off. Oh, I know what he's talking about, but I didn't expect him to be so direct. "Not now," he assures me, putting a hand on my knee. "But at some point?"

"Why?" I have to know. "It's not a pretty story."

"I'm sure it isn't, but it's your story, which means I want to know it."

Something about that hits me hard. The idea someone thinks I'm worth knowing is still so new. So strange to learn not everyone sees you as a means to an end, a *thing* to be used and discarded. I've had glimpses of it, especially the last few weeks, but from Tim it brings up a lot of emotions. Perhaps because it makes me realize he sees me as a whole and not as the sum of my *parts*.

"You like me," I blurt out, before I can catch myself. I'm mortified, but Tim chuckles softly.

"Not the first time I heard that," he says, shaking his head. "But yeah, I like you, Ruby. And I wasn't kidding when I said I don't know what I'm doing. I want to know you, but there's so much going on that I don't know where to start."

That little seed that had almost shriveled up in the past few weeks flares back to life with a fresh surge of hope. In my much younger years, before every last spark of hope had been carefully ground out, I'd sometimes fantasized about someone coming along, who might want me for more than just sex, but those dreams didn't last long. It makes me a little scared, a lot out of my element, but I force myself to look Tim square in the eyes.

"I don't know either, but maybe we can start with a drink?"

A slow smile spreads over Tim's face, brightening even his gorgeous blue eyes. "I'd like that," he says in a low voice. Then he gets up and I expect him to sit down on the couch, but instead he leans forward, his arms on the arm and backrest, caging me in.

His mouth brushes mine softly. "I'd like that a lot," he affirms, his lips moving on my mouth, before nipping my bottom lip. I'm completely mesmerized by the slow, sweet play of his kisses.

Abruptly he pushes up and steps back to reveal he's clearly as affected as I am. "Yeah," he says, adjusting himself unselfconsciously with a smirk. "Before I get carried away, I'm gonna splash some cold water on my face. Maybe you can grab those drinks?"

With my mouth still hanging half open and a hot flush on my cheeks, I watch him saunter into the hallway, realizing too late all I have in my fridge is milk and cranberry juice. A mad scramble to the kitchen shows me the sad truth. A jug of milk and half a container of juice, a few tea bags and decaf coffee Viv must've left in the cupboard. I'm going to have to make a grocery list the moment my brain starts working again.

I hear the toilet flush and a moment later Tim comes walking into the kitchen. "What are you doing?" he wants to know, watching me struggle to fold the paper towel in the coffee maker Viv left behind to serve as a makeshift filter. I'd bypassed the milk and tea as viable options for a drink, and settled on coffee being the more masculine option than cranberry juice.

"I, uhh…I'm making coffee. I wasn't expecting guests."

Noticing my embarrassment, he smiles before leaning down to kiss my lips again. "Coffee is fine, but what's with the paper towel?"

"No filters," I explain. "I haven't had a chance to go to the grocery store. I'll go tomorrow," I assure him. That's not exactly the truth, because I have been. It's just that I get flustered when I see the miles of aisles, with everything under the sun on offer. I hardly know where to start, so I end up grabbing what I can see and hurry through the register before I'm completely overwhelmed. I obviously haven't managed to find the coffee filters yet.

"Here—give me that." Tim deftly plucks the wad of paper out of my hands and proceeds to fold it neatly into the shape of a filter. In less than a minute, the coffee is perking.

"So let's start easy, okay?" he says gently, as he takes in my wringing hands. "I'm Tim Veldman, Timothy Michael Veldman, to be complete. I'm forty-three, have one brother and was born and raised in Portland. My parents still live here and I'm currently unemployed," he adds with a wink. "Now you."

"Oh. Uh, my last name is Soto," I share with him, a little relieved to find I'm only a year older. "I'm forty-four and don't have brothers or sisters."

"So not Betty Boop?" he jokes, before his smiling face turns serious. "And what about parents?" he asks carefully.

"They died a long time ago," I explain.

"I'm sorry," he says, reaching out and stroking the backs of his fingers over my cheek. I have to stop myself from curling into his touch like a cat.

"It's okay," I shrug, pulling away to grab the two mugs I have from the cupboard. "Like I said, it was a long time ago."

Tim stays quiet behind me while I pour coffee. Turning around, I find his eyes intently focused on me. "Tell me the rest when you're ready," he says softly. I nod in silent understanding. He's letting me off the hook, that's what he's telling me. At the same time, he's making sure I know that he still intends to find out everything about me.

Oddly enough, it doesn't scare me half as much as it probably should.

CHAPTER ELEVEN

Tim

"You're back?"

Ruby's voice sounds a little breathless as she opens the door for me. I'd managed to catch the entrance door as it was closing behind an older gentleman taking his slobbering little pug for a walk. I've never seen the appeal of those pint-sized failed bulldogs.

I'd made the decision to take Ruby to get groceries last night, when she mentioned needing some. She doesn't have transportation, and something about her having to tote her bags walking or taking the bus just doesn't sit right with me. The taste of that vile decaf crap solidified my idea. I've been living off takeout these last few weeks, too miserable to get myself into the kitchen, so I'm past due to stock my fridge anyway. It wasn't until I was halfway home I realized I'd forgot to mention it.

I'd been too preoccupied the rest of the evening. A little stilted at first, Ruby had started talking a little about her life. Mostly general stuff at first, a few movies she'd seen, some places she'd been to. When I asked her what place she'd most like to return to, she'd gone quiet for a bit. "To my parents' farm," she admitted finally, a hitch in her voice and a hint of wetness in her eyes. "I'd love to wake up to the sound of the tractor in the morning, when my father would go out to his fields. Mamá would be in the kitchen. She never sent my father off without a cooked breakfast. Or me," she said wishfully, her eyes getting that far away look of someone lost in their memories.

I didn't stay long after that. It was already late and she'd had a full shift on her feet. So I pulled her from the couch, had her walk me to the door where I kissed her goodbye. Took all I had to walk out of that door.

The same door that is now propped open by Ruby's well-rounded hip.

"Groceries. Let's go," I prod her, pleased to see a little smile tug at the corner of her mouth. "You probably start at ten or eleven? That gives us an hour and a half to get what we need and still have you there in time. Oh," I add as she buttons her coat and grabs her bag, before pulling the door shut behind her. "I also printed out a recipe for Chiles Renellos. I owe you a cooking lesson."

Not giving her a chance to react, I grab her hand in mine and aim for the stairwell. She tugs on my hand as we pass the elevator, and I stop. "We can take the elevator," she says nervously.

"We don't need to. I don't mind the stairs."

"I know, but I'd like to try the elevator," she insists, despite the fear in her eyes. "With you," she adds in a soft voice.

Immediately my free hand hits the button. I don't say anything but I'm pumping my fist on the inside. Not sure what drove her decision just now, but it feels like a milestone of sorts. One that she feels she can tackle with me. Makes me feel about ten fucking feet tall.

She jumps a little at the ding, announcing the elevator's arrival, and her breathing speeds up.

"Doesn't have to be today," I gently remind her when the doors slide open.

"Today," she firmly says, lifting up her chin and pressing her lips tight as she determinedly leads the way inside. I stand close, still holding her hand, which has grown decidedly clammy and is crushing the blood from mine. She squeezes her eyes closed when I hit the button for the lobby.

"Ruby. Sweets, look at me," I coax her when we start moving. Her panicked eyes shoot open and zoom in on mine. "Keep your eyes on me and breathe slower. You're hyperventilating. Just easy in and out, like this."

For what arguably is the longest elevator ride of my life, we breathe in tandem until the doors open on the ground floor. I let her exit in front of me but swing her around when I step off. Cupping her head with my hands, I tilt her face up and smile down at her. "Now that took balls," I compliment her, relieved to see her smile. "Proud of you, Boop." Her little eye-roll is cute as shit, so I kiss her in the middle of the lobby and damned if she doesn't kiss me right back.

-

I never thought of grocery shopping as anything but a necessary evil, but grocery shopping with Ruby was something else altogether. After her initial hesitation when we first walked in, she was like a kid in a candy store. When she tossed coffee filters and some real coffee in the cart, I couldn't resist dramatically rolling my eyes heavenward and making a sign of the cross. I'd never heard Ruby laugh before and the sound and sight of it was pretty damn special.

The cart was about full when we got to the register and we had a brief tussle over who was paying for what. I won, but only after assuring her that giving someone a housewarming present—which I had labeled it—was a normal custom.

"How about this," I suggest to her when we are buckling in. "We run over to my house, quickly unload my things and then back to your apartment. After that I'll walk you to work."

"Isn't it easier just to drop me off with my bags and take yours home with you?" she asks me, eyebrows raised and a half-finished danish partway to her mouth. That had been an impulse purchase at the counter of the coffee shop next door, when I discovered she hadn't eaten yet. Best purchase ever, because with every bite of the flaky pastry, crumbs would stick to her lips and her little red tongue would dart out for a cleaning sweep. Sweet torture.

"Not really," I manage, watching her take another bite before tearing my eyes away to focus on driving. "I'm meeting Gunnar at ten-thirty at the pub."

After yesterday's talk with Ike and then Mark, I wanted to pass my ideas by Gunnar as well. Having run his own business for many years, I want his take on my preliminary ideas. I actually need his advice on the business part of things, because if I do this, I want to do it right.

From the corner of my eye, I see Ruby looking at me with curiosity. "I'll explain when we get to my place," I tell her.

It takes less than five minutes to put away the groceries in the kitchen, then I take her hand and pull her toward the dining table. I can't help stroke my hand over the smooth finish. It had been a labor of love, made with old barn wood I had gotten my hands on and assembled with only glue, dowels, dovetail joints, and random butterfly splines. Not a screw in sight. The result was a beautiful, rustic harvest table.

"See this table? I made this," I proudly say to her, watching her eyes widen in surprise. "I used to work with my dad in his wood shop all the time as a kid and always loved making things with my hands. I like it, I'm pretty good at it, and I want to see if I can turn it into a business."

Ruby slowly walks around the table, every so often bending down to check a detail up close, and in doing so, affording me a nice view of her backside. Between that and the furtive licks of her lips in the car, I'm hard enough to hammer nails. She stops on the other side of the table, bending at the waist and running her hands lightly over its surface.

"It's beautiful." She smiles up at me, without any awareness of the effect she has on me.

Christ. Time to get out of here before I do something drastic, like bend her over that table. "Thanks." I manage a smile. "Anyway, that's what I'm seeing Gunnar about. I'm hoping he can help me get a business plan together." With my hand in the small of her back, I lead her firmly to the door, and out of my house.

Ruby

"Hey, Ruby?"

I turn around from the pile of veggies I've been cutting for the last hour. Since my disastrous attempt to manage the kitchen during Dino's weekend off, I've been thrown into full on prep duty. Basic kitchen training 101. I'm not complaining, I love how even here in the pub, the kitchen seems to be the center of the universe. Just like I remember from growing up on the farm.

Tim is leaning against the doorpost, the hint of a smile on his face. "Just wanted to let you know I'm off," he says, slowly straightening up and moving toward me. He doesn't stop until his body almost touches the length of mine. "What time are you done?" he asks, as he plucks the large knife from my hand, and lays it on the counter, before slipping his arms around me. Almost without thought, my hands come up to rest on his chest.

"Uhh…I think nine. Not sure," I mumble against his lips, as I pull his mouth down on mine. All rational thought is gone the moment he takes over the kisses. For someone with zero experience kissing, I've sure become addicted fast. When he raises his head, I lift my mouth for more.

"Nine tonight but you're off tomorrow, Ruby," Viv's amused voice cuts through the kiss induced haze, and has me trying to jump out of Tim's hold, but he doesn't budge. His eyes never leave mine, even as I peek around his shoulder to find Viv dropping her bag on the kitchen table, a big smile on her face.

"Good," Tim's deep voice rumbles as he presses a kiss to my hair. "I've gotta go see my folks today. Have some groveling to do for disappearing on them, but I'll be back at nine to walk you home. Tomorrow it's Chiles Renellos." With a last squeeze of his arms around me, he lets me go and starts walking out the kitchen. I haven't even opened my mouth yet.

"But…" I try when he's about to disappear out the door. "You don't have to…"

"I'm walking you home, Boop," he says firmly. "Anything changes, just give me a call. Okay?"

"I don't know your number," I blurt out, instead of insisting I can walk home on my own.

Tim takes two steps back inside and holds out his hand. "Where's your phone? I'll program it."

"I don't have one," I explain to him. I've never had one. There was never a need, since there was no one to call. There'd been a phone at Florence House, just like there's one at the apartment. For emergencies. It just never occurred to me someone might want to be able to reach me. Tears burn my eyes when I take in Viv and Tim, understanding softening their faces.

"Right," Tim softly says, moving up to me. With his index finger he traces a path from my hairline down to the tip of my nose. "We'll get that sorted soon. My number is up on the board in Gunnar's office, if you need me."

With a quick hard press of his lips against mine, he's gone.

"Whew!" Viv smiles, flapping her hands in front of her face. "I think I'll pull the chicken from the cooler. Gives me a chance to cool off," she teases, shooting me a wink in passing.

Tim

Kissing Ruby is amazing. Having Ruby be the one to kiss me is mind-blowing. Makes me feel like the fucking king of the world.

A part of me wants to pump my fist that a woman, who has every reason not to trust men in general, would voluntarily put her lips on mine. Hard to walk away from, but I wanted her to have a lingering taste of the power she has. My dick is not in agreement. Too bad. His day will come.

"Are you coming in or what?" My mother is standing in the open door, her hands on her hips, in a *don't-mess-with-momma* stance. Not one she adopts often, but I know I probably deserve it. I've been avoiding her for weeks.

"Hey, Mom," I say, as I lean down to kiss her cheek. There's no rib crunching hug that would normally follow. Those deceptively powerful arms stay down in a show of displeasure. Yeah. Momma's pissed.

"Two weeks, Timmie." I cringe at her use of my childhood nickname. "Two weeks of leaving messages, not knowing if my boy was lying dead in a ditch somewhere."

"Dramatic much, Jane?" my father snorts, while rolling his eyes. Probably not a great idea when Mom is worked up like this. Sure enough, her ire switches from me to Dad, who winks over her shoulder at me.

"Dramatic? I'll give you dramatic." Mom's volume goes up a few decibels, and I quickly close the front door behind me to spare the neighbors. "While you were sitting by that front window, lusting over that new bit of fluff that moved in across the street, I was pulling out my hair worrying about our son."

Oh Lord. I try to tune out the ensuing bickerfest between my folks. That bit of fluff is Mrs. Henderson, a seventy-year-old widow, who dresses like a gypsy and became an object of frequent discord between my parents since she moved in last year. New bit of fluff, all right. Dad had mentioned once that she reminded him of Mom when she was younger, which for obvious reasons did not go over too well. Mom is seventy-three.

My parents were both from what was called *a proper family* and married in 1965, at the very cusp of the flower power movement. For two people with their kind of upbringing and rigid social structure, it was a liberating time. One they were completely swept up in. I remember growing up that *free love* was a concept they continued to *enjoy* pretty openly. It wasn't until I was in high school, that their swinging days seemed to come to a grinding halt. An unexpected pregnancy and subsequent miscarriage at forty-three, when your husband had his boys blocked five years earlier, was enough of a reality check. From what I know, they've been monogamous since. Not something I particularly want to think about.

Mark and I had a great childhood. Never lacked for anything. I have to admit, I sometimes wonder whether the fact we are both in our forties and unattached might be significant.

"Come see what I've been doing." Dad breaks through my thoughts and I'm surprised to find Mom no longer in the room. I can hear her though, banging pots and pans in the kitchen. Definitely still pissed.

"It's that leftover barn wood you gave me," he says by way of explanation, as he ushers me out the back door into the cold.

"God, Dad, it's fucking freezing. Can't we grab a coat first?"

"Heater's on in the shop, quit yer whinin'."

Sure enough, the open coils of the old electric heater Dad has hung in the rafters of his wood shop are red hot. *Christ.* One of these days the place is going to go up in flames. The beam it's hanging from, and the surrounding wood of the ceiling, is already toasted dark. It wouldn't take much. Making a mental note to disable that fire hazard and get him a new heater, I turn to look at his worktable. Stacks of neatly bevelled and smoothly oiled pieces of wood in different sizes are covering the table.

"I may not be able to create masterpieces like you can," my father waves his hand over the collection of pieces, "but I can still bring out the beauty of old wood in these cutting boards and coasters," he concludes.

I pick up a cutting board and take a closer look and feel. Smooth as butter, without a ridge or splinter in sight. "They look great, Dad. Really beautiful, but what are you planning to do with all of these?" I ask him, only just now noticing the workbench against the wall is stacked with at least the same amount of neatly rounded and polished wood.

"Sell them," he says in a firm voice. "I've always wanted to take your mother on a cruise, but we never really had the money to spare. I want to sell these and use to proceeds to save up, so I can give her everything she's always wanted."

A lump lodges in my throat at my father's determination and his obvious devotion to Mom, when a thought pops in my head. "I think that's a great idea," I manage, sounding a bit ragged. "I think when I tell you what I've been thinking of doing, you'll see how perfect your timing is."

At first, when I tell Dad about losing my job, something I was grateful Mark hasn't let on about yet, he's predictably upset and angry on my behalf. But the moment I share my own hopes of making what was once just a hobby for the two of us into a business, his eyes light up in understanding. "*Veldman & Son*," I mumble, but Dad shakes his head vehemently at that.

"No. *Vintage Veldman*," he suggests. I have to admit, I like that even better.

"Perfect," I approve. "A family business. And I've already hinted to Mark that if he's interested, I would love for him to look after the business side. With his connections in the community, we'd already have a foot in a few doors."

When I spoke to Mark he hadn't been too convinced, but wait till he finds out what Dad's been up to. I already know of a possible taker for those coasters and some of the cutting boards.

"Be my dream, Son: building something together with my boys. My dream." I feel the corresponding burning in my eyes to the tears forming in his, but before either of us gets too soft, Dad clears his throat.

"Better go see if your mother has gotten over her snit, or we'll be eating our lunch from the garbage."

Chuckling at the truth of his words, I follow him out of the shop, taking one last look back at what must've taken the old man weeks to make.

Mom only has a hint of *snit* remaining when we troop into the kitchen and is quick to dole out tasks of hand washing, table setting, and drink fetching. Within minutes, we're sitting down to lunch the size of a proper Sunday night dinner. Like Dad, Mom reacts with fire to the news and circumstances of my dismissal, and just like Dad, she lights up at the thought of me chasing an old dream. She's less convinced about my father being part of this new venture, listing age and a slew of possible health reasons why it might not be a great idea for him to get involved. Dad just smiles and nods, knowing full well he's going to have his way on this, but doesn't breathe a word about his motivations. I don't say a thing either, it's not mine to tell, and listen to their usual bickering routine.

For the first time, I can hear the deep love they have for each other underneath the squabble. I realize I may well have allowed my views to be tainted by judgement.

By the time I wave goodbye and get into my car, I feel lighter and more excited about my life than I think I've ever been. And with a view to the future—before I tackle phase two in my life improvement: Ruby—I will be making a stop at the Audi dealership tomorrow.

Fuck!

Ruby

A steady stream of customers keeps me busy all day. Thursdays are popular, because it offers the all-you-can-eat special. Before Syd had her little boy, she was in charge of the day's special, but for now, Viv's taken over that task. It's usually a single pot item; something that easily stretches and is quickly served. Today's special is chicken pilaf, a sweet and spicy stew of onions, tomatoes, peppers, and chicken, with a sweet component: sliced peaches, served over a bed of rice. I had a taste before the dinner rush and begged Viv for the recipe. She said it wasn't hard to make, and I tucked her written instructions in my purse, excited to give it a try myself.

I'm busy wiping down tables when Viv calls me over to the bar. "Can you keep an eye on the bar for me for a minute? Been so busy, I forgot to place an order, if I don't do it now, it won't make Saturday's delivery."

"Sure." I drop my rag in the sink and head over to Arnie, a sweet old man who comes in for a drink and some company just about every night.

"Hey, gorgeous," he greets me with a twinkle in his watery eyes. "When are you gonna make me a happy man, huh?"

I'm used to his playful flirting by now. At first he made me feel very uncomfortable, but even if he noticed, he never let up with his teasing pick up lines. Once I started noticing he was no different with Sydney or Viv, I was able to relax; even able to tease him back from time to time.

"Don't think I'd be able to keep up with you, Arnie, but how about another beer instead?"

His raspy laugh in response puts a smile on my face when I turn to get him a fresh draft.

"Do me one of those as well, darlin'. And I'd make sure you'd keep up with me." The slick voice belongs to a cheap suit-sporting, dark-haired man, slipping onto a stool at the bar. A guy like so many I've seen in my days and just as soon put out of my mind. I don't say anything, just drop the draft in front of Arnie, who is not so casually observing the new customer, before grabbing another glass. Once full, I tap the side and scrape the top of the foam level with the edge of the glass.

"Ahhh, why'd you have to do that?" the guy drawls, leaning over the bar. "I like having my hands and my mouth full." His leer is unmistakable, as he eyes my body up and down, and I inadvertently take a step back.

"Keep it civil, will ya?" Arnie pipes up, obviously having heard his lewd remarks.

"What's it to you, old man?" Cheap Suit turns his body in Arnie's direction, leaning his elbow on the bar.

I can feel the tension cranking up to uncomfortable levels, and even Matt, who's been busy serving tables, walks up to the far side of the bar to keep an eye out.

"That's my friend you're talking to," Arnie bites off, and I put a restraining hand on his arm.

"It's okay, Arnie," I warn him off in a soft voice for his ears only.

"No, it's not, girl. Just cause you work in a bar, doesn't mean he gets to disrespect you."

"Ha!" The loud exclamation draws all eyes back to Cheap Suit. "Trust me," he says with a sneer. "In her profession that's the highest level of respect there is." His eyes turn to me and this time I get the feeling I have actually seen him before. His next words confirm my fears. "Besides, we go way back, don't we, darlin'? Sure didn't expect to bump into you here; a far cry from Club Innosins, though. Gotta say you've let yourself go a little, but I don't mind. I'll have a go for old-times' sake." He barely gets the last words from his mouth before Arnie is off his stool and lunging at him, and Matt is already rounding the bar. I just stand frozen, as some of the other patrons jump in to hold Arnie back, and help Matt hustle the guy out the door. I barely hear the crude insults he slings at me over his shoulders. Barely…but I still hear them. And so does the rest of the pub.

"Your cunt too good now, sweetheart? They know half of Boston had a piece of that?" And the last one, a real prize winner. *"Prob'ly need a fucking excavation crew to dig out the last idiot who paid good money to get in there."*

That's when Viv's face appears in my line of vision and I see her mouth forming my name. But I don't hear a thing as my eyes trail over her shoulder to spot a scuffle just outside the front door. Before I get further than a few steps, Viv grabs hold of my arm and pulls me along, straight out the back and into the office. "Sit," she orders, grabbing a glass and a bottle from the credenza against the wall and pouring a stiff drink of whatever. "Drink."

Accepting the glass with both hands, I'm shaking so hard the content sloshes over the rim. The strong scent of alcohol almost makes me gag. Instead of drinking, I try to hand the glass back. "I don't drink." My voice is hoarse, shock having dried up all the saliva in my mouth.

"You'll drink this," she insists, her hands folding around mine on the glass.

With her eyes trapping mine, and her hands urging the glass to my lips, I give in and take a swig of the amber liquid. The burn of it hitting the roof of my mouth is almost painful. I quickly swallow it down, focusing on the warm heat sliding down my throat.

"Again," Viv demands. Another sip and she takes the glass from my hands, setting it on the desk, before taking the other seat. "My guess is our *friend* out there knows you from before." Viv's words aren't so much a question as they are a statement, and there's little I can say in response.

"I'm sorry," is all I can come up with.

"Don't you be sorry," she scolds me, pointing her finger at me. "You had no choice. You never did. But that asshole, like so many other assholes, does have a choice. Then *and* now. He chose to get in your face and treat you like a piece of dirt. You didn't invite that. No use taking on shit that doesn't even belong to you." Suddenly she seems to register the tremors running through my body. "He scared you."

Taking a deep breath, I try to sort my raging thoughts into words. "What if he tells them where I am?" is the first thing that comes out. "I have to leave," I push out of the chair, just as the door swings open.

CHAPTER TWELVE

Tim

"Leave where?"

I hear her last words as I walk into the office and don't stop until I'm butted right up against her. She has to tilt her head back to see me. There's a throbbing in my cheekbone, and I lick at a little stream of blood dripping down from what I assume is a split bottom lip.

"You're hurt…" she manages to get out, before I grab her by the shoulders and give her a shake.

"Leave where, Ruby? Run? And then? Where are you going to go? You can't keep dragging your life behind you, like a block of concrete that holds you tethered, no matter how far you run." I'm angry. Fuck that, I'm hurt.

"I don't want to," she cries out. "But it keeps finding me!" Tears are shimmering in her eyes, but not one falls. She struggles to hold them back.

"I heard what that asshole yelled at you, Ruby. I heard every fucking vile word from his mouth, but I want you to understand something: he doesn't know shit. Not him, or any other motherfucker who pops out of the woodwork and thinks they've had a taste of you. They don't know you. They don't know that unless you invite them in, they can't get a damn thing from you. Don't even give them the time of day, Ruby," I drop my voice to a low whisper. "Because they don't deserve the warmth of your body, the taste of your lips, or the worry on your mind." I close my mouth over hers and barely notice the sting from my busted lip.

Standing in the safety of Gunnar's office, with Ruby's body wrapped around me and her kiss on my lips, I'm hoping she has heard me. That she understands running away won't solve anything. She deserves so much more than that.

"I'll try," she murmurs, when I finally release her.

"I know you will," I enforce.

At some point Viv must've left the room, because when I look around I find we're alone. "What happened to your face?" she asks, her fingers carefully feathering over my cheek.

"Was just walking in when Matt was trying to march the guy out. I gave him a hand. Guy didn't like it much and took a swing. I didn't like *that* much, not to mention the crap he'd just spouted moments before, so I made sure he was aware of my displeasure." I flex my fist in front of my face and only now notice the bloody scrapes on my knuckles.

"Let me clean that up for you," she offers, but I shake my head.

"First, I'm going to get you home," I insist, putting my arm around her shoulder and guiding her to the door.

"I've got a first-aid kit at home."

"Sounds good to me," I mutter, pressing a kiss on her hair.

-

We'd gone straight out the back, only speaking to Viv on our way. She gave Ruby a quick hug and kiss, and made me promise to look after her, which had me roll my eyes. Ruby asked Viv to make sure to tell Arnie and Matt thank you for her.

The walk to Ruby's apartment is silent, but comfortable, with my arm still around her shoulders. Once there, she makes me sit on one of the kitchen stools and fetches the kit from the bathroom cupboard. Both of us are silent as she clean my cuts, but when she tries to stick on a Band-Aid, I have to stop her. "No need for that," I assures her. "It'll probably heal faster if you leave them uncovered."

She tucks the Band-Aids back in the kit, when I slip my arms around her waist and pull her between my legs. "Thank you," I tell her, leaning my forehead against hers. "Are you okay?"

I watch the deep brown of her eyes turn a shade darker. "I'm okay. But I should thank you. I don't think anyone has ever thrown a punch over me before." She tries to make light of the situation, but the emotion behind it feels very real. She leans in with her body and fits her lips to mine. A move I greatly appreciate, and I show her by tightening my arms, pulling her body in even closer

Ruby

My lips open under the probing of his tongue. Although he resolutely takes over the kiss, the power of unleashing such a response in him, just by the press of my lips, is intoxicating. My hands slide up and around his neck, where my fingers tangle in his shaggy locks. His hands aren't still either, one sliding up under my hair and the other exploring my behind.

A deep, rumbling groan rolls against my mouth when I press my body closer, driven by this need to have his imprint on me. The feel of his hard dick, pressing in the soft of my belly, causes an unusual tingle between my legs. Abruptly, Tim pulls his mouth away.

"If I don't go now, I'm afraid I won't be able to stop before I'm buried balls deep inside you. And I'm not so sure you're ready for that." His voice sounds gravelly as both of us seem to be breathing hard.

"Okay," I reply, because he may be right, I'm not so sure I'm ready either.

He gathers his stuff and leaves me to close the door behind him after planting one last, lingering kiss on my lips.

Long after his footsteps have faded, I'm still standing with my back pressed against the door. Trying to process the unfamiliar heavy feeling in my breasts and the vague ache low in my stomach.

-

It had been a restless night, but unlike many nights before when I'd lain in bed scared of my future, last night my mind had been busy conjuring up images of what, at least my immediate, future might look like. I won't say I've never had fantasies before, because I have. But never ones that involved a real, live, breathing human being. Naked. I feel heat creeping up my cheeks at the thought of some of the things I'd imagined him doing.

Tim fully clothed is impressive. Tim in the buff, at least in my mind, is jaw-dropping.

Of course in my fantasies, I never quite see myself, just a vague awareness of where I am. Over the years, my body had become like a detached entity. There, and mine, but not really connected to the person I am. At first, it had been a way to cope. A way to distance myself from what I was subjected to. Later it had become a battleground of sorts. Carlos had been strict on our diets, wanting us to keep our bodies in prime condition. When I got older and was relegated to the much less desirable Johns, I realized I could perhaps use my own body to regain some power.

I began eating. A lot. Everything I could get my hands on. It didn't take long for my size to catch his attention. And his anger. Club Innosins had a reputation to maintain, he told me. He tried to beat it into me. Tried to starve me, but my body happily clung to all the pounds I'd gained. No matter what he dished out, I wasn't going to let go of that sliver of control I'd found. Finally, he put me to different use, had me tend bar, where my body wouldn't be on display, or tend to the new girls as they came in. It gave me a purpose. It made me a person and not just a body.

Ever since landing on Pam's doorstep, mainly under her tutelage, I've slowly started accepting my body as part of me again. The people I have in my life now, seem to see me as a whole person. None quite as clearly as Tim these past weeks, though. Maybe because I initially thought he didn't see me at all.

I'm still not clear on what brought about his sudden focus, but he makes me very much aware. Self-conscious in a way I've never really felt before, both emotionally and physically. Stranger still, I don't feel the automatic repulsion at his interest. No sick feeling in the pit of my stomach when he looks at me, or touches me, with lust in his eyes. Excitement—yes. Unfamiliar feelings when my body responds in ways that surprise me—absolutely. But not awkwardness or repulsion.

The buzzing of the downstairs doorbell pulls me from my thoughts, and I quickly dry the suds off my hands. My nervous energy had me empty out my sparse closet and wash my clothes. I know there's a laundry room in the building, but I've always washed my clothes by hand and have no desire to go down to the dark basement.

"Hello?" I say, when I pick up the phone.

"Buzz me in?" Tim's voice sounds slightly distorted over the intercom.

Two minutes later he's at the door.

"Hi." I sound a little breathless when I let him in.

"You sound surprised." He leans in for a quick brush of his cold lips on mine. "You forget we have some cooking to do?"

Right. So apparently he'd been serious about the Chiles Renellos. I'd spent a good amount of time convincing myself he hadn't really meant that last night and this morning. "I wasn't sure you were serious, and then when I didn't hear from you, I…"

"Oh, I'm very serious, Ruby," he interrupts me, suddenly pulling my body so close, all my soft parts are meshing with his much harder ones. He makes good use of my stumped silence by lowering his mouth to mine. This time, it's not for a brush of the lips. No, this time he goes for a full on assault that has my toes curl in my shoes. At some point, my arms wrap around his neck and my fingers become tangled in his outgrown hair. The brush of his short beard against my mouth and chin creating a delicious warm friction on my skin. Fully sensitized, I faintly register the rough pads of his fingers finding purchase on the strip of skin he's bared between my jeans and sweater, and then gently slip into my waistband. His other hand fists in my hair, pulling my head back and exposing my neck. I'm gasping for air as he nips and licks down my chin and over the soft skin of my neck, causing a charge to run down my back.

"Tim…"

"Serious as a heart attack, Ruby," he mumbles in the crook of my neck, before his mouth travels south onto the swell of my breasts.

I'm so lost in sensation, my eyes closed, that his sudden retreat makes me shiver. When I open them I find his blue ones staring back. "*Chiles Renellos*," he reminds me, but his voice is rough with need. "Get your coat."

It takes me a second to register, and then I move to follow his instructions, wondering why he just stopped. I'm pretty sure of what he meant by being *serious,* since evidence of that had been intimately pressed to my body just moments ago. I must've still looked a little lost, because his fingers come up to trace my swollen lips. "You make me lose control," he softly says. "I don't want to lose control with you, Ruby. Not yet. I'm trying to go slow, be mindful, even when all I can think of is how to get you out of those clothes fastest."

Oh.

I'm suddenly in a hurry to pull on my coat and grab my purse and keys. Plastering what I hope is a friendly smile on my face, I turn to the door. "Let's go." My voice comes out on a much higher pitch, and I'm pretty sure I look more deranged than friendly as I rush past him out of my apartment. Why the thought of being naked in front of this man suddenly terrifies me, when I never gave baring myself to a man another thought, is beyond me. Except—I realize as we make our way outside—I've never cared about what those other men thought. I care about what Tim thinks. I care about *him.*

Without a word, he takes my hand and leads me to an unfamiliar truck, and I look around me a bit confused. "Where is your car?"

"Traded it in," he says, a small grin forming on his lips.

"Really? Wasn't it almost new though?" I ask, looking at the not so brand-new truck.

"Yup. But it doesn't fit in with my plans."

"Plans?" I feel like an idiot asking question after question, but I'm having a hard time understanding why you would trade in a new car for an older truck. Sure, it was in good condition. No rust, or any major dents or dings, but still.

"I bit the bullet," he says with a big grin. "But there's more to tell you about it. I'll explain when we get to my place."

And he did tell me all about his visit with his parents, his talk with them about his plans to start a business, and the surprising news that his father and brother might join him. His excitement shows and I can't help but smile at him. "That's wonderful. So the truck is…"

"Hard to move wood, tools, furniture, and things like that in a sporty Audi. That was good for the old Tim. The truck is perfect for the new one." He smiles, and it occurs to me how much more relaxed he seems to be now than I've ever seen him before. Even before he lost his job. Of course it helps that he was a definite attention grabber in a suit, seeing him in jeans, boots, and sometimes even a flannel shirt, is a showstopper.

"It looks good on you," I compliment him, making his eyes crinkle.

"Yeah? How so?"

"You seem less buttoned up. Less stressed."

He slips his arms around me and pulls me in tight. "Like me less buttoned up? There's a lot of places I could take that," he says, before the persistent growling of my rebellious stomach draws his attention. "But I won't, because I've got to get you fed first. When did you eat last?"

I frown, trying to remember, but other than a banana with my coffee this morning, nothing comes to mind. "Oops," I tell him. "Breakfast?" The truth is, when I'm not being fed by Viv or Dino, I tend to forget. Or maybe I'm just too lazy to care. Either way, it's clear Tim does not approve, judging from the frown on his face.

"Gotta eat, Ruby," he says seriously, and I'm suddenly choked up. I'm used to Viv or Dino, even Syd, caring, but it's different from him.

I swallow against the lump in my throat and take a deep breath. "Okay," I reassure him, in as firm a voice as possible, but it still sounds pretty wobbly. I quickly slip out of his arms and lift the lid to check on the chicken. "Feed me then."

The heavy moment lifted, I turned to the recipe he'd printed off to which I'd added notes in the margin for my own future reference. "What's next?"

-

The food was out of this world delicious, and I can't believe I had a good hand in making that, or that I just ate seconds. Sitting back on his couch to relieve some of the pressure on my stomach, I watch Tim walk toward me with mugs of hot cocoa. He offered to make coffee, but with a light snow starting to fall outside, I had a sudden craving for something homey and warm. After the spicy goodness of the shredded chicken and cheese stuffed Poblano chiles, something rich and sweet will hit the spot. I accept the mug from Tim and sip cautiously from the hot liquid as he sits beside me on the couch.

"Oh, this is good," I hum in appreciation. "There's something in here besides cocoa, what is it?" I turn to Tim to find him staring at my mouth.

"Just a pinch of cardamom and a little bit of cinnamon," he says, his eyes never wavering.

"So delicious," I hum again, as I take another sip and suddenly find the hot chocolate taken from my hand.

"You drive me crazy with those sounds you make," he growls, as he puts both mugs on the table. Before I have a chance to object, I'm lifted onto his lap and he's kissing me. Fiercely.

I have no choice but to respond in kind. What his tongue is doing to my mouth is forcing all thought from my mind and leaves me to simply float on the sensations. My hands somehow find their way to the back of his head, where they play mindlessly through his hair. His hand strokes my back, and the other one travels all the way down my legs, where he wraps it around my ankle before traveling back to my waist. I feel like I'm melting from the inside out as his tongue makes love to my mouth. I groan, unable to hold back. In response, he tightens one arm behind me, while his other hand slips under my sweater, where it curves around my breast. So lost in my senses, I don't even register that he must've felt the rolls at my waist. Not even when he impatiently pulls the cup of my sturdy bra down and shifts his attention, with lightning speed, from my mouth to the breast he just exposed.

I feel more than hear, the deep groan rolling up from his chest, right before his mouth settles over the tip, pulling hard. It's like nothing I've ever felt before. Like a live wire running from where his mouth is sucking my breast to between my legs; every pull of his lips sends a charge of electricity to my pussy, leaving me wet and aching.

I've had hands and mouths on my breasts before, but never with this effect. I've experienced wetness between my legs, but rarely ever my own. With his upper body, Tim presses me back against the armrest until I'm almost laying down, splayed over his lap.

It isn't until I feel his hand make quick work of my button and zipper, and slips inside my panties, that I feel my first flutter of hesitation. What if I don't please him? What if he's disappointed?

"Stop thinking," he mumbles, with his mouth against my skin. "*Feel.*"

Oh, I feel. I feel his fingers slip through the wetness at the apex of my thighs, probing gently. I certainly feel the slight flick of his thumb in passing over my sensitive clit. I feel it all and I roll my hips, wanting more.

"Fuck, Ruby, so responsive. So slick and warm."

His finger slides tentatively into my opening a few times and I lift up for deeper penetration. A second finger joins and I'm deliciously full. Slow, deep strokes drive me out of my mind with a need that takes me by surprise. Tension tightens up every nerve and muscle in my body; it's almost unbearable. When his thumb finds my clit and presses down firmly, I feel myself free-falling with his name on my lips.

Soft kisses and gentle strokes: that's all I feel while catching my breath. Until I can feel all his movements still.

"Ruby? Are you crying?" My eyes open to find him just inches from my face, staring at me intently. "Are you okay?"

Breaking out in a huge smile, I lift my hand to stroke along his jaw. "I'm wonderful."

He closes his eyes briefly, the relief obvious on his face. "Thank Christ," he mutters, before turning that dark blue gaze on me again. "And yes. You're fucking phenomenal."

CHAPTER THIRTEEN

Tim

Fuck, she scared me with those tears. For a moment I thought I'd hurt her. Pushed her too far. The relief to see her smiling, through her tears, instantly slows down the pounding panic of my heart. Jesus, she's gorgeous, all that soft flesh flushed with arousal. The sounds coming from her mouth…I'd been so hard it was painful, but the tears served like a cold shower on my libido.

"Stay," I softly ask her.

"Oh," she breathes, suddenly scrambling to get off my lap and pulling her sweater down, regrettably blocking my view of her soft skin. Next thing I know, she's on her knees before me, struggling with the buttons of my jeans.

"What are you doing?" My words freeze her fumbling as her eyes lift to meet mine.

"You didn't…I thought…" After a few false starts, she closes her mouth and lowers her eyes shaking her head slightly.

"You gave me more than I expected, love." I gently remove her hands from my crotch, as her eyes flick up at my use of that particular endearment, her face betraying confusion. "Coming undone under my hands and mouth. Trusting me to take care of you. Your tears…" I take a deep breath. "I don't need you to get me off. Just stay with me tonight."

I'm don't really know if any of what I say makes sense to her. I can still see doubt in her eyes, and I don't blame her. That's why it's so damn important for me to keep my physical urges curbed. I'm no fucking saint. I'd like nothing more than to bury myself in that luscious body, but she's conditioned only to think about the other person's satisfaction and never her own. I need her to understand I'm not that person. I'm not those Johns.

Sitting back on her haunches, her eyes search my face for the right answer, but she won't get it from me. She needs to figure things out for herself. She needs to learn to listen to her own needs and not be afraid to voice them.

"Okay."

I barely hear her, her voice is so soft, but when she stands up and holds out her hand to me, I don't need to hear the words.

-

The first thing I notice waking up is the smell of coconut. The second is my morning wood pressed against the warm, pliable pillow Ruby's ass makes against my groin.

We haven't moved from how we fell asleep last night. Me curled around Ruby, who is lying on her side, her back against my chest, my nose buried in her mass of hair, and my arms keeping her there. She was comfortable there last night, but this morning with my dick ignoring my pleas for restraint and poking at her, I'm not so sure. I try to move my hips back a little, but she instantly scoots her ass back to where it has full contact. Did I mention I'm not a saint? I snuggle deeper into her soft body. If I'd known how fucking comfortable all those soft curves were, I'd have given up on the tall, skinny girls long ago. A guilty thought of Viv flashes through my mind, whose long athletic body had been fodder for my fantasies, even as the memory of it faded.

This, though...this feels like home.

Pulling her in a little closer and burying my face deeper in her hair, I feel her start to stir against me. Reluctantly, I loosen my grip so she can move. She immediately turns around and snuggles against my chest. *Fuck me.* I'd be an idiot not to recognize what a huge fucking deal it is for her to turn to me like that. My dick appreciates it too. Especially with the way Ruby's leg is pulled up across my hips.

Just as my mind is starting to blur with the physical sensations and resulting urges—mainly to strip the still fully dressed Ruby naked and slide into her soft body—my damn phone starts ringing on my bedside table. A quick look at the display shows my parents' number.

"Morning, Mom," I mumble, answering on a guess, since Dad rarely uses the phone. But the responding voice proves me wrong.

"Not the last time I checked, boy," my father's voice booms through the earpiece, and I lift my cell to a safe distance. Evidence Dad doesn't use the phone often is his need to shout at full volume, since he's never progressed from cans connected by a string. Cell phones are a total alien concept to him, since they aren't attached by a cord, necessitating the full capacity of his lungs. And that was impressive.

"Dad, not so loud," I plead, holding on to Ruby one-handed, as she's frantically trying to climb off me. "Inside voice please. I can hear you just fine."

"We're going to Freyburg," he booms, obviously not having heard me from the ringing in his own damn ears. He continues to tell me about this tip he received about a farmer looking to sell his barn wood for a steal. Dad apparently spoke to him at the butt crack of dawn, because the farmer mentioned that if we were able to come today and tear the barn down for him, he'd let us cart it off for free. In the meantime, Ruby's stopped struggling and is once again lying with her head on my shoulder and an arm slung over my stomach, but her leg remains straight at my side. Pity.

Free is a magic word for my dad. He believes everything that's free is worth having, which is why he has two spare and very ancient washers in the garage, the ugliest floral fabric couch in the basement, and an array of antique exercise equipment in the spare bedroom, gathering dust. Never mind it had needed three grown men to haul each and every one of those items inside his house. So the fact he had heard *free* and didn't waste a minute considering what it would take to bring down a barn, shouldn't surprise me.

"And it's gotta get done today, Son, so get your ass out of bed."

Ruby stifles a giggle against my chest.

"You want to come, Boop? Spend the day watching a bunch of men swearing and getting sweaty over a pile of free wood?" I ask her, watching as her head lifts and eyes light up.

"I have to work," she whispers, a little disappointed by the way her face drops. "Dino's off tonight."

"Who the blazes are you talking to? Who's Boop? You got a dog?" My father's voice blusters, setting Ruby's giggles off again.

"Dad! Inside voice, please!" Christ, my head's already starting to pound. "Too bad," he says to me.

"Honey?"

Oh great, now Mom's on the phone. "Hey, Mom."

"You got a dog?" She'd obviously been listening to Dad's side of the conversation, and not unexpected, decided to take over.

"No, Mom, no dog."

"But your father said you were talking to someone?" she persists, and I choose not to respond, letting the silence do the talking. It doesn't take long. "Oh…oh…ohhhh," she finally stammers before continuing in an excited whisper. "Do I know her?"

Not ready for a parental inquisition, especially with Ruby making moves to escape me again, I cut my mother off at the pass.

"No you don't, Mom. Can you put Dad back on again? The barn?" I helpfully add.

"Yes, yes of course. But, honey? I'm making pot roast tomorrow. Enough for an orphanage." Subtle, my mother is not.

"I'll keep it in mind, Mom," I reply, my eyes on Ruby's face, which has gone beet red. She heard, and she understands, what was implied too, judging by the panic in her eyes.

With my father back on the phone, I make quick arrangements for him to round up my brother, and assure him, I'll try to get at least another body along to help. Maybe one of my baseball mates. Ike might be game.

"Dad, I've gotta go," I interrupt my Dad's ongoing ramble. "I'll be there in thirty. Let me make some calls."

"Later, Son. Say bye to the girl." With a roll of my eyes, I end the call, turning back to Ruby, who has her hands covering her face, mumbling behind it.

"Ohmigod, *Madre de Dios.*" I hear the moment I pull her hand away from her mouth. I could say something to calm her down, but there's a much better way to silence her. Taking advantage of her moving lips, I cover her mouth with mine, and slide my tongue inside. She only struggles for a few seconds before she gives in on a big sigh, curling her hands behind my head.

Moments later I pull away, out of breath. The woman has no idea the power she wields. One soft touch of her lips is like a spark to a powder keg: explosive. Unfortunately, given my unexpected change in schedule, I don't have time to let it burn the way I'd like.

"I seem to be saying this a lot, but if I don't stop now…That barn wood, you heard my dad mention, would save us a fortune in expenses if we had to buy it from a salvager," I explain, but she puts her fingers on my lips.

"Go," she urges with a smile. "Go chase your dream."

Not quite sure how the fuck I got so lucky, I waste a little more time showing her my appreciation.

Thirty minutes after that, I drop her off at her apartment building, with a hard kiss to her mouth, and the promise I'll see her tonight.

Ruby

"Are you sure you'll be okay?"

Dino's large hand lands on my shoulder. He's been dawdling in the kitchen for at least ten minutes and his phone has rung three times already.

"I'll be fine," I reassure him. Again. "If I run into trouble, I promise I'll get Viv." Granted. Last time I took over the kitchen by myself had admittedly been pretty disastrous. I can't blame him for being a tad apprehensive.

With just a nod, he finally grabs his coat off the hook and shrugs it on. His face is drawn, haggard, and his movements are jerky. Without thinking I put my hand on his arm. "Is everything okay with you?" His eyes snap my way, and for a moment, they show a deep turmoil before he blinks it away.

"It will be," he says gruffly. "It has to be." The last is said on a whisper and I almost missed it.

"If there's anything I can do…" The rest of my words disappear in his thick winter coat as he pulls me into his chest.

"What you can do is stop running. Let the people who care about you help. Let them in." His voice is ragged, as he all of a sudden releases me and walks out the door without looking back.

I watch him go with a heavy heart before turning back to the stove.

"Hey. Viv said I could find you here." I turn to find Pam walking into the kitchen.

"Hi. How are you?"

"Good. Frozen. It's cold out and the snow is really starting to come down," she says, as she shakes out her coat. "Was that Dino just leaving?" she asks, tilting her head in the direction of the back door.

"Yes," I confirm, as I make a split second decision. "And Pam? There's something really wrong with him." Her eyebrows shoot up as she pulls out a chair at the table.

"How so?"

In between getting orders ready, I give Pam a description of the things I've observed. Do I feel guilty talking about someone who's become a friend? Sure, but I'm also concerned about him and know Pam is better equipped to help people than I am.

"I'll see if he'll talk to me. Lord knows, the man's knuckle dragging, alpha antics drive me up the wall, and he may well wipe the floor with me, but I'll give it a go. Now," she says straightening in her seat. "I came in here to find out how you were doing. I haven't seen you all week." I can't help the smile that spreads over my face and Pam clearly does not miss a thing. "It's like that, is it?" she says, the corners of her mouth lifting.

I start catching her up, skirting around a lot of the details, but she keeps looking at me with that one eyebrow raised high. She prompts me with, "And?" every time I take a breath, until finally I crack.

"Okay, fine. I had an orgasm," I blurt out way too loud, giving the big pot on the stove a good stir, too embarrassed to look at her.

"Oh my God, my ears! I'll never recover."

I swing around and look straight into Matt's horrified face. "Madre de Dios!"

"No shit, Sherlock. I come in here for a damn bowl of chili, and I'm slapped with an orgasm," Matt rambles, as he turns on his heels and walks straight back out the door.

In shock, I look at Pam who is trying, and failing, to contain her deep, rolling laugh.

-

"Ruby?"

I can't help the deep sigh of relief that escapes me when I hear the voice on the line. By the time I left The Skipper last night, I was trudging through snow already up to my ankles. There'd been no sign or sound from Tim. Although I knew it was possible he'd be home late, the weather had been cause for concern. It was coming down something fierce and wasn't expected to let up until sometime Sunday evening. When midnight came, and I was still waiting by the phone for a call, I'd had enough. Who knows what is *normal* in a situation like this? It's not like I have any experience being in a relationship. If that is what this is. I'm not even sure.

Frustrated and worried, I ended up going to bed, where it took forever to fall asleep.

Starting at ten this morning, I tried not to dwell on the fact I'd still not heard anything and went through my regular routine. The walk across to the wharf was even more treacherous than last night, even in daylight, I couldn't see a hand in front of my face. Snow was coming in sideways and strong gusts of wind swirled it around. My old boots were no match and my socks were soaked in minutes.

I'd barely gotten in the back door when the phone rang.

"Are you okay?" I blurt out the minute I hear Tim's voice.

"I'm fine," he chuckles, which somehow irritates me. He was fine, and I'd just spent half the night rolling around in bed, worried sick. "We ended up stopping at a roadside motel for the night, the snow was ridiculous. We're just grabbing a bite and then we'll be back on the road. Hopefully, plows have gone through, although it's still coming down." He must've noticed my silence, because he's suddenly quiet too. "Ruby? I'm sorry if you were worried. I tried calling late last night, but there was no answer. I was going to try again in five minutes, but I ended up crashing."

"It's okay," I placate him. I realize, he probably called when I was trudging home through the snow. But he's not buying it.

"No, it's not. Fuck, honey, I'm really sorry," he says, and he sounds it. "Look, it's going to take hours for us to get home in this weather, and then we'll have to unload, but I'll come see you as soon as I'm done."

"Really, it's okay," I assure him. Now I feel bad about making him feel bad.

"Ruby." He sounds firm. "I'll see you sometime this afternoon."

I don't get a chance to say anything because he's already gone.

-

"Excuse me?"

The snow had stopped around noon, letting a watery sun peek through every now and then. Gunnar had shown up shortly after I talked to Tim and was surprised to see me. He said he'd told Viv to stay home and that he was considering shutting down for the day. Then Dino walked in, and shortly after that Matt. Instead of sending everyone home, he suggested using the time to catch up on inventory, organizing, and give the place a thorough cleaning.

That's what I'm doing. Pulling bottles and glasses down behind the bar and giving the shelves a good wash and swinging my hips to the oldies rock Gunnar had been playing all morning. I've already cleaned out the three small fridges that held the bottled import beers, some wines, and a few other things. Other than a couple of my neighbors from across the street, who came in hoping for a bite, it has been quiet. So the voice startles me and I swing around.

A tall man, about my age, with dark hair showing streaks of grey, is eyeing me top to toe from the other side of the bar. Something about him is familiar, but I can't place it. All I know is his intense scrutiny is making me feel decidedly uncomfortable, and my eyes scan the bar to see where Matt is. Then I remember he went into the storage room to count bottles there. Dino is in the kitchen working on the pantry, and Gunnar is in his office. It's just me.

Fighting down my unease, I wipe my hands on a towel and plaster on a friendly smile. "Hi there. Can I get you anything?"

"Nice place," he says, looking around without answering me. "Didn't know it was here until a friend told me about it. Easy to miss if you don't know where to look."

The conversation feels all wrong as chills roll down my back. "Did you want to see a menu?" I try again, throwing a furtive glance toward the back hallway, in hopes one of the guys will show their face.

"You've come up in the world since I saw you last, *Abril*."

His use of my birth name freezes the breath in my lungs, and suddenly I know where I've seen him before. Club Innosins, heading into Carlos' office as I was coming out of the bathroom, only days before I ran from Boston like I had the devil on my heels. He was with a second man. Now *that* man I would've recognized in a heartbeat. I saw him days later, from behind a pile of pallets in a warehouse, and then again parked out front of the police station where I'd just given witness against him. *Eduardo Lima.*

"Ah, I see you recognize me. I was afraid of that," he says in a low voice. "You understand I can't risk leaving you. Loose ends and all that." He waves his hand casually. "If you quietly walk out with me, *Abril*, nothing will happen to your friends or this quaint pub. It would be a shame," he says, looking around the pub again. "Old structure like this, it wouldn't take much to bring it down. Perhaps an unfortunate kitchen mishap?"

The air that was stuck in my chest expels in a rush, as if I'm punched in the stomach. A deep groan involuntarily escapes as I think of my friends hurt, of this place that's become more like home these past months, destroyed. Despite the fact I want to run for help, fear for my new found family has me grounded to the spot. As if in slow motion, the man raises his hand and crooks his finger at me. My feet start moving before my mind has a chance to clue in.

I just step from behind the bar, throwing a last look at the empty hallway, when his hand snakes out and hauls me close by the neck. "Don't even think about it," he hisses in my ear.

A deep sadness settles in my chest when I meekly walk along beside him to the door.

"Hey, Ruby? Can you give me a quick hand?"

Gunnar's voice sounds behind me, just as the door in front of me opens, and Tim and his brother walk in. The hand in my neck squeezes in warning right before he forcefully shoves me in the path of the two men rushing forward. With nothing to stop the momentum, I fly forward and crash into them, before knocking into something and then hitting the floor. Hard. An involuntary cry escapes me as I feel something give way and feel instant hot pain blast my right side.

CHAPTER FOURTEEN

Tim

It had been a pretty grueling drive, coming back from Freyburg. The trip, normally a little over an hour, had ground to a halt last night about twenty miles in. The roads had been bad, but worse was the lack of visibility. You couldn't see where the road ended and the ditch began. Twice we'd barely been able to dig ourselves out of a drift on the side, when Ike spotted the brightly lit sign for an Econolodge through the snow. No one argued as I pulled onto the empty parking lot. It had been a fucking exhausting and very long day already, and driving home in this shit required a sharp head. Besides, Dad had worried me a bit, not wanting to give an inch to us younger guys, he'd worked his ass off all day. His breathing was still a bit choppy, though, even after we forced him to sit out while we loaded as much as we could of the wood on the truck and stacked the rest for pick up later in the week.

Since the snow had still been coming down steadily this morning, we didn't bother hurrying out. Made more sense to grab a shower, even if it meant having to get back in yesterday's dirty clothes, and grabbing a bit of breakfast, while hopefully the plows were out there doing their job. Still it took us a couple of hours to get home, where we first drop off Dad, before heading to my place to unload.

I haven't been able to get Ruby out of my mind all morning. It sucks to think she'd worried last night while I was out cold, snoring away. I just dropped Ike off at home and had planned to drop Mark at my parents before heading to the pub, but I can't wait.

"You mind hitting The Skipper first? Before I drop you off?" I ask my brother.

"Are you sure that's wise?"

I look at him, surprised at his reaction. "Am I sure what is wise, exactly?" My sharp retort is met with a firm set of his jaw.

"Do you even know what you're getting into? A woman with a history like that?"

Slamming my foot on the brake and coming to a stop at the curb, I turn my entire body to face him. "And what do you know of her history, huh? Do you really think that was some life-choice for her? Ending up where she did? She was branded, you bastard! At fourteen fucking years old, she was taken and branded like fucking cattle. I don't even know the full story yet, but it doesn't matter to me. None of that fucking matters to me. I'm disgusted that it would matter…"   With a cutting motion of his hand, Mark cuts me off before I can finish my sentence. Anger is etched on his face.

"Shut up, you idiot. Has it occurred to you that I'm worried about you?" With erratic movements he runs his hands through his hair. "Jesus Christ. The woman is a witness to a murder, Tim. She was associated with one of Boston's most renowned sex trade organizations. Saw one of its main players get killed. And is apparently on the radar of some less than law abiding members of the police force. You think I'm worried because she turned tricks?" He underlines his words with a frustrated groan as he leans his head back and closes his eyes. Stumped by his outburst, I only grunt in response. I understand where he's coming from, but part of me still rebels at the thought that Ruby would have to be tainted by something that happened *to* her. Something out of her control from the very beginning.

"You care for her." The statement is delivered with a hint of disbelief in his voice, but his conclusion is on the money. Fuck, yes, I care for her. Truth be told, the depth of it surprises me as much as it apparently does him.

"I do."

"Shit," he says, shaking his head. "I'm sorry, man. It's just, she's so different from your usual fare." It takes everything out of me not to take a swing at him after all. Instead, I white knuckle my hands on the wheel and grind my teeth.

"She *is* different," I manage, taking a deep breath and slowly letting it out. "She's more." I can feel his eyes on me but keep my focus on the snow bank on the side of the road.

"Right," is all he says.

"Right. So are we done with this now?" I want to make sure.

"All done. The Skipper it is."

-

There are only a handful of cars in the parking lot, which remains still covered in snow. Not a surprise really, even with the sky clearing, it's still a mess everywhere. You'd be nuts to go out if you don't absolutely have to.

Locking the truck, I slog through the snow behind my brother, who stops when we pass a dark sedan in the lot. Crouching down, he wipes some of the sludge of the rear bumper, revealing a *BPD, Boston's Finest* sticker. I get an uneasy feeling as I look down the alley toward the pub and start walking in that direction. Mark is not far behind me, putting a hand on my shoulder.

"Hold up. Lots of those stickers around. Doesn't mean anything." He tries to reassure me.

"Is that why it stopped you in your tracks?" I shoot back, not slowing down for a second.

First place my eyes go when I push open the door is the bar, where I'd expect Ruby to be. Instead Gunnar is standing there, tension radiating off his body. It's not until he calls out for Ruby that I notice her standing beside a lanky, tall guy. Her head down and her shoulders slumped. It takes a moment for me to register all is not well, when I feel Mark already moving to rush past me. Next thing I know, Ruby comes flying toward us, her arms windmilling. I try to grab for her when she bounces off Mark and crashes into a table before smacking hard into the floor. I helplessly watch as she lands on her side, her arm appearing to collapse underneath her with a sickening loud snap. Her pained cry has me shove Mark out of the way, and not paying any attention to anything or anyone else, I drop on my knees beside her.

Tears of pain swim in her eyes, but still she manages to force a smile. "I'm sorry," she whispers, and I cover her mouth with my fingers.

"Shit, sweets. Nothing to be sorry for. Lie still," I comfort her when she tries to move.

"Ambulance is on the way," Matt says as he crouches down beside us. "Cops too."

"No!" Ruby's violent reaction startles me, and before I can hold her back, she scrambles to her feet, her useless arm flopping at her side. White as a ghost, she backs away straight into Dino's massive chest.

Ruby

"No running, little one." I hear Dino's deep rumble behind me, as one of his arms bands around my waist, leaving me with nowhere to go.

"You don't understand," I whisper urgently, desperate to get away. "I have to go." My plea goes unheard as I watch Tim scramble to his feet and approach me with his hand out, but instead of grabbing onto me, he carefully brushes the hair from my face and tucks it behind my ear.

"The office, Dino," is all he says. Before I know it, I'm being frog-marched in that direction. Dino's arm still firmly around my waist. A deep throbbing pain crowds out my panic as every movement jostles my useless right arm, and I have to push down a wave of nausea. Once inside Gunnar's office, I'm gently, but firmly set on the couch, where Tim instantly takes a seat to my right, brushing his fingers lightly over the limp arm I'm now cradling in my lap. "Let me have a look, Ruby."

"It's fine," I bluster through teeth that have started to chatter. "I'll be fine. I heal fast."

"Honey…this won't heal on its own."

When I look down, the sight of my arm bending at an unnatural angle has bile rising so fast, I'm not able to stop from spewing all over myself. Tears I saved up for decades start rolling down my face as I slowly close my eyes.

I vaguely hear people moving in and out, talking, but don't really hear what they're saying. My mind is swirling with thoughts of hospital bills, police involvement, exposure, and defeat. It isn't until I feel something wet wipe at my face that I open my eyes to find Tim on his knees in front of me, cleaning vomit off my face and clothes.

"Hey," he smiles gently. "I'm taking you to the hospital. Don't panic," he says when I shake my head. "There's nothing to worry about. Mark and Gunnar are out there dealing with the cops, Dino and I will take you." He grabs my coat that Dino hands over and drapes it over my shoulders.

"I don't have insurance," I whisper.

"I figured as much," Tim says, his eyes steady on mine. "It's not going to be a problem." With that he stands up, and with an ease that belies my size, picks me up and carries me out into the hallway, ignoring my feeble protests. Dino is right behind him, talking on his phone.

I barely remember the car ride to the hospital, my mind is blissfully blank, but I'm constantly aware of the warm comforting body holding me, cradled in the backseat of the car, all the way there. My eyes stay firmly closed as I feel myself lifted and moved. I know I can't hide behind my eyelids much longer when I hear the whoosh of automatic doors opening and closing.

-

"His name is Terry Milano."

I look up to find Mark's face in the group gathered in Tim's living room.

After a few stress-filled, painful hours at Maine Medical Center, Dino was there to drive us home. To Tim's house that is. Neither of them seemed to listen to my assurances I'd be fine in my apartment. All I got was pointed looks at my arm, which is sporting a cast and sling that keeps it strapped against my body. Thank God for the clean shirt one of the nurses found for me.

Despite the shot they gave me beforehand, the setting of the broken bones had not been fun. That was after the doctor came in and showed two prior, improperly healed breaks on the X-ray. Tim didn't say anything, but I could see his nostrils flare and eyes get dark. When the young intern asked me, with half an eye on Tim, who'd refused to leave my side, if I wanted to talk to someone *alone,* I hurried to explain those were old injuries.

To my surprise, no one approached me about cost or insurance, but when I mentioned it in the car, Dino just said Pam was looking after things. Pam was one of the people waiting outside Tim's house when we got there, along with Gunnar and Tim's brother, Mark. The sight of all them made me nervous.

Once inside, Tim made sure I was comfortable on the couch, while Gunnar disappeared into the kitchen to *put on a pot.*

"At the pub, the guy who had a hold on you, his name is Terry Milano and he's a cop." Mark's eyes on me look almost sad. "I recognized him when he shoved past me and took off. I was at a conference in New Jersey last year and met him. Boston PD. The guy is the captain of the precinct you were questioned at."

"Son of a bitch." I hear Gunnar mutter from the kitchen as I stare in disbelief at Mark.

"Ruby." Pam's gentle voice draws my eyes to her. "I know you've been protecting yourself the best you know how, but I think it's time you let us in." At the words, which sounded much like those Dino used not that long ago, my eyes went around the room to finally come to rest on Tim. Aside from Mark, there is no one here who hasn't already proven to be trustworthy. I owe them the truth. Just as panic at the thought of exposing myself threatens to choke me, Tim's kind eyes and slight nod of approval convince me.

"I grew up in a small rural community, just outside of Tenancingo, Mexico, where my father was a farmer. When I was fourteen, my parents were murdered, and I was taken by force by a man I'd imagined myself to be in love with. I was kept in a house on the outskirts of Tenancingo, where for two years I was, as they called it, *broken in,* by any means possible. Drugs, beatings, alcohol, anything to keep us compliant. Carlos Delgado was a regular visitor at the *calcuilchil."*

"What's a *calcuilchil*?" Pam asks when I take a deep breath.

"House of ass," I explain, my voice sounding as flat as I'm forcing my feelings. "Tenancingo has many." I keep my eyes lowered, not able to tell my story while seeing so much emotion etched on the faces around me. Pity is an ugly thing in my experience, and I don't want to have to read it on the faces of people I've come to care about. So my eyes stay focused on the floor as I tell the rest of my story to the best of my ability. Lastly, I explain where I've seen Milano before and the significance of the person he was with.

"He was with one of the shooters?" Dino is the one to voice that. "The police captain? What the hell."

"He *was* the shooter. The only one I saw firing shots. His name is Eduardo Lima and he was a regular in the club."

Silence settles heavily over the room when I'm done. I find myself holding my breath in anticipation of what is to come.

"Why did you not run? In all those near thirty years, how come you never just walked away?" How ironic that Mark, the only cop in the room, would ask that question. It doesn't surprise me. I know, even if not always voiced, it's the first thing anyone would think.

I lift my head and look him squarely in the eye. "At first, fear of punishment held me captive. They were quite…clear in their expectations and brutal when we wouldn't live up to them." I shrug the memories of the merciless repercussions off. "Later, it was more a case of better the devil you know…Carlos Delgado was predictable in what he required, as well as his punishments. Knowing what to expect was the safer option. I still could've run, I guess, but I had nowhere to turn. *La jura,* his buddy cops, would hunt me down and send me back to the *calcuilchil*. He promised that's what would happen and…" I wipe at the angry tears blurring my vision as I keep my focus on Mark. "And today they did."

Tim

She's killing me.

Sitting there with her back ramrod straight and her eyes glued to the rug in front of her feet, her voice emotionless, as she recounts her horrific story…killing me. When my brother asks his question, I'm poised to jump up and finally lay him out flat, but Dino's large hand descends on my shoulder and keeps me pinned in my seat. "Wait," he warns, his voice so soft only I can hear. So I wait. Not that I would've gotten far, because I may be a big guy, but Dino's got even me beat.

When Ruby's last words finally register, I can feel clarity settle like concrete in my gut. I don't know how someone can survive what she has been through and still maintain such a sweet heart. You would expect someone to get hardened—bitter. Not Ruby, despite the injustices she's suffered, somehow she's retained an underlying innocence.

She turns to me, her face wet and her eyes large, almost hollow in her face. "I'm tired," she whispers. Without saying anything, I scoop her up and carry her upstairs, leaving the room to explode in voices behind me.

"I'm sorry," she mumbles against the skin of my neck. "I wanted to tell you but I was afraid."

"Hush. You get some rest and I'll bring you something to eat in a bit."

Sitting on the side of the bed, she lets me pull off her boots and socks, and doesn't even complain when I undo her jeans and help scoot her up on the bed, so I can remove them. The look in her eyes is vacant when I pull the covers up around her shoulders. When I move to leave, her hand darts from under the covers and grabs my wrist. "Don't be mad."

"Not mad, honey. Never mad. This is me, sad: for you missing out on the life of love and laughter you should have had." I lean over to kiss her lightly on her lips, and then again on her forehead. When I get to the door, I turn around to see tears rolling down her face again. *Fuck this.* Instead of walking out the door, I retrace my steps to the bed, kick off my boots and climb in beside her. Carefully shifting her, I wrap her in my arms and wait for her breathing to even out with sleep.

-

"I'll stay with her."

Pam's voice penetrates the half-doze I've fallen into, and I turn my head to the door. "I think you may want to get in on the conversation," she says in a cautious tone, but I can already hear the raised voices coming from downstairs. Once I've eased my arm from under Ruby's sleeping body, I get up and hurry out the door.

"Over my dead body!" Dino's booming voice greets me, as I walk into what looks to be a standoff between him and my brother, with Gunnar stepping between.

"What the fuck is going on? She just fell asleep. Idiots!"

Both men turn my way, matching sheepish looks on their faces and Gunnar seems to be fighting a smirk. I pick my brother to pin with a glare. "Wanna fill me in?" Dino harrumphs and disappears into the kitchen, while Mark runs a hand through his mop of already unruly hair.

"I was just suggesting calling an FBI buddy of mine. Someone I've been talking to about the Delgado case, about that young girl. See if they already have a bead on Milano, because it sure as hell looks like whatever the hell is going on, he's involved," Mark says, throwing a glare in the direction of the kitchen. "Bullneck over there, didn't take to kindly to the idea…"

"Fuckin' A, I didn't. Might as well put a target on her back." Dino walks back in with a bottle of water in his hands. "Did you not hear her? She's illegal here. They'll ship her back to Mexico and then what? She fucking has no one looking out for her there. Whatever sick business these bastards have going on, it's obvious they won't take kindly to her talking to anyone." I can tell he's getting worked up again, but he makes a good point.

"She's not going anywhere." I look at each of the men to make sure I get my point across.

Mark is the first one to speak up. "No. She's not," he agrees. "But unless you have a better suggestion, I trust Mike. He's a local guy, who went through the academy with me. After his first year with the Portland PD, he managed to get into the program at Quantico. We've stayed in touch, get together sometimes for drinks when he's in town visiting his folks."

"I remember him, Italian last name? His folks live on the south side?" I vaguely remember the lanky, quiet but very funny guy, who came with Mark to a family barbecue on the Fourth of July years ago. Cracked me up with his very dry humor. "Carmello or something? No shit, huh? FBI."

"You know him?" Dino wants to know.

"Saw him with my brother a few times. Can't say I know him, but if we have to trust someone, it doesn't hurt to know where the guy's family lives." I shrug my shoulders.

"Can't have her spend her life hiding, Dino," Gunnar finally speaks up. "The woman clearly has been through enough in her life. Be nice if she got to experience what real freedom feels like one day."

"Yeah, but what if she ends up being sent back across the border?" he repeats his earlier concern, when suddenly it dawns on me the answer to that might be the easiest of all.

"I'll just have to marry her."

CHAPTER FIFTEEN

Ruby

What?

I can't quite believe what I'm hearing.

I'm awake when Tim leaves the bed. He doesn't notice, but Pam does. "You can open your eyes now," she says. "He's gone." I blink them open to find her standing by the bed, wearing a smile. "I wanted a chance to talk with you, find out where your head is at, but things down there are getting a little heated. Did you sleep at all?" She reaches out when I struggle to sit up. Not easy with one arm unusable.

"Dozed a little," I confess.

"You looked comfortable enough," she says with a wink. "You know you'll have to deal with your situation, right? At this moment, there are four, big, chest-pounding males in that room downstairs, trying to decide by way of who can be loudest, what should be done with you. As much as I can understand wanting to roll up in a ball and hope it'll all go away, you realize that is impossible. Once that cat got out of the bag, there is no way in hell it's gonna go back in." She sits down beside me on the edge of the mattress. "No hiding. No running. This is time for Ruby to stand up for herself. Look," she says twisting her body toward me. "I understand that you've spent most of your life forced to submit to men, whose last concern was your welfare. I also get that when a good man, one who cares, comes along and offers to take on the world for you, it seems easiest to just let him. But Ruby, you didn't come this far just so you can let someone else make the decisions for you again. This is your future they are discussing. Don't you think you should have a vote?"

I hate it when she's right. I was lying with Tim's warm body shielding me, thinking how nice it was to just let someone else decide what comes next. It would be easier, but I owe myself more. I owe myself a voice.

I don't even bother answering her. I just get up from the bed and try to wrestle my jeans on with one hand. Pam is quickly there to give me a hand and follows me down the hall where the voices are getting louder.

That's when I hear Tim. "I'll just have to marry her," he says, forcing the air from my lungs as Pam bumps into my back.

"Oh, hell," she mumbles behind me.

Damn right, *oh, hell.* I feel a rush of anger burn up my face. He'll *have* to marry me? Like some kind of sacrifice? I don't even realize I'm moving until I'm halfway down the stairs. Holding on to the railing with my good hand, I almost run the rest of the way.

"Like hell you will!" Granted, my entrance may have been a little dramatic, but they were talking about me like I'm an inanimate object. I barely hear Pam's hearty laugh behind me through the blood roaring in my ears. Facing off with four oversized egos on legs, I propped my hand on my hip, watching their shocked faces take me in. It gave me a sense of power I'd never felt before. Gunnar was the first one to react, throwing his head back and busting out laughing. Dino was a little more subtle, but I could see the corner of his mouth tilt into a grin. It was the two brothers, who didn't seem to be able to wipe the shock off their faces. Tim just stood there, his mouth working but no sound coming out. My focus stayed on him. "No need to sacrifice your well-guarded bachelor status. As you well know by now, I'm not exactly known as the marrying kind. Besides, in the unlikely event I would ever consider that, I'd prefer to have a say in the matter."

"Ruby…" It seems Tim has found his voice, but by now, I'm so angry, I wave him off and stalk to the kitchen, hoping to find some coffee left in the pot. I'm not surprised to find him right behind me. "Boop, stop." When I ignore him and start opening and closing cupboards in search of a cup, he braces me against the edge of the counter, his head dipping down in my neck. He shifts my hair out of the way with his chin, before pressing his lips underneath my jaw. "Don't," he warns me, as I try to twist free of his hold. "Just listen to me for a sec, okay?"

It's not like I can move anyway, so I just give in with a slight shrug of my shoulders.

"I admit, that sounded bad. I'm sorry for that. I'm thinking you didn't hear what came before. We were talking about options. Not only how to keep you safe, but also how to keep you in this country, should it come to that. It was said out of practical consideration. But one thing it could never be is a sacrifice."

I'm find myself caving a little to what he says. Putting it into context certainly helps my perception, but it still doesn't feel nice.

Maybe he's sick of looking at the back of my head, or maybe he can feel a little give in my posture, but the next thing I know I'm being turned around to face him. One crooked finger under my chin tilts up my head so I'm forced to look up. "Never," he softly repeats. "Any time spent with you is a pleasure. If there's ever a time where the subject of marriage comes up again, I promise you will always have the final word." Without giving me time to react, he drops his head and drills his point home with the sweet pressure of his lips on mine.

"Sorry to interrupt." Gunnar is still sporting that grin when Tim finally releases my mouth, and I look in the direction of his voice. He doesn't seem fazed by the angry look Tim sends him, or the hot blush on my face, and calmly continues, "But I should get back to the pub. Your truck is in the driveway and keys are here." He dangles the keys before dropping them on the counter. He must have driven Tim's truck home. "I'm catching a ride with Dino. We can talk later," he says to Tim before turning to me. "And you, I don't want to see in the pub until that cast is off, and you've been given a clean bill of health. Unless, of course, you're looking for some food and a drink, in that case we'll be happy to see you."

"But I'm sure I can…"   My protest is swiftly silenced by Gunnar's stern look as he stalks toward me..

"No. You can't. I'm sure you'll have my wife and Viv knocking on the door. Both of those women would have my balls on a platter if I even entertained the idea. We'll sort it out…we'll sort *all* of it out, but not now." He gives Tim a friendly shove and moves into his place to give me a kiss on the cheek. Dino is right behind him, shooting a smug look at Tim, before he too leans in for a sideways hug and a kiss on my hair.

"Let him in, little one," he mumbles in my hair, before letting me go. The moment Dino steps away, Tim moves in again, sliding behind me and wrapping his arm around my waist. Dino just grins and shakes his head, before he walks out the door, with a wave and a polite nod at Pam but completely ignoring Mark.

"Do you feel up to a talk? Because I want you to hear what Mark has to say, Boop."

My anger mostly forgotten, and making sure Pam is staying for some emotional support, I nod my head and let him lead me to the couch. The next ten minutes I sit with my lips firmly pressed together, with Pam's calming hand on my knee and Tim's arm around my shoulders. I listen to Mark. Something I realize after a while; if I allow myself to forget for a second that he's a cop, what he says actually makes sense. Contact someone trustworthy in the FBI, talk to them about Milano, find out if they received any reports on Lima and where he is now. All sounds very reasonable, except that I'd once made the mistake of thinking my words would make a difference, and that didn't turn out so well. Funny thing is, after I'd given the detective Lima's name, and they'd sent me straight into the waiting arms of the man they were supposed to be hunting, I realized they'd never once asked for any confirmation of my background.

It all makes me very nervous.

"Do you have to tell him my name? Where I am?" Of course, I haven't really shared my birth name yet. I'm hanging onto that like a last little layer of protection. My eyes stay focused on Mark, who seems to be considering my question seriously.

"I think I can get away with being vague about who you are. Your picture was doing the rounds, but your name was never listed. Gunnar told the cops, who showed this afternoon, there'd been some trouble with an unruly customer but that he'd taken off. He never once mentioned you, just said the guy got into it with staff members." He walks closer and sits down on the coffee table facing me. "But Ruby, at some point, you're going to have to trust someone. This situation is not going anywhere, and I'm pretty sure Milano and his cronies won't suddenly forget you're here."

"He's right, you know," Pam says, squeezing my knee. "The reality is, even if they discover you are in the country illegally, they can't simply send you back to Mexico. But more importantly, they won't."

I'm confused. "Why wouldn't they?"

It's Mark who answers. "Because you're valuable as a witness. This case involves trafficking young girls from other countries into the U.S. for work in the sex trade. We now have a ranking officer of a large police force involved, and I shiver to think how much higher the rot goes. Besides," he says, with an unexpected wink. "From the sounds of it, my brother is more than willing to make you legal."

Tim

"Is Mark still with you? Where are you guys? Dinner is getting cold."

Pam left a few minutes ago, needing to get back to the shelter. With Ruby slowly relaxing in Mark's presence, Pam gave her a last pep talk and told her she'd call tomorrow. I walked into the kitchen when my phone rang, leaving the two of them hashing over any details Ruby might remember. She looks wiped out though. If Mark doesn't wrap it up soon himself, I'm going to step in.

"Mom, I'm sorry," I apologize, looking at the clock that shows it's already after seven.

"Your father stopped me from calling earlier, but I was worried."

"One of us should've called you. I'm really sorry. Something's come up that Mark is helping me with. We just lost track of time."

"Is everything alright? Have you eaten yet? I can bring something over." As usual, Mom rattles off her questions without stopping for answers, her nurturing instincts not even dulled a bit, despite the fact both Mark and I have been out of the house the last quarter of a century. I peek into the living room, watching Ruby stifle another yawn, and curb my irritation with my mother. Here's a woman who probably doesn't even remember what being cared for feels like. All these years Mark and I have scoffed at Mom's continuing need to *mother,* when Ruby had been forced to do without any warmth. Part of me wonders how Ruby would react to my mother's borderline invasive attention, but I'm thinking it might be a bit overwhelming right now.

"We're taken care of," I assure her instead. "I promise, I'll be there next week and I'll call you soon." A quick, *"Love you too, Mom, "* and I end the call.

I take my seat next to Ruby, who automatically leans into me with another yawn. "I suggest ordering pizza and shelving the third degree, Mark. What say you?" It's clear he catches my meaning when his eyes flick back and forth between Ruby and me.

"Sounds good," he concedes. "But I'll head out right after. Got stuff to do tonight."

Ruby is already half asleep by the time the pizza gets here, but manages to eat two slices before crashing on the couch. Mark and I make quick work of the rest.

"Calling a cab," he says, pulling out his phone.

"I can drive you," I offer, looking at Ruby's sleeping form beside me.

"No worries. My car is at Mom and Dad's, I'll get them to drop me off there. You don't want her to wake up alone and panic."

He's got a point, although I sincerely doubt a canon salvo would wake Ruby at this point.

"I'll give Mike a call tonight. Hopefully he'll be able to help. Some of the information she gave me will definitely pique his interest."

"But…" I start when Mark's raised hand cuts me off.

"Not going to use her name or our connection, Tim. Not without her say so," he assures me.

The moment he leaves, I lift a still sleeping Ruby in my arms and carry her upstairs. She may be small, but asleep she's heavier than I expected. Thank God for the occasional work outs I get in. She feels good in my arms—warm and soft—I don't want to let go.

-

A shift in the mattress wakes me up. In the semi-dark, I can see Ruby's outline as she makes her way to the bathroom. I silently bless the fact I took off her jeans again earlier, so she'd be more comfortable in bed. I hadn't quite wanted to go so far as to take off the rest of her clothes, but am grateful at least for the view of her scantily clad ass. Round, full, and soft, it jiggles slightly as she moves away from the bed, and an instant surge of lust stiffens my cock. There's something about the natural movement of her luscious behind that stirs me more than the many tight buns I've seen parade by over the years. It makes me wonder if self-preservation, against the now evident draw of the softer flesh, had me opt for the slimmer, tighter choices out there. But it's more than that. It's Ruby's emotional innocence that appeals. That seems to bring out a need to protect and savor.

I fold my arms behind my head and wait for her to return, but when I hear the water run, I realize she's in there for more than just a quick relief. Just minutes later, I hear the clang of the toilet seat coming down, along with a frustrated yelp. Worried she may have hurt herself, I jump out of bed.

"Ruby?" I softly knock on the door, trying not to startle her. "Everything okay in there?"

No answer, just a faint sniffle.

"I'm coming in," I warn her, as I push open the door. She's sitting on the closed toilet, her back to the door, and her shirt halfway off. A quick glance at the tub shows it's getting full, so I first turn off the taps, before sitting on the edge of the tub in front of her.

"Need help?" I gently ask. She lifts her tear-streaked face and looks so incredibly sad in that moment, it makes me swallow hard. There is shame in her eyes when she nods her assent. Without looking away from her face, I start untangling the t-shirt from the strap holding her arm immobile.

"I smell," she whispers, lowering her eyes. "I still smell of puke. I can smell it in my hair."

I don't smell anything but Ruby herself, but I think maybe there's more she needs to wash off in the middle of the night. "I'll wash it for you. You can't use that arm," I calmly remind her.

In just her cotton panties and a functional bra, she seems to curl in on herself. I figure sometimes the best thing to do with discomfort is just to push through it, so that's what I do. With swift movements, I have her out of her sling, her bra, and pull her up to standing so I can take off her panties. The entire time, her eyes are pressed shut. Only when I guide her to the side of the tub do her eyes open.

"Sit," I instruct her, holding her cast above the water. "I'm just grabbing a plastic bag for this, so it doesn't get wet." With lightning speed I'm back in the bathroom, having managed to unearth an old grocery bag from beneath the kitchen sink. A roll of duct tape, I remembered in one of the kitchen drawers, comes in handy and in seconds I have her arm more or less waterproof.

With one arm curved behind her shoulders, I encourage her to lie back so I can get her hair wet, trying very hard not to stare at the creamy curves on display. With economic movements, I manage to wet and shampoo her hair, letting her float back to rinse it out. It's thick and heavy, and I can't stop running my fingers through. When I finally help her back up in sitting position, I noticed she's started crying again. "What is it?" I ask, surprised when I get a watery smile in return.

"Thank you," she mumbles. "For being kind." Her eyes leave my face and travel down the front of her body. "You know, I wasn't always like this," she says, motioning her left hand down her body. "I was always curvy, but not fat like I am now. I wish you could've seen me then." She almost sounds wistful; I want to contradict her but can sense she's not done. "I did this on purpose, you know: packing on the pounds? Most men want the fantasy when they pay for sex, so I tried hard not to look like anyone's fantasy. Tried to make myself ugly." She's quiet for a second before she says something that cuts me deep. "I wish I could be yours, though."

Fucking hell. She wrecks me.

In seconds, I'm stripped down to nothing, and without a word I step in the tub behind her, sliding down so she is braced against my front. Leaning my chin on her shoulder, I gently slide my large hands over the swell of her belly, letting one wander up to lift the weight of her breast in my palm. "You have no idea, do you?" I mumble in her ear. "That when you tried so hard to make yourself ugly—as you say—you *became* my fantasy." Her breathing hitches as I press my mouth to the junction between her neck and her shoulder. "You are stunning. Whatever shape or size you come in doesn't change all the beauty that's you. I love the way your body can mold itself around me. I love how there is not one hard place on you, inside or out. But most of all, I'm becoming fast addicted to the depths you show me with those big brown eyes."

Her head falls back against my shoulder and she turns to look at me.

"Teach me how to make love?"

CHAPTER SIXTEEN

Ruby

I can't believe I just said that.

When I woke up, Tim's face had been buried in my hair. It made me immediately aware of my own body odor. Hygiene, ironically, had been something hammered into me over the years. No John likes to smell another guy on you. Having Tim so close, when I'd never even had a shower since this morning, made me uncomfortable. Like my senses were in overdrive, I could suddenly smell the pizza on my breath, the hospital on my shirt, and my puke from earlier on my hair.

I didn't think, I just thought I'd take a bath, so I wouldn't get my arm wet, but hadn't quite thought it through. That became evident when I tried to take off my shirt. Not sure where the tears came from. Crying after maintaining dry eyes for most of my life, and now I can't seem to stop. Same with talking. I start thanking Tim for his help and next thing you know I'm babbling. Then he climbs naked in the tub with me and soothes me with his hands, his words, and his deep baritone, which makes my body tingle.

Then it flies out my mouth and before I can even grasp what's happening, I'm standing beside the tub, and Tim is rubbing me down with a big fluffy towel. He's already stripped the plastic from my cast but doesn't put the sling back on. It doesn't matter, I'm not feeling much of anything except an unfamiliar hunger for his touch.

Although I'm embarrassed over my words, I don't feel self-conscious in front of him. Not now. Not after he seduced me with words I never in my life expected to hear. If that's not enough, there's always the evidence standing up straight from its nest of dark auburn curls. I didn't really get a chance to look at him when he joined me in the tub, but now I'm looking my fill. Strong muscular thighs with the same bristly auburn hair, but sparser, covering them. I'm almost relieved to see he doesn't sport a six-pack, but his pecs are nicely shaped, and his chest and shoulders are wide. He has a nice sturdy, manly look to him and it makes me feel small in comparison. My free hand automatically comes up to settle on his chest, exploring the surprisingly soft hair there. The dark pink disks of his nipples tighten into hard points when the pads of my fingers skim over one and his deep rumble vibrates underneath my hand.

"Boop…you're killing me," he groans. "Just having your hand on me feels so good."

Encouraged, I lean forward and lick around the tight nipple I was just teasing, biting softly, wanting more reaction. I've fucked more men in my life than I could even attempt to count, and yet I feel like this is all new.

When my mouth travels to the neglected nipple and sucks hard, Tim suddenly drops the towel he was still holding around me and lifts me straight off the ground, his arms banded underneath my ass, putting my tits in his face. "My turn," he mumbles, and latches on as he starts walking us to the bedroom where he drops me on my back on the mattress. Years of training has me arrange myself in, what I was made to understand, a seductive position. Tim stands beside the bed and follows my movements with a dark intensity.

"Don't." The single word from his mouth is enough to make me feel insecure. Suddenly, I don't know what to do with myself. "I don't want the practiced poses and a seduction act. I just want you. Just me and you feeling each other out. Discovering each other. You don't have to try so hard to seduce me, because I don't need it. You breathe, and turn those gorgeous expressive eyes on me, and I'm already gone. I see the slight jiggle of your ass when you walk, and all I can think of is sinking my hands into your hips and finding new ways to make that ass jiggle. I hear the rare sound of your soft laughter at something I said, and I feel like the fucking king of the world." He slowly climbs on the mattress, carefully covering my body with his, without ever losing eye contact. "Just be real, be honest, be you. It's more than enough."

My chest feels so full, and I feel so beautiful in that moment that I don't quite know how to respond. Tim solves that problem by slowly letting his weight settle on top of me and taking my mouth with his in a hungry kiss. The feel of his big body covering me—the slight abrasion of his hair against the sensitive peaks of my breasts, his lips on mine—creates a riot of sensations I can feel from the top of my head to the tips of my toes. His tongue is doing thorough sweeps of my mouth, and my body responds instinctively by squirming under his, looking for more friction. More contact. Just more.

I curse the lack of use of my arm, as I try to map out his back and ass with my other hand, running my nails over his back and down to the base of his spine. The responding shiver, running through him, bolsters my confidence as I palm his ass cheek. His cock is hard and long, pressing against my lower belly, leaving behind the sticky residue of precum. Instead of making me feel dirty, it makes me feel desired. I open my legs for his hips to settle between. The slow grind of his length against my heat, in tandem with the movements of his tongue in my mouth, has me lift my hips in invitation. Instead of plunging himself home, which I'm aching for him to do, he finally releases my mouth and stares into my eyes.

"I'm taking my time with you, Ruby." He underscores his words with soft, leisurely kisses over my face, my jaw, and down to my neck. I tilt my head away to give him better access, giving myself over completely to his thorough ministrations. "Gonna explore every damn inch of this glorious body," he mumbles, his mouth sliding over the swell of my breasts and down the valley between. Trying to suck in my stomach is ingrained, but I give up when he nuzzles my pouch with his nose and lips, nipping at the soft flesh and groaning his appreciation. I'm so lost in the pleasure of his touch, I barely notice the direction he's moving. Not until I feel his warm breath touching between my still widespread legs.

When I open my eyes and look down, I see his focus on the mark on my inner thigh. I immediately go to close my legs together, but his wide shoulders make it impossible. His eyes flick up to meet mine, over the swell of my belly, and I see heat in them. Heat and anger. It freezes me instantly. One of his hands comes up, and softly strokes my stomach, as the other takes a firm grip behind my leg, shoving it up and open further as his lips aim a kiss on the ugly brand. "Fuck the bastard who put this here. Hope he fucking rots in hell." His voice is rough and his eyes never leave mine. "I claim this spot. Just as I claim the rest of you," he whispers, moving his mouth to my center and taking a long, leisurely lick along my slit. Only then does he break connection by closing his eyes and so do I.

There've been only few Johns who got off on having a taste of me, something I've always hated. I'm not hating Tim's mouth on me, not when the appreciative grunts coming from him send tingles over my skin. Slow, almost reverently, he makes love to me with his lips and tongue. Probing and teasing—flicking and sucking. I find myself lifting up for closer contact, but the broad palm of his hand on my belly keeps me firmly in place.

"Do you like this?"

I open my eyes and find his blue ones on me once again.

"Talk to me, Boop. Tell me what you like. Do you prefer a soft touch?" He shows me what he means by using only the tip of his tongue to stroke along my opening and tease me around the tight junction of nerves at the top. An involuntary shiver runs through my body at the sensation. "Or would you prefer it a little harder." With that he slides two fingers inside my soaking pussy, while simultaneously sucking on my clit. Hard.

"*Madre de Dios*! Yesssss…" I hiss, bucking under his assault. "Please…" My ragged voice sounds strange to my own ears, as I squeeze my eyes shut and scream his name with my release.

His mouth is instantly tender again as he kisses me down from my climax, his fingers slipping from my heat. Cold hits me when he finally pulls away, but I can't quite bring myself to open my eyes just yet. The slide of a drawer opening and the soft crinkle of cellophane are all too familiar and my eyes snap open. Instead finding of an anonymous shape, I look into the beautiful, warm face I've become very familiar with. With my hand coming up to stroke his glistening beard, I lift my head to press my lips against his, tasting the evidence of my own arousal.

I can't even begin to explain the feelings that are swelling in my chest like balloons. Once again, my eyes well up with overwhelming emotions, and I struggle my tears down. Tim will start thinking I'm a basket case if I keep crying, like I seem to at every turn. I feel like I could float up if his body wasn't hovering over mine, keeping it firmly grounded.

I peek down between our bodies, only inches apart as he braces on his arms to keep his weight off me. The broad, dark purple head of his cock is shiny; suddenly, I want to taste him too. Shimmying down the mattress, I slip one arm through his legs and around his thigh, while keeping my cast braced on my chest.

"What are you doing, Ruby? I told you I—Ahhh." The moment my tongue flicks at the drop leaking from the small slit, his body jerks. Salty, smooth, and uniquely distinct, Tim's flavor floods my senses. The slight pleasant musk of his skin enhancing the taste of his body. By shifting my shoulders to wedge between his knees, and pulling his hips back so I can reach him, Tim is now sitting on his haunches above me. With a firm hand on his ass, I encourage him to move, welcoming the slide of his thick shaft down in my waiting mouth.

"Christ, babe…" The muttered moans from above me make me feel powerful and start a new throb between my legs. I love feeling the flex of his muscles underneath my hand as he struggles to keep his movements in check. I massage his length with my tongue, firmly pressing him up against the roof of my mouth as he slides in, swallowing his tip when he taps my throat, and sucking steadily as he pulls his hips back.

I moan around him as I rub my legs together, trying to find relief for my own ache and bring my hand down. Slipping my fingers through the wetness gathered between my lips, I find the little pearl of nerves. I roll the tip of my middle finger over and around the distended nub, before slipping down inside my opening, drenching the finger in my arousal.

Tim's grunts become louder as he loses the battle for control and his hips start bucking erratically. Suddenly he stops. "I don't want to come in your mouth," he manages through gritted teeth.

"Mmmmm," I hum against his skin. The responding hiss from his mouth almost makes me smile. I want him to lose it. I want to swallow him down and make him feel as wanted as I do right now.

His hips jerk when he feels my finger at his back entrance, firmly sliding in, pressing through the tight ring.

Tim

"Holy Jesus! Son of a motherfucker!"

I can't help the tirade of profanities flying from my mouth as I feel Ruby's finger slip up my ass.

Never. Not ever have I let anyone do that. My mind wants to revolt, but my body is instantly on board. When she presses the tip of her finger deep, an orgasm crashes over me like a tidal wave. My body, bucking and jerking, as the combination of my cock deep against her humming throat and her finger pressing on an ignition button somewhere inside me, hurls me into the abyss. I barely notice Ruby slipping her finger clear and licking my cock clean. My mouth is hanging open, as I gasp for air, after taking a higher plunge than I've ever experienced before.

With a gentle shove, Ruby rolls me on my back where I collapse; my arm slung over my eyes, not able to form a sensible thought or word. It's only when I feel the mattress move, and cold settle in when Ruby slips from the bed, that I open my eyes. Her naked, rounded figure looks as enticing from the back as it does from the front. I lay still as I hear the rush of water as she turns the tap on, waiting for her return. The moment she steps back into the room, I can tell she's surprised to see my eyes on her. The blue cast on her arm stands in sharp contrast with the pale olive tone of her skin. A slight flush covers her chest and cheeks, and along with the dark smolder in her eyes, proof of her arousal.

"Come here," I persuade her, my voice a bit gravelly. I watch as insecurity starts creeping in with every step closer to the bed.

Before she quite gets there, I scissor my body up and reach for her, pulling her off her feet and rolling her over me.

"I'm too heavy," she mutters when I press her head down to my chest, where my heart is still tapping out a rapid beat.

"Hush." I press my lips against the top of her head. "Feel what you do to my heart? You are incredible. *That*…was incredible. Your mouth…my God, Ruby. So good."

She's silent, but seems relaxed against me. It's nice to feel her skin all over me. "You okay?"

"Mmmm," she hums, sounding content, but the slight shifting of her thighs send a different message. My dick, despite the rugged workout, seems to hear it too.

There are so many things we need to talk about, or rather, I want to talk about with Ruby, but right now is not the time. Right now, we both seem to crave communication of a different language. One that is just as important. So I don't think twice before rolling Ruby on her back, stroking the hair back from her face, and dropping a kiss on her wet, swollen lips. Sitting back on my haunches over her thighs, I scan the sheets around us for the foil packet a dropped earlier, spotting it peeking out from under Ruby's hip. She lifts her butt off the mattress when I pull it clear, and I can't help placing an open mouthed kiss over her belly button. The scent of her excitement is strong, and I'm fully hard instantly. It takes me two seconds to roll on the condom.

"I'm claiming you, beautiful," I declare to her, right before I press the crown of my cock between her lips and in one smooth stroke, slide it home into her body.

Ruby's body arches off the bed, her head thrown back in full abandon. I've not seen a more glorious sight. Wild, dark brown curls fanned out over the pillow, a high flush staining her cheeks, and her mouth open, releasing a moan that seems to travel up from her toes.

I take my time, showing her the intimacy of a caring touch, a tender smile, the sweetness of a slow release.

Teaching her how to make love.

CHAPTER SEVENTEEN

Ruby

"So I'm guessing things have been good?"

Pam's voice sounds amused as she regards me from behind her coffee mug. I've just finished updating her since the last time I've seen her. I haven't gone into details, but I guess the fact the last few days have been the best I've ever known shows through.

When I woke up that first morning, the throbbing pain in my arm was an instant reminder of what occurred the day before. The sound of the shower from the bathroom explained the cold empty spot in the bed beside me. Tim is obviously an early riser, since the alarm on the nightstand showed barely seven o'clock. He's also thoughtful, since there was a steaming cup of what smelled like coffee, a glass of water, and a bottle of ibuprofen on the nightstand. I'd refused the hardcore painkillers they offered at the hospital, only too aware of the dangers of addiction. Been there, done that, and not about to tempt the devil. Over the counter would have to do. I popped two of the pills and swallowed them down with a swig of water when I heard the shower turn off. A minute later, a very naked Tim came walking into the bedroom, rubbing at his hair with a towel. I was immediately aware of my own nudity under the sheets as I watched him stalk toward the bed, his memorable package swaying with each step. His rumbled, "Mornin'," was underlined with a shit-eating grin on his face when he bent down to kiss me.

That day he went out for a bit, running some errands, and insisted I stay home. I spent my time watching some TV, something I haven't had a chance to do often. He found me a couple of hours later, totally immersed in a movie called *The Blind Side* and crying. Again. It didn't help that he walked in with a few large bags, containing all of my earthly belongings, which isn't saying much, but still. He'd apparently swung by my apartment with the key he absconded from my purse, and collected all my clothes and toiletries. The kindness of his gesture was a bit too much, on top of the already fragile emotional path the damn movie put me on. He dropped the bags, sat down on the couch beside me, and chuckled as he pressed my face into his shirt. Not that I minded, he smelled good enough to eat. One thing lead to another, but…we didn't get any further than some pretty intense kissing and petting. When I'd asked Tim why he stopped, he said he wanted to be sure I understood it wasn't all about sex for him. It's difficult for me to see my own value beyond what I have between my legs, but Tim sure has ways of getting his point across. My father was a kind man from what I recall, but he was also a man who was used to having his will catered to. One who believed in more traditional roles for the sexes. The men I've encountered, since starting at The Skipper, have been strong-willed, but at the same time they seem to treat the women they are with as equals. They respect them. Much like Tim seems to respect me.

I can't stop the smile from stretching my mouth.

"No need to answer that. The answer's plain on your face," Pam points out, breaking through my thoughts. "So have you guys talked? I mean, you did drop kind of a bomb." She shakes her head and her amusement is replaced with concern. "Heard anything from the brother? Mark?"

"We talked a little, but not much," I share shyly. Most of the past couple of days were spent in a total bubble, ignoring anything and everything outside the two of us. It wasn't hard to shut the world out, when I stayed inside Tim's house, even when he left for short errands. I was grateful not to have to go out in the now bitterly cold weather and was quite comfortable curled up on the couch, catching up on years of missed movies, while Tim sat at the table, working on his designs. So very domestic, and…normal. I'm not used to normal but I'm loving it. "Mark called last night, and he's going to be by this afternoon, after Tim picks me up."

Tim dropped me off at the shelter earlier. He'd received a call early this morning for some piece of equipment he'd been looking for. Must've been a good deal, because he was driving all the way to Boston to get it before someone else beat him to it. He suggested Florence House, and since I hadn't seen Pam since Sunday, I welcomed the chance to catch up.

"I feel guilty," I confess. "I don't know why I deserve all this concern." I cringe when I hear myself give voice to a nagging thought that I can't seem to rid myself of.

"What d'you mean?"

"It wasn't nice…what I did before. And I'm breaking the law just by being here. I don't want to cause trouble for anyone."

Pam leans forward and rests her chin in her upturned palms. "Let's see if I understand. You expected to be judged for working as a prostitute and being in this country illegally. The fact no one you know now seems to be angry at you is confusing?" When I nod in response, she shakes her head. "Not that any good person would judge you either way, but you realize you didn't choose to be a hooker? Nor did you enter this country of your free will. I don't think anyone looks at you as a burden or as causing trouble. What you don't understand is, all the people in your life right now care about *you*. Not what you've done or where you're from, but just you. They're your friends. We're your friends."

I'm trying to let what Pam's saying percolate. Friends. That's unfamiliar territory and I obviously have much to learn. Some days I feel older than dirt, only to discover that in other ways I'm as naive as a newborn.

"Your guilt, on the other hand, is understandable." I look up, surprised at that. Pam's eyeing me with one eyebrow raised. "Yeah. I'm not saying it's appropriate, I'm saying I get it. Shit went down and people got involved. They want to help you get out of the mess you're in. And you're hiding out in Tim's house, sticking your head in the sand. God forbid, even enjoying yourself, while others are worrying on your behalf. Am I right?"

I nod in response. She's right. I have been avoiding. Both Syd and Viv have called Tim's phone and I've let him talk to them. I didn't want to talk about the shitstorm that followed me to Portland. I just wanted to be normal for a while. "Yeah," I say out loud. "I just—"

Pam's hand comes up, palm out, to stop me. "No need to explain. You deserve a little time pretending there's not a world out there for you to deal with. But you can't hide out forever. I can't predict what will happen—don't know how things will end up—but I do know that you have a group of people around you who will do everything in their power to keep you safe and to keep you here. You owe it to them to look out for yourself."

Ouch. That one hit target. "I do," I softly admit, earning a gentle smile.

"Glad you're talking with Mark today. Let him and Tim help you sort through what steps you need to take to get through to the other side of this. Trust them."

Trusting Tim is becoming easier by the minute, since he's done nothing to indicate otherwise.

Trusting his brother, the cop? Now that's a real challenge.

Tim

"\$3,000 is my bottom dollar."

The guy puts a proprietary hand on the large, industrial-sized planer that looks well-used. Granted, the list price for the thing was probably closer to seven grand, but when he called this morning in response to my ad, looking for one of these babies for around two and a half grand, he told me he was in the ballpark. I'm pretty pissed he's talked me into driving all the fucking way to Boston, where he told me he wanted three and a half to start. The three he now offers is a good deal for the high quality machine, but I'd budgeted for five hundred less. I also still need a joiner kit and a hand planer. So I tell him.

"That's my entire budget. The extra five bills you're asking are for a couple of other tools I need."

"What else are you looking for?" the older man wants to know, waving his hand around the old warehouse. Used tools are everywhere, and I have to admit, I've been scanning the place for other deals. When I tell him what else I need, he walks over to a folding table in the far corner. "This is a DeWalt." He shows me the joiner, which appears to be in near new condition. "Hang on, I think I have a portable planer somewhere, same brand." Off he goes again, rummaging through boxes until he finally surfaces, a familiar black and yellow casing on the tool in his hand. "Yup, DeWalt as well. A little older than the joiner, but working fine. Everything I buy is checked and cleaned. Plug it in there, if you want to see for yourself." He waves in the direction of a workbench with a power block attached to the side. "Three G's for the lot. Final offer," he says.

"Done," I give in, shaking his proffered hand, after making sure all of them work. I'm pleased I stayed within budget and happy with the new contact I've made. Well worth the trip, even if it meant leaving Ruby behind. I've gotten pretty addicted to being around her. Not that I have much in experience, never really having had a relationship worth any mention, but Ruby's easy to be around.

It takes the two of us, plus one of his laborers, to load the damn planer on the back of my truck, but half an hour later, with the purchases strapped down and my wallet a lot flatter, I set course home to Portland. My mind is divided with thoughts on how to get this damn machine in my garage and the fastest way to get Ruby home and naked. Ruby naked wins.

There's a reason I've opted to just sleep with her in my arms these last two nights, but I'll be damned if I can remember it clearly. Something about wanting to show her she means more than just someone to bang. That first night was fucking amazing, but I didn't want to presume. The few hefty make out sessions we've had since, were killer to put a halt to. Not sure how many more times I'll be able to pull back. Ruby's become more and more enthusiastic in her participation, to the point where I almost feel I'm doing more damage than good by pulling back. If the cute little pout of her full lips is anything to go by. Damn if that doesn't make me want to start kissing that mouth all over again. For a novice kisser, Ruby sure has learned fast.

The more I know her, the more she surprises me. Mostly uneducated, she is still smarter than a lot of folks I know. A natural intelligence that only makes the package even more attractive. Especially when she showed an affinity with numbers and helped me work out not only the budget, but also a workable layout for the limited space in my garage.

Her soft giggles as she watches TV distract me from my work, but I could care less. Unsolicited responses like that are like little gifts. Small tastes of the lovable person she is developing into. And she *is* lovable. Not sure when I realized that I'd already fallen. Maybe it was when she asked me to make love to her. Or maybe it was long before that, the first time she curled, trusting into the protection of my body.

Fuck. I'm in love with her.

-

"Jesus that thing is a monster," Mark says, wiping his hands on his jeans.

We've just managed to wrangle the planer into the garage, with the help of one of my friendly neighbors, who saw us struggle.

Mark had arrived shortly after I'd come home, having picked up Ruby first. She's the one who suggested getting the machine unloaded before sitting down to talk. Now she stands in the doorway, nervously rubbing the palm of her hands on her jeans. I notice again that her clothes are serviceable at best. Not particularly fashion forward, and pretty sparse from what I could see when I packed up her things. Be nice to buy something nice for her sometime.

"Thirsty?" is the first thing out of her mouth when we step past her in the hallway, kicking off boots and coats as we go. She tries to scoot past me toward the kitchen, but I catch her around her waist and swing her around. The hard kiss I land on her mouth has her eyes glaze over. Suddenly, I want my brother to be gone so I can explore the fuck out of her warm body. A not-so-discrete clearing of the throat reminds me he's very much there, and watching with interest, apparently. "Beer would be great," I tell Ruby, at the same time shooting Mark, whose eyebrows are raised in question, a warning glare. I'm easily distracted by Ruby's backside making its way into the kitchen.

"You're so gone for her," Mark states half in jest, not expecting an answer, but I'll give him one anyway.

"I am. Deal with it," I warn him. "Any disrespect or hurtful comments and I'll take you out. Brother or not."

"You serious?"

"As a heart attack," I whisper, as I lean into his surprised face. Not that I think it would ever come to that, but he best be warned where my loyalty would be.

"You ready to bring her to see Mom and Dad?" I know it's a challenge. I know he's asking if I'm ready to face down any judgment that might come from them, should they find out her history, and I am. Not that I really believe my aging hippy parents would judge anyone much.

"Sure am," I confirm honestly. "This coming Sunday." That shuts him up, just as Ruby reappears with two beers in her hand, offering one to each of us. "What about you, Boop? No beer?"

"I put on some coffee. I want to keep my wits about me," she says, with a furtive look in Mark's direction. "Shall we go in?" She indicates the living room, evidently ready to hear what he has to say now. Still, she looks like a lamb lead to slaughter as she moves to sit on the couch. I sit down beside her and tuck her under my arm.

I can't quite identify the look Mark shoots me, but it doesn't fill me with confidence. Something that is confirmed when he opens his mouth. "Got good news and bad. What would you like first?"

"Good," Ruby says at the same time I say, "Bad".

Mark's eyes go back and forth between Ruby and me before he makes up his mind. "Good it is," he says, with a little smile for

Ruby. "Talked to Mike yesterday. A few times in fact, he needed to get clearance to discuss things with me. He was very interested, finding out I might have a lead for him. The name Terry Milano was not new to him. He's one of a few of Boston's finest that is apparently being looked into, Eduardo Lima is another. He's a detective in the SAU, the sexual assault unit. The task force Mike is part of is investigating the possible involvement of members of the Boston PD in the abduction and smuggling of women from South and Central America into the U.S."

"So far I fail to recognize good news in any of that," I interrupt Mark's description.

"Getting to it," he says, ignoring me otherwise, as his eyes stay on Ruby who sits near frozen on the edge of her seat. "He explained the girl I told you about, the one who took her own life while in FBI custody, had been offered a T visa, in return for her cooperation in the investigation. A temporary legal status in the U.S., specifically for victim's of human trafficking, who were brought into this country against their will. After three years, those with a T visa become eligible to become permanent residents."

I hear Ruby's sharp intake of breath as the magnitude of what he's saying hits her. Her hand reaches for purchase on me, and I quickly take it in mine, holding on tight. "I can stay?" she says, her voice breathy and disbelieving.

"Yes, you can stay. *But*…it would require you to assist the FBI in their investigation." He pauses for that to sink in. The sudden slump of her shoulders shows she is starting to clue into the meaning of that. "I haven't mentioned your name or where you are, but Mike is eager to sit down with you and talk."

"I guess that part was the bad news," she says, sounding a little shaky.

"Part of it. The other part is the possibility the FBI will want to put you up in a safe house for the duration of the investigation."

"Like hell," I grind out, standing up to face Mark. "Not letting her out of my sight, buddy. Not gonna happen." He holds up his hands in defense.

"Whoa, hang on here. I'm not the one calling those shots, Tim. Don't fucking shoot the messenger."

After an angry stare down, it's me who looks away first. He's right. I'm barking up the wrong tree. The moment I turn to find Ruby's shocked face staring at me, Mark's hand comes down on my shoulder. "I told him she's safe where she is. Hell, I'll offer to keep her safe myself, but there is no way to avoid talking to Mike," he calmly but firmly says.

"I know," I concede to him, but keep my eyes firmly on Ruby's panicked ones. "Ruby? You know I won't let anything happen to you, right?" The short, jerky nods of her head tell me she hears me, but she's not quite reassured. Frankly, neither am I and to make her, and myself, feel better, I pull her up and fold her in my arms.

"Can we have some time to decide?" I ask Mark over Ruby's head. He gives me a half smile and a nod.

"Yeah. Just don't take too long."

"Wait," Ruby turns her head. "Why did the girl kill herself if she was about to get help?"

Mark runs his hand through his hair, looking down at the tips of his stocking feet before lifting his eyes to meet hers. "Can't be sure, but after what you told us a few days ago, I'm guessing she had no reason to trust the FBI's promises. She was probably brainwashed to believe the authorities couldn't be trusted."

"I can't blame her," Ruby says in a thick voice. "I would've believed the same thing. Wouldn't have trusted anyone…" Her eyes come up to meet mine. "If I hadn't found friends, who prove to me every day there *are* still trustworthy people out there."

CHAPTER EIGHTEEN

Ruby

"Oh my God. What happened to you?"

I'm frozen on the spot when a woman with grey ringlets in a riot around her face comes barreling out of the house. I presume she's Tim's mother, wrapping her arms around me in a bear-hug of epic proportions. Next thing I know, she's shoving me back by the shoulders and eyeing the useless arm strapped against my body.

"Erm…" I manage to squeak out before feeling Tim's reassuring hand in the small of my back.

"Mom, this is Ruby. Ruby, meet my mom, Jane," he introduces her calmly.

"But what happened to her?" his mother insists, now talking over my shoulder at her son.

"She was…"

"I fell," I interrupt him, not wanting to get into any details. Jane snaps her eyes to me and raises a doubtful eyebrow, but she doesn't push.

"I'm sorry that happened to you," she says sincerely, making me believe she knows there's more to the story than that simple explanation. "Well, let's go inside and get comfortable," she suggests, spinning around on her heels, her long flowing tunic whipping around her body. "It's way too cold out here."

"You think?" Tim quietly mumbles behind me, but his mother must've heard.

"Don't smart mouth me, Timothy," she aims at him over her shoulder.

"Come on," he says for my ears only this time. "Nothing to be worried about."

I'm not so sure, as I let him lead me into the nice family house, in the quiet neighborhood. When he first told me *we* were going over to his parents' house for dinner on Sunday, I'd told him I wasn't ready. I wasn't. For one, I hadn't yet spoken with Mark since earlier in the week. Oh, I'd talked to Tim about it at length. The decision is not difficult; if I want a chance at any sort of life at all, that is. I'd just been postponing doing anything about it. Even Pam got on my case on Friday when I saw her again. She's the one who reminded me that the only way to get out of this situation is to move through it. One bite at a time. One step at a time. Going for dinner at Tim's parents place was a perfect opportunity. According to Pam…and Tim.

Then yesterday, Viv called and demanded to speak with me. No longer willing to stand guard for me apparently, Tim had shoved the phone in my hand and walked out the back to hide in the garage. Coward. Viv told me, in no uncertain terms, that since The Skipper was closed on Mondays, she and Syd were coming over. It wasn't a very long telephone conversation, since Viv didn't give me a chance to talk, and I was angry at Tim for putting me on the spot like that.

Truthfully, I'd been angry with him before that. Today marks a week since he introduced me to the surprising pleasures of sex, and I've been aching for a repeat. Yet, every time he gets me all steamed up, he pulls back. I know it's having an effect on him too. Hard to miss the large bulge behind his fly, no matter how much he's trying to hide it. I'm frustrated. I've never felt quite like this before, and it's making me cranky. What's worse is the little smirk that dances across his lips when I let him feel my displeasure. Like he's enjoying my frustrations.

Tim is hanging up my coat, and I smooth the front of the blouse I'd picked up for a steal at the thrift store a few months ago. It seemed like a good choice this morning when I put it on. A pretty floral pattern in pastels, with long gathered sleeves, and a high collar. Feminine and a little dressy, yet covering all the important parts. Most importantly, unlike anything I'd ever worn before. No plunging necklines revealing my ample cleavage. No skin tight T-shirts that leave nothing to the imagination, and certainly no mile-high heels to add some lift to my legs and ass. I paired it with my best pair of comfortable jeans, after Tim assured me this was just a casual weekly gathering for football and food. I thought it spelled dressy casual, but after spotting Tim trying to hide a grin behind his hand when I came down, I'm not so sure.

"Come with me." His mother grabs me by my good arm and drags me past an empty living room and into a large family kitchen. "Don't worry about the boys, they'll be stuck to the TV in the rec room downstairs until at least half time. We have time to chat. Have a seat." She waves at a stool by the kitchen island, and I hoist myself up. "Drink? Or would you prefer tea?" She wants to know. I'm not about to drink any alcohol so I opt for tea.

"So how long have you known my son?" she asks, as she pours a cup and places it in front of me.

"Maybe four months? I met him at The Skipper." I nervously sip at my tea and almost burn my mouth.

"You go there a lot?"

"No. Well, yes, I guess. I mean, I don't visit there, I work there." I know I'm rambling, but her intense scrutiny is making me squirm. "We never really talked until a few weeks ago, when he gave me a hand in the kitchen."

Her eyes light up. "Oh, you're a cook? I love cooking. You'll have to let me in on some of Dino's secrets. He guards his recipes like they come straight from the National Archives."

"No, no," I hurry to interrupt. "I'm not a cook. That's one of the reasons Tim was helping me. I wasn't doing so well in the kitchen."

"Really? You don't know how to cook? Perfect." She claps her hands. "I can teach you!"

"Teach her what, Mom?" Tim says, as he saunters into the kitchen, followed by Mark and finally a big burly man who must be their father. The older man's eyes are on me as he ignores the others and walks over to me in a straight line. The rest of my nerves twitch and shrivel when he stops a foot in front of me, tilting his head to one side and scrutinizing me from top to toe. In the next moment, he reaches out and wraps me in a tight hug. I can barely breathe, pressed against his barrel chest. Hugs are big in this family, apparently.

"Arthur!" Jane scolds her husband. "You're smothering the poor girl."

A nervous giggle escapes me. Hardly a girl. The relief I feel at the ability to draw a proper breath is short-lived, when Arthur holds me in place by the shoulders and goes back to his scrutinizing.

"Arthur," he says, his voice even deeper than Tim's. "My name is Arthur. Or you can call me Dad." Confusion must be evident on my face when he chuckles. "Maybe Dad is a bit too soon? What's your name, darlin'?"

"Dad, this is…" Tim starts, but is cut off when his father lifts his hand.

"Hush. Let her talk. I want to know if her voice is as sweet as she looks."

Of course my voice is stuck somewhere between my stomach and my throat, and other than gasping for air like a fish, not much sound comes out. I feel a bit better when Tim moves in behind me, his solid heat at my back. "My name is Ruby. Ruby Soto," I manage.

One side of Arthur's mouth tilts up as he grabs my hand and lifts it to his mouth, pressing a kiss to the back of it. "Delighted to meet you, Ruby. Ruby Soto." He's teasing me, judging by the twinkle in his eyes, as he repeats my name back to me.

"Your making Ruby nervous, Dad. Knock it off. Hey, Ruby. How's the arm?" Mark unceremoniously shoves his father out of the way, and then he too moves in for a hug. Definitely a family thing. I'd been nervous about seeing Mark, knowing he's been waiting for my call, but when I start to apologize he quickly stops me. "Later, Ruby." He tilts his head in the direction of his parents and gives me a wink.

Right. Maybe not a good time. Not with the curious looks his mother throws between us.

In the middle of an animated football discussion that develops in the kitchen, Tim leans his chin on my shoulder. "You okay, Boop?"

Am I? I feel a little shell shocked at the intensity of his parents. They seem very friendly, in an intrusive way. Not threatening, just really intense. Now that I'm no longer the focus of their attention, I can observe the loving way they interact. With each other and with their sons, who both seem so much more laid back. Loving and nurturing.

My mind jumps back to a time when I last experienced that. With my own parents in the large kitchen at the farm. *Mamá* stirring the *molé* sauce on the stove and *Papi* coming in, throwing me a wink and pressing a finger against his lips, to keep me quiet, as he snuck up and wrapped her up in his arms from behind.

Mamá angry at first, but then laughing softly as my father kisses her neck.

I'd forgotten how much they loved each other. How much they loved me.

For many years, my last memories were of my mother's screams and my father's enraged voice, only to be silenced by the deafening sound of the bullets entering them. It was the jerking of their bodies, the blood spatter, and the shock in their eyes as their life drained out of them.

Tim

"Shhh, baby."

I hadn't noticed she was crying, until my mom looked from Ruby to me, her hand pressed to her mouth.

She hadn't answered me when I asked her if she was all right. My folks are wonderful people, but a bit much at times. I'm not sure what triggered the silent tears tracking down her cheeks. I hate seeing them.

I scoot an arm under her legs and lift her off the stool. As if by rote, her hands wrap around my neck, and her face presses in my chest as I carry her out of the kitchen, ignoring the questioning looks of my family.

I sit her down on the counter in the powder room, closing the door behind us. Grabbing a towel, I mop at the steady flow of silent tears on her face.

"Talk to me, Ruby," I encourage her, as she appears to come back from whatever place her mind had been.

"Your family is nice," she says in a soft voice.

Not sure what I expected, but it wasn't that. "I know." It's all I can think of to say.

"I'd forgotten what it was like. My memories of mine have always been filled with pain. The only thing clear in my mind was the fear and panic right before they…" I patiently watch as she takes a deep breath and focuses her eyes on me. "They loved each other. I just remembered how good things could be before they went wrong. I miss them."

I don't say anything. What is there to say? I step between her legs and wrap her up in my arms, stroking my hand over her hair. I feel guilty. In my eagerness to bring her home to my parents, I hadn't thought about how it might affect her. Fuck, I'd basically forced her against her will. "I'm sorry," I mumble, with my face pressed to the top of her head. "Sorry I made you come."

"No." Her hands push at my chest and I take a step back. "I'm not sorry. It's given me back some treasured memories, I thought I'd lost. I want to remember my parents with a bittersweet ache, instead of the sharp pain and crippling guilt that I felt for years at their death. These are the tears they deserved all along," she assures me, cupping my face in her small hands and pulling me down for a sweet kiss.

A light knock on the door interrupts us. "Everything okay?" My mom's soft voice sounds from the other side.

"We're alright, Mom," I croak out, my throat a bit tight.

"You sure? Can I come in?" she persists, and I look at Ruby for guidance.

"Come in," she calls out, surprising me. Her eyes never leave mine, as she presses another soft kiss to my lips, and mumbles, "Thank you."

The powder room was never intended for three bodies simultaneously, so when my mom pushes her way in, I have no choice but to step into the hallway to give her room. Before I know it, the door gets shut in my face, leaving Ruby at the mercy of Mom, and me outside in the hall.

"Third quarter just started," Mark says, sticking his head around the corner before he disappears down the stairs. Reluctantly I follow him down.

At the two minute warning, with the Pats up by six on the Raiders, there's still been no sign of the women. Concerned, I get up to investigate when Dad calls me back. "Sit your ass down, Son. Your mother will take care of her."

Right. That's what has me worried, leaving Ruby with my less than tactful mother. "You don't understand, Dad. Ruby is…she's…"

"Don't underestimate your mother. Or me for that matter," he adds, pointing his finger at himself. "You really think with our years, we don't recognize your Ruby has had a rough life? It's all but spelled out in those big expressive eyes of her. Trust your mother."

Under my father's commanding stare, I sit my forty-three-year-old ass down as instructed. That doesn't mean my mind is on the game as New England manages to hold on to their lead. Years of experience have perfected my mom's call for dinner, which comes at the same time the last whistle is blown. Mark grabs the empties and heads upstairs as Dad turns off the TV, turning to me.

"Come on. Get your lazy ass up. Our women are waiting upstairs." With a wink, he follows the scent of Mom's Sunday dinner up the stairs. I take one last look around to make sure our mess is cleaned up before I turn off the lights and head up too.

Ruby

"You don't have to tell me a thing."

Tim's mom has stepped into the spot her son occupied, just seconds ago, and puts her hands on my knees. Her face is kind and her eyes show no judgement. I don't know if it is because I trust Tim wouldn't have exposed me to his parents, if he didn't think they'd be accepting, or whether it is the sudden craving for some nurturing of my own. Maybe both—but whatever it is has me put my forehead to her shoulder, and with her hand stroking my hair, much like her son did before her, I spill.

"So what are you waiting for?" is what she says when I tell her about the FBI offer on the table. I've just finished compressing thirty years of my life into a fifteen minute sound bite, and her abrupt question takes me aback. Her face doesn't show any of the judgement I imagined those words to hold. I realize there is none, just open curiosity to understand why I'm delaying what must seem to Jane to be the logical next step. That simple. No oohs or ahhs. No prying questions. Not even a reaction, other than the sudden shiny eyes and relentless, unwavering stroking of my hair.

"Nothing. There is absolutely nothing that I'm waiting for," I concede on a watery smile.

"Excellent. Then let's get dinner ready before those boys tear my kitchen apart." She helps me down from the counter and pulls me along behind her by the hand. "Oh," she throws over her shoulder. "By the way, we seriously need to go shopping. That shirt does nothing for you. In fact, I think the last time I saw anything like it, my mother was wearing it to her senior's social. That was twenty-five years ago."

I can't help it. The laughter bubbles from me. I'm finding it more funny than insulting. Or maybe it's funny because it's so insulting. In any event, the two of us stumble into the kitchen, giggling like loons, and a smile stays on my face long after the hilarity of the moment has gone.

Jane is taking her promise to teach me to cook seriously. Outfitted with an apron to keep any spills off me, she hands me a bowl and a bag of flour and step by step instructs me on how to prepare fresh biscuits. So when, by the time the men surface from their football game, I pull my one-handed creations out of the oven, I'm thrilled to see golden, fluffy biscuits staring back at me.

"Damn these are good," Mark says around a mouthful of one, just stolen off the baking tray I set down on the counter. It earns him a smack on the head from Jane.

"Still like starving animals, the way you boys attack any food in sight," she mutters, swinging a potholder in Arthur's direction, who's trying to sneak a biscuit for himself. The only one who is not focused on the food is Tim. His focus is squarely on me as Jane herds the other two with pots and plates to the dining room.

"You baked?" he says with half a smile, and I grin back at him.

"I did. With one hand," I happily tell him, with not a small amount of pride. "Your mother told me what to do, but I made them."

"You know…" he starts as he stalks toward me. "It's a little bit disturbing how incredibly enticing you are, wearing my mother's old apron, covered in flour." His face is inches from mine as he scans my features with tender eyes before slowly lowering his mouth to my very willing lips.

"Tim, grab the mashed potatoes on your way in," his mother's firm voice interrupts, but doesn't spoil the sweet moment. With a last peck on my mouth, he takes off my apron for me, shoves the plate of biscuits in my hand, and ushers me into the dining room, following closely behind.

Dinner is a casual affair. I find myself relaxing more and more amid the easy banter and light teasing around the table. I even smile back at Arthur when he directs his crooked grin my way. My biscuits are delicious, if I say so myself, and I ask Jane to write the recipe down for me. I could eat these every day. It's all very light-hearted and even Jane's not so subtle jabs at Mark, to find himself a good woman already, seem par for the course. Then she turns to Tim.

"You made me wait a long damn time, boy. But I'm glad you did," she says, turning her smile to me as she covers my hand on the table. "You two will make a beautiful family."

Just like that the happy bubble I imagined myself in bursts, as I feel the blood slowly draining from my face.

"Jane," Arthur's voice cautions his wife, but his eyes are watching me. All others follow his lead and I find myself squirming under the scrutiny of four sets of eyes.

"Ruby? Are you sick?" Tim asks. Sick? Sure I'm sick. Not the way he means it, but that doesn't make it less true. Grabbing the opportunity I nod at him with a wobbly smile—the only one I seem to be able to produce right now.

With requests for continuous updates and a stack of containers with leftovers, Tim hustles me out of the house not five minutes after.

That night, when Tim crawls into bed, long after tucking me in, I don't feel heat crawling through my body as he pulls me close. Instead, a numbing cold fills me to my fingertips.

CHAPTER NINETEEN

Tim

"Is Ruby alright?"

I look over to where Ruby is curled up on the couch, her eyes staring blankly at the screen of the TV. She hasn't been all right since dinner last night, and I don't think it has anything to do with feeling sick. She seemed distant last night and has barely said a word this morning. Something's definitely up.

"She's okay, Mom."

"Maybe I should come by and check on her." My mother is nothing if not persistent, but I don't want her over right now. I plan to get some answers out of Ruby first, and I don't need my mother's interference. So I bend the truth so I don't have to hurt her feelings.

"She's fine, Mom. Really. She's already got something planned with Syd and Viv. They should be here shortly. Another day?" I don't tell her the girls won't be here until this afternoon, which gives me the rest of the morning to try and get her to open up. Mom only grumbles a little, but promises to call back later in the week.

Setting my phone on the counter, I walk into the living room. Ruby pretends not to see me, but I can tell she does from the slight shift in her shoulders. Almost like she's steeling herself for what's coming. I turn the TV off and sit down on the coffee table, right in front of her.

"Alright, Boop. You've had the night to stew on whatever it is that's going on in your mind. Time to talk about it."

She tries on a look of innocence, but she's not an actor, and doesn't quite pull it off. Noticing I'm not fooled, she shrugs her shoulders, dropping her gaze to the ground. Ah. So avoidance is the next move. Well, not if I can help it. Before she can crawl deeper into her shell, I move to sit down beside her, and in one smooth move lift her on my lap.

"Tim," she protests softly.

"Ruby," I counter, bending so I can look into her downturned eyes.

"I'm fine," she says, equally unconvincing.

"But?" I try to prompt her to say more.

"Geeze, you're pushy! I'm trying to find a way to tell you I want to go home."

"And why would that be?" I want to know, not quite believing the sincerity in her eyes.

"It's best." This time I can hear resolve in her voice. Whatever is going on, she really believes it.

"Ruby," I coax. "I can guarantee not having you right here is not *best* for me. It's not even best for you, seeing as you still need help with your arm out of commission. Not to mention the fact, you're not exactly safe out there by yourself."

"I'm going to tell Mark I want to talk to his friend. I'll tell them everything, and then I think it's best if they take me to a safe house." I'm too stunned to stop her as she scrambles off my lap and stands in front of me with her arms folded around herself. "I'm sure someone there can help me strap on the sling or do my buttons."

The thought of some beefed up G-man having his grabby hands anywhere near my Ruby propels me into action. Grabbing Ruby's good arm, I pull her down and push her back on the couch, rolling on top of her with my elbows braced beside her head and my nose almost touching hers. Those liquid brown eyes of hers are teeming with emotions, but there's one I focus on.

"Do you love me, Ruby?" Immediately her eyes turn away.

"It's too soon," she mumbles.

"Maybe," I give her. "But even if it's too soon, I know how I feel. Wasn't looking for it but here it is: I love you." I watch as she searches my face with her expressive eyes before closing them, but not before I get a glimpse of the tears gathering.

"I don't feel the same." Her voice is hoarse with emotion, and I don't believe her for a second.

"Liar," I whisper against her lips. "Something happened last night that's got you running scared. I see that. But don't lie about your feelings. I don't deserve that."

"No. You deserve so much better." Her face is completely turned to the side as the pained words leave her lips. My mind is struggling to understand what she's saying as I try to curb my frustration. With one hand on her cheek, I turn her to face me again.

"What happened, Ruby?"

Her eyes fly open. "You. You deserve better. You should be with someone you can build a future with. A family with."

Clarity hits me as I recall my mother's teasing remarks last night at dinner. She'd mentioned family. Flooded with sudden relief, I throw my head back and laugh. I feel her stiffen underneath me before squirming to get loose. Fuck no. "Not letting go, Ruby," I warn her.

"You don't understand," she pleads.

"Then make me," I counter, holding her firmly in place.

"I can't give you a family. I can't have children!" she shouts, suddenly throwing me off enough that she manages to scramble out from under me. As I watch her disappear up the stairs, I realize that laughing may not have been such a good idea.

Fuck me. I can lie and say that I don't feel a pang of regret at the news she can't have children, but I do. Despite the fact I hadn't exactly been looking to settle down any time soon, I'd always figured I'd have kids one day. Of course, our years would perhaps have been a deterrent, but not to have any choice at all is harsh. Still, there isn't anyone but Ruby I'd want them with.

Shoving up from the couch, I follow her up the stairs, where she seems to have locked herself in the bathroom. No amount of pounding on the door or pleading for her to open up seems to work. I run down to the basement, where I have some tools floating around somewhere. Finally locating a screwdriver and hammer, I head back upstairs, only to be stopped by my phone ringing on the counter.

"Yes?" I answer, a little out of breath.

"Am interrupting something?" My brother's voice sounds amused. I'm not.

"Yes," I abruptly confirm.

"Who peed in your Cheerios this morning? I was just checking up on Ruby. Mom mentioned she'd given her the impression last night that she might be ready to meet with Mike."

"Look," I point out to him as I make my way up the stairs. "Got a bit of a situation here, can we call you back?"

"She okay?" Mark suddenly sounds serious. "Anything happen?"

"Just a little misunderstanding. Nothing that can't be fixed." With the phone wedged between my shoulder and my ear, I manage to brace the screwdriver against the top hinge and work it loose with just one good tap of the hammer.

"What the hell is that sound?"

The bottom hinge takes two whacks to loosen. "Taking out the bathroom door," I inform him, just as I drop the tools and lift the door from the frame.

That's when I see her. "Jesus—NO!"

Ruby

I spent the entire night awake.

I'm such a fool. I actually started to believe there'd be a normal future for me. A future with Tim. Something I'd not even dared consider until a short time ago. Seduced once again, but this time by the lure of a normal life. Except…I'm not normal. I don't know why I thought I could be. It seemed easy enough, right up until the moment Jane's words shook me awake. I'd allowed myself the illusion, just for a moment, that I was part of a loving family. But I'm not, am I? I'm a lost soul, just clinging on to any stability that comes my way. First, it was Pam and the shelter. Then, it was The Skipper and the kindness of friends. And finally, it's Tim.

Oh my God.

Already I've pulled down so many people in my life. Now I risk dragging down Tim and his family as well.

I feel like a cancer, infecting everything I touch with my disease.

You two will make a beautiful family.

No. We won't. And not just because of a botched abortion at sixteen that required a hysterectomy to stop the bleeding from a perforated uterus. It's because wherever I go, I drag this dark cloud behind me. My sordid history. I can't leave what I did and what I was behind. It's part of me. A part that I don't want to drag people I care about into.

But that's exactly what I've done. I've allowed people to care. Hell, I've allowed myself to care, against better judgment. Better to hurt a little now, than to hurt more later.

Morning came with a firm resolve to remove myself from the lives of good people, decent people, before they get lost in my garbage. I would've just disappeared, but I couldn't leave them to clean up my mess. That's something I would have to do myself. So I planned to talk to the FBI and do what I can to help clean up the sick business I'd been part of most my life, but first I have to get back to my place.

One look at Tim still sleeping soundly next to me, and I can't go through with it. I can't sneak out and leave him to wake up to an empty house. Worried about me. Instead, I'll wait until I can meet with the FBI and ask to be moved immediately to a safe house. That way I can disappear without anyone worrying.

I just didn't count on Tim calling me out.

When he gets off the phone, and I see him stalking toward me, I know he's done letting me get away with the vague answers I've been giving him all morning. Sure enough, he doesn't waste time getting to the point as he puts me on the spot. My play at ignorance doesn't fly and neither do my empty reassurances. I try to tell him I need to leave, but he makes it hard.

"Do you love me, Ruby?"

Oh God. Forgive me, but I do. Still, I attempt to deflect. When he tells me how he feels I look him in the eyes and am shocked to see the depth of his feelings reflected. It doesn't matter that I deny my own, he pushes and pushes until I feel something crack inside. That's when panic hits and I run.

Not many places to go, but the bathroom has locks. It doesn't take long for the pounding on the door, or the pleas for me to open up to start. I ignore it all. I saw his eyes when I told him I couldn't have children. I saw the shock on his face. It only confirms that leaving is the right thing to do. I just don't know if he'll let me go.

The pounding stops just as my eyes spot his razor sitting in a glass on the counter. A cold calm settles over me as I reach out for it. It seems like such a simple solution. Taking back control. The hurt would go eventually, along with all the problems. There's beauty in the finality. A sharp burn like the ripping off of a Band-Aid, but after that peace would follow. A clearing of the decks.

It doesn't even hurt. My body is already so cold it feels numb. The fingers of my right hand are barely functional enough with the cast hampering their movement, but I manage to squeeze the blade between my thumb and index finger. Slicing through the skin is deceptively easy. I know enough to run the cuts along the length of my forearm instead of across.

The warm blood slowly starting to drip along my skin feels almost soothing and for a moment I close my eyes, letting myself float on the peaceful feeling. But when I hear footsteps coming up the stairs, I snap them open, the sight of the thick red streams bubbling up making me light-headed. The renewed noises outside the door startle me into dropping the blade from my slippery fingers. When I bend down to pick them up of the floor, it's like falling into a dark hole with nothing to stop me. I vaguely hear a man's voice yelling, but can't quite make out what it says before darkness takes me away.

-

"Hey."

A familiar voice sounds beside me as I blink my eyes open. Pam's beautiful face leans over me as she brushes hair out of my face. I'm a little confused, but as she sits back and I have a chance to look around the sterile room, it all comes rushing back to me. I don't answer, but instead just turn my head away.

"I'm sorry, Ruby."

I'm shocked to hear emotion in Pam's voice. The woman is a pillar of strength that rarely shows emotion of any kind. Still, I resist turning around.

"I know you don't want to hear me now and believe me, I don't blame you. But I want you to know how sorry I am for failing you."

I don't understand what she means and before I have a chance to swallow it down, one question escapes me in a croak. "Why?"

I can hear a deep sigh and then a hand starts stroking my hair. "Because I wanted so hard to believe you'd already found your path to healing. Even if I should've known the damage done to you could never be so easily swiped away. It was too much, too soon, my lovely Ruby. You were reaching for the sky and I cheered you on. Instead, I should've made sure you were ready for each step you were taking."

Her hand stops suddenly, and I instantly miss the soothing motion, when a deeper, familiar voice sounds. "If there's any blame to go around, it's mine," Tim says, his voice ragged and broken. "I pushed too hard."

It's difficult not to turn around, but I persist in keeping my back turned. So many thoughts racing around, I can't handle seeing the pain I can feel in the room. Tim's large frame fills my vision as he crouches down beside the bed, his face only inches from mine. My heart breaks when I see tears pooling in his eyes.

"I'm sorry, Boop." His voice breaks on his nickname for me, and my throat closes up as my eyes close. "I love you so much," he whispers with his lips on my forehead, before I hear him walk away. The soft click of the door sounds so final.

"I'm going to let you rest, honey." Pam's soft voice is accompanied by a final stroke of my hair. The silence that follows the second click of the door is deafening.

I did this.

It doesn't matter that I didn't mean to—that I'd hope to spare them—not make them hurt. The blame is mine alone. Hot tears spill, rolling from the corner of my eyes to pool on the pillow. I wish I hadn't woken up.

CHAPTER TWENTY

Tim

It's been six weeks, and still the events of that Monday morning are all too fresh in my mind.

The blood, her pale face, Mark's voice shouting from the phone I'd dropped on the floor. The absolute terror that almost choked me as I frantically felt for a pulse. Pressing towels against her arm to stop the constant flow of blood, and my panicked plea to my brother to call an ambulance.

He'd been there in time to let them in. Probably only minutes, but it had felt like an eternity as my thoughts went over every little detail of the past weeks to find where I may have gone wrong. After that everything went into fast forward. The ambulance ride, the hospital wait as they wheeled her away, and the arrival of all our friends, apparently called by Mark as he followed the ambulance to the hospital. When Pam showed up, her skin had looked almost grey. Her hands were shaking. I'd never seen her so undone before. Mom and Dad, obviously also alerted by my brother, came in shortly after and sat down beside me, holding on to my hands for dear life.

She'd be okay, we were assured by the young doctor who gave us an update. Her vitals were stable and although she'd lost some blood, she'd completely recover. He made sure to clarify that he was talking about her physical condition. Psychologically, he indicated, it was the beginning of a long road ahead. She would be transferred to the psychiatric ward as soon as her physical injuries would allow, to properly assess her mental condition.

The only time I've seen her since then is when she was still in the ICU under observation. She didn't want to talk to me or see me.

I have talked with Pam. A lot. Seems both of us have some regrets. The same with my mother, who was initially convinced that she'd been the trigger for Ruby's suicide attempt. It had taken Pam's involvement there too, to convince Mom it hadn't been any one thing, but rather a ticking time bomb all of us had missed until it finally went off.

It had helped, discussing things with Pam. She pointed out that it's human nature to want to move away from traumatic events in our life as quickly as possible, without giving ourselves a chance to hurt, grieve, or to process our emotions. Ruby had been conditioned for thirty years to suppress all of those things, and when her life started moving in a positive direction, she was so eager—as were the rest of us—to step over them in a rush to get to the good stuff.

Sometimes you have to struggle through the bad before you can truly enjoy the good stuff. Or it might catch up with you. Just like it did with Ruby.

I'd decided to give her space to heal. I made sure, with cards and occasional flowers, that she knew I loved her and thought about her all the time. But I was done pushing her. Her suicide attempt had shocked me to the core. I hate to admit it, but it angers me too.

It had also hammered home the harsh reality that we aren't given much time. That we have to be responsible for our own happiness first. And to that end, I've thrown myself into pursuing the dream I'd shelved since becoming an adult.

My first commissioned piece is due to be delivered this weekend, when Ike and Viv will be celebrating the anticipated arrival of their baby and are planning to reveal its sex to friends and family. The harvest table is Ike's gift to Viv. She has no idea it's coming, and I can't wait to see her reaction. Ruby is scheduled to be there as well. Pam told me that.

Six fucking weeks: I haven't seen her beautiful eyes, felt the comfort of her body, or tasted her ripe lips. Six weeks of burying myself in wood chips and designs. Six weeks of taking myself in hand in the shower after another day of Ruby on my mind. I'm sick of the empty release with nothing but her memory to keep me company. I sure as shit am not going to see her for the first time in a room full of people. I need some time alone with her. Some time to make sure Pam's assessment that Ruby's made giant strides since she was released, means that she is ready for me in her life. I sure as fuck am ready for her, even though I'd wait forever if it took that long.

God, I'm nervous. My hands are clammy as I raise my fist to knock on the ornate door of the shelter, and I quickly wipe them on my jeans.

"Hi." I hear Ruby's soft voice, but I can't seem to get my own to work. I'm too absorbed in the sight of her in the doorway. She looks beautiful. Her hair is tied back in a ponytail, leaving her gorgeous face exposed. I take my time admiring every detail of her features. I missed her so damn much. My hand rises out of its own volition, my finger tracing the delicate swoop of her nose and the curve of her lips. Her eyes are big and shiny as she smiles nervously at me.

"Well, come the hell on in," Pam's voice sounds from behind her. "I'd like to keep the heat in here." Gone is the emotionally shaken and gentle Pam and in her place, the familiar no-nonsense, brusque, formidable woman she is. Ruby laughs softly at my grimace and grabs my clammy hand to pull me inside.

It isn't until I sit down in the offered seat that I notice. "Your arm…the cast is gone."

She stretches out her arm to show me, so I use the excuse to pull her a little closer and run my fingertips over her skin. "It came off last week." Her voice is husky and I see goosebumps breaking out on her skin. I'm fucking thrilled to see I still affect her. That'd been my greatest fear, that she'd lose interest. Wouldn't want me anymore. But the look in those brown eyes, and the slight hitch in her breathing, as I continue to stroke her arm tells me she's still in this with me. I try to avoid looking at the other arm, where the sleeve of her sweater covers most, but not all of the angry red scars.

"You two talk, I've got shit to do," Pam announces, as she looks from one to the other before walking out. I didn't realize she was even in the room.

"I missed…" I start.

"I'm sorry…" Ruby says at the same time. "Let me," she pleads. "I've got to get this out, or I won't have the courage."

"Okay." I nod, taking her hand a little tighter in mine and continuing my petting. I can't seem to keep my hands off her.

"I spent most of my life thinking about myself. How to get through another day—how to survive a week. I didn't think much further than that. Coming to Portland already turned into something I never dreamed for myself. Friends, a job, and then even a place for myself. Then you," she softly adds, turning her eyes away. "I couldn't believe my luck. Even with everything else going on around me, I soaked up all you gave me."

Reluctantly, I release her hand when she pulls away slightly, putting some distance between us without looking at me. The joy I felt earlier is slipping away. I don't like this distance. I also don't like the tears that are filling her eyes. This feels too fucking much like goodbye. "Ruby…" The sharp shake of her head shuts me up.

"I was so busy dreaming about a future with you, I didn't stop to consider if what I had to offer would be enough for you." Now she lifts her eyes and looks at me. "I'm so sorry. I never really weighed the impact I would have on your life, and it was a rude awakening." Again I try to interrupt, but this time she reaches over and places her fingers on my lips to silence me. "Meeting your family, your mother…it was wonderful. Nerve-wracking, but wonderful. Your mom put me at ease, and in minutes had me spilling my history, but she never once judged. She simply accepted and moved on. I couldn't believe my luck."

I'm starting to get the picture, so I keep my mouth shut when she takes a deep breath again. But I need to touch, so I grab her hand again, stroking my thumb over her knuckles. Her eyes focus there.

"*You two will make a beautiful family*…That line was like a punch in the stomach, and a mirror in my face at the same time. I realized that is something I can never give you. A beautiful family. I can't give you kids, I don't even know if I can make you happy. I don't know if I can really be happy." The tears are flowing and hers are not the only ones.

I've had enough. In one move, I have her on my lap. It's fucking torture not being able to interrupt and tell her; all that will make me happy is her. And that I'd spend my years working to make sure she's happy too. She doesn't fight, but instead settles in, putting her head on my shoulder before she softly continues talking.

"When you put a drop of white paint in a bucket of black, the color doesn't change. It stays black. But when you put a drop of black in a bucket of white paint, the white immediately loses vibrancy. The dark starts taking over." Her eyes lift to my face and she raises a hand to wipe at my cheeks.

"The black paint is me, and the last thing I wanted to do is turn your white world grey."

Ruby

I was so nervous when I opened the door. Many times over the past weeks, I've wanted to see him—talk to him. Pam had to remind me that the best thing I could do for him, and for myself, was to get to a point where I could see where my thinking had gone off the rails. But it was Dino's words that really hit home. He came to visit when I was still in the hospital and asked me if I was done running yet. When I started to apologize to him, something I seem to be doing a lot of, he stopped me.

"The only apology I'll accept is you staying right where you are, fighting for your happiness. Because little one, life is never perfect. Not ever. You have to claw and scramble and dodge, just so you can hang on. It's never perfect, but damn, it can be so beautiful."

I'd received so much support from my friends; it riddled me with guilt, but at the same time made my heart feel lighter.

This man, though: the beautiful, kind man who had the misfortune of falling for me. Who is crying hot tears over me. This man fills my chest to exploding.

"I caused so much pain," I whisper, my hand still on his cheek, and my face tucked in the crook of his neck.

"Don't," he says back, his voice ragged with emotion. "You're here. I can't want for anything more." His arms lock around me, so tight I can barely breathe, but I welcome the sweet burn of my lungs. A reminder that I'm still—very much—alive.

After a moment, he loosens his grip and moves his hands to cup my face. His eyes are red-rimmed and hot on mine, as he lifts my arm and lowers his mouth to the ugly scars in a torturously tender kiss.

The clearing of a throat has both of us look up. Pam is leaning against the doorpost, a small smile tugging at her lips, with a tray in her hands. "Tea, anyone?"

-

"It's beautiful."

I stroke my hand over the surface of the massive, gorgeously rustic harvest table Dino and Tim just carried in.

"Gotta say," Dino's voice rumbles behind me. "The man's got the magic touch."

My eyes search for Tim, the man in question, who's standing a bit sheepishly to the side. "He sure does," I whisper to Dino softly.

His visit to the shelter, only three days ago, had been intense, but I'm happy we had that time before facing our friends today. Tim had left shortly after we finished our tea, during which Pam carefully tiptoed through the swirling emotions in the room. He seemed to withdraw a little under Pam's scrutiny, which made me nervous. But when I was standing in the front door, saying goodbye, he'd taken my face in his hands again, pressed his lips to mine, and said, "You'll never be black to me. You color my world in rainbows." With that he'd turned and walked away, only stopping to look back at the gate with a wink, before he got into his truck and drove off. I was still standing there when Pam walked up behind me.

"You okay?"

"Mmmmm," I hummed. "I think I will be."

"Bet your ass you will. Now close that damn door already. Heat's getting out."

Across the room, Tim's eyes find mine and he smiles a little. I give it back to him, only bigger.

"Ohmigawd!" Viv's screech draws my attention to the front door, where she stands with her hands clapped over her mouth, Ike wearing a big grin behind her. "Where did you…How…"

"Tim made it," her husband announces, with a big grin.

"No way," Viv says, looking with disbelief at Ike before barreling for Tim, who smiles and endures being peppered with kisses. I watch him set his hands loosely on her hips as he smiles down at her. Their quiet conversation seems intimate, as Viv has her arms around his neck, keeping them standing very close. I feel a brief pang in the pit of my stomach, but when I check to see everyone else's reaction to what is clearly a very private moment, I find nothing but smiles. Even Ike observes their interaction with a warm indulgence, so I let go of the breath I've been holding.

The noise level goes up a notch when Syd, Gunnar, and the kids push in the door behind Ike, and in no time the house is filled with people. Even Dino's kids are there. The oldest boy a bruiser like his father, and his spitting image, is sitting next to Pam on the couch, talking animatedly. This, of course, is very much unlike Dino, who is far from a chatterbox. Only person missing is his wife, but no one questions her whereabouts.

"Everything okay?" I ask him quietly, as he keeps an eye on his rambunctious crew. He turns to me, and I see a dark emotion in his eyes that is quickly blinked away.

"My kids are here. My friends are here. It's all I need."

I wince at what his words imply. Something that doesn't go unnoticed as he puts his arm around my shoulders and leans in.

"I'll be okay," he says softly, so no one else hears. I grab his hand resting on my shoulder and give it a squeeze.

After three hours of laughter, constant noise. and restless children, I am pooped. I've found a spot on a cowhide-covered seat at the bar and take in the bustle around me. Viv had a special cake made that announced the baby's gender the moment she cut a slice. The pink frosting inside a clear indication of the little girl they're expecting. Apparently we were all finding out at the same time, even Ike and Viv themselves. They'd had no clue since their doctor had sealed the sex of the baby in an envelope, which Viv handed over to the baker. They are so happy. The strong bond of their friendships underlined by the fact they chose to share this special moment with everyone here. The fact I seem to be part of this tight group is a little surreal and a lot overwhelming. Especially given what I've put everyone through.

Melancholy blankets my earlier happy buzz. Something Pam had warned me would happen, from time to time, as my body was adjusting to the lack of emotion numbing drugs I've been fed. It's also a reminder that the depression I apparently suffer is not something that can just be *fixed*. It's a constant flying, falling, crashing, and getting up again, and it will likely always be part of my existence. That's been a hard pill to swallow.

"Hey, Boop," Tim says, as he leans in to kiss my cheek. "You alright? The steam seems to have run out on you just now."

I manage a smile and decide that instead of pretending I'm fine, I'm going to be honest. "It has. I'm a little overwhelmed and feeling a bit down on myself. I'm sorry."

"Gotta stop apologizing, Ruby. For the record, I'm glad you told me. Gives me an opportunity to take you home."

I start to protest, which Tim cuts off quickly. "I was heading out myself, babe."

Pam gives me a thorough look over, when I go to tell her I'm tired, and Tim's taking me home. Apparently satisfied with what she sees, she wraps me in a hug. Always interesting with Pam, since our height difference basically has my head buried in her cleavage every time. "Just a heads up that we have two new guests at the shelter," she reminds me quietly, referring to the domestic abuse victim and her little girl, who came in just last night. "But I'll make sure to keep the outside light on if you should be home late." I chuckle a little at her blatant implication.

Still shaking my head, I follow Tim around the room as we say our goodbyes. Dino gives me an extra tight hug. "Look forward to having you back soon. Been quiet without you." I smile my thanks. His words go a long way to settling my nerves over heading back to work this week. I feel like I'm starting over, once again.

With my hand firmly tucked in Tim's, we walk out to his truck, where he lifts me in my seat. I've missed his hands on me. Once he has himself buckled in, his hand finds mine again, resting them both on his leg as he slowly drives away.

"Wait," I plead, when he's about to pull into Preble Street. "Can we stop for a minute?"

With a puzzled look on his face, Tim nevertheless pulls over and parks at the curb. The drive has been quiet up to now, leaving me to my thoughts, only the comforting rub of Tim's thumb over my knuckles reminding me of his presence. I'm not ready to say goodbye. I want to fight off the darkness I feel encroaching on me.

Before Tim has a chance to react, I have my belt unbuckled and climb over the console onto his lap, straddling him. "Ruby…" I cut off his pained objection with my mouth as his hands steady themselves on my hips. Tracing the seam of his lips with my tongue, he finally relents and lets me in. I've never *needed* the way I feel need burning through my veins now. When the deep groan bubbles up from his chest, my hands weave through his hair, keeping our connection tight as I let my hunger feast. It seems to snap Tim from his, so far, passive participation. One of his hands slides under my hair and grabs a fistful, his tongue asserting his dominance, and I willingly let myself get carried away.

He finally pulls his mouth from mine and takes a deep breath in. "Jesus, Ruby. What you do to me."

I can feel what I do to him. I've been grinding myself down on the hard bulge in his pants that leaves no doubt of that. "Don't stop," I beg, sounding pathetic even to my own ears. "I need you. I want to feel alive. You do that to me," I whisper urgently when he tries to set me back.

"God, Boop. I've missed your taste. But not in the middle of the street in the cab of my truck. You deserve so much more."

"Not like I've never done this before," I remind him, which isn't a good idea, as I come to find out as he now firmly pushes me back to my seat.

"Exactly why I'm stopping now," he says in a stern voice, his eyes burning into mine. "I'm not that guy you have to get off quickly in a car." He stops and turns his eyes forward. "And you're not that woman who should be subjected to that."

Thoroughly chastised, I buckle my seatbelt back up, fully expecting him to drive me to the front door of the shelter. Which is why I'm surprised when he starts the engine and suddenly swings the wheel around, making a U-turn, so the truck is pointing back in the direction we came from. His next words spark the fire that was slowly dying inside me, back to its full flame.

"I'm taking you home with me."

CHAPTER TWENTY-ONE

Tim

Christ.

I hadn't planned on taking things this far. Not tonight. Not
that I really had any control over the situation; Ruby had been in
my lap before I was even clear what was happening. Now I'm
flooring it to get home in record time, just so I can bury myself in
her heat. What does that say about me? Well, other than that I'm
eager to get rid of a set of seriously painful blue balls.

She's fragile, dammit.

She doesn't seem so fragile the moment I close the front door
behind us. I don't get a chance to take off my jacket before she's
trying to tug it down my arms. The instant my arms are free, she
has my head pulled down and her mouth sealed to mine. Fuck,
I'm in trouble.

"Ruby," I try, gently grabbing her by the wrists to untangle
her hands from my too long hair. "Slow down, baby," I mumble
against her lips. Her frenetic pace grinds to a halt when she steps
back from me, her eyes big and shiny.

"Sorry," she mumbles, shame staining her cheeks red.

Great. Now I've upset her. I just want her to slow down and
see me. Not just some body she can *feel alive* with. Yes, I
recognize the irony. Before that day when I found her in my
bathroom—a day that will be forever burned in my brain—I'd
been holding her off, because I wanted her to know I didn't see
her as just someone to only fulfill my physical needs. Here I am
doing it again, but for the opposite reason.

She's not looking at me when I slowly unzip her coat and pull it off her shoulders. She's staring at the ground, which she continues to do as I pull her along to the couch, where I sit pulling Ruby on my lap.

"I want you so bad, I'm about to pop an aneurism here, babe. The operative word here is *you*. I just need to slow it down, so I can make sure you feel the same. That you want me because it's *me*. I'm…"   My words are cut off when the little fireball on my lap twists suddenly and kisses me with renewed vigor and a healthy dose of aggression.

"How dare you question that," she says. When she finally pulls her head back, I see anger in her eyes. "Knowing what you know about me. You are the only person I've kissed in thirty years. *Thirty years,* Tim. I never could bring myself to. Wanted to keep something for myself, even when the rest of me was public property. I give that to you. Give you all of me. No one else gets that."

I'm a fucking bonehead.

Even more so because Ruby's anger is seriously turning me on. Pointing that little finger at me every time she's talking about me, and in her own chest whenever she refers to herself. She's worked up. She's also making my head swell. The big one.

"Ruby…" I try to soothe her when the magnitude of what she's telling me starts setting in. She folds her arms over her chest, sits ramrod straight on my lap, and looks at me with fire in her eyes. "I hear you," I assure her.

"Good," she pushes through tight lips, before her face softens, and she reaches out to run her fingers over my beard. They come to rest against my mouth. "It's just…you make me *feel*, Tim."

I close my eyes against the surge of emotions welling up. It's not exactly a declaration of love, but it's close enough "Good," I mumble against her fingertips. "Now where were we?"

It would appear a little controversy heats the blood, because as soon as my mouth tastes hers, we spark into a raging inferno.

We don't make it to the bed that first time.

Clothes fly everywhere and our fucking is frantic. The need to imprint myself on her body so strong, I lose all control as I plunge inside her. My mouth is fused to hers, and I can barely brace myself on my arms as my hips pump furiously. With her small hands clawing at my back, and the soft groans coming from her throat, it takes only minutes before a tingle at the base of my spine spreads like wildfire through my body in a blinding climax. Ruby's cries heralding her own release ringing in my ear.

Sweaty, despite the chilly temperature, I finally lift myself off and carry her to the bathroom where I help her clean up. No words are exchanged, but our eyes appear glued on each other.

"Let's try that again, shall we?" I suggest in a low voice. The responding smile on her lips is answer enough, and when I scoop her in my arms again, her soft giggle against my skin feels warm in my heart.

I take my time with every dip and swell of her soft body, making sure to press my lips to the brand on the inside of her thigh. I briefly think about offering her to have it removed, but the moment my mouth closes over her heat, the thought is gone. Drowned out by her taste and scent as she squirms underneath my lips. I take her to the brink, using the tip of my tongue to tease the hood away from the hard little pearl it hides, without ever touching her clit. Before she can find her release, I slowly make my way up her body, tracing my lips over every inch of skin I encounter. By the time I reach her swollen mouth, I've eased her back from the edge.

"Look at me, beautiful," I whisper, with my lips against hers. Her hooded eyes lift up, her emotions on full display in those big brown pools. With excruciatingly slow determination, I slide myself home, feeling all of her close around me.

This time, the pace is lazy, almost reverent, and when Ruby finally comes around me on a sob, I'm not far behind. Fully sated.

With Ruby sleeping on my chest, her soft puffs of breath ruffling the hair there, I feel we've turned a corner. Where I may have had my doubts earlier, they're gone now.

This is what I want. She is what I want. Her history is irrelevant, just like mine is. Whatever struggles she still faces—or *we* still face—she won't be facing them alone.

Suddenly it hits me: Ruby didn't run—didn't even try. Instead she stood her ground and fought for what she wants. That puts a big-ass smile on my face as I let sleep wash over me.

Ruby

"Go back to sleep." I hear Tim's sleepy voice mumble when the persistent ringing of a phone wakes me up. "It can wait," he says, snuggling in closer behind me. In seconds, I hear his soft snore to indicate he's followed his own advice. But I can't.

Memories of last night's sweet moments come back to me with vivid clarity, and I can't keep the smile from splitting my face. I shouldn't be feeling this euphoric, and frankly, it scares me a little. Pam had warned me there might be times I'd feel like nothing was holding me back. That there would be other times, where I'd feel that darkness close again and to always stay prepared for that.

Our first frenzied bout of passion was desperate, a bit angry still, but in the bedroom he made love to me. I can't call it anything else. It had been agonizingly tender and intense in a completely different way. Where the romp on the couch had been dark, all about getting what we wanted, the second time, in bed, had been all about giving. Sharing. So exquisitely sweet, I swear it felt like I was floating.

I'm still there…floating.

Until the distinct click of a door downstairs has me land back hard to earth.

"Yo, Tim!" Mark's voice sounds from downstairs, followed by the pounding of footsteps, coming up the stairs. I barely have a chance to pull the sheet up to cover myself when Mark comes barreling in the bedroom, screeching to a halt two steps inside the door.

"Jesus!" His shock is clear as he looks from me, hiding behind the sheet, to Tim who suddenly shoots up in the bed, rubbing his eyes.

"Fuck me, Mark. What the hell?" he snaps angrily at his brother, who is already backing out of the room, his hands lifted defensively.

"Sorry, man. Sorry, Ruby…" His voice fades as I hear those same footsteps going in the opposite direction. "Making coffee! We have an appointment in twenty minutes!" he bellows upstairs.

"Fuck! I totally forgot," Tim mumbles, pressing a distracted kiss to my hair before jumping out of bed and disappearing into the bathroom. Leaving me, still in shock, staring after him. *Madre de Dios.*

Ten minutes later, after taking my own turn in the bathroom and doing my best not to think too hard about what just happened, I tentatively make my way down the stairs, wearing an old plaid bathrobe that was hanging on the back of the door. Hearing the deep rumble of voices coming from the kitchen, I decide in the direction of the living room, in hopes of snatching up the clothes I discarded there last night. Mark must've gotten an eyeful when he walked in this morning. Or maybe not, since he came right upstairs. No woman would've missed the clothes strewn haphazardly through the room, without knowing exactly what went on. But a man might have.

I manage to sneak into the powder room, where I quickly replace the robe with my jeans and sweater, tucking my dirty underwear in my pocket.

"Do you at least have those references printed off?" I hear Mark ask, as I walk into the kitchen, all too aware of the eyes that immediately turn my way.

"Hey," I say with a paltry wave. In two steps, Tim is there, pulling me firmly to his side. I automatically lift my face to receive his kiss, as if this was our regular routine. Mark smiles big, as he stares unapologetically.

"Glad to see it," he says to me. "The man has been an absolute bear, all this time. Good to see something other than a scowl on his face."

"Uhh, didn't you guys have somewhere to be?" I try to steer the conversation in a different direction, feeling more than a little uncomfortable. Not only because of the situation, but also because since I ended up in the hospital, I'd not once reached out to Mark to make good on my promise to help the FBI. I hope it hasn't put him in a difficult situation.

"No worries. Mark called and bought us another hour," Tim says, smiling down at me. *Well, damn.*

"Do you think Mike still wants to talk to me?" I tentatively ask Mark, knowing that I should deal with this head on. The alternative is avoidance, and I've learned how dangerous that can be. Sticking your head in the sand, doesn't make things go away magically.

"Very much so." His hesitant smile is not really reassuring. "Fuck, Ruby. Mike's gonna have my head for telling, if my brother doesn't get to me first, but he's had eyes on you the entire time."

"Excuse me?" Tim hisses beside me, glaring at him. He takes a threatening step in Mark's direction, but with a hand on his arm I hold him back.

"Wait. What are you saying?" I ask him, unable to keep the wobble out of my voice. It was difficult enough to consider all the people I would have to face, knowing what I'd done. Finding out some stranger—or God forbid, *strangers*—have known and been watching me, is humiliating.

"Honey," he softly coaxes. His eyes are tentative, searching, as he looks me straight in the eye. "I told Mike because I was worried about your safety. You needed some time to heal without any interference from Tim or anyone else, including me. But the information you hold is valuable enough to make it dangerous for you. You know that. Only way I could protect you was to let Mike know. He made sure you were always covered."

"Oh." Is all I manage to express. Part of me still feels humiliated and invaded, but his words also fill me with unexpected warmth. I'm just not used to this kind of consideration. I'm guessing it might take some time for me to get used to it, if I ever do. Of course, that makes me feel guilty again, the reality of what I've put these people through. Apparently sensing my internal struggle, Tim, whose rigid posture has relaxed somewhat on hearing his brother's explanation, pulls me into his chest and folds his arms around me protectively. With his chin on the top of my head, he addresses his brother.

"I still want to beat you up," he admits to Mark. "But considering you were trying to look out for my girl, I'm thinking thanks might be the appropriate response here."

I burrow my head further into Tim's shirt, clutching my fists in the fabric, as Mark chuckles softly in the background.

"Having said that," Tim continues. "Do you have anymore news about the investigation?" I lift my head to look in Mark's direction, curious to hear the answer.

"Actually. They're pretty much ready to bring the entire ring down. The only thing missing is proof of the connection with certain members of the Boston PD. If they shut down the human pipeline without it, chances are those guys will walk. That's not an acceptable outcome." Mark hesitates before he goes on. "That's why Mike is nagging for Ruby's testimony. He's hoping it'll be enough to obtain a warrant for their arrests. Something that'll surely make life safer for you." The last is addressed directly to me. "It might mean you need to be placed in protective custody until they effectively have everyone behind bars, but even if that's the way it plays out, it shouldn't be for long. Besides, it would provide you with your temporary residency."

"Okay," I say. I don't have to think very hard. "Call him."

"Wait a damn minute!" Tim bursts out, virtually shoving me back. "Let's talk about this."

"Honey…" I put my hand on his chest to calm him down. "I want it over with. Let me finish this. I've been selfish long enough."

"But…"

"No. I'm serious. I'm not the only vulnerable one, Tim. There are girls…" I don't finish the sentence. I can see by the way both men lower their eyes, that just like me, they are wondering how many like me are out there. Guilt is closing my throat as I think about all the young girls that crossed my path. Girls I could maybe have helped, if I'd had the damn courage to stand up for them, let alone myself. Well, I'm doing something now.

Tim doesn't say anything, he just pulls me close again. "Okay, Boop. We'll do it your way."

Tim

She's nervous. The moment we got in the truck, her hand reached for mine and for the past ten minutes she's been squeezing it so hard, I'll be surprised to have any blood flow left by the time we get to Boston.

Mark is riding in the backseat and two FBI agents are following us in a sedan. Just as a precaution, Mike Carmello suggested. I hadn't complained. These past few days, since Ruby spoke for over an hour with the FBI agent over the phone, I hadn't let her out of my sight.

Mark had called the real estate agent a second time to tell him something had come up, and we couldn't make it. He assured us that if someone else showed interest in the old small warehouse along Harbor Place, just on the other side of Casco Bay Bridge, he would call us right away. The place had been empty for three months and was the perfect space for us to set up shop. I'd discovered my garage had some serious limitations when I was building Viv's table, and my father's creations were fast filling up his shop as well. We needed more space, and Mark had found the place last week. The walk through would have to wait until I was sure Ruby was safe. Plenty of other spaces, should we lose out on this one, but only one Ruby and I'd like to keep her just the way she is.

She hadn't complained much when I insisted she stay at my house, with Mark staying as well. The timing was of the essence, according to Mike. He wanted to be ready to take immediate action as soon as Ruby gave her official statement at their Boston office. After which, they planned to set us up in a safe house until they had everyone behind bars. Something the agent suspected, if they had time to pre-plan, wouldn't take more than forty-eight hours at most. He hadn't been too excited when I insisted sticking close to her, but I'd made it clear he could take it or leave it. Mark had just laughed and grabbed the phone from my hand, after which he smoothed things over with his buddy.

Yesterday, Pam had come by again. The second time in so many days. Just making sure Ruby had thought everything through, she said. I've got to say, I was more than just a little irritated she seemed to think this was anything but Ruby's own idea. I made that clear to her when she accosted me in the kitchen. "I tried to stop her, you know?" I told her, when she walked in for a refill on her coffee.

"Don't get your panties in a twist, Veldman," she smarted back. "Wasn't implying anything. You think maybe you're projecting a little?" She ignored my loud snort. "I'm putting Ruby through the third degree, because she has a tendency to want to please others. That's something she knows she has to work on. She has to get out of that victim head space. I was merely making sure she wasn't making decisions she thought others would want her to make. She's carrying around a lot of guilt on her own, no need to add yours to it."

That was a bit of a cold shower on the nice head of steam I'd built up. Sometimes I don't like Pam, particularly when her arguments start to make sense. But most of the time I appreciate her brutal honesty—I just prefer it directed at someone else.

With a deep chuckle, Pam slapped me on the back and left me to stew on my own as she returned to the living room, fresh coffee in hand.

This morning the call had come in. Mike said everything was in place and they were ready for us. We were given directions to the FBI location in Boston, which ironically was located right around the corner from the U.S. Immigration Court. Ruby had fussed over what to wear, but Mom had come to the rescue with a few things she'd picked up for her. With bags packed for a few days, we'd hugged my mom goodbye, with promises to call.

"Baby, can I have my hand back for a second? I want to try and get some feeling back." Mark snickers in the backseat as Ruby drops my hand like it's on fire.

"I'm sorry! Was I squeezing too hard?"

"It's okay. You can have it back in a minute," I promise her, while flexing my fingers to restore blood flow. "We're almost there. See that building on the other side of the bridge? That big square looking thing? That's TD Garden. The Bruins are playing the Maple Leafs tonight, that's why traffic's so bad. It's only a couple of blocks further."

"I've seen the building before, the club is not too far from here, I've just never seen a hockey game," Ruby says, momentarily distracted as I'd hoped.

"I'll take you," I promise. Not that it's a hardship—it's been at least fifteen years since I was at a game. Her mention of the club reminded me she wasn't exactly new to Boston, something that hadn't occurred to me when we started driving. Her increasingly panicked grip on my hand made a bit more sense now. It's not just the upcoming interview, this is her first return to Boston since she ran.

-

"Can I have your full legal name for the record?"

Mike had been waiting when we came up from the parking garage, no doubt alerted by his team. Nice guy, although, not quite as funny as I remember him. Must be the job.

He'd suggested Mark and I grab something to eat while he talked to Ruby, but she wouldn't have anything of it. Even insisted I be with her during the interview, her back straight and her little chin lifted high. Mark caught my eye and winked, both of us well aware of Ruby's justifiable mistrust of law enforcement; amused if not impressed by the fact she was clearly stating her terms. The agent had no choice but to comply with her wishes and the smile on her face illustrated her little show of defiance went a long way to settling her nerves. Good for her.

"Abril Rubí Soto."

CHAPTER TWENTY-TWO

Ruby

My heart had been pounding in my throat the entire way into the city, putting me on edge. Oddly, it had been more about returning to a place I'd run from many months ago, than it had been about the impending interview. So when the nice enough FBI agent tried to send away Tim and Mark, I didn't hesitate telling him there'd be no interview unless Tim was beside me. Not really because I was scared to do it without him, but because I knew his presence would have a calming effect when I have to drag up things I don't necessarily want to revisit. Besides, he's the first to deserve to know everything about me. I won't shut him out.

I was a bit surprised at his easy capitulation and couldn't keep the smug smile off my lips, as I grabbed Tim's hand and followed Agent Carmello into the small interview room.

Anyone walking in can judge from the piles of wadded up tissues on the table and the white knuckled clench Tim's free hand had on the edge of the table, that this was not an easy interview. Some of the questions were really, really difficult. Especially those that dealt with the earlier years. Ironically, Mike's questioning had run backward. Starting with the appearance of the Boston cop at The Skipper and following it back to the murder I'd witnessed. These events weren't too difficult to discuss, since I'd spoken of them a few times before. But when it came to how I'd fallen in the hands of Carlos Delgado, it became more difficult. Especially when details are asked about my first introduction to the *calcuilchil.*

"Let me recap quickly to here. The man you knew as Ricardo came to your farm, trying to convince you to come with him. When your father tried to intervene, this Ricardo shot both your father and your mother in front of you. You were then taken forcefully to Tenancingo…"

"Not really," I whisper, feeling Tim's hand spasm in mine. "I didn't resist. I just let him take me." The shame was almost too much to bear. I'd just witnessed my parents killed in cold blood, and I never even lifted a hand. Never resisted when Ricardo grabbed me by the arm and pulled me from the house. I even remember buckling up my own seatbelt, as if what just happened wasn't even a blip on my radar.

"Ruby," the agent says sternly, drawing my attention as he leans over the table. "You were a child and you were in shock. When that happens, your mind is not in control, and the body reverts to instinct out of self-preservation. Had you resisted, had you fought him, he would have hurt you. Maybe killed you. At least as far as you would have been able to know. You did the right thing at the time. Believe me."

My eyes lift up and I see he is earnest. Tim slips his arm around my shoulders and gives me a squeeze. "Nothing else you could've done, Boop. Not a thing." His mumble in my ear is reassuring.

I think of all the guilt I've lugged around on my shoulders all these years, this was the heaviest. The hardest to let go of. The *what-if* question is a dangerous game to play with your emotions, and I've been playing it far too long.

"For the first few months, I felt it was my penance, each time I was *trained*. Ironically, it helped me distance myself from what went on with my body. Like some kind of warped rosary I had to pray to receive absolution." The memories seemed less difficult to relive with Tim's comforting presence keeping me firmly rooted in the now. "I think it was probably a few months after I'd been at the villa that a new girl was brought in. She was probably even younger than I was. Was barely developed, yet some of the regulars seemed to be especially drawn to her almost prepubescent body. By the second week, the fear had gone from her eyes and was replaced with an empty stare. It scared me. She stopped eating, stopped walking, and she'd void herself without moving from her spot. The guards tried everything, but it was like she just wasn't there anymore. Her body was, but her spirit had disappeared. After only two weeks she'd willed herself to stop living."

"Jesus," I hear Tim hissing beside me.

"And when I started fighting," I explain to them. "The furthest I got was to the corner of the street one time. They found me hidden in the bushes four houses down. That cost me a broken leg, but that didn't stop them from *training* me. Eventually, I gave up trying to escape. It was just easier to comply."

"How long had you been there?" Mike wants to know.

"Not sure, maybe two years?"

Several times Tim urged me to take a break, but now that I'd started, I didn't want to stop. It became easier to talk with each subsequent question. I wanted it all out. Be done with it. At least for now, since Mike made it clear that the likelihood I'd have to testify, at some point, was high. I wasn't going to worry about that now though.

A little over six hours after we started, Mike turns the video recorder off. "You did really well, Ruby. I'm going to make sure the team escorting you to a safe location is ready to take you."

I barely hear what he says. I'm exhausted. I lean into Tim's body and close my eyes.

-

The house they take us to is pretty nondescript. Like many of its kind in Boston, the brownstone is the same as the others in its row. Tim and I are installed on the second floor, with our own bathroom and small kitchenette, while the first floor and the third floor are occupied by agents. Three in all, by my count, but there could be more. One woman and two men, but I can't remember their names. I'm too tired to retain any information it seems.

It's suggested by the female agent that we rest a bit before dinner, which apparently is being made for us, despite the fact it's got to be close to nine at night. It all feels a little surreal, and a sideways glance at Tim makes it clear he's decidedly uncomfortable with the situation. It's a stark reminder to me of what he is willing to endure on my behalf.

"What's that look for?" He wants to know, lifting my chin with his index finger. I try to shrug it off, but he just lifts an eyebrow, obviously not willing to leave it at that.

"Just thinking…this can't be easy on you." I watch his surprised face from under my eyelashes, before he throws back his head and lets out a hearty laugh.

"Me?" he asks, still chuckling, before pulling me down on the bed and rolling on top of me. "You shitting me right now?" he adds, starting to piss me off a little. It's not nice to laugh at someone.

"No, I'm not *shitting* you." With my temper taking over it sounds more like *chitting*, which only serves to make him chuckle anew. When I try to wriggle out from under him his face turns serious.

"My beautiful, courageous *Abril Rubí Soto*… By the way, that is the sexiest name I know," he mumbles, sticking his face in my neck and making me forget what I was angry about again. "I won't deny today wasn't a cakewalk—having to sit there, quietly, while every word from your mouth was branding my soul like acid. But understand this, I'd gladly go through that a thousand more times, if it meant I could spare your even one second of what you've had to endure." His eyes burn into mine as he lowers his mouth in a soft kiss. Rolling on his back, he takes me with him, so I come to rest completely draped over him. "Rest," he whispers in my hair.

"I'm too heavy."

"Quiet, Ruby."

"Fine, suit yourself," I surrender, snuggling into his body and finally letting my body relax. Apparently my mouth isn't done yet, because right before I fall asleep I mumble softly in his chest.

"*Te amo…*"

Tim

We slept straight through until morning that first evening. I don't even know if they tried to wake us up, but the last thing I remember is those soft words I didn't need a dictionary to translate. They settled warmly in my chest, right where she dropped them, and I fell into a deep sleep right away.

This morning, maneuvering around the large kitchen downstairs was awkward, as everyone appeared to develop a need for caffeine reinforcements at the same time. Especially strange when three of the four people in there with you are complete strangers. Luckily, that was quickly resolved over breakfast, which Rhonda had cooked for everyone. Buck and Josh were the other two agents. Although Buck, an older man, wasn't big into sharing, Josh, who appeared the youngest of the team, did enough of it for everyone. Within twenty minutes, we knew all we had to know about all three of them and he'd elicited quite a bit of intel on me too. Ruby was quiet through it all, but she was eating so I left her space. Given that everyone likely read her file, no one bothered asking her questions and focused on me instead.

I haven't seen Mark since we were hustled out of the FBI offices yesterday. I'm not sure where he took off to. Ruby and I were taken down a service elevator and were shoved into the back of an old cargo van. Two black SUVs in front of us turned left out of the parking garage, rushing toward the highway, while we turned right and casually meandered through residential streets for about thirty minutes before stopping outside the brownstone. I should probably thank him as soon as I get a chance. Having him around these past days helped. I think I might have ended up whisking Ruby off to some remote island, where no one would be able to find us, had he not assured me time and time again that things would work out.

I can certainly feel the loss not having him around. Nice as the FBI team is, they are not volunteering any information about the case, leaving us completely disconnected. We handed off any cellphones before we left the office, and there aren't any landlines in the house. Nor is there any cable or radio, let alone computer access. Completely cut off from the outside world, even the doors and windows are all locked. We wouldn't even be able to crack a window for some fresh air. Not that we'd want to, judging by the steady fall of snow outside.

We spend our afternoon watching a few movies on the old DVD player they set up downstairs in the living room. After two movies, Ruby, who's been very quiet all day, quietly announces she wants to lie down. I follow her upstairs and watch her step out of her jeans before crawling onto the bed behind her.

"What's going on in your head, baby?" I coo against the shell of her ear. I don't miss the shiver that seems to run the length of her body as she shimmies her ass back against me. I groan, softly curving myself around her.

"I can't stop this feeling of impending doom hanging over me," she whispers.

I slide my hand down her stomach and between her legs, rubbing her slowly. "Want me to make you forget?" Her head turns to search my mouth, and she hums deeply as I slip my tongue between her lips at the same time my hand slides into the elastic of her panties. She's already wet when I plunge first one and then two fingers inside her. Needy moans vibrate against my mouth, and I can't stop my hips from pressing into her behind. Sweet and slow, I tease her, occasionally rolling her clit with my thumb as her hips rock against my hand. With deep contractions around my fingers and a long drawn out grunt, Ruby lets go. She turns her head to the pillow, with residual shudders running through her body and my fingers still buried deep inside her, she drifts off to sleep.

Dinner time is announced with a sharp knock on the door. Ruby stirs in my arms, and I reluctantly let her go to make use of the bathroom. By the time I get back, she's already gone.

She's sitting at the kitchen table, Chuck and Rhonda across from her, and this time Josh is apparently on kitchen duty, putting some kind of casserole dish on the table. Ruby throws me a smile as she pats the seat beside her in an invitation. A vast difference from the pensive woman earlier this afternoon. I lean down to press a kiss on her mouth.

"Josh made eggplant parmesan," she says with a hint of excitement, her lips mumbling under mine. "It's my favorite, and he says he'll teach me how to make it."

I pull back and look at Josh, who can't quite hide the smile on his face as he returns to the counter to grab a bowl of salad. I do my best to curb the flash of jealousy. Had I known the right food choice would put the smile on her face, I would have opted for cooking instead of having her come on my fingers.

"Lucky guess," he says on a shrug, as he catches me looking. Smug bastard.

"I'll keep it in mind." I smile as insincerely as I can, drawing a chuckle from Chuck. I'm being an ass. It's not even been twenty-four hours and already I'm growing bristles.

"Never mind them," Rhonda says. "They like to stir the pot." She serves healthy portions of the dish on each of our plates. I hate that it smells fantastic.

The nap, and possibly the orgasm I gave her, seems to have done Ruby some good. She's far more animated during dinner than she'd been the rest of the day. In contrast, I seem to have woken up with a chip on my shoulder. This kind of suspended animation we're in, being at the total mercy of others, is starting to grate on me. I don't like the feeling of not having a hand in the course of things. It makes me more vulnerable than I'm comfortable with.

Ruby notices my changed mood and leans in. "Are you okay?" she wants to know. I throw her a smile and grab her hand, covering it on my thigh, but I don't answer. I tell myself it's because I don't want to have to lie in front of the agents, but the truth is, I'm pouting like a damn schoolgirl. After that, the earlier excited mood quickly drains from Ruby, and soon she is back to quietly pensive again.

I'm the bastard.

"Boop…" I draw her attention after we finish the meal. A pretty fucking awesome meal, although I hate to admit it. Ruby's rinsing plates in the kitchen and I really need to apologize. In private. "Do you have a minute?"

With a small nod and a wipe of her hands on the towel, she follows me up the stairs. Once in our room, she walks right by me and sits down on the edge of the bed, her expression weary. I put that there.

"Sorry," I say, as I walk up and sink down on my knees in front of her, my hands bracing on the mattress on either side of her. Her big shiny eyes take in my features. "I'm being an ass. I don't like feeling this out of control. It's making me moody."

Tentatively her hand comes up, and with her fingers, she starts combing through my hair. "Okay," she says softly. "But why did you seem angry at Josh?"

On a deep sigh, I put my face in her lap where she continues to play with my hair. "He made you smile—happy. I want to be the one to do that. I want to be the one to cook you your favorite foods and make you smile in excitement and allow you to forget for one damn minute this goddamn prison we're in." I take in a deep breath and let it out slowly, before I continue in a low voice. "I don't like feeling useless. Especially, when it come to you. I don't ever want to feel useless again."

I'm surprised at my own words. They come from a place where I thought I'd carefully barricaded the sense of helplessness—the feelings of inadequacy. Starting with the moment I realized Ruby had tried to commit suicide, through the six or so weeks of her recovery, to right now: forced into a situation where I can't seem to do anything for her. A snort escapes me. How ironic to finally fall deeply, irrevocably in love, and have it not be enough.

"Are you crying?" Ruby's soft voice makes me aware of the hot tears leaking from my eyes, and slowly soaking into her jeans. I don't even care. When she shifts, I lift my head from her lap, and she scoots herself back on the bed. "Come here," she beckons, her hand outstretched. I crawl up after her, where she pulls my head to her chest and resumes the gentle stroking motions through my hair. "Do you want to know what pulled me back from the edge of darkness those first few weeks?" The question hangs for a minute as I press my ear to the steady beat of her heart. "Your tears," she whispers, wiping at the wetness on my face. "Every time I want to disappear into nothing, I remember the broken sound of your voice, when I just woke up in the hospital. It makes me want to live up to the person you see when you look at me, even when I don't feel worthy." Her soothing hands work silently for a while as I let her words sink in. What a pair we are. "You give me the promise of a life I hadn't even dared dream of, *Mi Vida*. Don't ever think yourself useless again, because you are the root I want to grow on."

I lift my head from her chest, and blindly, my mouth finds hers. I am raw with unfamiliar emotion and pour it all in this kiss. A melding of lips that starts out on a hint of bitter salt, but turns into the rich, sweet taste of promise.

Ruby

I'm so lost in the feel of him against my lips and under my hands, I've become oblivious to my surroundings.

So I don't notice Chuck until Tim pulls away from me.

"Grab your shoes and coat. We've gotta get out of here," he says urgently, peeking through the curtains to the street below.

"Did something happen?" Tim wants to know.

"Just hurry," he hisses urgently.

Before we have a chance to even get out coats, a loud bang sounds from downstairs.

"Goddammit. NOW!" Chuck ushers us into the hallway, but instead of going down, he directs us up the stairs. I'm wedged between Tim at my front and Chuck at my back, flinching at the shots and yelling coming from downstairs. Chuck doesn't give us a chance to think. He shoves us in the small room on the far side of the landing, closing the door behind him. He pulls on a latch in the ceiling and a set of stairs drop down. Tim heads up first, and reaches down for me. Chuck is the last one up and pulls the ladder back up. Pressing his finger to his lips, we can clearly hear the sound of footsteps coming up the stairs. With only hand gestures, he directs us to walk across a beam to a small round window on one side of the attic space we ended up in. Surprisingly, we all manage to crawl through. I panicked for a second when my hips seemed to get stuck, but a shove from behind had me tumbling onto a narrow ledge, where Tim managed to grab me before I slid off the side.

I can't breathe, panic is closing off my airway, as my heart is threatening to pound out of my chest. I freeze. The grim determination on Tim's face as he pulls me along the roof, three stories above the ground, and the fast and furious instructions from Chuck behind me, are the only things that keep my feet moving. The ledge is slick with the snow that hasn't stopped coming down. More than once I almost lose my footing, but Tim's firm hand on my wrist and Chuck's steadying grip on the waistband of my jeans, keep me upright.

As instructed, Tim pushes open a window of the corner house four doors down. "Hold on here for a minute," he says, as he shimmies himself through the open window.

"Now you," Chuck gives me a little push when Tim's hand reaches out. The sound of gunshots have me swing my head around in the direction we came, and I see someone hanging out the window we exited, some kind of long gun in his hands. "NOW!" Chuck roars as he shoves me through the window. Tim's hands grab at me and pull me against him. "A black SUV will be waiting in the alley off the side street. I'll hold them off—GO!" he yells, as he turns to return fire at whomever's been shooting at us.

This house has an actual spiral staircase going down to the second level and appears to be completely empty of any sign of life. I'm numb with fear and cold as I allow Tim to pull me behind him. I can barely keep up, and when we fly out the back door into the small yard, I stumble and fall on hands and knees. Before I have a chance to scramble to my feet, Tim has me lifted off the ground and is running for the back gate, as bullets start hitting the fence to my side.

The back door is open on the dark SUV sitting at the end of the alley. Tim almost throws me on the backseat, crawling in after me. It's only when Mike turns around from the front seat and tells us to buckle up and hold on tight, that I lift my eyes to Tim and my heart stops in my throat.

"You're hurt!"

CHAPTER TWENTY-THREE

Ruby

"It's just a scrape, Boop"

I shoot a sharp look at Tim, and he wisely clamps his mouth shut as I continue cleaning the gash in his scalp just above his ear. "You need stitches," I hiss impatiently, tossing the dirty sterile gauze on top of the others collecting in the garbage bin.

We're back in the bowels of the downtown FBI building, where Mike managed to get us. A surprise, since I was sure his NASCAR driving style, through the normally almost impassable streets of Boston, would leave us in a crumpled wreck more than once. Tim and I were locked into one of the interview rooms with a table, two chairs, and a thermos of coffee. The first aid kit was tossed in as an afterthought. I immediately started rummaging through it, eager to get a closer look at the cause of the blood on Tim's face. It almost gave me a heart attack when I first noticed.

"Ruby…" His hands settle on my hips as he pulls me close. "I promise, I'll be fine." I allow myself a minute to drown in his alert blue eyes before I tamp down the tears threatening. With brisk movements I finish tending to his wound, silently cursing his stubborn streak as I close the edges as best I can with the butterfly bandages, conveniently supplied in the kit. Tim's hands on my wrists stop me when I try to wrap his head in gauze. "That's enough," he says gently, but his hands are firm.

"Fine," I bite off, turning to the thermos next in my need to stay busy.

I've just finished pouring each of us a Styrofoam cup with the nastiest smelling coffee ever, when the door swings open and

Mike walks in. "Have a seat," he gestures at the empty chair for me to sit and edges himself on the corner of the table. "Sorry about that," he points at Tim's head, who just shakes it off.

"What the hell just happened?" I can't believe those words just flew out of my mouth, and apparently neither can Tim, judging by his surprised chuckle. Mike seems to find it amusing as well, which only serves to feed my temper. "Glad to know this is all very amusing to everyone, but can I remind you that my boyfriend almost got his head blown off just now?" Hysteria is creeping up in my voice. I can hear it, but I can't seem to stop it. "Is that what you consider a safe house?" I rant on, almost oblivious to the pacifying hand Tim places on my waving arm. "He's hurt! By a bullet!" I blurt out unnecessarily, since this is something that is clearly apparent to both of them already. Frustration finally breaks my hold on the tears, which now stream freely over my cheeks. Tim scoots his chair close and pulls me into his side.

"I know," Mike says apologetically. "Unfortunately, it appears we had a leak inside our department."

"You think?" Tim sneers, earning him a little squeeze from me. *You tell him, honey.*

Mike raises his hand. "Josh was added to our team three months ago, fresh from the five month training at Quantico. He had an exemplary record in his two years prior to that with the Boston PD. We never questioned his request to join this unit, since it seemed only logical he'd ask for placement in his hometown."

"Josh? The same Josh who…?" I'm incredulous. The fresh-faced young and enthusiastic agent would have been the last person I'd suspected. I ignore Tim's mumbled, *"I knew it,"* keeping my focus on my rolling stomach instead. Suddenly my body wants to revolt that delicious eggplant parmesan.

"Chuck got suspicious when he intercepted a few words of a phone call Josh was apparently conducting, locked in the kitchen pantry. Rather than confront him, he decided to get you to safety and sent me an alert. We were already on our way, when apparently, whomever Josh had been in contact with blew the front door right off and gained entry. Rhonda got hurt in the process, but she'll be okay," he quickly adds, seeing the alarm on my face. "She did manage to take down Josh, after hearing him direct the two men that entered up the stairs. My team managed to round everyone up, just as you were scrambling into the SUV."

"Is Rhonda going to be okay?" Tim asks the question that is burning on my lips.

"Shoulder shot. She was lucky but she'll be fine, as will Chuck who got nicked in his thigh."

"Jesus," Tim mutters. I'm just stunned.

Mike continues to explain that it had been Eduardo Lima and a second man at the safe house. They'd been able to arrest Terry Milano last night, but hadn't been able to locate Lima.

"I have to tell you," Mike turns to me as I huddle against Tim's shoulder. "Things could've gone an entirely different way, if we'd known all along who you were. Don't get me wrong," he hurries to clarify when he sees the guilt clearly on my face. "What I'm trying to say is that keeping your identity and whereabouts secret, may well have saved our case. And more importantly: your life. No one knew you were even here, until you were rushed out of here in the van."

It's near midnight when the door opens and Mark walks in, making a straight line for Tim and me, pulling the two of us in his arms at the same time. "Fuck, I'm relieved to see you both. Come on." He starts moving to the door, gesturing for us to follow. "We've been set up in the penthouse suite at the Nine Zero on Tremont. Views of the Back Bay and the Boston Common." His grin would be infectious, if the events of the day weren't just catching up to me. Barely stifling a yawn, I shuffle behind him out the door.

Tim

I've never really experienced this kind of opulent luxury.

I'm standing in front of floor-to-ceiling windows, watching the lights of the Boston nightlife below. It never seems to end, given that it is almost two in the morning in the heart of winter. Even a few horse and buggy rides are still carrying passengers around the Boston Common. I bet Ruby's never been on a carriage ride—something I'd like to do with her.

She's sleeping in the suite's master bedroom, already out cold when I carried her from the SUV that dropped us off, up the private elevator, and straight to bed. I don't think she got any of the last minute information Mike gave us on our way out the door. For the next day or two, while the main players are being interviewed and the last of the human pipeline can be rolled up by the various agencies involved, we'll be the FBI's guests at one of the most luxurious hotels in Boston.

The big difference with the safe house is that Mark will stay with us and that we have free access to phones, TV, and Internet. The luxury is fun as a one-time experience, but the freedom to connect with the outside world is priceless, even after only a short day and a half.

"What's going through your mind?" my brother, twirling his own glass of casket-aged scotch, asks as he steps up to the window beside me.

"That I'll never take my freedom for granted again."

"That bad?" I feel him turn toward me.

"I'm not just referring to the past few days. More like the past few months. Ever since finding out the kind of life Ruby's been forced to live. That she is still able to smile and laugh—even love—is an absolute miracle to me," I confess, as I turn to look in the direction of the open door to the bedroom where she sleeps. "You already figured that out, didn't you?" I turn to Mark, who is suddenly studying the amber liquid in his glass.

"Only just," he says quietly. "Working as a cop for all these years, you become almost blasé about the stuff you encounter. Brushing it off, because the reality is, we are just Band-Aids. Whatever it is we do doesn't change anything. We just mop up after the mess has already been made. Discovering that, for some of us, the numbness has worked itself so deep that slipping into the dark side seems effortless, that was a wake up call." He takes a deep swig of his drink and I follow suit, savoring the warm burn of the scotch sliding down my throat. After a moment of silence, Mark continues. "Did you know that that little prick, Josh, had been on the team protecting that young girl we found in the park?"

"Are you serious?" My mouth falls open as I turn to him.

"As a heart attack. Apparently he volunteered for the detail. At the time, they felt his youth was a perk. Would maybe make the girl feel more comfortable with someone closer to her own age. No one thought twice about the time he spent with her, because they'd specifically assigned him to try and get close to her. Trying to get her to give up some information. Mike speculates that instead of instilling trust, he used his position to whip up the fear in her, until she felt she had no other choice."

My heart constricts at the thought of that poor girl dying alone at her own hand. Much like Ruby had later attempted to do. The difference had been that Ruby had people caring for her. Had me already loving her. She did that. Her subtle strength, her naturally caring demeanor, even the edge of darkness she always seemed to carry around—they all served to have me throw aside my years long conviction to avoid the messy realities of love.

Suddenly I want to feel her body against mine and I set my glass down on the coffee table. "Will you be okay out here?" Mark mentioned he'd crash on the couch, which was a large sectional number, comfortable enough to sleep two, let alone one person.

"I'll be fine. Go on to bed," he says, clamping his hand on my shoulder, before pulling me in for one of those backslapping man hugs. Fuck if it doesn't choke me up. "We'll talk tomorrow," he says, strain marring his face as he turns his back, staring out into the Boston night.

This time, when I crawl behind Ruby and try to pull her body flush to mine, she turns around and presses her cheek to my chest, where my heartbeat settles down in a steady rhythm.

-

I wake up to the soft click of the bedroom door. I lift my head to see Ruby's distinct outline coming toward the foot end of the bed.

"Are you okay?"

"Shhh." She puts her finger to her lips as she reaches the mattress. The diffused light of dawn comes through a crack in the heavy curtains and casts a spotlight on her. Her eyes are dark on mine as she slowly pulls her nightshirt over her head, dropping it to the floor. My breath hitches in my throat as I watch the soft light stroke every curve on her glorious body. So damn beautiful, she literally takes my breath away. Her long, messy dark mane of curls falls down her shoulders, creating a teasing curtain over her breasts. The ends almost reach her waist. With each breath she takes, the ripe dark nipples peek through, making my mouth water. She's delicious and up to no good, as she slowly climbs on the bed on hands and knees, whipping the covers out of the way and spreading my legs apart as she crawls up. I want to reach out and touch, but something in her eyes tells me to let her take control.

I hiss and drop my head back as she deliberately runs her dangling breasts over my groin. My dick is already at full staff. Thank fuck I ditched my underwear before snuggling up to her last night. With her hands behind my knees, she pushes my legs wider apart, leaving me feeling almost obscenely exposed.

"Jesusss…" I can't hold back a curse as she teases me with the weight of her luscious tits between my legs, before sliding down enough to where her mouth can reach. The first touch of her tongue, along the underside of my cock, sends a shiver all the way to my toes and my mouth falls open. When she pulls back, my eyes shoot open at the cold air that hits the wet trail she leaves behind. She's softly blowing from my balls all the way up to the weeping crown of my dick. I grab a pillow and stuff it behind my head. This is a show I don't want to miss one second of.

Her little smile hits me first. It's seductive, but confident and trusting at the same time. She's enjoying this.

With a little flick of her eyelashes, she bends down again, and laves at my balls before tugging them in her mouth one by one. It's almost impossible to keep my eyes open as she rolls her tongue around the globes. Her hands slide down the backs of my legs and push them higher still, lifting my ass slightly off the bed.

Her tongue traces the seam on my scrotum until she reaches the taint. There she presses a thumb and her mouth finds its languid way back to the base of my cock. I don't miss the rocking and shifting of her hips, a clear indication she's as turned on by this as I am.

I watch, my own tongue about hanging out, as she slides her mouth over my rigid length. Massaging it in tandem, with the pressure on that spot below my balls, as she slides her hot mouth up and down. "Christ, Ruby…so good," I groan when she takes me deep and swallows on my tip. "Please let me come inside you," I plead, completely at her mercy as I feel the tingle start in my lower back. *"Please."* I have no shame, I'm her slave. I have no control over my body.

A soft plop sounds as she releases my cock from her mouth and braces her hands on my thighs, only to use her soft body once again to tease the now super-sensitized area between my legs. She rubs my length with her tits and stomach as she leisurely crawls up my body.

When her mouth reaches mine, she licks at the seam of my mouth. I willingly open, and not unpleasantly, taste myself on her lips. As our tongues tangle, I can feel the wet slide of her pussy against my stomach, where she is softly rocking, her legs on either side of me.

Unable to hold back any longer, I pull my hands from behind my head and grab her hips. My fingers bury in her flesh, helping her move. Preferably onto my waiting cock.

For a long moment she poises herself above me, my length throbbing in her hand as she plays the head through her slick lips. Reaching a hand behind her, she takes a gentle hold of my balls as she slams herself down on my erection.

"Son of a fucking bitch! You're killing me, Ruby…" The half-yelled, half-whispered words keep tumbling from my incoherent

lips, as she simultaneously tugs at my balls and rides me hard. My hips surge off the bed, chasing the warm vice of her body. I swear my heart stops when I feel my hot seed surge from my body into hers.

Ruby is undeterred in her movements, her eyes sharp on mine as she uses her body to milk me dry. Panting with the strain to reach her own completion, I press my thumb hard against her clit and roll it, while the other hand holds her hip firmly.

"*Madre de Dios!*" she exclaims as she throws her head back. With her hair wild around her face flush with climax, and her lips still swollen red, she is absolutely the most breathtaking thing I've ever seen.

CHAPTER TWENTY-FOUR

Ruby

"Orange juice or coffee?"

I still can't look Mark straight in the eye to his great amusement, apparently.

We'd been loud. I mean…*really* loud. Not once had it occurred to me, once I got swept up in what we were doing, that someone else was here. The only people in that moment were Tim and I, and it was unbelievable.

Until we walked out of the bathroom about ten minutes ago, after taking a nice long shower together, and Mark very pointedly, pulled two wads of tissue from his ears. I could've died.

"Boop?" Tim nudges me.

"Orange juice, please."

Very thoughtful of Mark, to provide some much needed *'sustenance'* as he jokingly called the order of breakfast he'd apparently just put in. I have to admit, the rolling cart that was wheeled in minutes ago, loaded with just about any item he could find on the menu, made my mouth water. I'm starving.

I'm shoveling my third pancake in my mouth, when the hotel phone rings. Mark's closest and snatches up the receiver.

"Hello?—Morning to you.—Just finishing up, actually. Come on up." He returns the phone to the cradle and sits back down. "Mike's on his way up," he says to us, before taking a bite of his toast.

I set my fork on my place, my appetite instantly gone.

It doesn't take long before there's a knock and Mark goes to let Mike in. After an exchange of greetings and a fresh round of coffees, Mike turns his attention to me.

"We've run into a bit of a problem," he says, his face serious. "We discovered where Lima had been holed up. His sidekick was the first to start talking last night, leading us to a small warehouse on K Street in South Boston. We organized a raid and apprehended two armed men, guarding a truck with two young women chained in the back early this morning. We were able to get them free and off to receive medical care." An inadvertent cry escapes me and Tim is immediately there, putting his arm around my shoulders. Mike looks slightly chastised when Tim throws him a dirty look.

"I'm sorry, Ruby. I wouldn't have put you through this if I didn't feel you could be of help." His regret seems genuine and I give him a nod to continue. "Lima had a room with a cot in the back. When agents came in, they found a girl shackled to the pipes in an adjacent bathroom. They weren't been able to get near because she kept slamming her head against the sink the moment they'd try to cut her loose. Finally with the place cleared, and the EMTs able to come in, they managed to subdue her and take her to the hospital."

"Oh my God," I whisper. "That poor little thing." I'm sick to my stomach at the fear she must've felt. I can still remember the acrid taste of it in my mouth.

"She won't stop fighting though. She's maybe thirteen, or fourteen. The other girls have been talking a little, told us her name is Nina and she was apparently Eduardo's favorite. I was hoping maybe you—"

"No," Tim interrupts. "Hasn't she been through enough already? Christ, two days ago she ripped open every old wound to help your investigation, bleeding herself empty for six goddamn hours. Now you want her help again? Fuck no!"

"Tim," Mark says in a conciliatory tone.

"Dammit, Mark. Enough is enough!" He jumps up, walks over to the window and leans his head against the cold glass. I slowly follow, running my hand from his side to his front as I press my body flush against his back, embracing him from behind.

"Remember the girl I mentioned? The one I couldn't save?" I mumble in a low voice against his back. "*Mi vida*, what if I can help this little one? What if by helping her, I can help myself?"

Gradually I feel his body relax. He turns to face me, looping his arms around my neck and lowering his forehead to mine.

"Let me try. Let me see if I can reach her. Who better than me?"

He slowly rolls his head from side to side, keeping our foreheads connected. "You blow me away," he mutters under his breath, then a little louder, "Are you sure?"

I lift up on my toes and press my lips to his, giving him a soft, grateful kiss. "Positive."

-

I can hear her screams from the end of the hall. The sound cuts me deep.

A rumpled nurse comes out of the room and shakes her head at our little group. "She's a little wildcat," she says as she passes me, and I can't help myself. I grab her by the arm and spin her around.

"She's a little girl, who was ripped from her family. Maybe even witnessed their murder. She was more than likely raped repeatedly, and in just about every possible way by evil, horrible men. She is traumatized and scared out of her mind. Show some fucking compassion!" My voice has gradually risen from a barely contained angry whisper to a full out yell, and it looks like I've drawn a crowd.

An older man in a white coat, probably a doctor, walks up. I fully expect to be thrown out and hang my head. I haven't even seen her yet and already I've failed her. Tim's arm slides firmly around my midsection, sending a clear message to me, and everyone else, that he has my back. Instead of questioning me, the older gentleman pulls the nurse aside and demands an explanation from her.

"Remind me not to piss you off," Tim whispers in my hair. "You are scary when you go momma bear."

I try to hide the smirk, but appear not to be too successful, since a quick glance at Mark from under my eyelashes shows him grinning widely. Even Mike has trouble containing the twitching of his mouth.

Oddly, the screaming from the room seems to have stopped, and I clearly hear the doctor's steps coming in our direction.

"I'm sorry for that." He vaguely waves at the nurse's retreating back before zooming in on me. "I'm Dr. Ambrose. Are you a relative?" he asks. I can see why he might think that, but I'm afraid to lie. Mark has no such compunctions.

"Absolutely. Her aunt," he says with a straight face, earning a raised eyebrow from Mike and a soft chuckle from Tim, who's hiding his face in my hair. It's clear the doctor doesn't believe him for a minute and turns his eyes to Mike instead.

"Agent Carmello?"

Mike shrugs his shoulders. "What he said," he says, tilting his head in Mark's direction.

"Hmmm." The older man looks from one to the other before his eyes find mine again. "All right. I'll give you five minutes," he says, turning on his heel and walking away, shaking his head.

I struggle from Tim's hold and beeline it to the door the nurse came out of.

"Ruby, wait," Tim calls after me, but I stop him with a hand in his chest when he reaches me.

"You can't come in, honey. As far as she knows, you are no different then any of the men who've hurt her so far."

He hangs his head, but nods in understanding. He slips his hand under my hair and tilts my head up for a kiss. "Careful in there," he says with a wink, before turning to join his brother and Mike on the chairs along the wall. Taking a deep breath I push open the door.

-

She's tiny.

The moment I step in the room and let the door fall shut behind me, she starts struggling against the restraints. It stops me on the spot. I don't want to upset her any more than she already is, and for a few minutes I stand there, helpless to do anything as her whimpers grow louder. The sheet, that at some point must've covered her, slips down the side of the bed, and I wince at a familiar sight. Almost instantly an idea forms.

I shuffle along the wall, making sure I don't get any closer to the girl, whose terrified eyes are now following my every move. Mike was right, she can't be more than maybe thirteen years old. When I reach a point where she can easily see all of me, I take a deep breath in. With shaking hands, I unbutton my jeans and slide down the zipper, making sure not to make any moves toward her. The fear is not gone, but her struggles still as she follows every move I make, until I lift my feet from the jeans, now pooled at my feet. Confusion marks her face as she looks up from my naked legs to my face. I hope to God no one barges in right now. I lift one foot on the chair against the wall and turn my knee out. Giving myself a little modesty with the hem of my sweater, I use my other hand to frame the brand burned on the inside of my thigh. The same kind of brand I noticed on the inside of hers.

It's clear she sees it the moment I hear her sharp intake of breath. Her eyes stay focused on the mark on my leg for a while, before her eyes lift to mine. I swallow hard when I see her lips start trembling and big fat tears begin to roll down her face.

"Nina?" I ask her softly, gently lowering my leg so as not to startle her and start pulling up my pants. Her eyes never leave my face. "*¿Su nombre es, Nina?*" I try again. I almost cry when I see the tangled of curls bob on her head as she nods sharply. I take a careful step closer, but she immediately freezes in the bed. "*¿Puedo venir más cerca?*" This time I ask her for permission to approach her and wait patiently while a war seems to be waged on her face. Finally she gives me another little nod, this one a bit more hesitant. I have to be careful not to push.

"*La misma marca,*" she whispers in a tiny little voice.

"*Si, mi pequeño,*" I reassure her, as I carefully pull up a rolling stool and sit down, careful not to touch her or the bed. Not yet. I let my eyes wander over her face, seeing the cut at her hairline, probably from her banging her head against the sink. It could use a few stitches, but we were told when we arrived at the hospital that they didn't want to traumatize her even further, if it wasn't absolutely necessary.

"*¿Estás herido?*" I ask her, needing to know if she's hurting anywhere else. She breaks my heart when her eyes fill with tears again as she nods.

No longer able to keep my distance, I carefully reach out and brush the pad of my thumb under her eyes. "*Estara bien.* It will be okay, Nina," I whisper softly, as she turns her face into the palm of my hand.

Tim

"What will happen to her?"

We've been sitting in the hospital hallway for half an hour. That doctor's five-minute limit had long since passed. Mark had gone to grab us some coffees from the Starbucks in the lobby, but other than that, we've been sitting here, each to our own thoughts.

Mike turns his head to look at me. "Depends on how old she is, and what we can find out about where she comes from. Worst case scenario, if she has no one waiting for her back home, she will likely be placed in foster care here. I've been able to hold off, but CPS will have to be contacted."

Suddenly the door opens and Ruby sticks her head out. I jump up and rush over to her, but the moment my eyes scan over her head into the room, she gives me a firm shove back. "Careful," she hisses. Then she easily puts on a smile and turns her face into the room.

"Está bien, Nina, él es mi novio. I'll be right back. " She steps out and closes the door behind her, but my eyes are still focused over her head, where the large-eyed little girl seemed only a blip on the bed. "You okay, Tim?" Ruby asks and I slowly drop my eyes to her face.

"Is she okay?"

"No. She's in pain." Ruby grabs my hand and pulls me over to where Mike and my brother are waiting. "Where is the doctor?" she asks, looking around. As if she summoned him, Dr.

Ambrose appears around the corner. I'm surprised when I see him smile at her.

"You did well," he says, when he gets close enough. The only one not surprised is Ruby.

"She showed me the camera. She's not stupid—she's hurt," Ruby points out. She quickly explains what she's learned and urges the doctor to find a young female physician to attend to her. "Can I stay with her?" Her face betrays her anxiety as she addresses him.

"Let me find one of our residents and we'll discuss things then," he says, his mouth twitching in amusement.

The moment he turns to leave, Ruby grabs my forearms. "I may be a while, why don't you guys go back to the hotel?" Before I have a chance to open my mouth, Mike pipes up.

"I'd feel better if they stuck around, Ruby. I have to get going, though, but I'll make sure you guys are covered," he says the last to Mark and me. He doesn't need to say anything else. He doesn't want to take any chances and neither do I.

Not long after he leaves to make his calls, Ambrose is back with a young Latino woman in scrubs beside him. "This is Doctor Claudia Medina, chief resident in our ER. I thought perhaps it would be easier to eliminate the language barrier." He smiles at Ruby.

Introductions are made and the older man turns to leave. "You'll be in good hands with Dr. Medina," he says, leaving Ruby looking a little disappointed as she edges closer to my side. The young woman looks too young to be a doctor, but she has a confident manner as she walks to the girl's room. With her hand on the doorknob, she turns to look back at Ruby.

"I thought you were coming?" she says with one eyebrow raised. I barely have a chance to pull her in for a quick peck before Ruby hurries through the door first.

-

It's near dinnertime when we get back to the hotel. Apparently room service has been there, because all the breakfast dishes we had spread around the suite have been cleared up. Mark immediately pulls out the menu and starts shooting off options, while Ruby kicks her shoes off and curls up on the couch. She's exhausted but smiling.

"Want a drink, Boop?" I ask her, shamelessly interrupting my brother. Ruby turns her smile on me.

"Would love just some water, please."

"Coming up," I answer easily. "Brewski, Mark?" I ask him, as I make my way over to the bar fridge.

"Sure. So what's it gonna be, little sis," he teasingly says to Ruby, who chuckles softly. "Pasta, salad, or steak?"

"Steak, medium-rare." She doesn't hesitate in responding.

"My kinda woman," I say, plopping down on the couch beside her, handing her a bottle of water and reaching Mark's beer over to him. "Order me the same thing. Baked potato, loaded," I add.

"Oh, yes. Me too." Ruby snuggles under my arm.

As soon as the dinner order is placed, the mood turns more serious, when Mark asks Ruby to fill us in on the girl's condition. I understand why he wants to know. Part of me wants to know, but another part doesn't want to hear more about how unfathomably cruel some people can be.

"Her name is Nina. She's fourteen years old and was taken from an orphanage near *Córdoba,* about six months ago, as far as she can tell. It seems to be the preferred age." My heart aches thinking about Ruby that young and vulnerable. Not to mention the number of young girls that may have been taken in the many years since then. "She doesn't know of any relatives. She thinks one of the people working at the orphanage may have been involved." She pauses and looks up at Mark. "Do you think we should call Mike?"

"Yes…" he nods, "but finish first."

" She has a brand similar to mine, on the inside of her leg, so I think she may have been held in a *calcuilchil* as well. I didn't want to ask her about what happened to her. I thought it might scare her —"

"Wait," Mark interrupts. "Sorry. What did you say about a brand?" He looks at me in disbelief. I guess we never shared that detail with him. Ruby is squirming in the seat beside me. so I take the question.

"Whenever new girls were brought to the place Ruby was at, and presumably others like it, they'd be branded. To show ownership."

"Branded how?" he asks, his voice a little rough.

"With a branding iron," Ruby answers this time. "Like cattle."

"Christ." Mark throws himself back in his seat and covers his face with his forearm. "Go on."

"Are you sure?" Ruby leans forward and puts a hand on his knee, and he lifts his arm from his face.

"Yeah, honey. Go on," he says, giving her an encouraging nod.

"Okay. Well, they did an MRI and a few X-rays. Claudia was really good with her, so she went in with her for those. They found some evidence of old injuries, but nothing looking to be within the last six months. No head injury on the MRI." Ruby suddenly stops and I know she must be getting to the most difficult part. "She wanted to hold my hand while Claudia examined her. She has some tearing that will heal on its own. But both her…" A sob escapes her and I pull her against me.

"We get it, baby. We get it. That's enough," I murmur in her hair. Over her head, my eyes meet my brother's and he looks as torn up as I feel.

"I dated a plastic surgeon last year," Mark says suddenly. "We still talk from time to time, I can talk to her. See what it would take to get those damn brands removed. For both of you."

"*No*." Ruby surprises me with her prompt answer, and even more so, when she slips from my hold and crosses over to sit next to my brother, leaning in to kiss his cheek. "Thank you so much for the offer. Maybe it's something we can offer Nina one day, but I'm keeping mine."

"Whatever you want to do, babe," I give in. "But why?"

She tucks her arm in to Mark's and looks from him back to me.

"Because that mark was what made Nina open up. There may be more like her—like me—who need to see in order for them to trust."

CHAPTER TWENTY-FIVE

Ruby

"Can I have two Thursday specials?" Syd sticks her smiling face around the kitchen door.

It's been two weeks since we were cleared to return to Portland; that was after spending our third night in the luxury suite. Mike had shown up during breakfast again and seemed very pleased with himself when he told us he'd been able to pit Milano against Lima. The former police captain realized, very quickly, that unless he turned state's evidence, he would not only be vulnerable to the general prison population as a cop, but as a sex offender too. The first could get him shivved, but the second, as he was well aware, could end much worse than a quick death. Mike had made sure he was very clear on that. He'd been singing like a canary since coming to that conclusion.

He said the tying down of all of the evidence would be at least another few months, but that we were free to leave.

I immediately thought of Nina, and the fact that I wouldn't be able to visit with her anymore. Claudia had called in CPS. Although she was keeping Nina for observation for another few days, CPS now controlled who and how long Nina could receive visitors. If not for Claudia, I wouldn't have been allowed back to see her. With her intervention, I'd been able to spend a few hours with her yesterday.

"Can we visit Nina before we go?" My voice had a little wobble when I directed my question at Tim. Understanding immediately spread over his face.

"Absolutely."

No hesitation at all. Just complete support, without any question. So damn beautiful, this man.

There were tears. Mine and Nina's for sure, but I suspect Claudia may have blinked away a few as well. I hugged Nina, who no longer was kept in restraints, something Claudia took care of right away. I handed Nina a box with a cell phone, one matching the one in my purse, that Tim had insisted on buying for us on the way here. "So you can stay in touch," he'd said.

"For real?" Nina said, sounding more like an American teenager than the little Mexican girl I met that first day. I smiled at her.

"Tim bought each of us one," I replied in English, as I showed her mine. Her eyes immediately went to the window where Tim was peeking in through the now opened blinds. Hesitantly she raised her hand and wiggled her fingers at him; his face cracked open in a wide smile.

Tim had asked me to go home with him, but I wanted some time to myself. Mainly to try and process the whirlwind events. He'd driven me to Florence House, where I packed up my belongings and promised Pam I'd give her a call the next day. After that, he helped me carry my stuff up to the apartment and gave me a sweet kiss goodbye, before leaving me to fend for myself. I could tell he wasn't happy, but other than demanding I call him before I go to sleep, he didn't complain.

Last week I'd started back to work and was just finding my feet again, after being off for about two months. The welcome I received had been heartwarming, with hugs from Dino, Gunnar, Matt, Ike, and even Arnie. There were emotional tears from Viv, whose belly had expanded impressively since I last saw her.

Today was the first time working with Syd, who ended up escaping the winter cold by visiting Gunnar's mother in Arizona with all three kids. She'd just gotten back the day before yesterday.

"I'll bring them out," I offer to her with a smile. "We're out of guac, I quickly have to make some more."

Today was my first hand at the Thursday Special. I'd spent most of last week practicing this easy recipe I found. Stacked nachos. It's pretty easy, you brown some onions and ground beef. Add some salt and pepper to taste, find the best salsa you can buy, and add it to the pan to simmer with the beef. Place six-inch metal rings on a parchment paper-lined baking sheet, and sprinkle some grated Monterey Jack on the bottom. Then you press in a layer of nacho chips, top it with the beef mixture, followed with some chopped green onions, jalapeños and more grated cheese. You repeat until you have three layers, ending with the beef and cheese. Bake for twenty minutes in a hot oven, top with fresh-made guacamole and a dollop of sour cream. I was so excited when Dino tasted it and suggested we make it for Thursday. A good call, apparently, since they've been flying out the door all night.

I make light work of the guacamole, pull two plates down and prepare the order. I'm rather pleased with myself. Dino is off again tonight, and so far I've managed the kitchen quite well. Orders had gone out smoothly and the evening rush had come and gone. I'd already started cleaning when this last order came through.

The pub is oddly quiet when I walk in, toting the tray of food. Syd is leaning against the counter, her eyes on the TV screen above the bar. So are everyone else's. No one seems to notice me, until I slide the order in front of Syd. She looks at me a bit startled before her eyes lift to the screen again, only to come back to me. I throw a look over my shoulder to see what has everyone glued to the screen and am shocked to see a picture of Carlos Delgado flash across the screen.

"Turn it up," I call to Matt, who's manning the bar. He turns to me, but looks over my shoulder before doing as I asked. I feel an arm coming around my shoulders and a quick peek beside me finds Gunnar with a concerned look on his face.

"*…held in the murder of Carlos Delgado, almost a year ago, was found dead in his cell at the Nashua Street Jail earlier today, where he had been remanded until his upcoming trial. Lima, a former SAU detective for the Boston PD…*" I don't have to hear anymore and slip right from under Gunnar's arm to the kitchen, where I sink down on a chair and drop my head on the table.

Dead.

I should feel horrified. Even shocked. But all I feel is a vague sense of relief—of justice. I remember what Mike had told us. How cops, and especially cops who were child molesters, were automatic targets in jail. I can't say I'm proud of the thought, but I hope he suffered. For what he had obviously put Nina through, and God forbid, how many other girls. I'd rather see him rot in hell over that, than have him live out his life in jail for killing one of his own kind.

I don't know that I've been crying until Gunnar, who has apparently followed me, tosses a box of tissues in front of me. "How are you doing, Ruby?" he asks in his gravelly voice, filled with concern.

"I'm good," I answer him, finding myself able to even smile. "I'm not sure what that says about me, but I feel lighter." Gunnar shoots me a crooked smile back.

"I get that," he simply says, before stepping around the table and leaning down to kiss my cheek. "Proud of you, girl," he mumbles, turns around and disappears down the hall.

I scramble to find my phone in my purse, suddenly feeling the need to talk to Tim. When I finally locate it, I see I have three missed calls from him. I quickly hit call.

"I'm on my way." Is the first thing out of his mouth when the call is answered after barely one ring.

"Honey…"

"Heard it on the news, baby. Hang in there, I'll be there in five." I hear a muttered conversation in the background and am only able to make out something about driving like a lunatic.

"Tim, listen to me," I hurry before he hangs up. "I'm fine. I really am. Please drive careful."

All I hear is a deep sigh followed by a pregnant pause. "I promise," he finally answers before a click announces he's ended the call.

I'm scouring the dirty baking sheets, lost in my thoughts, when familiar arms slip around my waist and pull me back into the hard wall of Tim's chest. His chin lands on my shoulder, where he presses his cheek against mine. "I feel better now," he says, making me snicker.

Wiping my hands on my apron, I cross my arms on top of his and lean my head back on his shoulder. "I'm really okay," I assure him. "I just wonder if someone will tell Nina before she accidentally sees the news or hears it on the radio."

Tim

Mark and I had finally rescheduled that meeting with the real estate agent, to have a walk around the warehouse. I was frankly surprised the place hadn't sold yet, until we did a walk through. To say it's old and needs a few improvements would be optimistic. Thing is, the space itself is perfect, with lots of natural light from the huge windows along the entire front. There's plenty of parking outside and would make for a fantastic workshop and showroom. That is, after I sink some serious money in it to replace half those windows, upgrade the wiring, have the plumbing fixed, get the roof repaired and call in an exterminator to deal with the rat problem. The last is not unusual, especially this close to the water, but I can't risk having some damn rodents chew the shit out of my wood.

The low price makes sense now too. Despite the broken windows, it eyes great from the outside, but you can't really see the rest until you walk through.

"I don't know," I say to Mark as we drive away, promising the agent we'll give him a call, whatever we decide. I have some money from my severance pay, and I also have a pretty decent amount in savings, but taking this on would decimate my assets. Not exactly the way I'd envisioned starting a new life with a certain someone.

"I do," Mark says beside me. "Let's pay Dad a visit and see what he has to say."

Not sure when my brother had become the voice of reason, but more often than not lately, he seemed to be. He'd come equipped with camera, measuring tape, and notebook, whereas I only had my half empty coffee cup. What happened to the buttoned up, borderline OCD, by the book Boy Scout I used to be? I can't help the smile spreading over my face, because I know exactly what happened.

"You're thinking of Ruby, aren't you?" Mark says, with no small measure of disgust in his tone. "You get that fucking goofy as hell smirk on your face. It's pathetic."

"I know," I say, now laughing out loud. "And I don't care."

We bicker and tease until we pull into my parents driveway. As per usual, Mom has the door open before we even have a chance to get out. "How does she do that?" Mark mutters under his breath.

"I think she either spends her days behind that curtain, waiting, or she has some secret alarm installed that goes off whenever someone comes within a hundred feet of the house."

"What are you kids talking about?" she asks, as we walk up to meet her at the door. Uncanny, the woman has a sixth sense.

"Hey, Mom." I lean down to kiss her cheek and quickly move past her, ignoring her question. Behind me, she greets Mark before closing the door behind us.

"You guys are staying for dinner, right?" It's not so much a question as it is an order.

My father is sitting at the kitchen table, flipping the newspaper. Something he does at least a few times a day. "Might as well say yes," he grumbles without looking up. "You know she'll not take no for an answer anyway."

"Oh hush," Mom scolds him, as she whacks a towel at him in passing.

Mark disappears behind her into the kitchen, as I pull out a chair and sit across from Dad. He walks back in with three beers and plonks them on the table in front of us, before sitting down beside me. Dad looks up from his paper and folds it calmly, his eyes going back and forth between us. "Get on with it already," he grouches, but the slight tilt of his mouth hints at amusement. "How was it?"

"A mess," I say.

"Perfect," Mark blurts out at the same time.

"I see." Dad smirks, folding his hands underneath his chin. "You first." He nods to Mark.

The next half hour, Mark and I take turns describing the warehouse with all its perks and downfalls. My father has grabbed a pen and pad and is making notes as we talk. When we're done, he flips the pad over and leans back in his chair, staring at each of us in turn before focusing on Mark.

"Tell me, what are the chances of you going back to law enforcement?" he asks him, and I turn to see Mark looking back at Dad without blinking.

"None," he says firmly.

"Is that so?" Dad fires back immediately.

"I've been offered early retirement. I'm taking it," my brother sighs, lowering his eyes to his folded hands on the table. "The thought of having to go back out there, being confronted with the dark side of humanity day in and out…I lose sleep over it. I want something different."

My own exposure to humanity's underbelly has been pretty sparse until recent months, but still I can understand how Mark feels.

"I'm glad," Dad directs at him. "Your damn shoulders were drooping lower and lower with the weight of the world piled on top. Your mother and I were getting worried."

"How about you?" This time, it's me who has his attention.

"Me?"

"Yeah. What are your plans with that little cupcake you're so hung up about?"

Mark snorts beside me, knowing as well as I do, if Ruby ever heard herself referred to as a *little cupcake*, we'd likely have to hold her back. I smile thinking of her rare but lethal temper. "She'll be part of my life, Dad."

"Don't think that was ever in doubt, Son. How do you envision this? She's avoided coming back here these past few weeks, despite your mother's near begging."

"Not gonna push, Dad. She'll come around, the woman needs a little breather," I inform him, letting my irritation show. All he does is raise an eyebrow and I blurt out, "She has 'til next week." Both other men at the table burst out laughing.

"Finally!" Mom yells from the kitchen, apparently shamelessly eavesdropping on our conversation.

"Okay," Dad says, completely ignoring his wife's outburst. "Now that we know where we're all at, let's put *Vintage Veldman* on the map."

He flips over his pad and starts firing off questions. It feels a bit like when we were young and he'd quiz us on our homework. Pretty soon, Dad has three pages full of calculations when he draws a thick line underneath the amount he feels is necessary to make this work. The number is a bit staunching, but Dad puts all three of our names down underneath, putting an amount next to each of them before lifting his eyes to me. "You tell me if you can do this, Son. I'm putting half the anticipated start up cost that includes the building next to your name, but that is only because you should have final say. The business starts and ends with your skills and designs. Mark and I each buy in for twenty-five percent, which will take some of the financial burden off you, so you're not left completely tapped out. Besides, it gives each of us a chance to help build something we can collectively be proud of." He tosses his pen on the table and folds his hands behind his head. "What say you?"

I turn to Mark, who looks back with a smirk on his face. Much like the one on mine. We can do this.

"Done," we say, almost at the same time. To which my father slams his fist on the table.

"Jane! Grab me that bottle of Dalwhinnie and a couple of tumblers, will ya?" The last word has barely left his mouth when Mom walks in, bottle in one hand and four tumblers in the other.

"And don't skimp on mine." She points a finger at my Dad who sits there, shaking his head at her. "I'm grabbing a snack."

"Ears must be burnin'," he teases her.

"Bite me, Arthur," she tosses over her shoulder.

Dad chuckles as he watches her disappear into the kitchen. "Love that woman."

-

Dinner, which had a celebratory feel to it, was enjoyed and cleared away when Dad flicks on the TV to watch the news.

Both Mark and I shoot forward in our seats when the first thing we see is a mug shot of Eduardo Lima. "Turn it up, Dad," Mark says urgently, while I pull out my phone and start dialing Ruby. With the fruitless ringing in one ear and the voice of the reporter outlining the events in the other, I finally get on my feet, and reach for my coat. Mom stops me with a hand on my arm.

"Is that…" she starts. Before she has a chance to finish, I give her a big hug.

"One of them, yes. I've got to get to Ruby."

"Of course," she says, watching me walk out the door, Mark following closely behind me.

I don't question him when he jumps in the passenger seat of my truck and calmly buckles up. "Maybe she hasn't seen it yet," he suggests.

"She's not answering her phone," I relay to him. Just then mine rings on the console beside me, Ruby's name popping up on the screen.

"I'm on my way," I advise her before she has a chance to speak. I'm trying to ignore Mark, who is loudly complaining about my driving, but I only have ears for Ruby.

Despite her assurances, I don't relax until I walk into the kitchen and see her standing at the sink. I take in her efficient movements for a minute, letting my heart settle down in my chest, before I walk up behind her and wrap myself around her body.

CHAPTER TWENTY-SIX

Ruby

I haven't spoken to Nina since she left the hospital, about a week ago, to be placed in temporary care by CPS. I've tried, but each time was relegated to an automated message. I'd spent some time talking to Pam about the girl last week, and she suggested perhaps to give her some time to adjust. Said she may not be ready to be faced with what happened to her every time she'd clap eyes on me. I never considered that. I guess it makes sense in a way. What brought me to her, and provided our initial connection, was everything she was probably trying hard to forget.

That's why I hadn't pushed, but I'm worried now. I don't know if her CPS worker or her foster family are even aware of the details of her ordeal.

I turn in Tim's arms and loop mine around his neck. "I want to call her."

He lowers his mouth and takes mine gently. I'm temporarily distracted by the masterful play of his tongue, but am dragged back to reality when Mark marches in. "Christ, you two. I'm starting to get a complex here."

Tim lifts his head and rolls his eyes at me. "Don't listen to him, please. Just go make your call." With a last sweet touch of his lips to mine, he steps back, letting me go.

I walk over to where my phone is still on the kitchen table, and spot Mark dip a few stray nacho chips in the fresh tub of guacamole. "Scoop some out in a bowl, please," I admonish him, while my finger hits the speed dial for Nina's phone. This time there is no ringing first, it immediately goes into the mechanical message. Dejectedly, I drop it on the table.

"Still nothing?" Tim asks concerned.

"Straight to voicemail now," I tell him. "You think maybe Claudia would know where she's at?"

"We can try," he says with a shrug.

"The doc?" Mark shakes his head. "If anyone would know where she's at it would be Mike. The investigation is ongoing, and he would need to know where he can find his witnesses." He immediately pulls out his phone and dials.

I never thought of that. Of course.

"Hey—Yeah, we just found out—She's fine," he says the last, looking at me as he listens. "I'm sure—Listen, Ruby is a bit worried about Nina. She can't get hold of her on her cell. Do you know where she can be reached?—Oh—No, I get it. So tomorrow?—Fine, I'll let her know." He hangs up the phone and turns to me. "He doesn't know her exact location because any contact with her has to go through CPS, but he'll contact the caseworker tomorrow first thing, and give you a ring back. That okay?"

It'll have to be. No choice really, if she doesn't answer her phone. But the worry remains. To keep busy, I finish cleaning the kitchen, while Tim and Mark hit the pub for a drink. By the time I'm done, it's almost ten thirty and I'm dead on my feet.

Mark has left, but Tim is in animated conversation with Gunnar when I walk up to the bar. Tim immediately pulls me between his legs, my back against his chest, and folds an arm around me to keep me in place. I squirm a little, not yet used to the easy public displays of affection. The conversation continues over my head.

"Drink, Ruby?" Syd asks from behind the bar.

"Just some water, please, Syd. Thanks."

Gunnar gets up from his stool. "Good news, buddy," he says, as he claps Tim on his shoulder, and with a wink for me, he slips behind the bar.

"Sorry about that," Tim mumbles in my hair. "You wanna head home?"

I wiggle out of his hold and hoist myself on the stool Gunnar just vacated with a deep sigh. My feet are killing me. "Where did Mark go?"

"Took the truck and went home. I'll call him when I'm ready to go tomorrow."

The implication is clear, he plans to spend the night. My eyebrow rises in question and he grins a bit sheepishly. "Hope you don't mind?" he asks as an afterthought, watching me closely for a reaction.

I put my hands on his knees and lean in close and he automatically does the same. "I'm wiped," I softly warn him. I'm not sure if I'm up to any bedroom gymnastics tonight, tempting as he is in his now standard flannel. "And my feet are killing me

"I just need to hold you for a bit," he whispers back. "Maybe I'll rub your feet." And just like that, my minor irritation melts like snow in the sun.

I've barely touched my water, and he hops off his stool. "Let's go. Where's your stuff?"

"Kitchen."

Syd chuckles as he jogs around the bar and down the hall. In a few seconds, he's coming back this way, carrying my purse and coat.

"Where's your coat?" I ask him as he helps me in mine.

"Must've left it in the truck." He shrugs buttoning up his shirt instead.

"It's cold out."

"I know," he says, crouching down in front of my stool, his back to me. "You can keep me warm. Come on, climb on."

"I'm too heav…"

In a flash, he's back up and in my face, his forehead leaning against mine. "Don't say it, Ruby," he says in a warning tone, before crouching down again, his arms reaching back. I throw Syd, who's watching us with a smirk on her face, an exasperated look, which only makes her smile bigger. Fine. If he wants to put his back out by lugging me across the street, who am I to stop him? I reach around his neck and let my body slide on his back, wrapping my legs around his waist. His hands immediately lock under my butt and we're off to the collective calls goodbye.

"You're crazy, you know that?" I mutter in his ear, as the cold outside air hits us.

"Only for you," he says, throwing a smile over his shoulder.

Tim

"Ohhh, that's so good…"

She has no idea what her moans and groans do to me as I dig my thumbs into the arch of her foot. I shift slightly to try and alleviate some of the pinch of my far too enthusiastic dick behind my zipper. She said she was tired, and I'm sure tonight was a shock, so he'll have to be on his best behavior. Not an easy feat, when the sounds she makes tease my baser instincts.

"You okay?" she says in a sleepy voice, her eyes peeking from under heavy lids.

"I'm good," I reassure her, shifting once again as I try to stay on task.

A little smile tugs at the corner of her mouth, as she carefully flexes her foot, causing her heel to slide over the bulge in my jeans. I hiss at the friction and firmly grab her foot, stilling the motion. I watch as she sucks in her plump bottom lip and bites down. Without moving her eyes from me, she starts doing the same thing with her other foot. Flexing and relaxing, pressing her heel down in a torturously slow rhythm, massaging my now painfully engorged dick.

"I thought you were tired," I try to throw out casually, but the slight hitch in my voice betrays my state of arousal.

"I was," she says, her voice not unaffected either. "But now I'm not."

"Little minx," I growl, lifting her feet and shifting out from under her, before leaning over and plastering my mouth to hers. Her arms come up instantly and pull me down further, until I'm covering her body with mine. I can feel her satisfied hum against my mouth when she spreads her legs and my hips fall between. I give up trying to control my body and instinctively rub myself against her heat as our tongues duel. With a small whimper, I feel her tilt underneath me, seeking friction, while her hands pull frantically at my shirt.

"Stay right there," I state firmly, when I push up and quickly strip the flannel down my arms, while she's already shoving up the T-shirt underneath. That's gone in a flash and tossed on the floor. Ruby's small hands play over my chest, setting my skin on fire. "Turnabout is fair play, Boop," I warn her, as I grab the bottom of her sweater and pull it right off her body. The moment her arms are clear, the hands are back to playing.

"I love this," she says, her eyes focused on her fingers that have found the small flat disks partially obscured by my chest hair. With a light flick of her fingernails, she sends a charge right to my cock. In retaliation, I pull the cups of her bra low, so her tits spill out and launch my own assault on her nipples, making her gasp. "So damn responsive," I mumble, as I lean down to have a taste, which leads to another. Before you know it, I'm back to being draped over her, but this time with my mouth latched on to her breast, while my fingers strum the other.

Our lovemaking is slow and sweet. By the time we are both naked and I finally slide inside her, the frantic earlier pace has burned off, leaving behind a deep glowing heat to fuel us. Ruby's half-lidded eyes burn into mine, as I rock my hips in a deep, stroking rhythm. Each time I fill her completely, a soft puff of air escapes her partially opened lips. So fucking beautiful, fully aroused, with her lips wet and swollen from our kisses, and a deep blush on her cheekbones. "Move in with me." I underline my demand with a powerful thrust of my hips, making her gasp. "I need you with me." Again I slam myself to the hilt. I see her eyes glaze over with her impending orgasm and still she manages to form words.

"Too soon," she sighs, but I thrust inside her again, making her eyes roll back before I pull back, staying poised at her entrance. Her eyes snap open.

"I…need…you…to…move…in!" Each word is emphasized by my bucking hips. Sweat dripping down my face in my struggle to maintain control, I pause at her entrance again.

"Please…" she whimpers, tilting her hips to try and force me inside, but I just pull back a little further. "I need…"

I drop my head and run my nose along hers. "I can give you what you need. Just say yes…" I mumble against her lips, while I slowly push inside her before pulling out and stilling again.

"This is blackmail," she wails, writhing underneath me.

"I know," I whisper. "I love you." As if that is a valid explanation but for me somehow it is. I'm not sure where this urgency comes from. I just know I don't want to spend one more night going to sleep, without her safely in my arms, or wake up one more single morning not having her beautiful eyes to look into first thing.

Again I tease her with a slow roll of my hips, not quite enough to push her over, only bringing her even closer to the edge.

"Fine! Yes. Please… Tim," she finally cries out.

"Yes?" I push one of her legs back for a better angle and flex my hips once.

"Yes, yes, yes! Please!"

I drop my head and let go of my control, hammering into her at a frantic pace until I can feel her inner walls start to ripple. With a loud, incoherent scream, Ruby's body arches up beneath me and the powerful pulsing of her pussy drags me over the edge with her.

"Ruby!" I shout hoarsely as I lose myself inside her body.

Ruby

He's really quite beautiful.

I just come back from an early morning bathroom visit when the solid man, sprawled out in my bed, takes my breath.

My eyes trace over his face and his body at leisure. His dark blond hair has a reddish hue and is a bit on the long side, but I love tangling my fingers in it. The red comes in stronger in his beard, framing a perfect set of full lips, which he knows how to put to good use. A strong forehead, the beautiful blue pools of his eyes behind his closed lids, and a prominent, mostly straight nose.

He's still fast asleep, the steady rise and fall of his broad chest proof of that. I lay back down with my head to his chest and my arm resting on his stomach. I love the little bit of softness to cover the muscle on his midsection. It makes him all man to me.

My man.

Who managed to blackmail me into moving in with him. *Bastardo*. I smile at the memory of his particular method of coercion. He had me almost bursting out of my skin with want before he gave me what I needed. I know I said I needed time to be alone, but truthfully, unless I was with him I felt unsettled. We also seem to naturally veer toward his house, spending most of our time together there. Other than that one time before Christmas, the first time he saw my brand, which resulted in an unpleasant morning to end our first rather innocent night together, he hadn't slept a night here, until now

A slight tightening of the hand that automatically had seemed to find its way back on my ass is the only warning I get. I must've fallen asleep again, because daylight is now streaming in.

"I like this bed," his gruff morning voice gently stirs the hair on my head. I just snuggle closer in response as his hand almost absentmindedly massages my backside. "I sleep well here, but we're sleeping in mine tonight." I can't stop the smile pulling at my face.

"Ours," I whisper with my lips pressed against his skin. I feel him jerk slightly at my declaration before his strong arms pull me on top of his body. I lift my head and am instantly pinned by his soft gaze.

"Ours," he confirms, before following it with an order, "Kiss me."

Scooting up his body, my lips find his in a lazy, early morning kiss.

Before it can turn into a lazy, early morning anything else, we're interrupted by the incessant ringing of a phone. "That's yours," Tim mumbles against my mouth, reluctantly letting me up. I throw on my sleep shirt, which had stayed, unused, under my pillow and am about to leave the room when he calls out. "I'm hopping in the shower, quick."

"Knock yourself out," I suggest before padding toward the kitchen, where I'd dumped my purse last night. Fishing out my phone, I notice a missed call from an unknown number. It's a Boston number, though, and I wonder if it's perhaps Nina calling? I'm about to hit dial when I hear Tim calling.

"Boop. Do you have a spare toothbrush somewhere?" I take a few steps to look down the hall to see Tim sticking his head out the bathroom door on the other end. "Shit. Never mind." He waves me off with a smile as he steps buck naked into the hallway and opens the door to the linen closet, rummaging around inside. "Found it," he says, triumphantly waving a toothbrush still in its packaging. One that I know for a fact, I never purchased.

With morbid curiosity, I slowly walk toward the closet, pulling the door open. Behind the stack of folded towels, I just put on that shelf last week, I spot the corner of a brown paper bag I had not paid attention to before, sticking up. Inside is a five pack of toothbrushes. Now with two missing.

-

I'm not sure how long I sit on the couch with the paper bag clenched in my hands before I hear the shower turn off. My ears register each and every sound coming from the bathroom. The hair on my arms is standing up straight and I struggle for each breath, trying to stay calm. Finally the door opens and I hear the soft sound of his bare feet coming down the hall.

"Hey, beautiful. Who was that on the phone?" He kisses my head and pads on into the kitchen. I don't move. I can't. I'm afraid to make a sound, for fear a question slips out I don't want to know the answer to. "Ruby?" He sticks his head back into the room, and I notice he's just wearing a towel slung low on his hips. He really is quite beautiful, and seems to feel quite at home here. "What've you got there?" he asks, looking a bit puzzled as he walks up and takes the bag from my hand.

I know the moment he realizes. First curiosity, when he peeks in the bag, followed by confusion and then he snaps his eyes to mine, filled with concern and maybe fear. "Ruby…" His voice is soft, pleading, and I can't stand it.

"Funny," I manage, my voice sounding flat even to my own ears. "Until last week I'd never even opened that closet. Pam took me to Wal-Mart to pick up some towels, which I washed and was putting away. I didn't even notice the bag there. I never knew it was there." I let my words hang, watching regret settle on his face. But I'm not done. I'm hurt to the core that while I've been forced to bare myself completely, he's been less than forthcoming with me. So I hammer my point home.

"It would appear you really do like that bed. Seems you were in it enough." My tone is vicious, matching the boiling of my blood.

"Ruby…" he tries again, but I jump up off the couch and run to the bathroom locking the door behind me. "*Fuck!*" I hear him yell before I sink to the floor and curl myself into a ball. Tears burning tracks on my cheeks.

Tim

"Fuck!"

I throw the stupid bag of toothbrushes at the wall where it bursts apart, spilling it's contents to the floor. I wasn't thinking when I marched up to the closet, where a long damn time ago, Viv had sent me to grab a spare toothbrush after our one night together. In that same bed. That'd been a mistake of epic proportions. Something we both willingly admitted to, although I never quite could give up wondering what if. Then she found Ike, and now that I've found Ruby, what happened with Viv is just a shadow behind me.

I sit down on the couch where she was just sitting and drop my head in my hands. Any time during the past months I could have told her, but each time I thought I should, I held back for fear of hurting her. I feel sick to my stomach now. She's crying behind that door. I can hear her.

Suddenly I'm propelled off the couch in a surge of panic, remembering the last time I left her behind a locked bathroom door.

Charging through the hallway, I throw my shoulder into the door, splintering the frame as the lock breaks away. *Son of a bitch!* Ignoring the burning in my shoulder, my eyes immediately spot Ruby curled up on the floor, her arm covering her head, and the sight steals my breath. Slowly she lifts her arm, that I realize was thrown up to protect herself when I barreled through the door like a raving lunatic. She turns her tear-filled eyes to me and gives me a full dose of the pain and betrayal she feels in one look. It slices me open and leaves me bleeding. I slump down on the floor beside her legs and wince as my back hits the vanity, but my burning eyes never leave hers.

I reach for her ankle, and she allows me to wrap my hand around it, sensing, more than feeling, her pulse underneath my fingers. I take a deep shaky breath in. "Only one woman has ever had the power to destroy me. To drag me through fire. Only one who can crush my heart as easily as she fills it." My voice is raw with emotion and I don't give a flying fuck. The pain in her eyes is like an acid burning through me. "Ruby," I plead. "There was never anyone who could've caused more than a blister before you. Please let me explain."

"How will you explain?" she rasps. "I trusted you with everything. In return, I find out that not only you, but at least Viv as well, have kept something pretty significant from me. I don't see how there can be any explanation for that."

My right shoulder is killing, throbbing right down to my finger tips, but I lean over and pull Ruby's limp body on my lap with a wince anyway. "Let me try," I beg, with my nose pressed in her hair. She just shrugs. Fine, I'll take it as a yes. "Viv and I have been friends for quite a few years. One night, we'd been talking a bit. She'd been telling me some of the crap her ex had put her through. We had too much to drink and what was supposed to be comfort turned into something else. One night, Ruby. And as soon as it was over, Viv made it clear it was a mistake. That it was not worth losing our friendship over."

I look down to see her studying my face. "Did you think it was a mistake?"

Fuck me. I don't want to answer, knowing it might make things more difficult, but I won't lie. I band my arms a little tighter around her. "I do in hindsight, but maybe not so much at the time." I clearly feel her body freeze up as she drops her eyes to the floor. "Look at me, baby. I need you to look at me, so I know you understand." Slowly her eyes find mine again. "I know now, what I felt for her all along was a deep friendship. For a while, I liked to imagine that it could be something else, but the reality is, I never pursued it. Probably, because on some level, I knew all along it wasn't the way I was supposed to feel for a woman I wanted to spend the rest of my life with."

"How do you know?" I can barely hear her voice when she asks.

"I know, because that woman is sitting in my lap, and I'm holding on with all my might so she can't leave me. The one I can't see myself living without for even one more day. The beautiful soul, who has taken a lifetime of avoiding commitment and obliterated it with one blink of her stunning eyes, into an overwhelming need to tie her to me permanently."

I could cry in relief when her hand comes up to stroke my face. "You love me," she says, as a statement more than a question. I cover her hand with mine and turn my head to press my lips into her palm.

"So much, at times it's painful," I confess to her honestly. "I'm so sorry. I didn't want you hurt, but in keeping quiet, I hurt you so much more."

She covers my mouth with her fingers. "Hush. It's done," she whispers, tucking her head underneath my chin.

We sit like that for I don't know how long, just slowly existing in the moment, when the sharp peal of Ruby's phone rings again. I help her up and she runs to reach it in time.

"Hello?" I hear her a little out of breath as I slowly get to my feet, taking in the mess around me.

"Nina, honey—*Cómo estás*?" Ruby sounds relieved and frankly so am I, until I hear her yell, "They did *what*??"

CHAPTER TWENTY-SEVEN

Ruby

"We'll get it sorted. You've got to calm down." Pam leans in from the backseat, with her hand on my shoulder.

Tim is driving like the hounds of hell are at his heels. I try not to pay too much attention or I'll be hyperventilating even more. I'm furious. The moment I heard Nina's terrified little voice over the phone, my instant relief was quickly replaced with anger. I relayed what she was telling me to a very concerned and, eventually, equally angry Tim. He finally just took the phone from my hand.

"Nina, sweetheart?—Yes, it's Tim. Is Mike there with you?— Okay, honey. We're coming. You hang tight, okay?—Good girl, now can you put Mike on?"

What followed next was a tremendous amount of swearing and threats, all from Tim's side. In the end, I guess Mike managed to calm him down, because when he put down my phone, he lowered his head and took in a deep breath. "Get dressed, baby. Mike's keeping her with him, and I'm calling Pam."

We're on our way to Boston after we had to wait for Mark to bring the truck, dropping him back off at his, and swinging by to pick Pam up. I didn't realize she had connections to the CPS, but Tim wasn't surprised.

I'm still seething after finding out the stupid, idiotic caseworker had placed Nina in a good, Catholic foster home, with three older teenage boys. *Three!* The excuse she made to Mike was apparently that she felt the influence of good Christian boys might help her get over her unreasonable fear of the other sex. *Unreasonable!* I'm beside myself. "I hope I never meet that woman," I say to Pam over my shoulder. "I hate violence, but her I'd gladly take apart, piece by piece."

"I hear you, honey," Pam soothes. "But I'll warn you. I don't do jails, so you're on your own there. I hear they make you take off your underwire bra. Damn, woman, they'd have to pry those off my cold, dead, girls. No way in hell are they allowed out without proper protection."

I snort as Tim bursts out laughing at Pam's well-timed injection of humor.

The rest of the ride to the FBI offices, I try to get my blood pressure back under control, while Pam makes a few phone calls in the back. Pulling into a parking spot in the underground garage, I see Rhonda walking up to the car with a large Denzel Washington lookalike, smiling from ear to ear when Pam gets out of the car behind me. I'm surprised to see her throw her arms around the man, accepting his kiss on her cheek readily. The only time I've ever seen her hug a man was Ike at their baby announcement party. Then my attention is drawn to Rhonda, who seems to be shuffling her feet, looking distinctly uncomfortable.

"Hey, Rhonda," I say, slipping down from my seat and walking up to her. "So glad to see you up and about. I was worried about you." I try to ignore the surprised look on her face when I stick out my hand. She hesitantly grabs it. "I never had a chance to thank you," I mention to her quietly.

"I…thank you," she stutters a little, appearing a little flustered before she straightens her shoulders.

"Good to see you," Tim says with a friendly nod, throwing a casual arm over my shoulders, before turning his eyes on the other couple, no longer embracing but involved in a very impassioned discussion. "Who's that?" he asks Rhonda, tilting his head in their direction.

"CPS supervisor. He showed up twenty minutes ago. Mentioned he was waiting for someone? That must be her."

"I want to see Nina," I announce, only slightly impatient.

"Sure," Rhonda says. "She's been asking for you."

-

I'm not sure what I was expecting, but it wasn't almost being tackled to the ground by the surprisingly long-limbed teenager, who I'd only seen in the hospital, when she was always lying down. Guess her little girl voice and pixie face made her seem so much shorter than she really is. Or maybe I was just projecting my own vertical challenge onto her. Tim manages to brace me from behind, so I don't actually hit the floor. I'm grateful for his strength at my back, because right now, I just want to wrap this girl up and run.

"Tim?" She lifts her eyes over my shoulder and I step away, giving them some room. Should be interesting since they never even spoke, except for when Tim confiscated the phone from me this morning.

"Yes, sweetheart," he says in his rumbly voice, which combined with the warm smile he directs at Nina is enough to melt me on the spot. She ignores his outstretched hand and puts her hands on his shoulders instead, giving his cheek a little kiss.

"*Gracias…*" she smiles shyly, "…for coming."

When Pam and her acquaintance walk up with Mike, Nina sidles up to me, grabbing on to my arm.

"Why don't we all sit down?" Mike suggests, ushering everyone into a large boardroom at the end of the hall. Nina sticks close to me, settling in to my right, and Tim claims the chair on my left. Everyone else seems to find a seat around the table except for Mike, who stays standing. "Nina, this gentleman here is Scott Paisley. He's a supervisor with Child Protective Services."

The stunning man's introduction is met with a suspicious stare from Nina as she scoots a little closer to my side, but I have to bite my lip to stifle a giggle when I hear his name. Not quite what I expected for Denzel's twin brother. I catch Pam's eye, who raises her eyebrow at me, and I have to suppress another giggle. Instead of looking at anyone, I keep my eyes on the glass of water in front of me and continue listening to Mike.

"The lady next to him is Pam Brunard, she's a friend of Ruby's and a counselor. Now give me a minute to get everyone on the same page, and then we'll sort this mess out," Mike says with a nod and a smile at Nina, who seems to be listening closely. "Want to go first, Scott?" Mike nods in his direction.

"No need, you're doing a good job," he says in return, the broad smile never far from his face.

"Fine. Here's where we stand. I called the caseworker's supervisor, Scott, when I found they'd placed Nina in a house full of hormonal teenage boys. Not only that, Nina wasn't allowed to use the phone. Her own was confiscated. Turns out, the family may have created some of their own theories about why a fourteen-year-old Mexican girl might be in need of foster parenting. Let's just say they were worried about *bad influences*. Sad, isn't it? Anyway," Mike continues as he shakes his head. "I brought her here with all her things, she didn't want to stay there any longer. I just don't know where to go from here. I have no real authority here."

"But I do," Scott pipes up. "I was surprised, when not ten minutes after hanging up with Mike, Pam called me. Long story short. If agreed on by Nina," he directs at the girl again, making sure she has veto. "I'll contact my counterpart in Portland and recommend she be placed in Pam's care in the short term."

Nina turns her face toward me and pulls at my arm. "I want to stay with you," she pleads, breaking my heart.

"I want that too, *cariño,*" I comfort her. "But I'm not an American citizen yet. Pam looked after me when I had no one else, and she helped me so much. I know she can help you too."

"Is it far from you?"

"Not at all. I go there all the time. And you can come visit me too."

I feel Tim's hand slide up my spine and gently squeeze my neck. I'm almost losing the battle with my tears. This morning has been an emotional meat grinder.

Tim

That little girl about floored me.

I was still simmering when we arrived in Boston, but the brave little thing completely wiped any lingering anger out when she stood on her tiptoes and kissed my cheek.

From that moment, my mind had been going a mile a minute. I have an idea, but given what happened earlier between Ruby and me, we have some stuff to sort out before I can even contemplate the ideas floating around in my head.

It takes less than ten minutes to sort out an acceptable solution for everyone and another fifteen for Scott to clear things with the Portland office. With some serious thanks-yous for Mike for stepping in like he did, and to Rhonda for keeping the girl calm until we got here, we start our drive back to Portland only an hour after we pulled in. Except this time, we have Nina in the back quietly talking with Pam, who is sitting next to her. Ruby has another death grip on my hand, but her eyes are looking straight out the window in front of her. I don't think anyone else can see the occasional tear run down her face as she listens to the conversation in the backseat. I give her hand a little squeeze back. "You okay, Boop?" I whisper, just loud enough for her to catch and watch as she turns her shimmering brown eyes to me.

"I will be," she replies almost soundlessly. I simply wink. There's not much I can say right now.

When we pull up to Florence House, Nina has her face almost pressed up to the window. I smile at her barely contained excitement. Ruby, on the other hand, seems to look a bit more dejected, if possible. But the moment I give her hand a little squeeze again before releasing it, her face straightens into a forced smile. While Pam and Nina make moves to get out of the car, she quickly pulls down the visor to check her face.

"Come on, baby. Let's get our girl set up." It just kind of slips out, but Ruby's head swivels my way so fast, I'm afraid she'll give herself whiplash. I shrug and smile at her a bit sheepishly.

"Okay," she agrees easily, this time with a genuine, full-wattage smile that I can't resist pressing my lips to.

"Can't wait until you get her home?" Pam sticks her head back in the door and Nina stands behind her, giggling. "Get your asses in the house," she dictates, tossing the door shut with dramatic flourish.

-

It's only two o'clock by the time we get back to Ruby's apartment. Feels like we've been gone the whole day.

The moment we spot the splintered doorpost, both of us freeze on the spot. "I'll fix that," I promise Ruby, who looks at me with her head slightly tilted to one side, as if she's trying to figure something out.

"You thought…you were worried…"

I quickly step up and close her in my arms. "Not gonna lie, Ruby. I didn't give myself any time to think, or I might've realized I was overreacting, but the moment the thought even entered my head, I panicked. I'll fix it."

"Do you think we can go to your house now?" she asks, taking me completely by surprise.

"For real? Fuck yes, Boop. Let's get you packed."

By three, we're back on the road. This time with most of Ruby's stuff in the back. She didn't have much to begin with since the place came furnished. "I'll have to let Viv know. Give my notice. I hope she won't be upset."

"We'll talk to her together. I don't think she will be upset at all."

"Okay." She throws a hesitant smile my way. "Thank you, by the way, for calling Gunnar this morning. I wasn't even thinking about my shift. I guess I could have made it after all."

"We didn't know," I reassure her. "Besides, this is better. I think maybe we need tonight to get settled in." She just nods at that, but I get the impression she understands I'm not just talking about her moving in. Something I still can't quite get my head wrapped around after this morning's revelations, but I'm not going to question it. "You okay with ordering pizza for dinner?"

"Sounds good."

Just like that her smile is wide and bright again.

-

While Ruby putters about in the kitchen, adding her stuff to mine, I quickly make some room in the dresser and walk-in closet. Good thing I just have the basics in the kitchen, a set of four of everything, same apparently as she does. Between us we can host a party. I smile at the prospect, wishing spring was here so we can maybe have our friends over. I'll have to buy a new grill. With my head going full steam ahead, I don't hear Ruby come in.

"Wow," she blurts, startling me. "Big closet for not very many clothes."

"I know," I confirm, as I move my flannels to the same side as my suits, just so she can have the entire wall to herself. "My clothes tend to last, and I mostly wore suits. I may need to get some more jeans and Henleys though. That enough room for you?" I ask her and watch as she dissolves into giggles. Now that is something I've not seen before, and I can't hold back my own chuckles at her hilarity.

"I can't even fill a quarter," she snorts, as she watches me stalk toward her, slowly backing away.

I have her trapped with both my arms braced on either side of her head against *her* wall. There's still a light-hearted twinkle in her eyes when I lean down and kiss her. "Maybe we should go shopping together," I suggest, running my nose along hers.

"You like shopping?" she sounds surprised, and I shake my head vigorously.

"Fuck, no. I hate it, but with you I might learn to enjoy it. We could help each other try on stuff." She collapses with her head on my chest, full out laughing now. Best fucking sound in the world. I just hold her shaking body against me, feeling pretty happy right now.

"You know." She lifts her head, looking at me with a mischievous glint in her eyes, still snickering softly. "Your mother might have something to say about that."

"She's not coming," I declare firmly, but she just snorts.

"I'd like to be a fly on the wall when you tell her she can't come shopping."

It's an opportunity I can't pass up, since Ruby hasn't been back since that night. She's only seen my mom once, when she dropped off some clothes for Boston, but she didn't even really meet her eyes. And she's not seen my dad at all. "Okay. Deal," I say with a cocky smirk. "Sunday dinner, two days from now, you can watch."

Her mouth falls open in disbelief. I once again see an opportunity I'm not gonna pass up. Pulling her against me with one arm around her back and the other in her hair, tilting her head just right, I launch an assault on her mouth. Her hands come up and clutch at my shirt as I walk her backwards, slowly moving her to the bed.

When the back of her knees hit the mattress, her eyes snap open. I see both surprise and heat smoldering there. A little shove and she falls back on the bed. I drop down and pin her down, my hands pulling hers up and holding them over her head.

"You make me happy." My voice is hoarse as I pepper her face with kisses. "I thought I was happy before, but I was wrong." I drop my head down and latch onto the soft skin at the base of her neck. I feel her tilt her head to the side to give me better access. When I let her skin slip from the suction of my lips with a soft plop, I'm pleased to see a red mark appear where my mouth touched her. My mark. I lift my eyes to watch Ruby's face change with understanding. "I will spend the rest of my life erasing every single mark, every single touch, every single gaze any other man has ever left on you, until all you can remember is me." Her eyes are no longer smoldering, but brimming with unshed emotions.

"*Mi vida*…I love you," she whispers, tangling her fingers in mine.

"I know," I affirm to her, my eyes closing as my mouth settles on hers, tasting the salty tang of her feelings from her lips.

CHAPTER TWENTY-EIGHT

Ruby

The house is quiet when I find my way downstairs, carrying an empty pizza box.

We were tangled up in the sheets and each other all night. Except when Tim had to open the door for the pizza, which he brought straight back upstairs. We ate, sitting naked in bed, talking about anything and everything. Some of it interesting or funny, some of it painful, but according to Tim, all of it valuable.

I smile. It was a perfect night that ended with me falling asleep, half sprawled on his chest, his usual tidy bedroom looking like a tornado hit it. I was surprised when I found myself alone in bed this morning.

I drop the box on the kitchen counter and check the clock. Nine-thirty, I have lots of time to get ready for my shift. I start the makings of a pot of coffee. Wherever Tim went, he didn't make coffee this morning, because the old grinds left in the filter are stone cold.

I'm just sipping my first drops, watching some really eager birds looking for material for a nest. It's not even spring yet. Getting closer, though. A blast of cold comes in when Tim stumbles in the front door, bags in his hands and a tray with take-out coffee.

"Damn," he says, spotting me in the kitchen. "I was hoping to surprise you in bed." He kicks off his boots and walks in, depositing his load on the counter before turning to me and ducking his cold nose in my neck.

"Eeeek, you're freezing!" I try to push him off but he won't let go. "What's all that?" I ask him when I finally give up the struggle.

"We never got around to getting any groceries, so I picked up some necessities for breakfast. Then I passed by that Standard Bakery, and I decided their necessities for breakfast looked much better, and they also have very excellent coffee." Keeping one arm around me, he proudly presents his purchases. Everything from eggs and milk, to what looks to be half the display case at Standard.

"Why are there two bags of chocolate croissants?" I ask him, my mouth full of cherry danish, still picking through the pile of bags.

"Because, my beautiful Ruby," he says, tightening his arm around my waist and leaning down to rest his chin on my shoulder. "We're expected at Viv and Ike's in half an hour."

"I don't have time, I have to get ready, and then I'm scheduled for a shift." I don't know if I'm ready to face Viv yet, but I don't say that out loud. "Can't we do it another time?"

Tim turns me around and gives me a warm look. "Too late. I already told them we need a talk to clear the air."

"You did what? Why would you do that?" Now I'm completely mortified. I drop the danish on the counter behind me and try to push Tim off. A fruitless endeavor.

"Look at me," he says in a stern voice. "Remember what I told you last night? About erasing every single…"

"Yeah, I remember," I cut him off, not in the mood to have him melt my heart again.

"Okay, well I was thinking this morning, perhaps I should first show you that you already erased any of my memories that came before. You did that the first time we kissed."

Every protest on my lips turns to dust. "Why do you have to go and say something perfect when I was just working up a good temper?" He throws his head back and starts laughing. Nothing for me to do but drop my face to his chest, feeling every shake and rumble of his body.

-

I rub my clammy hands on my jeans when we pull into Ike and Viv's driveway. Tim turns off the engine, unbuckles, and twists his body toward me, reaching out to cover my hand with his.

"It's gonna be fine, Boop. I swear. Sometimes, the best way to make sure a wound doesn't fester is to rip off the Band-Aid and let it air. It was my mistake not telling you before, but now that it's out there, let's deal with it head on." He lifts my hand and presses his lips in my palm, and then he tugs me closer, bending his head for a soft touch of his lips on mine. "You have my heart, and I promise you…you have all of my memories."

We barely get to the door and it swings open, revealing a radiant, and very pregnant, Viv. Tim's warm hand in the small of my back keeps me from running.

"So what's the occasion?" Ike smiles when he accepts the familiar Standard bag. Viv's behind him, pouring coffee. He leans in over the counter. "You know I have to hide these from her, right?" he whispers conspiratorially, as his wife sneaks up behind him and manages to snatch the bag from his hand, a big smile on her face.

"Try it, and you'll find yourself on the couch, mister!"

"Actually, we have some news," Tim volunteers and I shrink down on my stool. This is going to be so awkward. Both Ike and Viv raise their eyes questioningly. "First off, Ruby moved in with me yesterday."

"Yay!" Viv squeals, clapping her hands. "I'm *so* happy." She rushes around the counter and almost pulls me off my stool in a bone-crushing hug.

"Congrats, man." Ike pounds Tim on the shoulder.

"Of course, I'll give you proper notice. Pay out this month and next."

Viv drops her arms from around me instantly. "Are you nuts? The timing couldn't be more perfect. My brother and his husband just announced last week they're coming out from San Francisco for an extended period of time. They want to be here for the birth of this baby and are looking into setting up a second gallery here on the East Coast. I was getting anxiety attacks at the thought of them staying with us for any longer than a couple of days at a time. Don't get me wrong, I love them, but in small doses." She moves to the other side of the counter and hugs her husband from behind. "You know what this means, right, baby?" Ike covers her hands on his stomach with his own.

"What's that?" he smirks.

"We won't have to be quiet for our morning constitutional," she mumbles into his back. Somehow I think she's not talking about a rigorous walk as my eyes snap to Tim, who is suddenly finding the ceiling very fascinating. Ike just chuckles as he turns and plants a kiss on his wife that instantly raises the temperature in the kitchen.

"Good news, baby," he mumbles, the smile big on his face.

"Alright guys, enough of that," Tim chuckles. "You're making Ruby blush."

Oh, Ruby is blushing all right. I can feel myself turning beet red as I throw him a dirty look.

"While we're on the subject," he continues, stepping closer and hooking an arm around my front and pressing his body to my back. "And already uncomfortable," he adds, giving me a squeeze. "This is probably a good time to let you know Viv and my history is no longer a secret."

I close my eyes, not wanting to see the looks on their faces, but I can hear Viv.

"I see," she says softly. "Ruby, honey. Can you look at me?" After a heavy pause, I reluctantly raise my eyes to find hers tearing up. "Don't mind the tears, I'm told it's hormones." She distractedly snatches the paper towel Ike hands her and rubs at her face. "Honey, I'm glad the moron finally found the balls to tell you. It was a stumble in time, and already long forgotten, but you deserved to know."

"Okay," I reply stupidly, not sure what else there is to say. Tim moves in even closer and leans his chin on the top of my head.

"I *am* a moron, because I didn't actually tell her—she found out by accident. It wasn't pleasant for her." I'm pretty sure it wasn't pleasant for him either, since his shoulder is bruised and swollen from crashing the bathroom door, but I guess it's a good reminder for both of us that honesty is always the better choice.

"Who wants to see the nursery?" Ike breaks through the slightly painful silence that follows Tim's admission. Eager to get some air, I raise my hand.

"I would," I say. With a dramatic gesture, Ike invites me to lead the way.

"Second on the right," he says, as he follows me up the stairs. I ignore the low rumble of voices coming up from the kitchen as I push open the door Ike indicates.

"Oh." I clap my hand over my mouth, it's just so pretty. Part of me expected pink, but instead the room is done in soft sage green and dark lilac, with splashes of yellow. "It looks like spring," I tell Ike, who walks past me into the room and runs his hand over the railing of a crib in the same color as the green from the walls. The bedding is lilac and yellow, tying the entire room together.

"I'm sure Viv will like that better than Pam's description of an Easter basket," he chuckles, and I smile.

Inside my heart feels a little heavy. I never thought much about not being able to have children. It was never something I was missing, given the life I led. But standing here, looking at the love and the excited anticipation that was poured into this room, I miss it. I think Ike may have misinterpreted my silence, because he walks up to me and lifts my chin with his thumbs, a hand on either side of my neck. "There is nothing between them but friendship, Ruby. I have to admit, I didn't feel too good about it at first, but the truth is, Tim's been a good friend since school and Viv…well, Viv's everything. I love them both."

Stupid me, I burst into tears at his words. Not because of what he says, although it's beautiful, but because I realize how blessed I am to feel so cared for. I don't know if I'll ever get used to that.

Tim

"There you are!"

As per usual, Mom has her spidey sense on full blast as she comes charging out the door at the precise moment I lift Ruby down from the truck. When I feel Ruby stiffen under my hands, I turn to intercept Mom, but she easily sidesteps me and smothers Ruby, in what looks like a distinctly uncomfortable hug.

"It's so good to see you!" Mom gushes as she squeezes Ruby's face in her hands. Seeing the hint of panic in her eyes, I pull her from Mom's hands tightly against my side.

"You too, Mrs. Veldman," Ruby mumbles, earning a stern look from Mom.

"It's Jane," she snaps, but then her face softens. "Or Mom, whichever you prefer." I roll my eyes heavenward. Mom's determination knows no bounds.

"Hello to you too," I draw her attention to me, leaning in to kiss her cheek.

"Hey, honey." She smiles way too innocently for my peace of mind.

"Are we hanging out in the driveway all day?" Dad's ruddy face is sticking out the front door. "I thought you were grabbing me a beer, Jane." The last is directed at my mother and seems to immediately jar her into action. As she hurries back inside, with us following at a slower pace behind, Dad throws us a quick wink. He knows her well.

The closer we get to the door, the slower Ruby moves, not sure what to expect from Dad. But I do. It doesn't surprise me when he steps out on the porch and pulls her straight from underneath my arm into his signature bear hug. "Good to see you, doll," he rumbles, before turning Ruby to the door and basically marching her inside. Completely ignoring me.

"You made it." Mark waves his beer from the couch when I make it to the living room, where Dad's already trying to sell Ruby on some of his homemade wine. Good thing Ruby rarely touches alcohol, because that stuff would turn her off it completely. Even Dad doesn't really like it, his preference being beer, but still every Sunday he tries to pawn one of his bottles off on us. Poor Mom is stuck drinking it, since Dad has now banned all other wines from the house. Claims it's a waste of money to buy her preferred bottles of Moscato with a cellar full of perfectly good wine.

Another typical Sunday afternoon at Casa di Veldman.

Armed with a beer and relieved to see Ruby's insisted on her glass of water—much to my father's chagrin, I'm sure—I sit down beside her on the couch. Dad flips through the channels for the game and settles back in his recliner. As usual, both Mark and I pop our feet on the coffee table and settle in, but this time I do it feeling pretty damn good with my life. And that has everything to do with the slightly stiff, delicious smelling, woman butted up against me.

"Why are you all down here?" Mom wants to know, panting as she comes down the last steps. "Turn that thing off!" She flaps her hand at the offensive big screen TV. Dad's pride and joy. "We've got company," she hisses at my father, who calmly watches her come unhinged.

"We don't have company. We've got family. Just like every other damn Sunday, woman."

"But…" Mom starts to object when Dad cuts her off. I can feel Ruby squirming uncomfortably in the seat beside me. She's not used to my parents' tiffs yet, but I'm sure she will be.

"No buts." There's no mistaking the authority in my dad's voice. Something he's always been able to shut any one of us up with. "Look around the room, Jane? See anyone who doesn't belong?" Automatically Mom's eyes go from Mark, to Ruby, to me, before flicking back to Ruby and a soft smile spreads over her face as understanding dawns.

"Nope," she says, with the tiniest of winks at Ruby, before turning on her heel and huffing and muttering all the way upstairs.

Yup. Not much changes here. Except perhaps the feel of Ruby's body relaxing against mine, her head tilting to lay against my shoulder, and her hand coming around to rest on my belly. Yeah, except that.

-

Ruby falls asleep about two minutes into the Bruins' second period. When Mom comes down to see if she'll lend a hand in the kitchen, I shake my head no. I don't want to wake her up. God knows these past days, since that report on the news, it's been one drama after another. I know my Boop is emotionally drained. So I let her sleep through the entire game. She barely even flinches when Connolly gets boarded for the second time in the game, making both my brother and father loudly voice their displeasure. Something I'd normally have gladly joined in, but doesn't seem half as important as the woman snuggled up to me.

The moment the final minute ticks away on the game, Mom's head pokes down the stairs. "Dinner!" she yells, unnecessarily, since just like she somehow manages to get it ready at the perfect time each Sunday, we know that when the final whistle goes, the food's already on the table.

I let Dad and Mark go up ahead, holding Ruby behind. Mom's holler woke her up. "Shouldn't we go upstairs?" she asks, tilting her head to look at me.

"In just a minute," I mumble, my mouth already on hers. "I need my appetizer first."

-

Mom's already served us by the time we sit down at the table, and I pointedly ignore the snickers from across the table where my brother sits. Sometimes, it's like we're still in high school.

"I got you some more water, Ruby. Unless you want something else?" Mom holds up a bottle of Dad's wine.

"I'm good with water. Thank you." I squeeze her knee in relief.

"So tell us about this Nina?" Dad asks, and I flick my eyes at Mark, who must've told them because I sure as heck didn't.

The question seems to melt the last of Ruby's inhibitions, though, because before I have a chance to respond, she launches into a spirited account of our impromptu trip to Boston just this Friday. Feels like a lot more time has passed. I sit back and let her tell the story, a smile playing on my lips when I notice the more passionate she becomes, the thicker her normally almost undetectable accent becomes. Her vowels are rich and round, and her consonants seem to roll off the tip of her tongue. With the color high on her cheeks and fire in her eyes, she's more beautiful than ever. "Can you believe it?" She ends her impassioned monologue with a dramatic snort.

"When she gets settled in," Mom says, sniffling suspiciously. "You bring that girl for a proper Sunday family meal." She finishes on a sob and Ruby leans in and buries her face in my shoulder.

"We will, Mom," I promise, feeling fucking blessed.

Unfortunately, Mom is not done.

"And we'll all go shopping soon," she adds, clapping her hands.

This time, Ruby dissolves in giggles, leaving everyone around the table stunned at the unexpected outburst. I can't hold back and give in to my own bout of hilarity, which only serves to confuse them more.

-

Ruby falls asleep on the way home and barely stirs when I try to lift her out of the car. Unfortunately, the condition my shoulder is in, there is no way I can carry her all the way upstairs.

"Baby, we're home," I try, stroking the hair that's fallen in her face out of the way.

"I'm home?" she mumbles, cracking her eyes open as she battles back sleep. I help her on her feet and keep my arm firmly around her waist as she stumbles beside me to the front door. I have to lean her against the wall, while I dig around my coat pockets for the keys. Ruby spreads her arms, palms flat against the siding, rubbing them up and down. "I like our home."

"I do too, baby. I do too," I say, as I finally manage to get her through the door.

Once upstairs, Ruby flops on her belly on the bed and is almost instantly asleep, leaving me to rid her of her clothes. I stand back to look at her face, soft with sleep, and regret having to pull the covers up over her glorious ample ass, the slight dip of her waist and the swell of her full breast peeking out on the side. She fits me perfectly.

CHAPTER TWENTY-NINE

Ruby

"You'll love them, *cariño*" I look over my shoulder, where Nina is huddled nervously in the backseat.

These past three weeks have brought us to spring, and Tim's parents are throwing the first BBQ of the season. Still just a Sunday family dinner, Jane assured me on the phone, but this time with hamburgers and hot dogs. The invitation to bring Nina along had been a repeat of a standing invitation since she asked the first time. The difference this time, I'd had a chance to spend some time with Nina. Some with Pam, when she felt my presence would be helpful, and some time just for the two of us. Getting to know each other better, hanging out for lunch at The Skipper a few times, and talking about school. Nina was understandably hesitant to start school here, so for now Pam is home-schooling her, with the approval of CPS. Assessing her knowledge level and preparing her for the standard curriculum. I'm glad for her. Glad she'll have the chance to make something of herself. I want to make sure she doesn't waste it.

The last few times, I brought Tim into the mix, who hadn't seen Nina since we dropped her off at Florence House. Careful to keep his distance at first, he'd had no problem making her feel safe, just as he'd done with me. We'd just seen her yesterday morning when we took her out for breakfast. Jane's call had come in the night before, and after a quick chat with Pam, we're hoping that we might be able to convince Nina to come.

I think we were both a bit shocked when, after Tim regaled her with some childhood stories, and I described how easily I'd been accepted, she seemed to readily accept the invitation. That was yesterday. Today she is nervously biting her nails in the backseat, her leg bobbing up and down so much, I can feel it in the front.

"How do you know?" she asks, her English getting more secure with every passing day.

"Because you're family," Tim says simply, conveying the same message his father had to me only a few Sunday dinners ago. I reach out and grab his hand, which he folds around mine instantly. A quick peek in the rear-view mirror shows Nina following every move.

I lean back in my seat, my own nervous energy slowly disappearing.

This time, we don't even have a chance to pull in the driveway before the door flies open, and Tim's mother, her long tunic fluttering behind her, comes barreling down the steps. Tim chuckles in the front seat and lifts his eyes to look at Nina in the rear-view mirror. "I warned you about my mom, right?" I turn just in time to see her nod with more than just a hint of trepidation. I don't blame her. I don't think I've quite gotten used to Jane's exuberance myself. "She's just…excitable," Tim says with a smirk in my direction, before he gets out of the car. I can't help but snicker when he tries to intercept his mother, who is going for the back door.

"Come on, Nina girl," I smile over my shoulder. "Let's give Tim a break. I'll distract her and you slip out behind me." Nina looks out the window and giggles at Jane's apparent struggles against Tim's hold. The sound is music to my ears. I'm still smiling ear to ear when I get out and slip between Tim and Jane, surprising her by throwing my arms around her, knowing full well she wouldn't be able to resist. "Be gentle with my Nina," I whisper in her ear. She slowly pulls back and looks at me warmly. "Of course, honey. I love her already."

The sound of a door slamming shut behind me has us turn around, where Nina is half hidden behind Tim, clutching his hand in both of hers. "Hi, sweetheart," Jane says softly, her voice sounding a bit shaky. "I'm so glad you could come. I don't know what you like yet, so I made Chiles Renellos on top of the regular BBQ stuff. My boy tells me it's Ruby's favorite, but I've never made it before." She turns and starts walking toward the house, casually throwing over her shoulder, "Maybe you can taste it, tell me if I did it right."

"Okay." It's soft, but I hear it. So does Jane, whose stride hitches but doesn't stop.

Tim doesn't let go of her hand all the way to the house, and I follow behind, working hard to get my tears in check.

-

"Not spicy enough?" Jane looks at Nina wide-eyed. "Girl, are you sure? I think I have blisters on my teeth!"

Nina, who finally let go of Tim's hand when his mother came downstairs at the Red Sox's seventh inning stretch and asked if Nina would help, is giggling at Jane's antics. Arthur has been very quiet, observing Nina when she wasn't aware he was looking and only casually asking her once if she wanted more juice. She softly replied, and since then, has kept her eye on him too. For Mark, she'd even smiled a little when he and Tim did their usual sibling bickering.

We're sitting outside on the deck with sweaters and jackets because it's still a bit chilly. Dinner was delicious and I'm feeling nice and toasty cuddled up with Tim on a chaise, my back against his front. It's becoming a favorite position. For Tim, because he can keep me close and still be part of the conversation around him, and for me, because I feel completely blanketed in Tim. I love him so much, even though it's still a bit scary to say it out loud. It's not just Tim, I'm falling in love with his family too.

"What do you call a grandmother in Spanish?" Jane asks Nina, as the rest of the family does their signature eye-roll, probably able to guess what is coming.

"*Abuela,*" Nina says. "And for grandfather, *Abuelo.*"

"Hmmm." Jane is obviously not impressed as she scrunches up her nose. "I was hoping something a bit more…fun-sounding."

"My grandparents died when I was really young, but I remember I called my grandmother *Yaya,*" I suggest.

"That I like," Jane smiles at me. "What about your grandfather?"

"*Tito. Yaya* and *Tito.*"

"Perfect." She turns to Nina and smiles at her broadly. "Then if you want, you can call me Yaya." Nina looks at me quickly before turning back to Jane and nodding. Encouraged, Jane takes it a step further. "And you can call the grumpy old man here, Tito," she adds with a wink, knowing full well it would have Arthur up in arms.

"No one is calling me Tito, woman." I laugh when he almost spits out the name like something distasteful. And what follows I could've predicted; a long drawn out bicker fest between Tim's parents that had us all in stitches. Even Nina.

But Arthur has the last word—and it's a good one.

"You call me anything, girl, you call me Pops. You hear me?"

It earns him his first beautiful smile from Nina.

Tim

My parents are exasperating. They are also the most loving people I know, despite their unique morals and quirky ways.

I honestly didn't think, with only a few family dinners, they'd have Nina talking a mile a minute about logo design with Dad or making plans with Mom for a shopping expedition.

Nina has been in Portland for a little over six weeks and seems to be adjusting well. Exactly as long as Ruby has been living with me, and other than a few flare ups of either one of our tempers, we seem to be adjusting well too. I still spend some nights lying awake, trying to find ways to give back to Ruby what was taken from her, despite her repeat assurances that I've given her more than she ever dared hope for.

Nina and Ruby have been chattering all the way to Mom and Dad's, giving me time to disappear inside my head. These past few months, Vintage Veldman is starting to make a bit of name. Ironically, it's not so much my designs, although I've been keeping busy with what is coming in, but rather Dad's coasters and cutting boards that have been drawing major attention. It helps that The Skipper, a very popular hangout for the locals in Portland, now sports custom-made coasters, branded with the signature ship's wheel. Dino had tried out and approved Dad's cutting boards and had some connections in the restaurant business he was able to get interested as well. A website has gone up, courtesy of my brother, who proves to be quite handy on the computer and new online sales are coming in daily.

Friday, the first big order came in from a small, regional chain of seafood restaurants, wanting custom-made serving boards for their surf and turf presentation. They approved one of my designs and immediately ordered three hundred to start. With all three of us working, we can have that order done and ready to ship in a little over a week. It may take us through the last of our current stock of barn board, but with the profit we'd pull in, we'll be able to order more.

Of course, Mom has the door open already, before I can turn the key on the engine, and my girls are already climbing out of the truck. I shake my head as I lock up and calmly follow behind the chattering trio into the house. What awaits me inside stops me in my tracks though. Memories of childhood birthdays come to mind, when I look around the amount of garland and balloons making the living room virtually impassable. Somewhere in there I hear the sliding door open and my father complain. "Christ's sake, woman. Told you not to go overboard. How the hell did you manage this in the time I've been dicking around the workshop?"

"Language, Arthur," Mom scolds, and somewhere behind the wall of balloons I hear the distinct giggles of Nina and Ruby.

"Holy shit!" That would be Mark, walking in behind me.

"Mark! Watch your mouth."

The ridiculous situation, along with the increasing giggles from what I guess is the kitchen, is starting to work on me. What starts as a silent chuckle quickly works its way up to a belly deep laugh that has tears running from my eyes. Mark is no better, hanging on to my shoulder to stay upright.

"Jesus Murphy!" my father bellows, and next is the sound of loud popping as I guess Dad has found a solution.

"You're spoiling my surprise!" Mom squeals, quickly adding; "And stop swearing!"

"Jesus Murphy is not swearing," Dad counters, not doing anything to diminish the general hilarity in the room. With the incessant popping and the remainder of the balloons floating up to the ceiling, I finally get a bead on everyone's whereabouts. Mom is hovering over the dining table, where a large cake takes center stage. She's using her body to protect it from the bits of rubber Dad's ministrations fling around. Ruby and Nina are indeed in the kitchen, hanging over the counter with tears running down their faces.

"Mom, how in God's name did you manage to do all this?" I ask, gesturing around the room. She tries to look hurt, but I can see even the corners of her mouth twitching.

"I may have a tank of helium in the laundry room," she admits with a grin. "I wanted to celebrate your first big corporate order. I even baked you guys a cake."

I manage to walk up to Ruby and pull her, still laughing, in my arms. "My family is crazy," I tell her, attempting to keep a straight face. "Bat-shit crazy," I emphasize. "Are you sure you still want to be part of it?" Her eyes twinkle with humor as Nina continues to chuckle as she helps Dad try and clean up the mess.

"Absolutely," she says, a smile on her face so wide, I'm afraid she'll hurt herself.

I guess this is as good an opening as ever.

I've been working on something that is taking much longer than I'd hoped. There were some things that just needed more time to dig up. It also required the cooperation of quite a few people. That part wasn't hard. Everyone I talked to, so far, was immediately on board. But the most important people I've had to wait to ask, until all information was in.

Well, yesterday I received the final piece I needed and was able to get the very tearful and very enthusiastic endorsement of my plan. Today, come hell or high water, I was planning to ask the final and ultimate decision maker.

"Nina?" I motion the one co-conspirator, other than my brother, present here to come closer. She nods in understanding and easily slips under my free arm. Ruby seems confused, looking from one to the other and when Mom tries to speak up,

Mark sneaks up and covers her mouth, silencing her. He knows what's coming too. Dad doesn't need any explanation, he probably guessed what I've been up to.

"What's going on?" Ruby asks nervously, looking around before her eyes finally find mine again.

"Abril Rubí Soto—I did my best to ignore you for months, something I'll regret for the remainder of my days, but there was something about you that spoke to me from the first time I saw you." Behind me, I hear Mom gasp behind Mark's hand and slowly understanding dawns for Ruby, who claps her hands over her mouth. "I love you with everything I am. I could stand here and say a whole lot more about the why, but I think I'd rather spend the rest of my life proving it to you." I let go of Nina, who hands me the ring, and go down on my knees. I almost lose my composure when I discover I'm still pretty close to eye level. It's a bit of a struggle to peel her hand away from her face, but she finally relents. "My family is here, because they already are your family as well. With or without this ring." I hold up the simple one-carat engagement ring Nina helped me pick out. She managed to convince me less would be more for Ruby. "They say the only way to escape hell is to go through it. You've done that…and Nina's done that. Which proves something else: the strongest bonds are forged by fire. You have my heart, Ruby, and I'd gladly walk through the fires of hell, if it meant I could walk with you. Will you let me walk with you?" She shakes as I slide the ring on her finger. "*¿Te casarias conmigo?*"

I know I probably butchered that, but you wouldn't be able to tell from the brightest smile she is hiding behind her hand. "*Si. Yes, mi vida…*" She can't say more, because my mouth is already covering hers.

"This calls for champagne!" I guess Mark's let go of Mom, but there's something we still have to cover. Reluctantly, I let

Ruby's lips go and turn to give Nina a wink. "Mom, hang on a sec." I stop the loud banging of kitchen cabinets.

"Guess no baseball this afternoon," Dad grumbles behind us.

"You've got the floor, Nina-girl." I nod at her ignoring the rumblings around us. Ruby's attention is intently focused on the girl.

"Will you be my family?" Nina asks, handing her a piece of paper, but Ruby barely notices.

"*Cariño*—we already are," she replies, not once taking her eyes off the girl.

"Please—read it." Nina gestures to the paper.

The three of us, sitting on the kitchen floor, it's as if time stands still in this moment.

Until Mom pipes up behind us. "What is it?"

"Hush, Jane," Dad, who probably guessed, admonishes her.

"Don't you shush me, Arthur."

"I don't understand." I almost miss Ruby's low whisper, but Nina is already leaning in. "Tim wants to make me part of your family…for real." Ruby's eyes come to me.

"I've put in a request for us to become Nina's official foster parents, which I discovered *is* possible because I am a U.S. citizen and we live together. What you are holding is the letter confirming that as off the first day of summer vacation, Nina can come live with us. That's only a few weeks away, baby."

"For real?" I thought her smile would be painful before, but it's even bigger now.

"You bet," I assure her. "And after six months, provided we're married by then and the visits from CPS have gone well, we can apply to adopt Nina legally."

Both girls throw themselves at me, knocking me clear on my back, but I don't give a fuck. I'm holding my life in my arms.

CHAPTER THIRTY

Ruby

"Oh my God! That boy doesn't waste any time, does he?"

It takes Viv approximately two seconds to clock the ring on my finger.

"You're one to talk." Dino walks up behind Viv and has a look over her shoulder. "You go to the West Coast to testify at a trial and end up getting married in Vegas. You hadn't known Ike for much longer, from what I recall," he says with a wink to me. I'd heard the story in bits and pieces over time.

"Oh hush," Viv says, rolling her eyes. "Old news, Dino." The big man walks off chuckling, having made his point. Not in the least offended, Viv gives me a big smile and hug, and over a cup of tea has me recount how that ring got on my finger.

Dino's rather abrupt, "We doing any work here today?" from behind me, alerts me to the time. I scramble into the pantry to get out the veggies, but by the time I get back, Viv's gone. With Dino obviously not in a mood to talk, I start chopping and my mind wanders.

For the first time since I started at The Skipper, I'm not looking forward to my shift.

Sunday blew me away. What was supposed to be a celebration for Vintage Veldman, turned into a celebration of a different kind altogether. I had to keep looking at my finger, and then to Nina, who was never far from my side, to check if it was all real. Then yesterday, Tim and I spent the day planning what to do for Nina's room. He's the one who suggested the rec room in the basement, only partially finished, but with a full bath right next to it. Considering Nina will be fifteen in a month and a half, I had to admit it was probably the best solution. It wasn't just having her own bathroom that was the decision making factor here. Tim took great care to demonstrate how easily sound carries from the master to the spare bedroom. Repeatedly. Plus, he showed me some very creative uses for the mirror and vanity that he wouldn't feel right utilizing if we were to share the bathroom with Nina.

I'm a reasonable person. It only took me two orgasms to come to the same conclusion.

This morning, I was treated to a Standard Bakery breakfast—delivered in bed this time. I didn't want to come out. I just wanted to stay in bed with Tim, scanning through some options for the bedroom layout on his laptop and generally lazing about like we'd done most of yesterday.

Tim had to go to work, though, this big order needed taking care of and he'd already taken Monday off. As it is, it looks like his plans for the basement are going to be difficult considering the timeline for that order runs about parallel. But this morning, he'd wanted to make sure we both had a good start to the day, which he certainly took care of, in more ways than one.

"Diced, girl. Not minced," Dino's voice pulls me from my daydream, and I see that I have very much minced the onions. With a deep sigh, I scrape them into a container to be used for something else, and fetch a few more onions from the walk-in cooling.

Peeling the first onion, I throw a look at Dino, who's putting a rub on some steaks. His shoulders look slumped, like he's trying to disappear into himself. "How are you really doing?" I say in a soft voice, but loud enough for him to hear. At first, my only response is a deep sigh and thinking I'm being shut out, I turn back to the onion on the cutting board.

My mind is already wandering again by the time he starts talking. "She walked out," he says, surprising me with the broken rasp of his voice. I struggle not to react, feeling instinctively that if I do; he'll shut back down. So I dice my onion, patiently waiting for him to say something more. I don't have to wait long. "Things weren't right for a long time. Fuck, maybe they never were. Somewhere along the line, she got hooked on meds. Didn't matter what I said, or how often I forced her to agree to detox, the moment she was home and I left for work, she was back at it again." He takes a break and I chance a quick look. His head is tilted to the ceiling and he's swallowing hard, so I quickly turn back to my cutting board. "We had an envelope with cash for the kids' Christmas presents in our dresser drawer. She blamed Jonas, and for three fucking weeks I gave that kid hell." His voice is steadily growing louder. "Then I discover she'd been lying. She'd taken it herself, bought drugs, and blamed her own fucking son for it!" I drop the knife on the board, startled by his sudden volume. When I turn to him, he's leaning heavily on the counter, his head hanging low. But the moment I start moving in his direction, his hand comes up, warding me off. "Don't."

"Okay," I agree, sounding much more flippant than I feel. I turn back to the cutting board and tackle the next onion, trying hard to ignore the footsteps that eventually come my way.

"You know what the final straw was?" he asks from right behind me. It doesn't really require an answer. "She said it had been the only way to survive her nightmare of a life." His laugh is low and lacking any humor. "I'm surrounded by women, who crawl on hands and knees through hell and still come out fighting for another go, and she thinks her life is a nightmare? She gave up before she even started, Ruby. Had a guy who would do everything for her, two amazing kids, a decent life. You didn't even know a life like hers could exist, but you fought for it anyway. So did Syd, and Viv. Not Jeannie. She never had it in her. And I was too stupid to see."

I finally turn around and simply wrap my arms around his big body. It takes a minute, but then his big arms close around me.

"Everything okay?" Gunnar's voice sounds from the doorway. I drop my arms immediately but Dino takes his time letting go.

"S'all good," Dino mutters, going back to his steaks without even looking at Gunnar.

I put on my best smile, and look a concerned Gunnar straight in the eyes. "Everything's fine," I assure him, and I watch him grant Dino one more look before he gives me one back.

"I hear congratulations are in order," he says, as he walks over and gives me a hug. "Tim is a lucky man."

All I can do is nod my thanks as he gives me a little pat on my shoulder before leaving the kitchen.

By the time Tim comes to pick me up, I'm dead on my feet and therefore emotional. Today turned out much better than I thought. I'm sad Dino is hurting, but I know he deserves much better than what he's endured. I'm grateful I was able to be a friend to him, like he's been to me so many times now.

"Want to have a drink or go straight home?" he asks.

"Home," I echo him, still getting a little thrill each time I use that word.

Tim

When I get to the warehouse, Dad and Mark are already hard at it. A decent stack of the special design trays are stacked on a trolley. Mark actually surprised me in the last few weeks. For a guy who never showed much interest in woodworking, not like Dad or me, he seems to know what he's doing with the new planer. All the trays are perfectly smooth and level, ready for the custom brand.

"Good work," I compliment him before turning to Dad. "How many did you get done?"

"Seventy five yesterday and almost fifty today," he says, a big grin on his face. The old man is having fun, but I don't want him to overdo it.

"Awesome. And it's just three o'clock now. Why don't you head home, Dad? I'm staying until I have to pick Ruby up from work. If I can keep at the rate you guys are pumping them out, we can probably get an even hundred done." I mentally calculate how long the whole process will take and realize it might give me just enough time to get that special project I have in mind for Nina done.

"Let me finish up the full fifty, Son, and I'll go see what your mother's been up to all day without me keeping her in check," he says with a twinkle in his eye.

Mark snorts. "You sure it's not the other way around?" he teases Dad, who looks at him with squinted eyes.

"Guess you already forgot that heavy-assed tank you returned to the rental place yesterday, didn᾿t you? Fucking helium balloons. Half the time I don't know what that woman's thinking," he mutters, making it sound like doesn't enjoy my mother's brand of crazy, when we all know he'd be bored without her. My guess is that's why their marriage survived. They would miss the bickering and the crazy antics; it keeps life interesting.

Dad leaves as agreed when he's fulfilled his self-imposed quota, but Mark stays and we work well together in silence for a few hours. I'm surprised to find it's already seven.

"Are you not hungry?" I ask him. He's been here all day. "You should head out, get some rest. Between yesterday and today, we've got well over half done."

"Nah. Nothing waiting but an empty house. I'll stick it out here, but call for pizza," he answers with a wink before bending back to his work. I hear a wistfulness in his voice I'm not used to. Not like my cocky brother.

I order us some pizzas and grab a pencil and my sketchpad, while Mark finishes running the last of the trays through the big machine. I'm so engrossed in my design, I don't notice he's done until the cavernous space is suddenly plunged in silence. Mark hurries to the door, where a disgruntled pizza delivery kid appears to have been banging on the door for a while. Shit. Mark grabs the boxes and the bag of drinks and I quickly pay the boy, and give him a tip for his trouble. Need to get a loud bell or something installed. I leave the door open. It's not too cool out, and a light breeze blows in the smells and sounds from the bay. Mark hoists himself up on a stack of lumber and I follow suit, grabbing one of the boxes on my lap.

"Hope you tipped him well. You should know there's little more important to keep a good relationship with the pizza delivery boy," Mark jokes, but it tells me a bit about where his head's at.

"Course I did. Was single for forty-three years, remember?"

"Yeah." Suddenly he gives my shoulder a shove and smiles. "Mom went nuts, didn't she?" he chuckles.

"With the balloons? You're not kidding. Ninety-five fucking balloons," I shake my head.

"That too, but I mean when she finally clued in that she'd not only gained a daughter but a granddaughter too. Thought for sure she was gonna break that poor girl's bones."

I smile thinking about Nina's face while Mom was assaulting her. Poor girl had been shocked as shit at first, but ended up patting Mom on the back a bit awkwardly, in an attempt to get her to stop wailing. She can't have had much physical love, growing up in an orphanage. Something Ruby already started making up for. I'm being a bit more cautious, for obvious reasons, letting it all come from her.

"Are you ever scared?" Mark, who's been eating quietly beside me suddenly asks. This time I instinctively know what he's asking.

"Often," I answer honestly. "I'll lie awake at night, listening to Ruby breathing, and I realize how fucking much I have to lose now. It's terrifying. But then she shifts against me, and I realize she has even more to lose. Yet there she is, deep asleep and at peace as long as she has me to hang on to."

"I thought I had that once," he says. "But I can see now it wasn't even in the ballpark. I don't know, man," he says, biting off half a slice of pizza, but chewing doesn't seem to interfere with talking. "Been keeping myself pretty unavailable, but recently I've been wondering…"

"Scary as shit, and not always easy, but worth every fucking second." I pause for a minute before I ask. "Who's she?" His head swings around.

"What?"

"Don't bullshit a bullshitter." I smile when he rolls his eyes.

"Claudia. Talked to her a few times, she's nice," he says, shrugging his shoulders.

"The doc? Yeah. She's nice. I've got a great recipe for Chiles Renellos you can impress her with," I tease him, as I jump down and wipe my hands on my jeans and down the last of my drink. "Don't try and find the safest way first—just jump." He watches me for a second before he nods. "Alright, enough of this fucking girl talk. Let me show you something I want to work on for a few hours." I grab the sketchpad and show him the design.

"Home," she says with a little smile on her pretty mouth. No way I can ignore the invitation, so I lower my head and kiss those lips, sliding my tongue between them for a taste.

"Say goodbye, then," I prompt her, pulling back a little before giving her another hard, closemouthed kiss.

We're home fifteen minutes later. Ruby goes straight for the kitchen to grab us drinks, and I flick on a few lights, making myself comfortable on the couch, feet up on the coffee table. I watch her walk in, a bottle of water and a beer in her hands. I lift my arm in invitation and she settles herself beside me on the couch, handing me my drink before she pulls my arm around her and snuggles in.

"Dino's wife left," she quietly says. "I knew something was off and he finally told me. He's so sad. I don't think he's told anybody yet, although everyone knows something is up with him."

I feel for the big guy. I'd only met his wife a few times, and she seemed unnaturally quiet. Not at all what I would've expected for him. Nothing I can say, so I squeeze Ruby's shoulder. "Mark is lonely," I confide to her. "Did you know he was married before? Long time ago—he was still young—but it left a mark."

"That's sad too," Ruby muses.

"Yeah. He asked me tonight if I was scared." Ruby tilts her head back to find my eyes on her.

"What did you tell him?" She seems to understand the question instinctively as well.

"The truth," I explain to her with a smile. "I'm terrified. Afraid to lose this." I emphasize my words with a kiss on the tip of her nose. "But with you in my arms, I'm more afraid of not having it at all." Ruby tilts her head up to press a kiss to my lips.

"Me too," she admits, snuggling back into my shoulder. "It's a bit of a rude awakening to discover the world keeps on turning around us. Things happen we have no control over and leave a mark, but if at the end of the day, I can come home to you, I can handle whatever comes my way."

"Ditto," I mutter with my face pressed in her hair.

Ruby

"Are you ready?"

Tim sticks his head around the bedroom door. Today we can go pick up Nina at the shelter, and I want to make sure her room is perfect. Oh, she's come shopping—there wasn't a chance in hell Jane would not drag her new *granddaughter* with her—but she's not seen it all put together. That's something Tim and I wanted to do ourselves. Jane was not pleased, but Tim put his foot down and told her she was welcome to organize any shopping with me, but the first one to see the room finished would be Nina.

It's been two weeks since Tim gave me something I'd never really had a chance to miss. A little family of my own—forged by fire. Sure, I know it won't be smooth riding from here on in, and not just because Nina has a lot of work left to do. I do too. There are days where I'm so overwhelmed with everything that's going on in my life, I become paralyzed with fear something bad will happen to take it all away. All normal according to Pam, who had me sit in on a few sessions with Viv's anxiety group.

We've been busy. Finding time between my shifts at The Skipper and Tim's business to work on Nina's room had been a challenge. We managed though, with a bit of help from Mark, finishing the drywall and putting a proper floor down and door in. It had been my first time painting, and I found to my surprise, I have a knack for it. I already warned Tim that once Nina moved in, I might tackle our bedroom. Tim just chuckled and told me to have at it.

I take one last look around the bright, sunflower yellow room, Nina's favorite color. The crowning touch is the beautiful last minute addition Tim brought home last night. The one he spent until two in the morning putting together. I close the door and grab the hand he holds out to me.

Tim

"I'm gonna miss you."

Pam folds Nina in a hug, the slight girl disappearing in the statuesque woman's arms. I swear I see a glint of tears in her eyes, but when Pam notices me watching, she throws me a dirty look. She's a ball-buster, but with the way she cares for my girls, damn if I haven't grown to love that woman too.

"I'll miss you too, baby." Pam softly strokes Nina's curls from her face. "But we'll hang out once a week as promised, and you can always call me. Day or night."

"I know." Nina snuggles into Pam one last time before letting go.

"Ready, Nina-girl?" I ask her, holding the door open. Ruby's already in the truck, fighting a losing battle with the tears that have been brimming in her eyes from the moment we started loading up Nina's sparse belongings.

"Ready." The smile she sends me, full of hopeful trust, knocks the air from my lungs. *Fuck me*. Two women now who can bring me to my knees.

Nina climbs up in the truck, and as I close the door behind her, I notice Ruby and Pam sharing a long look through the passenger side window. Pam is the first to turn away. Instead of getting in the truck and driving off with just a wave, I walk straight up to her and pull her into a hug. She holds her body rigid at first but slowly relaxes.

"Thank you," I whisper for her ears only. "For loving my girls back on their feet and trusting them to me." Her shoulders shake a few times under my arms before she pushes back, furiously wiping at the stray tears running down her face.

"Pain in my luscious black behind, you are," she snaps, only serving to make me grin. "Better forget you ever saw a tear on me, you hear? Or I'll make you sorry," she threatens, her finger poking my chest. "I've got ways." I'm full out laughing now. For all her bluster, Pam is one of the most soft-hearted women I know. Ignoring her sputtering, I hook an arm around her neck and kiss her cheek with a loud smack.

"Love ya, Pam," I voice to her with a wink before letting her go. I'm halfway around the truck when I hear her call my name.

"Take care o'my girls."

"With my life, Pam," I call back without turning. "With my life," I repeat softly.

-

"Keep your eyes closed, *cariño*, okay?" Ruby's buzzing with excitement, and fuck if I'm not a bit jittery myself.

It had taken my father to put his foot down to prevent Mom from turning this into an all out family event, bringing Nina home. She'd been planning another one of her surprise parties, but Ruby and I decided we want one day of just the three of us to get settled before we let Mom loose with a full on celebration. Dad's suggestion of having Sunday family dinner at our house for a change went a long way to smooth her ruffled feathers. "As long as I'm cooking," she snapped. No one dared argue that and we'd left her free reign in the planning of Nina's welcome home party, which resulted in her inviting a lot of our friends. "The more the merrier," she claimed. It was all good by me, as long as we had one day to ourselves.

Nina is descending the stairs behind me, keeping her hands on my shoulders because Ruby doesn't want her to look until she's actually *in* the room. I don't even try to understand the difference, I just go with it. When we reach the bottom of the stairs, Ruby scoots around to open the door and I lead Nina right in.

"Stop here, but don't open them yet." Ruby leads Nina to exactly where she wants her before rushing back to where I'm waiting by the door. Her eyes are shining and I can't resist pressing a quick kiss to her smiling lips. With my arm draped over her shoulder and hers tight around my waist, she tells Nina; "You can open your eyes, Nina."

For a minute, she just stands there, not moving, not speaking, not making a sound, and it's making me nervous. Ruby put her right at the foot end of the large, rustic-looking canopy bed I built my girl, so it would be the first thing she sees.

"Oh my God!" With an ear piercing, very girly scream, Nina flings herself forward, landing in the middle of the mattress. The breath I discover I'm holding, explodes from my lungs as I watch her roll around the bed, giggling and crying. As is Ruby, who can't quite contain herself anymore and rushes toward the bed, tugging me along behind her. Nina is looking at us, just beaming.

"Hop on," she says, making room and patting the mattress. Ruby gives me a little shove to go first and I crawl up beside Nina, who doesn't hesitate even for a second to snuggle up against me. When my Boop scoots close on my other side, my heart feels close to bursting from my chest.

"Did you make this?" Nina asks, her head on my shoulder.

"I did," I confirm.

"It's perfect," she says, snuggling her head under my chin. "It's my dream come true."

I press a kiss on her curls before turning to Ruby, who looks like she's as close to bursting as I am. "No, baby," I say to Nina, but never losing eye contact with my Boop. "This here? This is my dream come true."

EPILOGUE

Ruby

"*Mami*! We need you for the pictures."

I shrug an apology to Pam, who was in the middle of a sentence, and turn to look for the source of my summons. My eyes scan the crowd, a collection of friends and family, who've been here for every major and even minor event since my life started for real. Barbecues, birthdays, holidays, and my simple—but beautifully perfect—wedding day in this same backyard only three years ago. Gunnar and Syd are sitting in the grass, watching their youngest, Caden, playing ball with Dexter, while their daughter Emmy is distracted by her phone. Viv is trying to wipe the chocolate from three-year old Francessca's cheeks, while the little girl struggles in Ike's arms. Dino, leaning against the railing of the deck, his arm around his daughter and is smiling in our direction—a much happier man these days. Jane and Arthur, the parents I never knew I so desperately needed in my life, are bickering as usual. Beside them; a very happy Mark, his arm possessively around Claudia, both are laughing out loud at his parents' antics. Finally, in the shade of the old tree beside the garage, I spot Tim smiling behind our beautiful daughter.

I raise my hand in acknowledgement and excuse myself to Pam before making my way over.

"Mike says we should both grab our certificates," Nina says when I'm within earshot.

Mike Carmello had also become a dear friend to all three of us. In the months following the discovery of Nina in that warehouse, he'd been in touch on a regular basis to check up on both of us. The first time, he asked for my help with a young girl again, Tim wasn't too happy. He didn't want me drawn back into that part of my life. But I was able to convince him that I really wanted to give some meaning to the thirty years I'd lost. Making sure others like me would get the same opportunities that I was given, without judgment. There have been a few more occasions where Mike has asked me to help. Although gut-wrenching at times, I never failed to walk away feeling a tremendous amount of satisfaction.

I'd like to think that may have been in part what made Nina decide to follow in Pam's footsteps, and study psychology, in hopes of becoming a social worker or a therapist.

I smile at my beautiful, headstrong girl. "Okay, *cariño*. You know where they are—run in and get them," I reply, watching her skip across the grass and dart inside before I turn my eyes to my smiling husband. "Where did Mike go?"

"Went to grab his camera from the car. Apparently he came prepared." I lean my ear against Tim's chest, loving the way I can feel the vibration of his words.

"Thank you," I say, as I slip my arms around his middle.

"For what, baby?"

I watch the sliding doors open back up and Nina step out, waving both the Certificate of Citizenship I received in the mail just two weeks ago, as well as her own brand-new, high school diploma. I tilt my head back and look my beautiful husband in his warm blue eyes.

"For filling my life so that all that remains are memories I built with you."

341

THE END

NOTE FROM THE AUTHOR:

My Portland, ME, novels all have something in common aside from the location. They tell the stories of women who have dealt with trauma, tragedy and devastation in their lives, but who manage to fight their way through to a better, brighter future.

THROUGH FIRE is such a story. Like the other two novels before, THROUGH FIRE is loosely based on a real life story of a young, Mexican woman I once read about in a newspaper article. A story that haunted me because I could not begin to imagine what this woman had gone through. But more than that I was at a loss as to how one would overcome such incredible events? This woman was lucky in that she managed to find a way out, but countless more like her may never have had an opportunity to break free.

Human trafficking is not a thing of the past. It happens today, where predominantly children and women are taken from their perceived safety and traded like nothing more than cattle. Without identity, without power and without dignity, they are bought and sold for the singular purpose of serving someone else's needs and wants. A sickening concept for most of us, but a brutal reality for those unfortunates.

I believe in hope.

I don't know if I have been able to adequately portray the emotional (and physical) trauma a woman like my Ruby has endured, but I hope I have at least shown the amazing fortitude and adaptability of women in the face of adversity of any kind.

Thank you all, for reading THROUGH FIRE. My heart is in this book and if it touched you only a fraction of how it has touched me writing it, I have done my job.

ACKNOWLEDGEMENTS:

As always I have a list of people to thank.

First and foremost a massive thank you to my readers. You are the inspiration that drives me to write—to write better. I am still in awe of the support I have and continue to receive for my books. You have no idea how much it means to me—how much it has done to build my confidence, both in writing as well as life in general. I may not be a big name, but you make me feel like a winner each and every day.

Of course the amazing Barks & Bites group that is always ready to support, guide and lift me up. These women are a constant source of strength and inspiration and have my love and appreciation for all they mean to me.

My wonderful beta-readers who are always ready at a moment's notice to pick apart my often disjointed scribbles and help me create a better, more coherent story. You amaze me with your enthusiasm, sharp eyes and generosity. I love you all.

To my editor, Karen Hrdlicka, who has become a close friend and respected guide in my literary endeavors. Thank you, my friend, with all my heart. You are an absolute rock in my existence and I keep hoping your confidence and wisdom rubs off on me. I love you lots.

Francessca Webster, my absolutely fantastic assistant who keeps my brain organized. I don't know what I'd do without you. You are my touchstone…. Xox

I also want to thank my agent, Stephanie DeLamater Phillips, who works hard behind the scenes, always looking for creative ways to bring my books to a bigger audience. I adore you, you lift a heavy weight off my shoulders.

Thank you to all the amazing blogs who are always ready to help promote and/or review. The time you invest in this industry—

in these books and us authors—is invaluable. Not one of us would be able to sustain without your ongoing support. If I don't say it enough, please hear me now: You are SO appreciated!!

As always, I need to thank my family. Everyone of them is supportive in their own way, making me feel so proud. I am blessed and I damn well know it! No need to express my love for all of them: they know it.

Mom, you have been my rock, my example, my inspiration throughout the years. Thank you…just, thank you.

ABOUT THE AUTHOR

Freya Barker inspires with her stories about 'real' people, perhaps less than perfect, each struggling to find their own slice of happy, but just as deserving of romance, thrills and chills, and some hot, sizzling sex in their lives.

Recipient of the RomCon "Reader's Choice" Award for best first book, "Slim To None," Freya has hit the ground running. She loves nothing more than to meet and mingle with her readers, whether it be online or in person at one of the signings she attends.

Freya spins story after story with an endless supply of bruised and dented characters, vying for attention!

Freya

https://www.freyabarker.com

http://bit.ly/FreyaAmazon

https://www.goodreads.com/FreyaBarker

https://www.facebook.com/FreyaBarkerWrites

https://tsu.co/FreyaB

https://twitter.com/freya_barker

or mailto:freyabarker.writes@gmail.com

ALSO BY FREYA BARKER

CEDAR TREE SERIES:

SLIM TO NONE
HUNDRED TO ONE
AGAINST ME
CLEAN LINES
UPPER HAND
LIKE ARROWS
HEAD START

PORTLAND, ME, NOVELS:

FROM DUST
CRUEL WATER
THROUGH FIRE
STILL AIR

NORTHERN LIGHTS COLLECTION:

A CHANGE OF TIDE

A CHANGE OF VIEW

A CHANGE OF PACE

(Coming soon!)

ROCK POINT SERIES:

KEEPING 6

CABIN 12

(Coming soon!)

SNAPSHOT SERIES:

SHUTTER SPEED

FREEZE FRAME

IDEAL IMAGE

PICTURE PERFECT

(coming soon!)